Praise for Irene Hannon's Books

"Hannon is a master at character development."
Library Journal on *In Harm's Way*

"Nail-biting suspense."
Booklist on *Deadly Pursuit*

"An ever-climactic mystery . . . engagingly sure-footed."
Publishers Weekly on *In Harm's Way*

"A love story that will melt your heart."
RT Book Reviews on *An Eye for An Eye*

"Romantic suspense that pounds your pulse."
USA Today on *Deceived*

"Teems with action."
St. Louis Post-Dispatch on *Labyrinth of Lies*

"Unputdownable."
Write-Read-Life on *Dark Ambitions*

"Hannon expertly writes characters
who embody human vulnerability and strength."
Publishers Weekly on *Tangled Webs*

INTO THE FIRE

BOOKS BY IRENE HANNON

HEROES OF QUANTICO

Against All Odds
An Eye for an Eye
In Harm's Way

GUARDIANS OF JUSTICE

Fatal Judgment
Deadly Pursuit
Lethal Legacy

PRIVATE JUSTICE

Vanished
Trapped
Deceived

MEN OF VALOR

Buried Secrets
Thin Ice
Tangled Webs

CODE OF HONOR

Dangerous Illusions
Hidden Peril
Dark Ambitions

TRIPLE THREAT

Point of Danger
Labyrinth of Lies
Body of Evidence

UNDAUNTED COURAGE

Into the Fire

STANDALONE NOVELS

That Certain Summer
One Perfect Spring

HOPE HARBOR

Hope Harbor
Sea Rose Lane
Sandpiper Cove
Pelican Point
Driftwood Bay
Starfish Pier
Blackberry Beach
Sea Glass Cottage
Windswept Way

UNDAUNTED COURAGE · 1

INTO THE FIRE

IRENE HANNON

Revell

a division of Baker Publishing Group
Grand Rapids, Michigan

© 2023 by Irene Hannon

Published by Revell
a division of Baker Publishing Group
Grand Rapids, Michigan
www.revellbooks.com

Printed in the United States of America

Library of Congress Cataloging-in-Publication Data
Names: Hannon, Irene, author.
Title: Into the fire / Irene Hannon.
Description: Grand Rapids, Michigan : Revell, a division of Baker Publishing
    Group, [2023] | Series: Undaunted Courage; #1
Identifiers: LCCN 2022056706 | ISBN 9780800741884 (paperback) | ISBN
    9780800745158 (library binding) | ISBN 9781493443543 (ebook)
Classification: LCC PS3558.A4793 I67 2023 | DDC 813/.54—dc23
LC record available at https://lccn.loc.gov/2022056706

Baker Publishing Group publications use paper produced from sustainable forestry practices and post-consumer waste whenever possible.

23 24 25 26 27 28 29   7 6 5 4 3 2 1

To Tom Becker,
FBI veteran and retired police chief,
who has been my premier law enforcement source
since my first suspense novel was published in 2009.

With his dual background at both the national and local levels,
he brings a wealth of expertise and experience to the task—
and his detailed responses to my many questions
have put the final polish of authenticity on countless books.

Thank you, Tom, for your generous and gracious assistance.

I will be forever grateful.

PROLOGUE

FIRE WAS CLEANSING. SACRIFICIAL, ALMOST.

And soon . . . very soon . . . the flames would come.

But first, my souvenir.

I crossed to the dresser. Flipped up the lid on the jewelry box. Poked around with my latex-covered finger.

Frowned.

Where was the ring?

It had to be here. There was no way she'd let that go. Not after all she'd done to get it.

Maybe it was tucked in one of the small drawers underneath the main display area.

One by one, I pulled them out.

Ah. There it was.

I picked up the heavy ring, weighed it in my hand, and turned back to the bed.

She was still watching me, eyes wide, waves of fear rolling off her.

So satisfying.

Lips flexing, I wandered back to the bed, leaned over, and ran a finger down the side of her face.

She flinched and averted her head, whimpering behind the duct tape I'd slapped over her mouth.

Also satisfying.

I pinched her cheek for good measure. Hard.

A tear spilled past her lower lashes, and she gave me a pleading look.

Didn't work.

In fact . . .

Folding my arms, I considered her. The fire would erase evidence of surface damage, including any bruises from our tussle when I'd pinned her down to mash the chloroform-soaked rag against her face. She'd put up quite a struggle during the five minutes it took for the drug to render her unconscious, but I was bigger and much, much stronger than she was. The fire would also destroy the ligature marks from the zip ties I'd used to bind her hands and feet while she was out—along with any other cuts or contusions I might choose to inflict now.

But I wasn't a mean person.

I just wanted justice.

Leaning close again, I patted her arm. "This will be over soon."

My reassurance didn't seem to comfort her.

Nevertheless, it was true. I'd scoped out her place, studied her habits. Knew she spent every Tuesday night alone in her house after she returned from her counseling session. Now that she was a widow, her social life was in the toilet. I didn't have to rush this job.

Yet there was no reason to linger.

I picked up the second syringe I'd retrieved from her fridge and swiveled back toward the bed.

Her eyes got even bigger, and a mewing sound vibrated deep in her throat. She attempted to wriggle away, but her efforts were pathetic. The first insulin injection had already kicked in. She was sweating, and her squinting and rapid blinking suggested her vision could be blurring.

The next dose ought to give her a whopping case of hypo-glycemia.

Such a shame.

Yet a distraught, grieving, diabetic widow could make mis-takes with medication—and judgment. Like mixing up her fast-acting and basal insulin, and forgetting she'd already given herself one injection.

Especially after downing two prescription sleeping pills. Even if she'd needed a bit of convincing to swallow them.

My concealed carry permit had proven to be quite useful. Again.

She began to writhe with more energy, and I straddled her legs. Yanked up the bottom of her tank top. Clamped one hand against her shoulder to hold her in place as I plunged the syringe into her abdomen and injected the insulin. Pulled out the needle.

As she whimpered again, I stood and transferred the waste can from the other side of the bed to the front of the skirted nightstand, close to where she lay. Then I plucked a tis-sue from the box on the small table. Wadded it into a ball. Dropped it into the half-full can. Repeated the process over and over.

The tissues would provide excellent kindling.

A few other flammable items wouldn't hurt, though. Like the magazines on the dresser.

I gathered them up, reading the titles as I returned to the bed. Snorted. Every one was crammed with self-help psycho-babble. However, they did provide more evidence she wasn't herself, which was useful.

After dropping three of them into the waste can, I added more tissues. Scattered the rest of the magazines on the bed.

Now for the accelerant.

I bent and rooted through my gym bag. Pulled out a bottle of hand sanitizer, opened it, and saturated the paper in the waste can, as well as the edge of the comforter. When the bottle was half empty, I tossed it in the trash, tucked the bottom of the table skirt into the can, and checked on Pookie.

What a gag-worthy, insipid name.

Her eyelids had drifted closed, and she'd stopped thrashing. It was possible she was already unconscious.

After I finished the setup, I'd verify that.

I moved to the window beside the bed, reached behind the blinds, flipped the lock, and raised the sash several inches. Nothing would seem amiss about an open window, not with the pleasant spring temperatures St. Louis had enjoyed over the past few days. After being confined during the endless, cold winter, everyone liked fresh air.

So did fire.

It thrived on oxygen.

I secured the long, filmy curtain to the table drape with liquid stitch. While the breeze from the open window should be sufficient to blow it into the flames—and that would be the obvious conclusion later—why take chances?

Next, I detoured to the foyer to get the partially unwrapped gift that had been my entrée tonight.

Back in the bedroom, I pulled the scented pillar candle from the festive paper, set it on the bedside table, and flicked a lighter against the wick. Within a few seconds, the scent of orange blossoms began to waft through the room.

Very pleasant.

I ought to get one of these for my own house.

Wadding up the wrapping paper, I angled toward the bed and assessed Pookie.

She was limp and pale, her breathing shallow but even. Hard to fake if you were stressed.

But just to confirm she'd slipped into a coma, I unhooked the safety pin brought for this very purpose from my shirt. Pricked her forehead.

No response.

I jabbed the point into her lower lip.

Nothing.

She was out of it.

It was safe to remove the ties and duct tape.

After tossing the gift wrap into the trash, I quickly dispensed with the restraints.

Now to finish up and get out.

I zipped the top of my gym bag, picked it up, and set the candle, on its side, in the waste can.

For a moment, the flame flickered. Then the paper caught fire as the hand sanitizer did its job. I also held the lighter to the edge of the comforter until flames began to lick along the saturation line.

Before I was finished with that task, the table drape was ablaze.

Excellent.

Everything would progress fast now, thanks to the open window, the wood and upholstered furniture, and the other combustibles in this room. But on my way out, I stopped to open the door of the double closet to help accelerate the carnage. Fabric also burned well.

Aww. She'd kept all her husband's clothes.

How sweet.

But he didn't need them. And soon, she wouldn't need hers, either.

I exited the bedroom, closed the door, jogged down the hall, and slipped out the back door, into the darkness.

No one had seen me come. No one would see me go.

Gym bag gripped in my hand, I edged along the shadows at the back of the house and peeked around the corner.

The street was deserted.

Not surprising. Most people didn't hang around outside after dark in late April. Even on balmy days, temperatures tended to dip once the sun set. And this was a quiet neighborhood, anyway, based on the drive-throughs I'd done in preparation for tonight.

Besides, it would be difficult to spot smoke seeping from the house in the darkness, should anyone pass by or look out the window of an adjacent home.

And once the flames were visible, it would be too late.

At the corner of the property, I paused to give the small contemporary structure a final once-over. Nothing appeared to be amiss—yet. The bedroom was in the back, overlooking the shrub-enclosed yard. No one would be able to see the glow behind the blinds.

The location of the room couldn't have been better.

I started forward again, heading toward my car in the parking lot of the neighborhood quick shop less than three short blocks away.

It was a shame I couldn't hang around to enjoy the show, though. There was nothing like a fire to juice a person's adrenaline.

But successfully pulling off a risky job produced its own high.

At the street corner, I glanced back.

Still no external sign of the blaze, but at this point it would be raging inside the bedroom. It wasn't necessary to wait for visible confirmation of the inferno.

I knew how to set fires.

Smiling, I turned my back on the house and picked up my pace. This one had gone like clockwork, as had the others. It was time to enjoy the moment. Bask in the exhilaration.

And think about the final release to come, when the purge would be complete.

ONE

ARSON INVESTIGATORS WEREN'T SUPPOSED to die in fires.

Bri Tucker shoved her hands into the pockets of her jacket and clenched her fists, the acrid smell of smoke prickling her nose. Up and down the quiet suburban St. Louis cul-de-sac of modest homes, flashing lights from emergency vehicles pierced the darkness as small clusters of neighbors watched the roaring flames consume Les Kavanaugh's house.

All at once, a dormer window on the second floor exploded. Moments later, a portion of the roof shuddered . . . buckled . . . and collapsed in a cascade of fiery sparks that rose like a swarm of demon hornets toward the inky sky.

Collectively, the onlookers recoiled.

From her spot in the shadows, Bri appraised them. All part of her job as the St. Louis Regional Bomb and Arson Unit investigator assigned to this fire. Bystanders could help her put the pieces together once the flames were extinguished. Determine if the fire was accidental or intentional.

Under any other circumstances, her money would be on the former. Ninety-five percent of residential fires were due to innocent causes.

But most didn't take place at the home of an experienced arson investigator who knew all the fire hazards and would have taken pains to eliminate them.

So if this blaze turned out to be deliberate, the spectators could be key.

Because arsonists liked to stick around and enjoy the show.

No one in the immediate vicinity raised any suspicions, however. Most were older couples, huddled close together, watching in shock as the tragedy unfolded. The few lone people were also more advanced in age, one in a bathrobe, another watching from a front porch and using a walker for support.

If this was arson, and if the guilty party was close by, they were either an atypical suspect or hiding in the shadows.

"How long have you been here?"

At the question, Bri swiveled to her right. Deep creases lined Sergeant Frank Connor's forehead.

"A few minutes. I didn't expect to see you tonight." Then again, until his retirement, Les had been a fixture in the Bomb and Arson Unit. If ever her boss would show up at a fire scene, this would be the one.

"Les and I go way back. We may have clashed on occasion, but I had tremendous respect for his skills. Everyone did."

"So I heard." A gust of unseasonably cool September wind whipped past, and she shivered despite the heat emanating from the blazing house.

"You talked to anybody yet?"

"No bystanders, but I touched based with the captain." She motioned toward one of the fire trucks.

"He's next on my list. Is there any news about Les? Was he home?"

Sarge didn't know.

Bri took a breath. Gave a slow nod. "Yes. They found him in the back of the house. Too late to save."

A muscle tightened in Sarge's cheek as he scanned the burning structure, and his voice hardened. "I want the ATF in on this one. They have resources we don't. If it's arson, let's find out ASAP."

The irony of a fire investigator dying in a fire must have set off an alert for him too.

"You think this was deliberate?"

"It's possible. I imagine Les made a few enemies through the years. He was like a dog with a bone while he was on the trail of a suspect, and he didn't worry about social niceties or political correctness in his quest for truth."

"I heard that too."

One side of Sarge's mouth flexed. "He was a character. And he never left a stone unturned in an investigation. Pardon the second trite, but apt, cliché. Nor did he hesitate to pull in people he thought could help him put a case to bed."

Hmm.

Bri averted her face from the fire as a billow of heat surged toward them. "He called me yesterday morning. Asked me to meet him. I was supposed to drop by tomorrow afternoon."

The pleats on Sarge's forehead deepened. "Why?"

"I don't know." But a ripple of unease snaked down her spine as she processed the coincidence. "I mean, he retired a month after I joined the unit, so I didn't really get to know him. He was in wrap-up stage. I did assist once at a scene he was working, but it wasn't like we hung out together. I was too busy learning the ropes and digging into the warehouse fire that landed on my desk a week into my job."

"The one that could have been ruled accidental if you hadn't found out a guy with a drone had been in the adjacent field the day before. The footage he had of the subject's car was the turning point. That was a stellar launch to your career with the unit, in case I haven't told you that."

The unexpected praise sent a rush of warmth through her. Being the new kid on the block was never easy, and an occasional compliment eased the transition anxiety. Not that Sarge had given her many during her four-month tenure.

"I believe in being thorough, but there was also an element

of luck with that one. If the kid who gave me the drone tip hadn't shown up with his skateboard to practice kickflips in the empty parking lot while I was there, the owner could have gotten away with the insurance scam."

"Nevertheless, a slam dunk. Assuming the prosecuting attorney does his job." He squinted at the fire. "I wonder if that case could be why Les called you."

"How so?"

"He hated loose ends and puzzle pieces that didn't fit. Those kinds of cases ate at him. Whenever he had a spare minute, he pored over the files, searching for clues he might have missed." Sarge shrugged. "Could be he was impressed with your work on the warehouse fire and wanted to pass on to you a few of the cases that troubled him."

Like she wasn't busy enough already.

"He could have done that before he left."

"Unless he'd found a new clue."

She hiked up her eyebrows. "You think he was still working cases after he retired?"

"Wouldn't surprise me. Unofficially, of course."

"That seems like a stretch, even for someone as diligent as Les." She didn't try to hide her skepticism, though the man's out-of-the-blue call did raise questions.

"You didn't know him as well as I did. But it's a moot point now." He motioned toward one of the fire trucks. "I'm going to talk to the captain."

"And I'm going to make a circuit of the crowd. See if I can dig up any useful information."

"Keep me in the loop. I'll contact the ATF and have them get in touch with you." With a wave, he strode toward the truck.

While the flames arced against the night sky and the fire continued to hiss and crackle, Bri frowned at his retreating back.

Why was he siccing an ATF agent on her? Hadn't he just

18

commended her for solving the warehouse fire? Didn't he trust her to handle this one?

Shoot.

That wasn't exactly a confidence builder.

On the other hand, one of their own was dead. That made it personal. And she was new to the unit. Had admitted her quick resolution to the warehouse fire was due in part to luck.

Instead of grousing, maybe she ought to be grateful Sarge hadn't yanked her from this one and assigned a more seasoned investigator.

Stop overanalyzing, Bri. Just do your job and quit trying to prove yourself. Your work will speak for itself.

The pep talk she always gave herself when a new challenge arose replayed in her mind. It had served her well in her previous careers, and it would serve her well in her new job—even if she'd never quite managed to convince herself that an offer of help wasn't necessarily a criticism of her abilities.

That's what came from hanging with the alpha males in the McCall smokejumper unit, who hadn't been at all certain she could pull her weight.

But she'd proved herself more than capable of holding her own there, and she'd do the same in this job and on this case.

With or without the help of the ATF.

Refocusing on the scene, she gave the onlookers another survey and psyched herself up for the long night ahead. Some of the questioning could wait until tomorrow, but fresh impressions tended to yield more detail. That could be vital if a crime had been committed.

And in light of the timing of tonight's fire on the heels of Les's call, plus Sarge's speculation that the man may have unearthed a new clue on one of his vexing investigations, arson was feeling more and more like a reasonable possibility.

Had Les been digging into old cases?

If so, could that have made someone nervous enough to take drastic action?

Like commit a murder?

She swallowed past the taste of soot permeating her mouth. Moistened her heat-parched lips.

While that was far-fetched, it wasn't impossible. People who did bad things often went to great lengths to keep their crimes from surfacing.

Meaning this could be one of the rare residential arson fires.

And once the embers burned themselves out and the smoke wafted away, it would be her responsibility to sift through the charred remains of Les's home for clues about what had happened here tonight.

Well, hers and the ATF agent's.

A daunting task in any situation, but more so with such a high-profile death. Sarge would want updates every day.

So she'd dive in and pull out all the stops to come up with answers.

But as she withdrew her creds and approached the older couple on a lawn two doors down from the burning structure, her stomach clenched.

Because every instinct in her body said that solving this one wasn't going to be as simple as finding a skateboard-toting teen whose single, providential tip had given her a win in the early days of her new job.

A HOUSE FIRE.

Quashing a sigh, Marc Davis hung a right and eased back on the gas pedal as the morning light filtered through the maple trees lining the quiet street, their leaves showing the first faint hint of red.

What a comedown after four years on the ATF's National Response Team and the major investigations he'd overseen in the Chicago office for almost a decade.

But the transfer to St. Louis two weeks ago had been his choice, and as the low man on the totem pole, he couldn't expect to get all the plum assignments despite his experience and credentials.

So he'd suck it up and give his all to whatever jobs landed in his lap. And he'd do it with a smile. For Nan.

"In fifty yards, turn right. Your destination will be on the right."

He followed the instructions from his cell, but once he swung onto the street, he didn't need his phone to direct him to last night's fire. The blackened wreckage that had once been a house was like a smudged thumbprint on the cul-de-sac of small, well-tended homes. Much of the roof had caved in, and while the scorched brick walls were still standing, most of the windows had shattered.

As he stopped a few yards from the back bumper of the patrol car parked in front of the ruins, an officer got out of the vehicle and walked toward him.

Marc slid from behind the wheel and held out his creds. "I'm supposed to meet a fire investigator here at eight to do a walk-through. Brianne Tucker."

The officer skimmed the ID and inclined his head toward a dark sedan parked in the curve of the cul-de-sac. "That's hers. She's been here since first light. You'll find her in the back." He handed over the scene log.

"Thanks." Frowning, Marc signed in and ducked under the yellow police tape. If the County investigator had wanted to start earlier, why hadn't she told him that in her response to the text he'd sent her last night, after his boss handed off this assignment?

Tamping down his annoyance, he skirted the remains of the structure, cinders crunching under his sturdy boots. Until he put on the rest of his safety gear, he'd keep his distance from the house. But first he'd make his presence known.

He rounded the corner. Paused.

A tall woman in loose coveralls and a hard hat was examining the back door. As she leaned closer, homing in on the lock, a breeze teased her long, wavy blond hair. She brushed it aside, leaving a smudge on her cheek.

When it became clear she didn't intend to straighten up anytime soon, he cleared his throat.

She jerked upright and spun toward him, posture coiled and taut. Like she expected trouble.

Curious.

"The officer out front told me you were back here." He closed the distance between them, held out his hand, and introduced himself.

She regarded his outstretched fingers, then lifted her gloved hand. "I don't think you want a fistful of soot. But it's nice to meet you, Agent Davis."

Was it? The words were cordial, but her tone was reserved. Wary.

Maybe she had jurisdictional issues. Not all local law enforcement officers welcomed an intrusion by the Feds.

Or was she just tired?

As he returned the sentiment, he studied her. Fine lines radiated from the corners of the cobalt-blue eyes behind the safety glasses, and faint shadows hung under her lower lashes.

One explanation for her weariness? She'd been here during the fire . . . and beyond.

"Make it Marc. How late did you stay last night?"

Her eyebrows arched a hair at his assumption, her gaze measured as she let a few beats pass. "Until the firefighters left and I was confident the scene was secure."

According to his boss, the fire had been called in about nine thirty. Meaning she'd had a late night.

"Prompted by diligence or suspicion?"

She shifted her weight. "Securing a scene is normal protocol."

Not a direct answer. But if she did have suspicions, why not share them?

A question he'd have to explore over the coming hours—or days.

"Let me suit up and you can fill me in on what you've got so far." As he pivoted and retraced his steps across the cinders littering the yard, his spirits ticked up a few notches.

Working a house fire might not be on his top ten list of exciting assignments, but doing it with someone who looked like Brianne Tucker—even if her welcome had been less than effusive—could add a bit of zing to his life for the few days it should take to wrap this up. The cause of most house fires, even ones with loss of life, could often be nailed down fast.

But while they were sorting out the pieces of the puzzle, why not also see what he could uncover about the woman in charge of investigating it? Concealing as the bulky protective gear was, it hadn't been able to camouflage the caution in those vivid blue eyes. Nor had it masked her overly startled reaction to his approach. Why was she—

He stopped as he approached the front corner of the house. Peered down. Through the ashes stirred by a gust of wind, a small, bright object winked at him.

Marc dropped to the balls of his feet to examine it.

Next to the stone garden edging that had once protected a singed, wilted row of hostas, a piece of faceted glass glinted in the morning light like a diamond. He leaned closer. It wasn't a broken bottle shard. The fragment appeared to be cut glass.

Worth preserving, after he had an evidence envelope in hand. Anything that seemed out of place deserved scrutiny.

He stood and continued toward his car, his thoughts shifting back to Brianne Tucker.

What was her story?

Purely an academic question, of course, since he had no time or inclination to socialize. Off the job, his priorities were Nan and settling in.

Yet as he unlocked the trunk of his car to collect his gear, it was impossible to ignore the faint flutter in his nerve endings. The kind he'd experienced once upon a time, in his early days with Serena.

Odd that it would rekindle in the most unromantic of settings, beside the burned-out hulk of a house, and thanks to a stranger who hadn't been any too happy to see him.

He shoved his legs into the dark blue coveralls.

Weird how life worked.

But as Nan was fond of saying, while God's timing was often a mystery to mere mortals, there was always a purpose behind it.

So he'd go with the flow and see how much he could learn about the blond fire investigator while the two of them sorted through the rubble. If nothing else, some personal reconnaissance could liven up an investigation that would likely pose few other challenges.

Because for whatever reason, he had a feeling the puzzle of Brianne Tucker wouldn't be solved as easily as the mystery of this house fire.

TWO

"SO WHERE DO YOU WANT to start, Ms. Tucker?"

As Marc spoke, Bri angled toward him from her spot by the back door.

The ATF agent was now attired in garb and equipment similar to hers, but the shapeless coveralls couldn't camouflage his broad shoulders or diminish his height—about six-one or two, using her five-eight frame as reference. Nor did his safety goggles mask those discerning, coffee-colored eyes. The man exuded lean, leashed strength, along with confidence and competence.

A faint fizz flicked along her nerve endings, and she frowned. Not appropriate. The fire that had taken Les's life deserved her total focus.

Besides, letting a surge of hormones distract her would be unprofessional.

She tugged off her gloves and brushed back a few rebellious strands of hair. "It's Bri." May as well reciprocate on the first name suggestion. "And I was waiting to hear your thoughts."

"You're in charge here."

Technically true, but Sarge was going to expect her to treat him as a partner.

"I doubt a former ATF National Response Team member is used to taking orders from a local fire investigator." She tried for a casual tone, but a touch of irritation crept in.

"You've done your homework on me." He appeared more amused than offended by her subtle testiness.

That rankled, for reasons that eluded her.

She stifled her irritation and shrugged. "I'm thorough."

"I am too." He folded his arms. "You're new on the job here."

So he'd checked her out too.

The insecurity she kept on a tight leash reared its ugly head, and she lifted her chin. "Yes, but I've had other fire-related experience." In all likelihood more unique than his, though she left that unsaid.

"I assumed as much. I doubt County would hire a green investigator."

He waited, as if he expected her to recite her resume.

Not happening. If he wanted to know details about her credentials, he could dig for them.

She waved a hand toward the house. "Why don't I bring you up to speed on what I know so far?"

"Sounds like a plan."

His manner remained pleasant, his tone conversational, but his sharp, probing gaze continued to assess her. As if he was wondering why she was prickly and defensive.

This man didn't miss much.

Quashing the latent self-doubt that always tried to chip away at her confidence in the presence of intimidating men, she shifted into her official persona. "I spoke with all the residents of the cul-de-sac last night. No one saw anything or anyone out of the ordinary. I also talked with the fire crew after the blaze was out. All doors were locked when they arrived. There was no sign of forced entry. The window in the room where they found the victim was open a few inches, but they saw nothing to suggest it had been jimmied or was an access point. Neither did I during my perimeter check."

"How was the fire reported?"

"An alarm from the smoke detector in the kitchen."

"Any indications it was incendiary?"

"No. According to the fire crew, there was no sign of multiple fires, trailers, or fire-starting devices. Nothing in the smoke color was inconsistent with what would have been in the house. They believe it started in the room where the victim was found."

"Where was he?"

"Sitting in his recliner."

Marc's eyes narrowed. "So he made no attempt to leave the house."

"That was their assumption." And hers. "He did have surgery a month ago for a broken ankle and was wearing a boot, but that wouldn't stop a person from fleeing a fire if his life was in danger."

"Agreed. Have you been inside yet?"

"No."

"You ready to take a look?"

Without responding, she fished a ponytail band from her pocket, gathered up her hair, and tucked it under the hard hat. After pulling her gloves back on, she edged through the back door into a world dominated by shades of black and smoky grays, especially in the upper third of the room. Typical, since heat and smoke accumulated at ceiling level.

"The fire crew said that was closed." She motioned toward the singed end of an open sliding door that separated the kitchen from the hallway. "So was that one." She indicated the matching door on the other side of the fridge, also open.

Marc gave the room a sweep, homing in on the soot-covered wallet and keys on the counter, as she had.

If this was an arson fire, it didn't appear theft had been on the perpetrator's mind.

"I noticed that too." Important to mention in case he thought she'd missed the significance. "Let's do a walk-through."

She took the lead as they traversed the house, boots crunching on carbonized fragments of drywall and collapsed ceiling.

Nothing jumped out as suspicious, although an untampered-with safe in an upstairs closet put any further speculations about theft to rest. As did a high-end watch and a money clip containing a few bills on the dresser in an upstairs bedroom.

After completing a circuit of the house and basement, she finished in the room where Les had died, Marc on her heels.

"The victim was found there." She motioned to the upholstered chair beside the shattered window. The seat and back were still intact, protected by Les's body, but everything else in the room was charred almost beyond recognition and covered with ash and debris.

Marc moved around her, edging past what appeared to be a collapsed wooden desk, and dropped to the balls of his feet beside the chair. Studied that area. Stood and did the same with the wall next to it. "I can detect a V pattern here."

She could too, though it was barely there given the extent of the damage in the room. And it was the only such pattern in the house.

The firefighters' conclusion about where the fire had started seemed to be sound.

"I think we have our point of origin." She folded her arms.

"Yeah." He swiveled toward her. "You ready to dig in and see what we can find?"

"After I document the scene with photos, video, and sketches."

"Naturally." He flashed her a grin. "Would you like me to handle one of those?"

No. She'd prefer to do it herself. But since Sarge wanted the ATF in on this, she'd have to relinquish a bit of control.

"How are you at sketching?" Delegating her weakest skill wouldn't be a huge sacrifice.

"Passable."

"Why don't you tackle that?"

"Done. I'll get a few supplies from my car and we can re-group after we finish."

Once they launched into their tasks, they worked in si-lence for the next couple of hours except for occasional brief exchanges.

Just as Bri snapped a final photo of the collapsed desk, he rejoined her and handed over his sketches. "See if there's anything else you want."

She let the camera dangle around her neck and took the notebook. Flipped through.

His skills in the sketching department put hers to shame.

"These are excellent. You captured a lot of detail." She passed the notebook back.

"I've had a fair amount of practice." He ripped out the pages and handed them to her. "You've got me for the whole day. I assume you want to concentrate on this room?"

In other words, after today he didn't plan to hover or try to take charge.

Good. Having Sarge looking over her shoulder was bad enough.

"Yes. Let me haul in my tools and evidence containers."

"I'll give you a hand."

She didn't argue.

He fell into step beside her after they exited, but as they neared the front corner of the house, he stopped and dropped to one knee.

"What's wrong?" She halted too.

"I spotted that earlier." He indicated a shiny object in the grass next to the stone garden edging, partially hidden under debris from the fire.

"Why did it catch your attention?" She leaned down.

"Seems like an odd place to find such an intricate piece of glass. Look closer."

She maneuvered herself to the ground beside him, ignoring

the protest from her hip and knee, and got up close and personal with the irregular, one-and-a-half-inch triangular shard. "It could be cut crystal." And the location was odd.

"I wonder if it's part of a drinking glass. Someone could have dropped it during an outdoor party."

"I think it's too thick to be from a glass. Besides, most people don't entertain outdoors with fine crystal. If that's what it is."

"Do you think it's worth documenting?"

Clearly he did, or he wouldn't have brought it to her attention.

Was this some sort of test? An attempt to get a handle on her abilities?

She sent him a sidelong glance and found him watching her, his face mere inches away. At this proximity, it was impossible to miss the gold flecks in his irises or the faint aroma of aftershave that tickled her nose. And the magnetism he'd exuded earlier was amplified tenfold.

He tipped his head and raised an eyebrow. "No?"

What?

Forcibly shifting gears, she replayed their last exchange.

Oh. He'd asked about documenting the glass.

"Yes." Her voice rasped, and she swallowed. "I, uh, agree it seems out of place." Though truth be told, she'd walked past it all morning without ever noticing it.

Maybe her skills *weren't* up to par.

He spoke again, as if he'd read her mind. "The sun caught one of the facets as I passed by earlier. Otherwise, I would never have spotted it."

His reply was matter-of-fact, but his comment felt like a reassurance.

More than a tad unnerving to think he could pick up on her thoughts so easily.

"Sometimes fate works in our favor." Like the skateboard-toting kid who'd told her about the guy with the drone.

"As my grandmother likes to remind me, never underestimate the power of serendipity."

She pushed herself to her feet. "I'll have to jot that down in my book of wise sayings."

A glint of humor sparked in his eyes as he stood. "You write down wise sayings?"

"They come in handy on days when I need inspiration or encouragement." Enough on that subject. "Let me snap a few photos before we put the glass in an evidence bag."

He moved aside as she took care of that chore, then followed her to her car to gather the supplies and equipment.

As she opened her trunk and began handing him items from her scene investigation stash, the subtle tension in her shoulders began to ease.

So far, Marc Davis had not only been quite agreeable but useful. Perhaps the old adage about two heads being better than one would prove true on this case.

Which could be helpful.

Because the agent standing a few inches away had already demonstrated he had a keen eye by spotting that piece of glass. The small fragment might or might not end up being relevant, but the fact he'd noticed it suggested few details got past him . . . as did a number of his other perceptive observations during their walk-through.

And if this fire did indeed turn out to be a crime, the smallest details mattered.

So hopefully, between the two of them, no piece of evidence that could bring an arsonist to justice—if this was arson—would escape their notice.

BRI HAD A LIMP.

Juggling the boxes and equipment he was toting, Marc appraised her as she took the lead back to the house. While her slightly uneven gait didn't call a great deal of attention to itself, it was definitive.

Did it reflect a recent injury that would heal, or was it permanent?

One more intriguing piece of her puzzle.

If the opportunity arose, why not see if he could fit a few of those pieces together before the end of the day?

Back inside, the nitty-gritty work began as they sifted and raked through the rubble in search of answers. Knowing where the blaze had begun allowed them to concentrate their efforts around the easy chair, and one by one pieces of evidence emerged.

A melted disk that could once have been a waste can. Shards of glass that might be the remnants of a tumbler and liquor bottle, based on their shape. A ceramic curtain rod above the window, the few strips of burnt fabric clinging to it indicating it had once held draperies.

"Was the victim a smoker?" Marc inspected a blackened metal lighter he'd excavated from the wreckage.

"I don't know." Bri flipped up the remains of a rug in front of the chair, revealing a char pattern on the floor underneath that should be sampled and analyzed.

"Drinker?"

"No idea." She folded the rug back, leaving the floor exposed, and faced him. "The tox screen will be helpful."

Same conclusion he'd come to, meaning they were tracking the same direction. Booze and smoking were a dangerous combination, and the fact the victim hadn't tried to escape suggested alcohol could have played a role in his death.

They continued to poke around the room for another hour, their exchanges sparse and confined to business. After she rebuffed several of his attempts to make small talk, he gave up. So much for finding—or creating—an opportunity to learn more about her. It was obvious the fire investigator he'd been paired with had no interest in conversation. With him, at least.

By late morning, they went their separate ways at the scene, doing a second pass inside and out to ensure they hadn't missed anything that could be relevant to the fire.

But as far as he could see, they'd found the single point of origin, and nothing else was amiss.

When one o'clock came and went with no indication from his reluctant partner that she had any intention of stopping for lunch, he went in search of her.

He found her back in the room where the victim had died, brow furrowed, hands on her hips as she gave the space a once-over.

"You turn up anything else?" She swiveled toward him as he entered.

"No. You?"

She shook her head and waved toward the door. "That was burned through when the firefighters arrived, but it was closed."

"Is that significant?"

"I don't know—but he lived alone. There wouldn't have been any reason to shut it for privacy, or to block out noise from another part of the house."

"Maybe he wanted to let in a little fresh air through the window but preferred to keep any wayward pollen or leaf mold in this room."

The creases on her forehead deepened. "The doors to the kitchen were shut too."

He did the math.

"You're wondering if someone wanted to keep the smoke and flames and heat confined to this room as long as possible so the smoke detectors would go off too late to save the victim."

"That thought did cross my mind. I like to consider every scenario."

Laudable. But nothing he'd discovered indicated this was a crime scene.

He kept his inflection neutral as he responded. "Have you seen any evidence of arson?"

"Nothing concrete. But this doesn't feel right."

"Based on what? Intuition? Instincts?"

That earned him a narrow-eyed glare. "Don't discount those."

He held up his hands, palms forward. "I wouldn't think of it. I listen to my gut too."

"What's it telling you about this fire?"

The truth? A big fat zero. If he were a betting man, he'd put his money on an accidental cause at this stage.

"My suspicion meter hasn't spiked into the danger zone." He chose his words with care. "If this were my case, I'd reserve judgment until I saw the autopsy report."

She bristled a bit as she adjusted her hard hat. "I intend to. But I knew Les . . . sort of. For a month, anyway. He didn't strike me as the careless type. Stories I heard about him from colleagues confirmed that impression. Plus, for a fire investigator to die like this . . ." She surveyed the burnt wreckage, her troubled gaze lingering on the remains of the chair.

"I'll grant you it's ironic."

"At the very least." She adjusted her goggles. "Are you finished with the rest of the house?"

"Yes. And I'm getting hungry. Are you planning to eat lunch? It's after one."

"I have a granola bar and apple in the car if I get hungry later."

Translation? She wasn't stopping.

He camouflaged the low rumble in his stomach with a cough. "I'm going to take a break and grab a burger somewhere."

"Okay." She shifted her weight. Gave a slight wince. Grasped what was left of the edge of the windowsill. "You may as well call it a day. I can finish up here. I want to nose around for a while in this room."

He was being dismissed.

"I'd be happy to come back and help after I eat." Though there wasn't much more to do, as far as he could see. They'd been over this room with a fine-tooth comb already. Or a fine-tooth rake, in this case.

"I don't want to waste your time."

"Like I told you this morning, I'm at your disposal all day. I'm also happy to consult throughout the process."

"I appreciate that. I'll stay in touch."

Only because her boss had requested ATF assistance.

But she didn't want him hanging around today.

Fine. He could take a hint.

"In that case, I'll head out. You want any help carrying the evidence to your car?"

Not that there was much of it. A section of the burned rug and a piece of flooring from underneath for accelerant testing, the items they'd found beside the chair, and a scorched laptop. There'd been nothing obvious to suggest arson was a factor. Nothing to fingerprint that wasn't already ash covered. No sign anyone but the victim had been in the house. Nor had there been anything else suspicious.

Except that odd piece of glass next to the garden, which likely had no bearing on the case.

"No. I can manage." She straightened her shoulders. "Thanks for your help today."

"Happy to assist." With no excuse to linger, he turned and exited the room. Paused in the hall. Swung back to offer one final thought.

She was bent slightly, massaging her leg between her knee and thigh, features pinched.

The instant she realized he was watching her, she stood and neutralized her expression. "Forget something?"

"No. I just wanted to give you a heads-up about the bottom step in the basement, in case you venture down there again. The riser collapsed on my last circuit."

"Duly noted. Thanks."

So what's wrong with your leg?

The question hovered on the tip of his tongue, but he bit it back.

He did, however, ask the next one that came to mind. "Are you certain I can't carry those to your car for you?" He motioned to the small pile of evidence containers. "Or haul out some of the equipment?"

She did that chin-lift thing again. "I've got it covered."

No thank-you was tacked on this time.

Unaccustomed as he was to walking away from anyone in need of a helping hand, his gut said that was the wisest course with Bri Tucker. The woman oozed independence with a capital I.

And as he'd told her earlier, he listened to his gut.

"Okay. Talk to you soon."

No response.

Yet much as she might resent his intrusion into her investigation, she'd get in touch with him again to dot the i's and cross the t's, if nothing else. She was too new on the job here to risk miffing a boss who'd brought in the ATF.

Unfortunately, that didn't mean he'd have any further opportunity to find out what made her tick or what had caused her limp.

Too bad.

Beautiful, intriguing women didn't enter his orbit every day.

He picked up his pace as he left the house and struck out toward his car, trying not to let her lack of interest and encouragement dent his ego. In truth, he should be glad for her coolness. In a few months, after he settled into life in St. Louis and Nan was in better shape, he could think about reentering the dating game.

For now, though, it would behoove him to forget all about his social life in general and Bri Tucker in particular.

Marc stopped beside his car, removed his hard hat and safety goggles, and unzipped his jumpsuit. The early finish at the scene would give him a chance to log a few hours at the office and continue getting up to speed on local cases, protocols, and personalities.

But as he slid behind the wheel and put the car in gear, his gut told him one more thing.

It wasn't going to be easy to forget about the enigmatic blond fire investigator whose intuition was prodding her to keep digging in a burned-out room that, as far as he could tell, had already yielded all the clues it was going to relinquish.

THREE

BRI EXPELLED A BREATH and moved aside to let a waiter with a laden tray pass by.

She was not in the mood to socialize.

If she'd known Les's toxicology report would land on her desk this morning—much faster than the usual four-to-six-week turnaround, thanks to her constant calls to the County medical examiner's office and Les's position with the unit—she would never have set up this lunch.

Especially since the results pointed to an accidental fire, as had the autopsy report. Les had died of smoke inhalation. You didn't survive with high amounts of soot and smoke in your upper and lower respiratory system and a carboxyhemoglobin level of 81 percent. Yet he'd stayed in his chair, making no attempt to leave the house while the fire raged around him.

Now, thanks to the autopsy report, she had a potential explanation for why he'd done that.

But none of the ME's findings aligned with her suspicions. Suspicions that had grown in the ten days following Les's tragic death.

Because it didn't make sense for a diligent, seasoned fire investigator to die in a fire at home in his recliner.

She hoisted her purse higher on her shoulder.

Something still didn't feel right.

Call it intuition, as Marc had, but even the experienced ATF agent had said he listened to his gut.

Without proof, though, instincts took you only so far. Unless specific evidence surfaced that suggested a crime had occurred, she could be at a dead end.

And dead ends stunk.

Bri stepped onto the patio of the popular café and surveyed the diners who were enjoying this sunny October Friday. Tempted as she'd been to cancel after reviewing the report on Les, this lunch had been set up more than a week ago. If she made a habit of bailing on her friends, they wouldn't be her friends for long.

From a table on the far side, Alison Stephens waggled her fingers.

Calling up a smile, Bri wove through the lunch crowd and joined her. "Sorry I'm running a few minutes late."

"No worries." Alison dismissed her apology with a wave. "I'm off today, and fall is in all its glory. Soaking up rays while sipping a margarita was no hardship, trust me. You should have one."

"I'm on duty. Besides, lemonade's more my style."

"I know. I'm giving you a hard time. But seriously, you seem stressed."

"Goes with the job."

"Tell me about it." Alison wrinkled her nose and took a sip of her drink. "We had a bad one yesterday in the middle of that thunderstorm. A lightning strike at one of the century houses in Webster Groves. All the adjacent municipalities responded."

"Any injuries?"

"No, but it was a long day. I treated myself to a bubble bath after I got home. This girl had more than a few sore muscles, let me tell you. Wielding a fire hose can be like wrestling an alligator."

"I know." The very reason the two of them had clicked when they'd crossed paths at a fire three months ago. Female firefighters were in the minority, and that sisterhood produced strong bonds.

"I bet. But my job is tame compared to the stuff you've done. You're my role model."

Bri fidgeted in her seat. Role modeling carried way too much responsibility. "Why don't we just be friends instead?"

"Whatever you want." Alison took another sip of the margarita and perused her. "But you do look über-stressed today. Everything okay?"

The temptation to talk about Les's case with Alison was strong. As a firefighter, her friend would understand the dynamics far better than Bri's siblings. Yes, Jack's detective experience was relevant. But fire investigation was a unique animal. As for Cara . . . while her younger sister had empathy to spare, the sort of research a historical anthropology professor did was a world removed from the kind of foraging and analysis required in a potential arson situation.

Nevertheless, sharing information with anyone on an in-progress case—even one that appeared poised to wrap up—should be need-to-know based, colleagues included.

Her lunch companion tipped her head. "Does your funk have anything to do with the Les Kavanaugh fire?"

Bri straightened the cutlery on her napkin. "Why do you ask that?"

"Because I know it landed on your desk, everyone at County is talking about it, and the case hits close to home." Her forehead crimped. "It's such a tragic situation."

"Yeah, it is. Did you know Les?" Maybe she could glean a few pieces of back-door information about the man that would be helpful.

"I ran into him on occasion at fire scenes, but we weren't best buds, if that's what you mean."

"What was your impression of him?"

"Hard worker. Meticulous. A bit crusty. He had no qualms

about yelling at firefighters who put extinguishing the fire above protecting evidence. And according to scuttlebutt, even in retirement he continued to unofficially stir the embers of cases that bothered him. Pardon the pun." Her lips twitched. "He was a character."

"So my boss said."

"Are you still investigating?"

"Yes, but I'm getting close to wrapping up."

"I heard your boss sicced the ATF on you." Alison squeezed the lime wedge from her glass into her drink and rolled her eyes. "Those Fed types can be a pain in the you-know-what."

"Not in this case. The agent showed up the first day at the scene, but that's been our only contact."

"Lucky you. They tend to want to run the show. Sounds like he may leave you alone."

"We can hope."

But if she really didn't want to see him again, why did images of him keep flitting through her mind—and through her dreams?

She quashed that annoying question.

"So did you ever find out why Les wanted to meet with you?" Alison took another sip of her margarita.

Bri erased the latest picture of Marc Davis her brain had called up and switched gears.

Since she and Alison had been chatting by phone the day Les's incoming call popped up on her cell screen and she'd put her friend on hold to take it, that made this topic fair game.

"No. I hoped I'd find a clue at the scene, but that didn't happen. The oddest thing we found was a misplaced piece of crystal that—" Her phone began to vibrate, and she pulled it out. The number on the display didn't register, but letting calls roll—particularly during normal working hours—wasn't her style. What if someone had a lead to report on one of her cases?

"Go ahead and take that if you need to. I'll continue to enjoy my margarita." Alison swirled her drink.

"Thanks." Bri pressed talk and greeted the caller.

"Detective Tucker, this is Sandra Morris."

Les Kavanaugh's daughter.

She hadn't talked to the woman since two days after the fire, when Sandra had confirmed that Les did indeed smoke cigars on occasion and often indulged in a glass of bourbon in the evening.

Now, with the tox report in hand, there were tougher questions to ask. But posing them in a crowded café wasn't ideal.

It might be more prudent to see why Sandra had contacted her and arrange another conversation for later in the day.

"Hello, Ms. Morris." She held up a finger to Alison, who nodded and began to peruse the menu. "I was going to call you today or tomorrow with an update on my investigation. How are you doing?"

"I'm hanging in." The last word scraped, and she cleared her throat. "But the past ten days have been very difficult. My husband had to go back to Phoenix for work on Sunday, and trying to deal with everything alone has been hard."

"I can understand that. I know losing your dad was a tremendous shock. We're all still reeling from what happened too. He was a legend in our ranks. Tell me how I can help you."

"I've been through the house—or what's left of it. I was able to salvage a few personal objects, but the one I most wanted wasn't there. It was in Dad's study, where the fire started. I realize it may have been destroyed, but I wondered if by chance you'd found it during your investigation and kept it for some reason."

Nothing she'd removed from the scene would have any sentimental value as far as she could tell, but who knew? One person's trash was another person's treasure.

"What is it?"

"An engraved desktop Waterford clock. It was a retirement gift from the St. Louis County PD. He'd always wanted a piece of Waterford, so the clock was an ideal present."

Waterford clock.

Fine crystal.

Bri's antennas went up, and a warning began flashing in her mind.

Could the shard Marc spotted have been from that clock?

And if it was, why had it been outside?

Deferring this call suddenly wasn't an option.

"Can you hold, Ms. Morris?"

"Yes."

Bri rose. "I have to find a more private spot. Give me a few minutes?"

"Of course." Alison picked a few grains of salt off the rim of her drink and grinned. "I can always order another one of these if I get bored."

Pressing the cell back to her ear, Bri wove through the tables and tucked herself into a secluded, vine-bedecked alcove by the door that led to the inside dining room.

"Sorry, Ms. Morris. I wanted to step away so we could talk without distraction. Tell me about the clock."

Bri listened as Sandra described the memento that was cut in the intricate Lismore pattern. The lab hadn't yet weighed in on the fragment from outside Les's house, but they ought to be able to tell what Waterford pattern it was. It was possible she might be able to tell herself, if she compared the photos she'd taken to the piece Les's daughter had described. And someone at County should know what clock had been ordered.

"Detective Tucker?"

The woman's prompt pulled her back to the conversation. "Yes, I'm here. I didn't see anything like the clock you described in your father's study. As you said, it may have been destroyed in the fire." It was too soon to mention the broken piece of crystal they'd found outside. Until she was certain it was from the clock, why jump to conclusions or raise questions in this distraught woman's mind?

"That's what I was afraid of. I guess it was foolish to hope it had survived, but it meant the world to him. He put it on his desk after the retirement party and told me that's where it would stay until the day he died. He loved his job, Detective." Her voice broke.

Bri's throat tightened at the woman's palpable grief. "I know. I joined the unit a month before he retired, and I had the privilege to work with him briefly. I also heard from multiple sources how dedicated he was."

"That was Dad to a T." A sniffle came over the line. "I also wanted to let you know I found your phone number in Dad's wallet, on a small slip of paper with a few other notations. They make no sense to me, but I thought they might mean something to you."

Alison passed by en route to the door that led inside, mouthing "ladies room."

Giving her friend a thumbs-up, Bri pivoted away from the dining room, pulse spiking. Could this be a clue about the purpose of the meeting Les had requested? "What's on the paper besides my phone number?"

"Nothing but dates and letters. I'd be happy to snap a photo and text it to you."

"I'd appreciate that, but I'd like the original too. If you'll tell me where you're staying, I could swing by in the next day or two and pick it up."

"I'm actually flying home this afternoon, but I could leave it for you at the front desk."

"That works." Bri jotted down the name of the hotel as Sandra recited it. Then she took a deep breath. May as well tackle the hard issues while she had the woman on the line. "Ms. Morris, I got the toxicology report back from the medical examiner's office this morning. It raised a few questions."

"Like what?"

"There were elevated levels of oxycodone in your father's blood. Do you know if he was taking a strong painkiller?"

"He told me his doctor prescribed Percocet after he broke his ankle, but he only took two pills the first couple of days. He hated medicine. How much was in his system?"

"More than a usual prescription dosage." Like double.

"That's strange. I talked to him the morning of the fire, and he told me his ankle was feeling better."

Another red flag began to wave in Bri's mind.

"There was also a small amount of diphenhydramine. That's a sedating antihistamine used in over-the-counter allergy medications and sleep aids."

"This isn't making sense. Dad hated medicine. He would never take a sleeping pill, and despite his bad allergies, he had other coping mechanisms. Like never, ever opening the windows in the house. That was a sacrosanct rule while I was growing up, and it never changed."

If that was true, why had medication been found in his tox screen? And why had the study window been open?

The flag waved harder.

"There was one other notable finding. Your dad's BAC was .12."

A few beats ticked by. "You mean he was . . . drunk?" Incredulity raised Sandra's pitch.

Bri shifted her weight to relieve the ache in her leg. "The legal limit is .08."

"No." Sandra's tone was vehement. "That can't be right. Dad never drank to excess. I know he started having trouble sleeping after Mom died last year, and I know he was bummed by the broken ankle, but he wouldn't resort to alcohol or drugs to get through. That wasn't how Dad was wired. Something's wrong with this picture."

"If what you're telling me is true, I see the disconnect."

"So what does this mean?"

Bri cherry-picked her next words. "I don't know at this stage, but I promise you this. I'm not going to give up until we have an answer to that question. Please send me a photo of that slip of paper you found in the wallet as soon as possible."

"I'll do it the minute we hang up."

"Thank you. I'll keep you apprised of my progress. And if I find out anything about the clock, I'll let you know. Have a safe journey home."

As they said their goodbyes, Bri wandered back to the table, weighing her phone in her hand. If she hadn't been in the mood for lunch before, she was definitely not in the mood now.

Her cell pinged as she retook her seat. The photo from Sandra had arrived. She opened it.

Alison slid into the seat across from her, a second margarita in hand. "I swung by the bar for a refill on my way back."

Not the best idea, even if it was her day off. But how did you tell a friend trying to deal with a separation initiated by the man she loved that it might be wise to cut back on the booze?

Besides, if the man in question did have a problem with controlled substances, as Alison had confided recently, maybe her anguish about the breakup was misplaced. Maybe the split would be to her benefit in the long run.

Also not an easy subject to introduce.

"What's up?" Alison took a sip of her drink. "You look very serious."

"A new development." Bri redirected her attention to the photo. At first glance, the cryptic jottings didn't mean anything to her, either. She'd have to study them more closely after lunch.

"On Les's case?" Alison motioned toward the cell. "From your conversation, I got the feeling that was his daughter."

"Yes, it was. She had a few thought-provoking nuggets to pass on."

"Thought-provoking as in worthy of further investigation?"

"Let's just say I'm not quite ready to put this case to bed."

Alison's mouth bowed. "Your tenacity reminds me of Les."

"I'll take that as a compliment." She skimmed the dates and letters again. It was gibberish to her, but maybe someone else would notice a pertinent fact, pick up a pattern she was missing. Couldn't hurt to ask a few random people for a first impression. Like her lunch date. Bri angled the phone toward Alison. "Any thoughts on what this might mean?"

The other woman leaned closer and peered at the screen. "It kind of looks like a code. Or maybe some sort of personal shorthand?"

"Do you see any connections between anything here?"

After a moment, Alison shook her head. "No. Sorry."

Bri sighed and closed the image. "Me neither. I guess I'll be burning the midnight oil trying to connect the dots."

"Better you than me." Alison lifted her glass. "Good luck."

"Thanks."

But in truth, it would take more than luck to figure this one out. While Sandra's new information did spike her suspicion meter, to use Marc's term, a hunch wouldn't prove the fire had been set on purpose. That would require compelling evidence—and all the help she could get finding it.

The slip of paper Sandra had found in Les's wallet was a potential starting point, and she'd give it her undivided attention after lunch, but it couldn't hurt to get another opinion on the jottings and the situation in general.

And she knew exactly who to call for that.

Marc Davis.

Besides, she owed him a follow-up call. Sarge would expect

it, and the ATF agent had spent a large portion of a day getting his hands dirty on this case. Bringing him up to speed would be a professional courtesy.

You're rationalizing, Bri. Grasping for an excuse to call him again.

Bri muzzled the annoying voice in her head as Alison raised her glass.

"You sure I can't interest you in one of these? It would get rid of those frown lines."

"I'm not certain alcohol solves problems."

If Alison got her subtle message, she gave no indication. "Suit yourself. It helped me get through a mouse infestation a few months ago." She gave a mock shiver. "If there's one thing I can't abide, it's furry little creatures that come out at night. I had nightmares about them nibbling on my toes until the exterminator took care of the problem. Margaritas helped me sleep." She flagged the waiter. "Let's order lunch."

As he approached, Bri skimmed the menu and settled on an entrée. Lemonade would have to suffice for a beverage.

Because even if the stress-reducing effect of a margarita would be welcome about now, an alcohol buzz would provide nothing more than a short-term respite from the challenge facing her.

Only one thing would smooth out her brow permanently.

Solving the mystery of a fire in which more and more pieces of the emerging puzzle weren't fitting together to form a coherent picture.

And in which the possibility of murder had just moved from long shot to maybe.

FOUR

"THAT WAS A DELICIOUS MEAL, MARC." Nan patted her mouth with her napkin and set it beside her plate. "But all this fancy takeout food since you moved back has to stop. I'm perfectly capable of cooking dinner for us every night. You've already done too much."

Marc forked the last bite of his chicken divan. "Nope. I could never repay you for all the sacrifices you made for me."

She huffed out a breath. "That's nonsense, as I've told you over and over again. It's no sacrifice to love a grandson. And after all the joy you've brought me, I'm in debt to you."

"Not true." Not by a long shot. Where would he have been twenty-five years ago if Nan and Pops hadn't been willing to dust off their parenting skills in middle age and take in a bereft and grief-stricken ten-year-old?

His grandmother's eyes began to twinkle. "Which part isn't true? The joy or the debt?" A glimmer of her old animation sparked in Nan's irises.

"The debt for sure. As for joy . . . I recall a number of my antics that almost gave you apoplexy instead."

The twinkle intensified, tinged with affection. "You did have your moments." She leaned closer and patted his arm. "But you were always a good boy at heart. Still are. I can't believe some lovely lady hasn't claimed you by now."

"She has." He grinned and stood. "You."

49

"Oh, stop." She gave the back of his hand a light smack as he reached for her plate. "You know what I mean."

"I do. And I'll give the dating scene another go one of these days."

"Remember the immortal words of Babe Ruth. 'Never let the fear of striking out keep you from playing the game.'"

Marc stifled a groan.

He should never have told her about Serena.

"Fear isn't holding me back." He picked up his plate too.

"Then it must be me." Her forehead puckered. "I told you not to upend your life and move back to St. Louis just because I have a little health issue."

"Breast cancer isn't a little health issue."

"It's Stage 1. Very treatable."

Also very scary, whether she was willing to admit that or not. If the diagnosis had given *him* sleepless nights, it had to have played havoc with her peace of mind.

"I know it's treatable. But that treatment includes surgery, radiation, and five years of medication. That's a big deal."

"I'm done with the surgery and I'm already a week into radiation. I'm doing fine. Do you know how guilty I feel about all the changes you made in your life for me? I bet I ruined your romance too."

"No, you didn't." He sat back down, set their plates on the table, and took her hand. It was past time to clear up that misperception once and for all. "You saved me from making a huge mistake. I want what you and Pops had, and to build on your baseball analogy, my relationship with Serena wasn't in the same league. It wasn't a priority for either of us—and that's telling. Your news two months ago was the wake-up call I needed to realize Serena and I weren't meant to be."

"You're just trying to make me feel better."

"Wrong. I'm being honest. I came home because I wanted to. For you, and also for me. You're all I have, and Chicago was too far away. When an opening came up here, I considered it providential. A chance for a fresh start on several fronts. Don't ever feel one minute of guilt about my decision to come back."

She searched his face. "I don't want to cause you any regrets, Marc."

Taking a leave from the National Response Team was his only one, but he could return to that after Nan was back on her feet and he was settled in here. An opening would come up again at some point.

He picked up their plates again. "At the moment, my biggest regret is the delay in our dessert. I stopped and got us macarons from that high-end French bakery you like."

"You're going to spoil me."

"No more than you spoiled me while I was growing up. To this day, whenever I eat a chocolate chip cookie, I remember the homemade ones you had waiting for me after school every day." He deposited the plates on the counter beside the sink and lifted the white bag he'd stashed behind the coffeemaker. "I got four flavors. Vanilla bean, raspberry, pistachio, and salted—" His phone began to vibrate, and he pulled it out.

Huh.

After nine days of radio silence, Bri Tucker had decided to touch base.

"If you need to take that, go ahead." Nan pushed herself to her feet. "Nature is calling. Besides, anticipation will add to my enjoyment of our splurge dessert." She winked and squeezed his arm as she passed.

Marc leaned back against the counter and put the cell to his ear, a smile tugging at his lips. Talking to a beautiful woman was never a bad way to end the week.

Especially a woman he'd begun to assume he'd never hear from again.

Bri returned his greeting and got straight to business. "I realize it's late in the day, but if you have a few minutes, I'd like to bring you up to speed on the Les Kavanaugh fire. There have been a few new developments."

"I was beginning to think you'd put that one to bed."

"No—and I may be working it for a while in light of information I got today that raised several red flags."

"I'm all ears."

He listened as she filled him in on the autopsy and tox reports, as well as her conversation with the victim's daughter.

The warning flags were easy to spot.

A possible ID for the piece of crystal they'd found, raising questions about why it had been outside. A man who hated medicine and always kept his windows closed due to allergies, but who had died with high-powered drugs in his system in a room with an open window. A victim who never drank to excess but was legally drunk.

"In addition to all that, his daughter found a slip of paper in his wallet with my phone number and a few dates and initials I haven't been able to decipher. I'm wondering if they have anything to do with why he contacted me to set up a meeting."

As Bri concluded, Nan rounded the corner from the hall into the kitchen. "Why don't I put on a pot of coffee to go with—" She came to a halt inside the doorway and pressed her fingers to her lips.

Marc mouthed "it's okay" and waved her toward the coffeemaker.

"Um . . . maybe this isn't the best time to talk." On Bri's side of the connection, a chair squeaked and a drawer closed. "It's Friday night, and this is long past working hours. I can call you on Monday and—"

"You're still working. In fact, I'd wager you haven't left the office." He strolled over to the back window and propped a shoulder against the frame as Nan set about brewing their java.

"I haven't. But as my siblings often remind me, I tend to

be a workaholic who has trouble leaving the job behind even while socializing. I don't want to intrude on your evening."

In other words, she'd heard a woman's voice and thought he was on a date.

Time to correct that impression.

"You're not intruding. My grandmother won't mind if we delay dessert a few minutes."

Dead silence.

His lips flexed again. Throwing Brianne Tucker curves was kind of fun.

"Um . . . okay. In that case, I'd like to take you up on your offer to stay involved in the case. Based on what's come to light so far, I'm not ready to let this go."

"Understandable. What are your next steps?"

A sound of papers shuffling came over the line. "I plan to talk with the neighbors again, verify they didn't notice any strangers or unfamiliar cars in the cul-de-sac the night of the fire. I want to have another conversation with Les's daughter, see if there was anything in the locked safe that could possibly relate to the meeting he and I were supposed to have. I'm also going to talk to a few of his coworkers and friends, get their take on his drinking habits and aversion to medicine."

"That sounds reasonable. How can I help?"

"I'd like to email you the autopsy report and the note his daughter found. See if any of that material sparks an idea or two."

"I'll review it and get back to you ASAP. Or would you rather wait until Monday to talk? I wouldn't want to infringe on your weekend—or any engagements you might have." Why not see what he could find out about her social life, since he'd shown his cards to her?

"Anytime is fine. There's nothing on my calendar except church on Sunday and a family dinner."

Nice to know she was a churchgoing woman—but did that

family dinner mean she had a spouse and children? The absence of a ring on her left hand at the fire scene didn't necessarily mean she was single.

Short of asking a direct question, however, there wasn't any way to find out.

"I'll try to get back to you tomorrow rather than interfere with your Sunday plans."

"No worries on that score." Her chair squeaked again. "My brother and sister won't mind if you call while we're together. None of us have a nine-to-five job. We're all used to work interruptions."

Brother and sister, not husband and kids.

Despite the darkness outside the window, his day brightened.

"I'll try to review everything tonight anyway. If you want to discuss the case in person tomorrow, we could always meet at a coffee shop. My morning is free."

Pushy, perhaps, but much as he loved Nan, spending an hour with a beautiful woman closer to his own age would liven up his weekend.

"Um . . . why don't we touch base after you go over the material and decide then?"

A disappointing response, but not surprising in light of her wariness during their first encounter.

"That works. I'll call you later this evening."

"The documents and photo will be in your inbox in the next few minutes."

"I'll watch for them."

"Enjoy your dessert."

"Guaranteed."

As the line went dead, he pocketed the phone and turned back to the kitchen.

From her spot beside the coffeemaker, Nan arched her eyebrows. "That sounded like an interesting call."

He flattened his mouth and shifted his features into neutral. "It was work related."

"Uh-huh." Smiling, she picked up the coffeepot and began filling their mugs.

Marc mentally replayed his conversation with Bri. Near as he could recall, he hadn't said anything that should give Nan romantic ideas.

"Interesting how?" He opened the fridge and rummaged around for the cream. "All we talked about was work."

"It wasn't what you said but how you said it—and how you looked when you turned around."

Good grief.

His grandmother's intuitive powers were every bit as strong as they'd been decades ago when she'd been able to give him a fast once-over after a tough day at school and know he needed a hug.

But it was safer to go with the-best-defense-is-a-good-offense strategy.

"I think those radiation treatments are affecting your brain, Nan."

She held out her hand for the cream. "Are you telling me that wasn't a woman on the other end of the line?"

He passed her the carton. "I have a lot of women colleagues."

"I bet you don't get together with many of them on Saturday at a coffee shop."

Nan would have made a formidable prosecuting attorney.

"This is an unusual case." He picked up his mug, grabbed the white bag that held their dessert, and returned to the table.

"How so?" She retook her seat too.

He gave her a topline as he opened the bag and pulled out the macarons. "I'm only involved in a consulting capacity. Which flavors do you want?"

"Too hard to pick. Why don't we split them?"

"Fine by me, but I'll let you do the honors. I'd crush those fragile shells." He rose, pulled the small paring knife from the block on the counter, and handed it to her as he reclaimed his chair.

"So tell me about this woman."

They were back to that.

But rather than evade the question, why not be up-front? Nan had already picked up on his interest. Downplaying it wouldn't fool her.

"Tall, blond, blue eyes. Very attractive."

"Also nice, I take it." She began cutting the macarons in half.

That would be stretching it.

"More like professional." And prickly. And easily spooked.

Nan finished dividing the macarons and passed over his share. "Not the sort of description most men would give about a woman they found appealing."

"I can't argue with that."

"So what was it about her that drew you?" Nan took a sip of coffee, watching him over the rim of her mug.

The very question he'd been pondering for the past nine days.

"I'm not certain. It wasn't as if she gave me any encouragement. We didn't even talk all that much. But there was something intriguing about her."

"Intriguing isn't a bad place to start. It's better than superficial sparks."

There'd been plenty of those too—on his side, at least.

No reason to share that tidbit, though.

"It may be a moot point. She didn't jump to accept my invitation for coffee, and I have enough on my plate anyway. Relationships complicate life."

"They also make it worthwhile, even if they arrive at inconvenient times. Your grandfather and I never expected to find a ten-year-old under our roof in our fifties, but you ended up being one of our greatest blessings. My advice? Don't close any door too fast. Some only open once." She picked up the vanilla bean macaron. "Now let's have our dessert."

"I'll second that."

He went with vanilla too. May as well eat the blandest one first.

One bite in, however, his taste buds exploded. This macaron in no way fit the plain-Jane vanilla stereotype. The confection was bursting with intense flavor—vanilla, amaretto, and a hint of . . . cinnamon?—that added complexity and depth.

Whoa.

"These are amazing." Nan chewed slowly. "Who knew there would be so much goodness to savor inside?"

"I agree."

And unless his instincts were off, the same would be true about Bri Tucker.

But getting past her defenses to test that theory would be a challenge.

Not that he minded challenges. Tackling them head-on had always been his MO, even when the odds of success were formidable.

So if she agreed to meet tomorrow, he'd give it one more try. Worst case, she'd keep her guard up and they'd go their separate ways after this case. Maybe they'd do that even if she did open up. Because unless they clicked beyond the electricity level, a relationship wasn't worth pursuing. Sparks alone eventually fizzled.

Been there, done that, with Serena.

Nan was right, though. Closing doors that could lead to fascinating places and might never open again was a mistake.

So while it was possible Bri Tucker would slam this one in his face, he had nothing to lose by trying to nudge it open.

IT WAS TIME to take care of the last person on my list.

Past time.

But was orchestrating two deaths so close together wise?

I paced over to the window, shoved aside the curtain, and scowled at the murky midnight sky.

Curses on Les Kavanaugh.

If he hadn't persisted in turning over rocks that should never have been disturbed, I wouldn't be behind schedule. Why couldn't the man have walked away from his job and forgotten about it after he retired, like any normal person would do?

But no. Instead, he'd not only doubled down on cases that had been a burr in his saddle, he'd called in reinforcements.

Now Bri Tucker was picking up where he'd left off.

I spat out a few words not suitable for polite company.

The newest County fire investigator was a distraction and a constraint I didn't need.

With Kavanaugh gone, I should have been able to safely complete my mission. If Bri Tucker hadn't started poking around, justice would soon have been done, as it should be.

Because people who did bad things didn't deserve to go about their lives as if they were innocent. Betrayal should be punished.

The delay was maddening.

A patrol car appeared around the corner, and I let the curtain drop back into place. Retreated a step. Frowned.

Could that be a warning? A sign that I should wait longer than I'd like to move on to my next target, give the dust a chance to settle?

But the opportunity in the offing was ideal. And there wouldn't be any connection between Kavanaugh's death and this one. The jurisdictions didn't overlap, and the setup wouldn't fit my usual pattern.

Still . . . there would be other windows to get the job done. Ones I could manipulate to my advantage. Ones that would allow me to develop my strategy at leisure. It was never wise to rush these things. Mistakes could happen.

As they had with Kavanaugh.

I gritted my teeth and fisted my hands.

There'd been too little time to plan that one. To think through every element, every step, every contingency.

Like what to do if the doorbell rang.

I shouldn't have run out without closing my gym bag. Nor should I have tripped over the stupid stone edging around the garden in my haste to escape. That had complicated matters considerably.

Waterford crystal didn't like getting up close and personal with rocks.

And hanging around to search for the missing piece wouldn't have been wise. The FedEx truck had already been driving off, but who knew if someone else might come to call?

I pivoted away from the window, crossed the bedroom, and opened the closet. Pulled out the shoebox that had once held my well-worn Nikes. Flipped up the lid.

The clock was right on top, the largest item in the box.

I picked it up. Ran a finger over the jagged, broken corner of the base. The missing piece didn't bother me, but the fact someone had found it did. Seeing the small fragment amid the carnage would have required an eagle eye and considerable attention to detail. Traits that could cause me problems, especially when those traits belonged to a woman who was already suspicious about the fire at the Kavanaugh house.

I settled the clock back into the box. Fingered Pookie's ring. The nautical emblem from Larry's cap. Adam's monogrammed money clip. The necklace I'd given Renee.

There was just one more item to add.

Then I could bury the box, along with the painful memo-ries, and start fresh.

I wouldn't wait long to tie up the last loose end, either. Couldn't wait long. I needed to be done.

Because only then would I be free.

So maybe I'd take the unexpected opportunity that had come up. After all, the risk should be low—as long as I didn't make any other mistakes.

As for Bri Tucker . . . it was a shame she'd been pulled into the middle of this. While I had no grudge against her, I couldn't let her derail my plans.

So if she got in the way, or got too close to fitting the puzzle pieces together, she'd have to be discouraged.

And if whatever deterrent I decided upon didn't distract her?

She'd have to be stopped.

Whatever that took.

FIVE

A GUY WHO NOT ONLY spent his Friday night with his grand-mother but admitted doing it.

Nice.

Nicer yet?

He wanted to have an in-person meeting tomorrow.

All of which suggested he was single and available.

Hard as Bri tried to focus on the slip of paper Les's daughter had left for her at the hotel earlier today, tingles of anticipation kept short-circuiting her concentration.

Which was dumb.

Hadn't she made a rule that for the first year in this job, she'd put her social life on hold and concentrate on building her career at County? And after her last workplace interpersonal disaster, hadn't she decided to walk a wide circle around professional colleagues going forward?

Yes, she had—and she ought to stick with that plan.

Even if a perceptive, smart, handsome, and apparently well-grounded ATF agent had caught her fancy.

But following rules kept you safe. Helped eliminate surprises. Gave you a modicum of control. Made you less apt to get into trouble. All of which had been critical during her firefighting careers.

And during her early childhood years.

Dark, suffocating memories squeezed the air from her windpipe until she forced them back into cold storage where they belonged and refocused on Marc's offer. A much more pleasant subject.

Even if she wasn't open to any sort of personal connection, maybe she could accept his invitation. After all, a coffee shop meeting to discuss business didn't really violate her rule about—

"Still here, I see." Sarge poked his head into her office.

She shifted mental gears yet again. "Just like you are."

"Goes with the big bucks." He flashed her a grin. "If you're trying to impress me, don't bother. Your work speaks for itself."

"Thank you. For the record, I didn't stay to brownnose. I've been mulling over the latest information on Les's case."

Sarge dropped into the chair at the adjacent desk, long since vacated by her unmarried office buddy who'd been eager to dive into his weekend. "I saw the autopsy and tox report. There were a few surprises."

"What jumped out at you?" Rather than highlight her concerns, it would be smart to hear his thoughts first.

"The BAC. I didn't socialize with Les except at an occasional department function, but I never saw any indication at those or in his job performance that he drank to excess."

"I talked to his daughter again today. She confirmed that."

Sarge leaned back in the chair and laced his fingers over his stomach, grooves etching his forehead. "I wonder if that could have changed, though. I know the sudden loss of his wife knocked him for a loop. The two of them had all kinds of plans for his retirement, including a trip to Ireland. The broken foot had to be a downer too." He shrugged. "Without a job to worry about, or the need to keep a clear head, it's possible he began overindulging on occasion."

Hard to refute her boss's rationale on the drinking score.

"His daughter had other concerns too." Bri relayed the information the woman had shared about her father's medication aversion and allergy issues. "Do you have any insights about either of those?"

"I can confirm he had bad allergies. Whenever we had occasion to be in a car together, he kept the windows closed tight and the air cranked up, even on cool days." The indentations on Sarge's forehead deepened. "The open window at his house is an anomaly."

"Unless someone wanted extra ventilation to stoke a fire, and a breeze to push the curtains toward the flames in the trash." May as well put her hunch on the table.

He tapped his index fingers together, his expression noncommittal. "An open window isn't proof of deadly intent."

"No, but the other facts that have surfaced could indicate my suspicions have merit."

"What's the ATF's take on all this?"

Bri straightened a stack of papers on her desk. He would ask about that. "I just passed on the new information. I may meet with the agent to discuss it tomorrow."

"Good. It can't hurt to get input from an experienced third party who has no personal connection to the case." He stood. "Did you ever figure out why Les wanted to meet with you?"

"No, but his daughter did find this in his wallet." She picked up the slip of paper from her desk and handed it to him. "Does it mean anything to you?"

Sarge studied it. "All I see is a list of numbers and letters." Drat.

"That's all I see too." That's all anyone she'd shown it to throughout the day had seen.

So unless Marc had a thought or two to offer about Les's jottings, the cryptic note would be useless. And any hope that the retired fire investigator had information in his locked safe relevant to their meeting had been dashed with a follow-up phone call to Sandra, who said she'd found nothing but personal papers inside. If there was other pertinent printed material, it had probably been in his desk—and that had been destroyed. As had the hard drive on his laptop.

Sarge propped his fists on his hips. "I know you don't want to hear this, but unless you find some concrete evidence soon to support your suspicions, we'll have to back-burner further investigation."

No, she did not want to hear that.

"I may discover a few other avenues to explore." Hopefully ones that weren't dead ends, as every trail so far had been.

"You remind me of Les." Her boss hitched up one side of his mouth, extracted a folded piece of paper from his pocket, and held it out. "On a different subject, would you touch base with this guy? He's the father of a victim in a fire Les investigated a few months back. Apparently he was in contact with Les on a regular basis. The fire was ruled accidental, but he's not satisfied with that conclusion. He saw the story about Les in the paper and wanted to connect with someone here. Make sure we don't drop the ball."

Bri stifled a sigh. One more item to add to her to-do list. "What's his beef?" She took the paper.

"He suspects foul play."

Wonderful. Now she had two suspicious fires to deal with.

"What kind of case was it?"

"House fire back in April. Victim was a Michelle Thomas."

"I'll review Les's case report and call"—she consulted the paper—"Mr. Wallace."

"Thanks. Seemed logical to have you follow up, since you're involved in Les's case. Have a great weekend."

As he disappeared out the door, she set the slip of paper on the desk. James Wallace would have to wait for a reply until Monday.

Because for once, she wasn't taking work home for the weekend. She was going to walk out this door tonight and chill for the next two days.

Except for a possible meeting with Marc tomorrow.

That could heat up her weekend—if she was able to convince herself that spending an hour with him qualified more as work than pleasure.

A fifty-fifty chance at best.

BRI TUCKER WAS TROUBLE.

And someone who caused trouble deserved trouble in return.

Travis Holmes slid lower into the shadows of his rental car as his nemesis walked through the pools of artificial illumination in the parking lot outside police headquarters.

His lip curled.

Given the hour, she was still going above and beyond in her job. The very quality that had endeared her to their boss, bolstered her credibility, and ultimately destroyed his career.

He spewed out a string of venom and pounded the heel of his hand against the rim of the wheel.

At least he'd found a relatively safe way to harass her, thanks to his surfing skills and diligent networking.

The story in the St. Louis newspaper about the fire investigator's death, including the quote from Bri, had screamed opportunity during his Google search. The blaze was suspicious enough to play into her dogged determination.

Meaning that if a crime had been committed, someone who didn't want that discovered could come gunning for her. A conclusion she would doubtless reach if bad things started happening, leaving him free to make her life miserable with little risk of detection.

Sweet.

And he'd covered his tracks. Left his car in Idaho and drove to St. Louis in the newly purchased clunker he'd sell as soon as he returned, with a wad of cash in his pocket so there was no credit card trail. Parked his car in Marcia's garage here after claiming he had engine trouble. Had her rent a car for him under her name and credit card through a smaller, off-radar service using local hosts. Brilliant. No one would be able to easily track his movements.

Only Marcia knew he was here, and she was in his corner.

Travis slid a hand into his pocket and touched the trigger of his Glock. Yet after one feather-light stroke, he left the pistol where it was.

There would be no shooting tonight. Whatever happened to Bri had to appear accidental, and that required careful planning.

Like the kind he'd done for—

His cell began to vibrate, and he picked it up off the seat beside him. Grimaced at the screen.

Marcia was fast becoming a nuisance.

While her offer of a place to stay during his "vacation" in St. Louis had been welcome—as had the perks that ended up coming with it—who knew his college crush would turn into a divorcee on the prowl for a new long-term relationship?

Not in the cards. Not with him, anyway.

However, renewing their acquaintance gave him an excuse to be here. It would be foolish to rock that boat until he was finished with his mission.

Quashing his annoyance, he infused his voice with as much warmth as he could muster. "Hey, babe. What's up?"

"Nothing. That's why I called. I'm missing you."

"I'll be back soon. I told you I had business to take care of today."

"Today's over. And I thought you were on vacation."

As Bri slid behind the wheel of her car, he twisted the key in the ignition. "I am. This was personal business."

"Do you have another girl here?" Suspicion colored her words.

"How can you think that after the reunion we've been having?"

"Yeah." Her manner softened. "It reminds me of the good old days. Whatever happened to us, anyway?"

He put the car in gear and fell in behind Bri, keeping his distance. "You met Allen and dumped me."

Which had been fine by him. Otherwise, he'd have had to dump her. Marcia had been fun but too demanding. A realization that Allen had apparently arrived at too late.

"My mistake. But now that he's history, we could always wind back the clock."

Travis rolled his eyes. How could she be hinting at anything serious a mere five days into his visit?

Maybe he'd have to accelerate his timetable. Get out of here before she started picking out china.

"Why don't we see how it goes while I'm in town?" He hung a right, keeping Bri in sight. If she stayed in pattern, she'd go straight home to her duplex apartment on a quiet residential street—also consistent with her history. She'd never been much of a socializer.

"We were together for eight months back in college. It's not like we don't know each other." Petulance crept into her voice. Typical if she didn't get her way, and another one of her less-alluring traits.

"That was more than a dozen years ago. People change."

"You seem the same to me. Tall, dark, and charming as ever." A beat ticked by, and when she continued, her tone was cajoling. "I picked up an excellent cabernet after work. I also made lasagna. Everything's waiting."

Travis flipped on his blinker.

Bri's pattern was holding. She was following her usual route home. At this rate, she'd be pulling into her garage within fifteen minutes. Much as he'd prefer to hit a few bars tonight, find a no-strings-attached companion for the evening, keeping his hostess happy had to be a top priority.

"I should be there in half an hour. How's that?"

"I'll be waiting. See you soon, handsome."

He punched the end button and tossed the phone onto the seat beside him.

If only he could toss Marcia away too.

But that would happen soon. Once he finished the job he'd come to do, he was out of here.

Marcia might think the old spark between them was back—and he'd play along while it suited his purposes—but the instant he was done wreaking havoc here, St. Louis would be a speck in his rearview mirror.

And Marcia's romantic fantasies, along with Bri Tucker's perfect life, would be reduced to ashes.

BRI HAD ARRIVED.

Marc took a sip of his Americano as she pushed through the door, his corner seat offering a clear view of the entire coffee shop she'd suggested as a meeting place. A stereotypical table choice for law enforcement types, perhaps, but it had paid off for him on more than one occasion.

You couldn't be prepared to fight an enemy you didn't see coming.

Bri, however, was not an enemy.

He lifted a hand to draw her attention, and she responded in kind before striding to the counter.

Exactly what he'd expected her to do, given the independent vibes radiating from her at the fire scene.

After placing her order, she wove through the crowd of Saturday customers, her skinny jeans, soft-looking sweater, and heeled boots a definite improvement over the baggy jumpsuit she'd worn the day they met. Several people moved out of her path as she crossed the shop, clearly intimidated by her strong, purposeful, I-have-important-business-to-take-care-of bearing.

Only when she drew near did her pace falter for a millisecond. As if she was having second thoughts.

Offering her an encouraging smile, he rose as she regained her rhythm. "Good morning."

She returned his greeting, hugging a notebook against her chest. "This shouldn't take long. I don't want to monopolize your day."

"I don't have any pressing plans." He motioned to the empty chair, waited until she claimed it, then retook his seat and indicated the scone and muffin on a plate in front of him. "I thought you might enjoy a pastry." If she wouldn't let him buy her drink, he could at least provide food.

"I already had breakfast. Thank you."

"I bet it wasn't as healthy as these."

She cast a dubious eye at the pastries. "You lose. I had a veggie omelet."

"Nope. I win."

Her eyebrows peaked. "How can you say that? Those are loaded with sugar."

"What's wrong with sugar?"

"Nothing. But it's not as healthy as veggies."

"Depends on how you define healthy."

She set the notebook on the table. Squinted at him. "How do *you* define it?"

"Same way the World Health Organization does—complete physical, mental, and social well-being, not merely the absence of disease. And part of my mental and social well-being comes from indulging my sweet tooth."

One corner of her mouth quivered. "That's an interesting take."

"Works for me. Have I convinced you to join me in a sugar

fest to launch the weekend? Or were you born without a sweet tooth?"

"Sadly, no. My sweet tooth is alive and well and very demanding."

"Not based on evidence."

She broke eye contact and brushed an invisible speck of lint off the arm of her sweater. "Trust me, it's a constant battle. Usually I win. But you managed to pick one of my splurge items." Catching her lower lip between her teeth, she surveyed the plate. "They have amazing blueberry muffins here."

He took the scone, set it on his napkin, and eased the plate with the muffin toward her. "It's all yours."

"Bri, your drink is ready."

As the barista called out her order, he rose.

So did she.

"Why don't you let me get that for you while you dive into the muffin?" He indicated the plate.

"No. I'll grab it. Thanks."

Before he could protest, she was off again, winding through the tables as he watched her progress.

While the County fire investigator wasn't model-skinny to go with her model-like height, she appeared trim and fit. In light of how she'd hefted and toted debris and heavy equipment with ease at the fire scene, any extra weight she might carry was likely muscle.

Did she frequent a gym? Bike? Swim? Lift weights? She could also be a runner—unless her slight limp was more than a temporary inconvenience due to an injury rather than a permanent condition.

Was it?

She rejoined him less than a minute later, broke off a bite of muffin, pulled out a pen, and opened her notebook. "You said on the phone you'd had a chance to review all the material I sent."

So much for small talk and exploring his growing list of personal questions.

"Yes. As I mentioned last night when we confirmed this meetup, I agree the findings are a bit suspicious, based on your conversation with the victim's daughter. Beyond that, I don't have much to offer. No new insights have come to mind, but I hoped a face-to-face conversation would produce a few ideas. Maybe we could walk through our experience at the scene again, factoring in everything you've found in the interim." While that might prove useful, it wasn't his sole motivation for this in-person get-together. In fact, with any other woman who made the air around him crackle with electricity, he'd initiate a little flirting about now.

But the wariness in Bri's eyes, the sudden tautness in her shoulders, sent a clear keep-your-distance message.

She set down her pen and picked up her coffee. Took a slow sip. "I doubt that will help."

If she wasn't inclined to pursue his idea, pushing could be a mistake.

"So what's your next step?" He took another bite of his scone.

Her brow crinkled. "I'm going to find out what clock County gave Les for his retirement and see if I can verify that the piece of crystal you found in his yard could be from that."

"What if you do? That doesn't prove anything."

"No, but it would be very suspicious." She set her cup down, folded her hands, and leaned forward. "Why would a broken piece of Lismore crystal be in Les's yard? If the pattern is a match, it has to be from the clock. His daughter said that was the only Waterford item he owned."

"That does raise questions. Did the lab find any fingerprints on it?"

"No." She dropped back in her seat, unclenched her fingers, and massaged her forehead. "None of the pieces are fitting. Yet none of them hold a clue about who could have been behind the fire, either. I keep wondering if we missed something at the house."

"I don't think so. We were thorough, and the cause of the fire was obvious."

"Maybe too obvious."

She wasn't letting go of her arson theory.

"Okay. If a crime was committed, what was the motive?"

"Self-preservation? Les had a reputation for being dogged in his investigations. He could have made a few enemies through the years. It's possible one of them didn't want him digging into a certain case."

"But he was retired. If anyone had been concerned about exposure, wouldn't they have tried to get rid of him while he was an active investigator?"

"Maybe they would have if he'd stayed on. My boss suggested he may have continued to look into cases that bothered him after he left. Informally, of course. Someone could have found that out."

Marc didn't try to hide his skepticism. "Pursuing cases in retirement would be very unusual, even for someone who was dedicated and diligent. Besides, as a retiree he wouldn't have the resources to do much. Would anyone consider informal poking around enough of a threat to commit murder?"

"Depends on how concerned they were he might stumble onto something. And the poking around isn't informal now that I'm involved." She picked off another nugget of her muffin and chewed it slowly. "But I can't argue with your overall logic. At the same time, I'm not ready to throw in the towel. Les contacted me for a reason, and the timing of his death relative to our meeting is spiking on my radar. Everything about the whole scenario feels off." She took a sip of coffee and dug into her muffin in earnest. "I don't expect the ATF to devote manpower to this, though. Because you're right. There isn't much to go on."

Like nothing, other than a few disconnects and a stray piece of crystal. None of which pointed to a motive or a suspect.

Yet she was going to continue to pursue her theory, with or without him.

You had to admire that kind of perseverance, even if you'd walked that road yourself on a case far more personal than this one and hit nothing but brick walls.

But bottom line, there wasn't sufficient evidence in this situation to justify a continued investigation, as his boss would no doubt agree. They were stretched too thin to expend limited resources on wild goose chases.

Unfortunately, he was going to have to bow out.

After downing the last bite of his scone, he swigged his coffee. "If anything new develops, feel free to reach out. I'll be happy to help."

"I appreciate that." She wadded her napkin into a tight ball and dropped it on the empty plate. Picked up her notebook and half-empty cup. "Thanks for giving up part of your Saturday to meet with me."

She was leaving already?

"You don't have to rush off."

"I have a list of errands to run today." She stood.

He rose too. "And our meetup here intruded on those. I'm sorry for wasting your time."

"It wasn't wasted." Her gaze locked onto his for a brief, electric second before she tugged it away. "I'll, uh, let you know what happens with the case. Enjoy the rest of your day."

Before he could respond, she strode through the coffee shop to the exit and left without a backward glance.

As she disappeared out the front door, Marc lowered himself into his chair, picked up his coffee, and took a slow sip.

While the business part of their meeting had been a washout, producing new questions rather than new information, one uncertainty on the personal front had been resolved in those parting moments.

She felt the high voltage between them as much as he did.

But she was fighting it mightily.

Why?

And how was he supposed to find out, since there wasn't any work-related excuse for him to initiate further contact?

Maybe he ought to forget her.

He picked up his napkin and wiped the scone residue off his fingers, but the sticky caramel drizzle was hard to expunge.

As thoughts of Bri would be.

Yet short of some new, significant development, their work together on this case had come to an end.

SIX

"EARTH TO BRI. Come in, Bri."

At the playful elbow nudge in her ribs, Bri shifted toward her sister, seated on the picnic bench beside her. "Sorry. What did I miss?"

Cara motioned toward their brother, who was manning the barbecue pit on the patio behind his house. "I said I hope Jack doesn't char the steaks, like he did on the Fourth of July."

"I heard that." He waved his tongs at them. "Those steaks were not charred. They were seared, my dear Cara, which gives them excellent visual appeal and enhances the flavor of my secret rub. If you ever learned to cook more than soup and omelets, you'd appreciate my masterful grilling technique."

She dismissed his comment with a flip of her hand. "You make grilling sound like rocket science. I'm sure if I studied the technique, I could produce a delicious meal. Research, as you know, is my forté. In fact, when it's my turn to host the family meal next month, maybe I'll barbecue and—"

"No!" Bri and Jack spoke at the same time.

"It's not that we don't appreciate the offer, Cara." Bri sent Jack a sidelong glance. "But I have a craving for one of your cheese and mushroom omelets. They're always delicious."

"And they won't break our teeth." Her brother grinned and adjusted the flames.

"Jack!" Bri rolled her eyes.

"What? It's true. I was afraid I was going to have to visit

my dentist after Cara's one and only grilling attempt last spring." He directed the next comment to their sister. "How the heck did you manage to produce ribs that were dry as jerky, anyway?"

"Thanks a lot, Bro." Cara stuck out her tongue at him.

He chuckled. "Just giving you a hard time, kiddo. My teeth survived. Besides, you have many other talents, and we love you even if you can't cook. Right, Bri?"

"Goes without saying."

"If you ladies want to get the side dishes from the kitchen, we're about set."

"We're on it. I'm starving." Bri rose and tugged Cara up. "What else did you prepare for this feast?"

"Baked potatoes with all the fixings and Mom's green bean casserole—for old time's sake. She gave me the recipe a couple of years ago."

Pressure built in Bri's throat during the silence that followed. The green bean casserole had been a staple at family holiday dinners for as long as she could remember, until Mom had finally succumbed to her worsening heart issues eight months ago.

"It will almost be like Mom is with us." Cara sniffed and pulled a tissue from her pocket.

"She *is* with us. We just can't see her anymore." Bri gave her sister a hug.

"It's not the same."

No, it wasn't. With both Mom and Dad gone now, there was a hole in their lives that would never be filled.

"She'd be happy we kept up the tradition of monthly family dinners, though." Jack averted his face and fiddled with the grill settings. Cleared his throat. "Even if some are less palatable than others."

Leave it to Jack to wisecrack when emotions started to run high.

But if that coping mechanism helped keep their detective brother sane on the stomach-churning cases he often dealt with, he could wisecrack all he wanted.

"Come on, Cara. Let's get the rest of the food." Bri towed her sister toward the house. "And if Jack keeps yanking your chain, we can gang up on him about the leaky faucet repair he botched last summer that you helped him sort out."

"Yeah." Cara smirked at him as they walked toward the house. "Fixing a faucet is much more complicated than fixing dinner. How could you have forgotten to replace the O-ring? And using the wrong-sized cartridge didn't help, either."

"I'm not a plumber."

"Neither am I, but I do my homework on repairs."

"That approach could work with cooking too, you know."

"Jack." Bri shot him her big-sister scowl, an intimidation technique that was often effective despite her mere six-month age advantage.

"Sorry." He held up a hand, mirth dancing in his eyes—and not looking in the least contrite. "Truce, Cara?"

She folded her arms as she considered his peace offering. "At least until after dessert. I wouldn't want to be deprived of the chocolate mint squares I saw in the fridge."

Their typical bantering continued throughout the laughter-filled meal, each sibling contributing equally. But as Jack and Cara got into a debate over the Cardinals' performance for the season, Bri's thoughts wandered to her coffee date with Marc yesterday.

No. Not date. Business meeting.

Yet the undercurrents of attraction had been strong, and fighting them had been like swimming against a riptide.

Still, letting that revealing comment slip when he'd apologized for wasting her morning hadn't been smart. It could encourage him. And after the fiasco in Idaho, it wouldn't—

". . . zoned out earlier too. Our dear sister seems to be distracted today."

Bri tuned back into the conversation at the table and found both her siblings watching her with amusement.

What had she missed?

"Did you ask me a question?" She chased a green bean around her plate, keeping her tone nonchalant.

"Yes, but you were off in la-la land." Cara tipped her head. "What gives?"

"She could have a case on her mind." Jack shrugged and went back to eating.

A tailor-made out.

"I do have a troublesome case." True, if not the subject of her daydreaming.

"I bet it's the Les Kavanaugh fire." Jack arched an eyebrow at her. "Right?"

"How did you know?"

"I'm an ace detective, remember?" His mouth quirked. "And in this situation, it's elementary, my dear Brianne. The case is well known in the department, and people in the highest places will be tuned in to the progress. That would be nerve-wracking for anyone, and worse for someone new to County. To tell you the truth, I was kind of surprised they assigned it to you."

"Gee, thanks for the vote of confidence."

"Hey, no insult intended. But I would have expected a more seasoned investigator to take the lead on this one."

"Maybe they wanted someone unbiased." Cara went back to eating too. "Someone who didn't know the victim well and could examine all the evidence without any of the filters that come from familiarity or organizational culture or department history."

"Spoken like the historical anthropologist you are." Jack acknowledged her comment with a jaunty salute. "You could be right. Or her boss may have been impressed by that ware-house case. I know I was."

"I don't think a case would have her gazing off into space with that daydreamy expression." Cara pursed her lips. "Have you met someone?"

Bri shifted in her seat, warmth creeping across her cheeks. "I meet lots of people every day."

"That's not what I mean, and you know it."

Jack stopped eating to join the inquisition. "You mean met someone like . . . a guy?"

"Uh-huh." Cara speared a green bean.

"*Have* you met someone?" Jack's eyes narrowed.

"What is this, the third degree? You're not interrogating a criminal, you know."

Cara looked at Jack. "She's avoiding the question."

"I noticed." He set his fork down. "Who's the guy?"

"I never said there was a guy. You're jumping to conclusions."

"Not without evidence." Jack leaned forward.

"What evidence?"

"You're blushing." Cara singsonged the response, mischief flickering in her hazel irises.

Curses on fair skin.

"You know . . ." Bri set her cutlery down on her empty plate. "If you keep this up, I may skip our next get-together."

"Wow." Cara stared at her. "This must be serious."

"Tell me who the guy is. I want to check him out." Jack whipped out a notebook and pen.

Bri gaped at him. "You've got to be kidding."

"Do I look like I'm kidding?"

No. He didn't.

Sheesh.

She should never have mentioned the Idaho mess to him. All that had done was activate his already formidable protective instincts.

"Listen—no crime has been committed here. Put away your detective badge. And you"—she poked Cara in the arm—"stifle your unruly imagination. If I ever get serious about anyone, I promise you'll both be the first to know. Until then, back off. I'm not going to discuss every man I date."

"Ah-ha! She *is* dating someone!" Cara clapped her hands.

Bri huffed out a breath and stood. "I'll clear the table while you two get your act together." She picked up her plate and Cara's. Grabbed Jack's.

"Hey! I'm not done." He lunged for it.

"Yes, you are." She swung the plate containing a lone green bean out of his reach. "I'll put on coffee and be back in a few minutes."

With that she marched into the house.

And no matter how much they pestered her when she came back, she wasn't going to say anything about the man who'd been dominating her thoughts for the past ten days.

Because both of her siblings were smart, intuitive, and knew her too well.

Meaning the more she denied their theory, the more they'd be convinced she'd met a person of interest.

So until—or unless—there was a substantial piece of news to report about any budding romance that might happen in her future, her new motto with regard to her personal life was going to be simple and straightforward.

Mum's the word.

WELL, WELL, WELL. Wasn't this an interesting and perhaps useful development.

I pulled up the collar of my jacket and slid lower behind the wheel in the spot I'd staked out. No one was about at this midnight hour on Bri Tucker's quiet residential street—except for the crouched figure that was staying in the shadows of the mature trees and bushes and moving steadily in the direction of her duplex.

Very curious.

Also providential.

Lucky thing I'd extended my surveillance later than usual tonight or I'd have missed this potential opportunity. One that could play into the plans I was formulating for my distraction campaign.

The way I saw it, no law enforcement organization had enough staff to indulge a fire investigator who wanted to pursue unprovable suspicions, so at some point Bri Tucker's boss would pull her from the Kavanaugh case. And if she was occupied off duty dealing with other aggravations, she'd have no spare time to pursue her theories.

I'd already come up with a few ideas, but this new twist might put another resource at my disposal.

The figure stopped at the bottom of the duplex's driveway, and I lifted my binoculars. Fitted them against my face.

In the darkness, it was impossible to tell the gender of the person wearing a baseball cap pulled low on their forehead. But based on height and build, it appeared to be a male.

And whatever he was up to probably wasn't legal if he had to skulk around in the middle of the night to do it.

I set the binoculars down and picked up my phone. Filmed the area to identify the location, then zoomed in. The quality wasn't great in the low-light situation, but only I would know that. And there were tons of enhancement tools out there.

After giving the neighborhood a scan, the guy pulled something from a pocket in his jacket and walked across the apron of the driveway. After pausing twice to bend down, as if he was setting objects on the concrete, he stuffed whatever was in his hand back in his jacket and jogged toward a black Chevy Cruze parked several doors down.

I homed in tight on the license plate, memorizing the numbers and letters as I filmed him getting into the car. It wouldn't be hard to trace the owner. I had excellent resources if I needed them.

But why not follow the guy? See what else I could find out? All had been quiet at the duplex since the lights went out at ten thirty, and there was no reason to think that would change before I was back on surveillance duty at dawn for daylight reconnaissance.

I set the cell on the seat, twisted the key in the ignition, and gave the other driver a head start before falling in behind him. It wasn't hard to keep the Cruze in sight at this hour of the night given the sparse traffic. The trick was remaining undetected.

I'd had plenty of practice at that after the shadowing I'd done on my prior targets, though.

The car wound through the streets, stopping fifteen minutes later in front of a modest home in a respectable suburban neighborhood.

Odd that he didn't pull into the driveway.

The lights on the car went off, and the driver slid out from behind the wheel.

I'd killed my lights a few streets back after the meager traffic that had helped mask my pursuit evaporated, and now I too parked by the curb. Picked up my binoculars again and trained them on the dark figure.

Now that he'd ditched the cap, I could confirm it was a man. But he was angled away, making it impossible to get a clear view of his profile.

Didn't matter. I had all I needed. This address and the plate number would tell me everything I wanted to know.

I waited until he disappeared through the front door, put my car in gear again, and tooled toward home, my brain processing this new development.

Two things were clear.

Someone besides me appeared to have Bri Tucker in their sights.

And with the incriminating evidence I had against that someone, it was possible I could get him to do my dirty work as well as his if I played my cards right.

I settled back in my seat, lips flexing.

This had been a good night. For me, if not for the unlucky guy who'd just become my unwitting accomplice.

SEVEN

AS FAR AS SHE COULD TELL, Michelle Thomas's death had been accidental.

Bri read the last few lines of Les's origin and cause report, skimmed the autopsy findings again, and sat back in her chair.

Tragic though it had been, there was nothing in the official documents to suggest foul play in the young widow's death, despite what the woman's father might suspect.

So why had Les continued to talk with him?

Only one way to find out.

Bracing herself for what could be a difficult start to the work week, she punched in the man's number.

He answered on the second ring, his greeting muted against what sounded like a TV blaring in the background, but as soon as she introduced herself, the extraneous noise ceased.

"Thank you for calling, Detective Tucker. I was afraid you people would forget about me now that Detective Kavanaugh is gone. He was a good man."

"Yes, he was. A legend in the department." Bri clenched her fingers around the phone and plunged in. "My boss asked me to follow up with you regarding your concerns about the fire at your daughter's house. Before I called, I did review Detective Kavanaugh's file and the coroner's report. The findings appear to be straightforward." And hard to dispute. It wasn't difficult to understand how a grieving widow undergoing counseling could mix up her insulin or inject too much, especially if she was taking sleeping pills.

"That's the problem. It's too straightforward. The pieces all seem to fit together, but they don't." A touch of agitation crept into his voice. "My daughter was super careful with her medication, Detective. Almost to the point of paranoia. She would never have made a mistake like that. And I've studied the reports too. She was in the wrong room. She stopped sleeping in the master bedroom after her husband died."

Curious, but not conclusive.

"Isn't it possible she could have decided to sleep there that night for some reason?"

"Even if that was true, it wasn't very warm the evening of the fire. Why would a woman who was always cold open the window?"

Bri straightened up.

Another unexplained open window?

She leaned forward, speed reading the report again as she spoke. "I can't answer that question, Mr. Wallace, but from what I can tell, Detective Kavanaugh did a thorough investigation. He was known for leaving no stone unturned. If he didn't find cause for suspicion, I'm not certain it can be found."

"But I think he did have suspicions. Especially after I talked to him about my daughter. Why else would he promise to keep this on his radar in case any new information came along?"

Because he was trying to be kind to a distraught father?

Or had Les actually believed there was more to the story than the evidence was telling?

Had he felt as troubled about Michelle's death as she felt about his? A death that also involved an open window?

Strange coincidence.

Or was it?

"Detective Tucker?"

James Wallace's query pulled her back to the conversation.

Despite the tickle of unease in her gut, raising this man's hopes without more to go on would be unfair. For now, it would be kinder to stick to facts.

"Yes, I'm here. The case is considered closed, Mr. Wallace, so unless new evidence appears, there isn't anything left to investigate."

A few moments of silence ticked by.

"Look, Detective—I'm sure you're busy, but Michelle was . . . she was all I had." His words grew ragged, and he cleared his throat. "Before you check me off your to-do list, could you spare an hour to talk with me in person? I'd like to tell you more about my girl. That may help you understand why this whole thing smells to me, and why Detective Kavanaugh was receptive to my concerns."

Bri squeezed her cell, closed her eyes, and tried to muster up the fortitude to politely decline. Much as Mr. Wallace's grief might pull at her heartstrings, without proof, his suspicions would amount to nothing. If an investigator with decades of experience hadn't been able to find any evidence to support the man's concerns, how could she hope to do any better? And it wasn't as if she had a spare minute to—

"Please, Detective."

At the desperation in his entreaty, Bri massaged her forehead. She'd always been a sucker for people in distress. People who needed a sympathetic ear. Who felt alone and helpless.

Easy to understand, in light of her history.

If nothing else positive had come from that trauma, it had at least given her a heightened sense of empathy that translated to a caring heart.

Which meant she was going to cave to James Wallace's request.

"All right, Mr. Wallace." She searched out his address on the report. A quick detour on her way home wouldn't be too much of an imposition. "I can swing by at the end of the day. About five or five thirty, if that's convenient."

"I'd be happy to come to your office if that's easier for you."

"No." She had more control over the length of the visit if she went to him. "I don't mind stopping by. I'll be in your area later today anyway."

"I'll see you this afternoon, then. And thank you."

The line went dead, and Bri set her cell on the desk. Read Les's report again.

There it was. The notation about an open window. Also a mention of the remnants of what appeared to be a trash can close to the victim.

Eerily similar to what she and Marc had found at Les's house.

But while those parallels spiked her suspicions, they weren't in themselves evidence of criminal activity.

So unless Michelle Thomas's father had more concrete information to offer—unlikely, or Les would have been all over it—today's visit would be nothing more than a compassionate gesture to placate a grieving father.

"HOME SWEET HOME." Marc swung into the driveway and glanced over at his passenger. More than two weeks into radiation, Nan's growing fatigue was evident in the lines at the corners of her eyes and the shadows beneath her lower lashes. A normal side effect, according to her doctor, but stomach-churning for a loved one nonetheless.

"It wasn't necessary for you to cut your day short to ferry me to and from my treatment, Marc." Nan released her seat belt as he stopped the car and set the brake in the garage. "I could have called Uber or another friend after Betty had to cancel out on chauffeuring me."

"The afternoon was winding down, and I was ready to call it quits. Sit tight and I'll get your door."

"You don't have to treat me like an invalid, you know."

"I'm not. I'm treating you the way you taught me to treat a lady." He winked and called up a smile.

Her features softened as she looked over at him. "You're a fine man, Marc Davis. But I feel guilty about taking you from your work."

"Don't."

He slid from behind the wheel and grabbed their dinner from the back seat, his lips flatlining as he juggled the takeout bag while circling the car.

If anyone should feel guilty, it was him. Not about Nan, though. He was here for her and always would be. Never again would he be absent when someone he loved needed him. That was the legacy of the guilt he'd been unable to banish, even after all these years.

But why burden Nan with that? It was his load to carry. She'd had enough to deal with guiding a traumatized young boy through a maze of messy emotions and dealing with all the other challenges that had landed in her lap over the decades. Including this health crisis.

He stopped on the passenger side of the car, recomposed his features, and eased her door open in the tight garage. "Watch your head getting out."

"Thanks for the warning, but I've been doing this for most of my life. I think I can manage." She swung her legs out, but as she struggled to stand, it was clear her youthful spryness had been another victim of her treatment regimen.

Without comment, he gave her an assist.

"Mercy." She brushed a hand down her jacket once she was on her feet. "That shouldn't take so much energy."

"It should if you're having radiation treatments." He shut the door and lifted the bag he held as savory aromas swirled around them. "This may give you an energy boost. It's a bit early for dinner, but we could eat now if you like."

She took his arm as they walked toward the door that led from the garage into the mudroom. "To tell you the truth, I wouldn't mind taking a catnap first if you don't mind waiting."

Another indication of the toll the radiation was taking. As far as he could recall, Nan had never once slept during the day in all the years she'd mothered him.

"I'm good with that. I can catch up on emails and texts while you rest. We'll nuke our food whenever you're ready."

"If you're hungry you could always nibble on one of those blueberry muffins you brought home from your coffee shop date on Saturday."

"It was a business meeting, not a date. Probably our last one."

She turned toward him after she entered the house. "Your business is finished?"

"Yes. Unless there's a new development. But I doubt that will happen." Sad, but true.

"So why not set up a real date at the coffee shop with this intriguing woman?" Her eyes began to twinkle. "Your description of her, not mine."

Radiation certainly hadn't messed with Nan's memory . . . or her romantic inclinations.

"She'd have to be willing—and I didn't get the impression she was."

Nan arched her eyebrows. "How is that possible? She couldn't do any better in the fine young man department than you."

He managed to dredge up a chuckle. "You may be a mite prejudiced."

"No, I'm not. But if she can't see your stellar qualities, she's not worth pursuing, anyway." She clapped a hand over her mouth as a yawn snuck up on her. "The bed is calling. Give me an hour."

"Take your time. I have plenty to do."

They parted in the kitchen, and while Nan slowly traversed

the hall toward her bedroom in the tidy ranch house he'd called home for most of his growing-up years, Marc stowed their dinner in the fridge, returned to the car for his laptop, and booted up at the kitchen table.

Emails first.

He scrolled through the half dozen that had come in over the past forty-five minutes, searching for a name that wasn't there, as he'd been doing for two days.

Of course Bri hadn't contacted him. She'd assured him she didn't expect him to stay involved in a case that lacked substance, and he hadn't pushed to remain engaged.

Too bad he didn't have something more to offer.

Unless he could think of something. An insight, perhaps, that would give him an excuse to call her again.

He rose and strolled toward the coffeemaker, rereading her last message to him from Friday night about their coffee shop meeting. Maybe a jolt of caffeine would kick-start his creative juices.

Because given the low odds that he'd ever hear from Bri Tucker again, it was up to him to come up with a plausible justification to initiate further contact.

And hope she was receptive.

THERE WAS NO EXCUSE TO CALL MARC.

Was there?

As she pulled out of the police headquarters parking lot and accelerated toward the highway entrance ramp, Bri flicked a glance at the cell on the seat beside her.

While she'd received confirmation that the piece of crystal he'd noticed in Les's yard was, indeed, cut in the Lismore pattern and did match the corner of the Waterford clock County had given the former fire investigator as a retirement present, that didn't constitute a breakthrough in the case or merit further discussion.

Nor was there news on any other front. No questions had been answered. No suspects had been identified. No solid evidence had emerged to substantiate her suspicions.

She tapped her finger against the wheel as she merged into westbound I-64 traffic, his offer from Saturday echoing in her mind.

"If anything new develops, feel free to reach out."

The clock was all she had, and it didn't qualify.

End of story.

Except it would be really nice to hear his voice.

Bri rolled her eyes and pressed harder on the gas pedal.

That was not a sufficient reason to call him. On the contrary. It was a dangerous reason to call him. One that violated the hard-and-fast rule she'd adopted after McCall.

She should forget about Marc. Put all her thoughts and energies into finding concrete proof that Les's fire hadn't been the accident it appeared to be.

And in the short term, she ought to concentrate on psyching herself up for the looming meeting with James Wallace and shoring up her resolve to make no promises, no matter how much his story touched her heart or—

Thwump, thwump, thwump.

The steering wheel pulled to the right, and she tightened her grip as a loud flapping noise came from the back of the car.

What on earth?

Flipping on her trouble lights, she maneuvered the car onto the shoulder of the highway.

Could she have a flat tire?

Once parked, she waited for a break in the rush hour traffic, then exited the car, which was now listing to the right.

She circled around the hood to the passenger side.

Yep. The front tire was flat.

Well, crud. What a—

Wait.

She squinted toward the rear of the car.

Was the back tire flat too?

She strode down the length of the car and confirmed the bad news.

Double crud.

Planting her fists on her hips, she expelled a breath. How in the world could she get two flat tires at once? And what good was one spare when you needed two?

What an end to a Monday.

She shoved her fingers through her hair, angled away from the road dust being churned up by passing trucks, and debated her next move.

Either of her siblings would come to her rescue, but asking Cara to drive up from Cape Girardeau would be too much of an imposition. Her Monday teaching schedule at the university was packed. And according to the delayed response he'd sent to her text this morning, Jack had pulled an all-nighter after being called in late last evening to assist with a double homicide.

She'd have to call a towing service. Without wheels, she'd also have to reschedule her meeting with James Wallace.

Heaving a resigned sigh, she trudged back to the front passenger door, pulled it open, and leaned in for her cell. Somewhere in her emergency contacts was a number for a towing—

She blinked at the screen.

She'd missed a call from Marc? Less than a minute ago?

He must have phoned while she was inspecting the damage to her tires.

Why?

Shifting her priorities, she punched in a return call. The towing service could wait.

"Bri?" He answered on the first ring.

"Yes. Sorry I missed your call."

Silence.

She frowned and cupped a hand around her free ear to muffle

the sound of the traffic whooshing by mere feet away. "Marc? Are you there?"

"Yes. You said you had a call from me?"

"A minute or two ago." The air horn from an over-the-road semi blared behind her, and she winced.

"Where are you?"

"On the side of the highway, with two flat tires. Wait a sec while I get away from the noise." She opened the front passenger door and tucked herself into the car. "Much better. Now I'll be able to hear you."

"Did you say two flat tires?"

"Uh-huh."

"Did you drive through a construction zone?"

"No. Must just be my unlucky day."

"Have you called a towing service?"

"Next on my list. But I saw your call and thought maybe you'd come up with a new angle on the case."

A beat ticked by.

"I wish I could say I have, but the truth is I must have dialed you by mistake while I was scrolling through my messages."

Quashing a foolish surge of disappointment, she called up the brightest tone she could manage. "In that case, I'm sorry I bothered you. I'll let you get back to whatever you were—"

"Why don't I pick you up and give you a lift home?"

A truck with a familiar swoosh logo rumbled by, and the company's Just Do It motto flashed through her mind, tempting her to accept his offer.

But that would be breaking her rule. Wouldn't it?

"I, uh, wasn't going home."

"Still on the job?"

"More or less." She filled him in on her call with Michelle Thomas's father and their scheduled meeting.

"Why did Kavanaugh stay in touch with the man?"

"I don't know, and the origin and cause report didn't offer

a clue. It was pretty cut and dried. Maybe he just felt sorry for the guy."

"Or maybe Les suspected there was more to her death, despite the evidence. In fact, I wonder if that case could somehow be connected to the meeting he set up with you."

She gazed toward a line of row houses adjacent to the highway. A light flicked on in the upper window of one, illuminating the interior.

Could that be true?

And if it was . . .

"Hold on a sec."

Pulse quickening, she pulled up the photo of the list Les's daughter had found in his wallet. The one that had appeared to be a jumble of letters and numbers strung together in no coherent pattern. Like a private code, as Alison had suggested.

But suddenly, on one line, the letters and numbers clicked into focus.

MT420.

Michelle Thomas. April 20.

The date of the fire.

"Wow." She sucked in a lungful of air. "I think I found the connection." She explained her discovery in one sentence.

"I'd say you're on to something. Meaning the other letters and numbers may also be cases, which could suggest he thought they were somehow linked."

"That's my take too."

"In light of this development, why don't I pick you up and we'll both meet with the victim's father? I promised I'd be available to assist if any new evidence came to light with the Kavanaugh case, and this qualifies."

Bri hesitated, but only for a moment. Interacting with an ATF agent in the line of duty didn't break any of her rules.

Even if the man in question had temptation written all over him.

"If you can spare the time, I wouldn't mind having company during the conversation. Two heads and all that."

"Where are you?"

She gave him the location. "I can call the towing service while I wait for you."

"Sounds like a plan. Expect me in less than twenty minutes. Are you carrying?"

"Yes." Curious he would ask, since most fire investigators didn't. "Why?"

"You can't be too careful these days, and being stuck on the side of a highway in that area isn't the safest place to be."

He was worried about her?

A surge of warmth filled her heart. Since Mom and Dad had passed on, no one but Jack and Cara had ever expressed any concern about her well-being.

"I'll be fine. I'm more than capable of taking care of myself."

"I have no doubt of that. You have a weapon, and I know you'll keep the doors locked. See you in a few minutes."

He ended the call, and Bri slowly lowered the cell. Locked the doors as cars and trucks continued to whiz by.

Strange how this had worked out.

A call placed by mistake minutes after she'd fought off the urge to call him, leading to a joint visit to James Wallace that could give her a clue or two to follow in Les Kavanaugh's case.

Fate . . . or something more?

Mom, of course, would have said something more. She'd been a firm believer that everything happened for a reason, even if that reason was known to God alone.

So if that was true, what was the reason behind this?

And where was it about to lead?

EIGHT

BRI WAS WAITING INSIDE HER CAR when Marc pulled onto the shoulder behind her, but as he braked she opened the passenger door and climbed out.

He met her by his hood. "Did you connect with a towing service?"

"Yes. I duct-taped my key in the wheel well for them." She motioned toward the front tire.

"You keep duct tape in your car?" He hitched up one side of his mouth while he edged around her to view the damage.

"Doesn't everyone?"

His kind of woman.

He gave the tires a quick look.

Both were flat as the proverbial pancake.

Very strange.

"Have you made someone mad recently?"

Her eyebrows rose. "You think this was deliberate?"

"Two flat tires is unusual."

"I know, but it could happen."

True. Yet it wasn't leaving him with a warm and fuzzy feeling.

"Anyone come to mind who might want to mess with your life?"

Her forehead puckered. "If you're asking whether I have any enemies, everyone in law enforcement does. I'm sure you know that. I haven't been back in this area long, but I imagine the arsonists I've identified aren't too happy with me."

"Anyone in particular? Any threats?"

"No to both."

"Have there been other incidents like this?"

"No. I do appreciate your concern, but I think this was a fluke. You ready to listen to James Wallace's story?"

She thought he was overreacting—and overstepping.

Maybe he was.

But as he'd told her, he listened to his instincts, as she did. And right now they were pinging with negativity.

Nevertheless, he followed her lead.

"Yes." He moved to the passenger door of his car and opened it for her, earning him another eyebrow hike.

"That's not a courtesy much in evidence in today's world." She skirted around him and slid into the car.

"My grandmother gets the credit for my chivalry. She taught me old-school etiquette."

"Kudos to her. The world could use more courtesy and civility."

"Thanks for that. Not all women have been receptive to my attempts to be polite. Some view it as patronizing."

"Good manners have been a casualty in our politically correct society."

"Amen to that." He shut the door, circled the car, and took his place behind the wheel. "If you'll give me the address, I'll get directions." He pulled out his phone.

"No need. I'm familiar with the area. You'll want to continue on I-64 west."

"Got it." He eased back into traffic and picked up speed. "Why don't you fill me in on the gist of your conversation with Mr. Wallace?"

He listened as she recounted their exchange and passed on the news about the clock.

"The confirmation that the fragment we found matches the Lismore pattern is interesting, but it doesn't prove anything."

She shifted in her seat, as if seeking a more comfortable position. "That's how I feel about our conversation with Michelle Thomas's father. It may be interesting, but I doubt it will lead anywhere."

"What's your game plan for that meeting?"

"Let him have his say. See if anything he shares triggers an idea or two. As I already warned him, though, if he had anything relevant to offer, Les would have followed up."

"Yet something he said was significant enough to earn his daughter's name a place on the list in Kavanaugh's wallet."

"The question is what. My first priority tomorrow is to search our files for cases that match up with the dates and initials on the list and review those. See if I can find any commonalities." She motioned to the right. "Take the next exit south."

Marc switched lanes. "Kavanaugh would also have done that, and it apparently didn't lead him anywhere except to you. Since your phone number was on his list, it's looking more and more like he was going to enlist your help with this puzzle."

"Problem is, if he couldn't figure it out, I have no confidence I can. He was much more experienced than me."

"Tenacity can compensate for lack of experience. He could have realized you weren't the type to give up." He flipped on his left turn signal, stopping at the red light at the bottom of the ramp. "Your arson theory with regard to his fire is also beginning to grow on me. It's possible someone related to one of the cases on his list realized he was getting too close to the truth. They could have heard about his meeting with you, were afraid he was going to share whatever intel he had, and decided to come after him. Silencing someone who's a threat is a solid motive for murder."

She surveyed him in the deepening dusk. "So now you're thinking my suspicion that his death may not have been accidental has merit?"

"Let's just say I'm open to the possibility, especially in light of your tire incident today." May as well put his concerns on the table.

"Are you suggesting that the person who killed Les could be targeting me?"

"I'm not ruling it out."

"But what would be the point? I have no clue what Les wanted to talk to me about."

"You're digging in, though. If someone did target Les, they could be getting nervous."

Several seconds ticked by, and he could almost hear the gears whirring in her brain.

"Assuming that was true, what would sabotaging my tires accomplish?" She spoke slowly, as if she was analyzing the question while she spoke. "That's penny ante stuff compared to what happened to Les—if foul play was involved in his case."

"I can't argue with that, but I don't like the double blowout. My gut tells me someone wanted to cause you grief, and the timing suggests it could be linked to an ongoing investigation. Like Kavanaugh's."

She settled back in her seat. "I'm not discounting your instincts, but if the tires were sabotaged, it feels more like petty vandalism than a serious threat."

That was true. The scale was out of whack.

"You may be right." Pressing the issue would accomplish nothing, and it was possible his instincts were off for once.

That could happen when you had a personal interest in someone who was being threatened.

Their conversation during the remainder of the drive to James Wallace's house consisted of directions and related questions. Only after they pulled up in front of a small bungalow in a neighborhood of manicured lawns and stately oak trees did he return to the meeting at hand.

"Does he know I'm coming?"

"Yes. I told him when I called to explain why I'd be delayed. He was more than receptive to having an ATF agent in on the discussion."

"Unless you'd like me to play this otherwise, I'll do more listening than talking."

"That's my plan too. He has information he wants to share, and I promised to hear him out. I'll ask questions if anything he says strikes me as pertinent. Feel free to do the same. I'm not expecting much, but if I can identify the other cases on Les's list—and if any of those raise questions related to his daughter's death—I may want to pay him a follow-up visit."

"Okay. Let's do this."

She met him in front of the hood, notebook in hand, and he fell in beside her during the short walk to the front door.

Thankfully the darkness hid the smile tickling the corners of his mouth.

It was hard to say what, if anything, this meeting would produce. As Bri had noted, the visit could be a bust. James Wallace had already relayed whatever information he had to Les Kavanaugh, and apparently it had led nowhere.

But if nothing else, two positives had come out of today's news and insights.

First, the investigation had legs.

And second, he now had a legitimate excuse to stay in touch with the beguiling County fire investigator who'd captured his interest.

Not a bad end to a Monday.

JAMES WALLACE LOOKED like he'd been through the wringer.

As the slender older man welcomed them into his tidy, modest home, Bri surveyed the deep crevices around his eyes, the gaunt cheeks, the dark circles beneath his lashes.

He seemed in need of a caring word, a comforting hug, and an infusion of hope.

Unfortunately, it was doubtful she'd be able to provide anything but the first one.

After she introduced herself and Marc, the man motioned toward the living room. "Please have a seat. May I offer you a beverage?" He paused on the threshold as they entered the room.

"No, thank you." Bri sat on the sofa as Marc also declined the offer and dropped down beside her.

"I appreciate you both coming today." The man perched on the edge of a chair across the coffee table from them and leaned forward, hands clasped, distress etching his features. "I sure was sorry to hear about Detective Kavanaugh."

"It was a shock to all of us." Bri opened her notebook.

"It's strange how he died in a fire. Like my Michelle." His voice caught.

Bri pulled out her pen. Prolonging this visit wasn't going to make it easier for anyone. "Yes, it is. Why don't you tell us about your daughter?"

His shoulders slumped, and he stared down at his clenched fingers. "She was a wonderful person. Never gave me or her mom a lick of trouble her whole life. Straight A student, talented pianist, volunteered at the church food pantry every week. Resisted peer pressure and stayed away from drugs and alcohol as a teen. She watched over me real careful after her mom died three years ago too. I wouldn't have survived without her and Daniel. That was her husband." His Adam's apple bobbed.

"I saw in the report that she was a widow." Bri gentled her tone.

"Yes. Daniel died a year ago after suffering a traumatic brain injury in a car accident that left him in an extended coma. That was a few months after Michelle was diagnosed with diabetes."

Bri glanced at Marc, whose wince said it all. That was a boatload of tough breaks to cope with in a very short period.

No wonder the woman had needed sleeping pills and counseling.

But that also meant the obvious explanation for the fire was plausible. If she'd been in a groggy state from the pills, it was reasonable to presume she'd not only double-dosed on her insulin and mistakenly taken her more potent morning dose, but that she'd also knocked the candle that had started the fire off the table beside the bed and into the trash.

That had been Les's conclusion, and after reading his report, Bri saw no reason to question it.

Just as no one would see any reason to question her report on Les's death, either, nor an accidental ruling if she chose to go that route should her doubts prove untenable. The case would be closed, filed away, and forgotten unless someone down the road found cause to raise concerns about the conclusions, as James Wallace had in Michelle's situation.

"I'm so sorry your daughter—and you—have had such a difficult time." Bri twined her fingers together on top of her notebook.

James Wallace raised his head, and the anguish in his eyes tightened her throat. "Some days I wonder why I get up in the morning. But the goal to see justice done keeps me going. The fire in my daughter's house wasn't an accident, Detective."

"How can you be that certain?"

"Because I knew Michelle." He raked his fingers through his thinning gray hair and took an unsteady breath. "There was too much of that sleeping drug in her system. She never took more than the prescription dose, and in the weeks leading up to the fire she'd begun cutting back on it. She was finally beginning to come to terms with her grief. And she never, ever made a mistake with her insulin. Also, her being in the master bedroom, and the open window, don't make sense, either—as I told you. For someone who knew her, there are all kinds of pieces that don't fit."

"Why is the master bedroom an issue?"

Bri turned toward Marc to answer his question, but Michelle's father spoke first.

"She and Daniel were high school sweethearts. True soulmates, like her mom and I were. She told me that sleeping alone in their bed made her cry." The older man's eyes began to shimmer. "I felt the same after my wife died. I stopped using our room too."

"Where was your daughter sleeping?" Marc asked.

"In the guest room, down the hall."

"Did you tell that to Detective Kavanaugh?"

"Yes."

"What did he say?"

"He agreed the location seemed odd. He also asked questions about the remnants of what appeared to be a candle in the bottom of the trash can. He got even more interested when I told him that as far as I knew, Michelle never burned candles in the house. She thought they were a fire hazard."

Bri rejoined the conversation. "During any of your conversations, did Detective Kavanaugh happen to mention other cases he was working on?" A long shot, but worth asking.

"No. During our last call, though—about a week before he died—he told me he was beginning to make connections that could prove helpful. I tried to find out more, but that was all he offered. Do you know what he meant?"

"Nothing specific." Bri slipped her pen back into her shoulder tote. Unless she was able to match the notations on Les's list to specific cases and search the reports for commonalities, it would be imprudent to say more. "I expect Detective Kavanaugh asked this, but did your daughter have any enemies you were aware of?"

"No. She was sweet and kind. Everyone loved her."

"So what would be the motive to do her harm?"

"I don't know. Maybe it was an intruder. She could have been a random target."

If that was the case, the odds of finding the culprit plummeted.

But Bri left that unsaid.

"Do you have anything else you'd like to share with us?"

"Yes." He pushed himself to his feet, crossed to a large bookshelf, and withdrew a photo album. When he returned, he held it out. "If you can spare another three or four minutes, I'd appreciate it if you'd page through this. I know you folks are busy, and this case isn't a high priority, but a face and a story can bring a set of cold facts alive. Put a human touch on it that makes it more real. A lesson I learned in my days as a history teacher."

Marc took the album. "We'd be happy to." He flipped it open, scooted closer, and positioned it so they could both see the photos.

With him mere inches away, it was hard not to fixate on the flecks of gold in his dark-brown irises and the firm lips playing havoc with her respiration.

While Marc turned the pages, James Wallace hovered over them, offering brief explanations about what they were seeing. Michelle as a baby in her mother's arms . . . dressed as a Disney princess and clutching a treat bag on Halloween . . . playing a piano on stage at a recital . . . mugging for the camera with friends from behind a sweet sixteen birthday cake . . . diploma in hand at high school graduation . . . on her wedding day . . . in a beach setting with her husband and parents before tragedy became their lot.

Bri tried to focus on the photos and the narrative, but the subtle, masculine scent of Marc's aftershave swirling around her was reducing her brain to mush.

As the man beside her reached the last page and closed the

album, she scooted a few inches away. Maybe distance would help clear her head.

James Wallace took the album back as Marc held it out. "Thank you both for stopping by today. I hope I can count on you to keep Michelle in mind and take another look at the case as time permits."

With a glance, Marc deferred that question to her.

"Yes." Bri forced her brain to engage. "I can promise I'll dig deeper and keep this top of mind in the near term."

"That's all I ask." He returned the album to its place on the bookshelf and faced them. "If either of you have lost people you love, you can understand how difficult it's been for me to cope with the back-to-back deaths of the three people who meant the world to me. And to lose Michelle in such a terrible way . . ." He swallowed. "A person never gets over a tragedy like that."

"I understand. And you have my deepest sympathy." Bri stood and gave him a business card. Marc did likewise. "I'm the lead on this case, but feel free to contact either of us if you think of anything else you'd like to share." Then she took his hand and cocooned his cold fingers in hers. "Please know I'll keep you in my prayers."

His eyes grew glassy again. "Thank you for that, and for your kindness today. Both of you." He reached out and shook Marc's hand.

"I'll be in touch with any news." Bri took the lead toward the foyer.

After they said their goodbyes at the front door, Marc fell in beside her as they walked back to his car. "Sad situation."

"Very."

"It's easy to think you have a corner on sorrow until you meet someone in worse straits."

She peered at him in the darkness, but his features were shadowed. "Are you saying you've had a tragic loss in your life?"

His step faltered for a millisecond, but he quickly recovered his gait. "I doubt anyone reaches their thirties without experiencing some measure of sorrow or loss. I'll get the door for you." He picked up his pace toward the car, moving ahead of her. Ending their conversation.

Hmm.

What trauma was he nursing that he didn't want to talk about?

He didn't give her a chance to probe, because as he slid behind the wheel, he changed the subject. "Why don't you direct me to your house while we discuss our meeting with Mr. Wallace?"

Despite her curiosity about his past, she went along with his suggestion. "Go straight on to the T intersection, then hang a right. What did you think of his story?"

"If what he told us is accurate—and I have no reason to doubt his sincerity or truthfulness—there are disconcerting inconsistencies in his daughter's case, just like there are in the Kavanaugh fire."

"I know. My top priority tomorrow is to dive into Les's list. If I can match up names and cases, I'll go through the case reports with a fine-tooth comb, searching for parallels or similarities. Les would have done that too, but I have more information than he had—from his own case."

"If you want me to review any cases you find as well, I'd be happy to."

"I'll take you up on that."

"Moving on to practicalities for the moment, would you like a lift in to work tomorrow? Your office isn't far from mine. I could also give you a ride after work to pick up your car, if it's ready."

Bri hesitated. Jack would be happy to do both, but for all she knew, he was still working the double murder. When he finally did get home, he'd crash. Asking him to rise at the crack of dawn to deliver her to the office would be inconsiderate. Especially with another offer on the table from a man who wouldn't have to drive all the way downtown from his usual County beat to help her out, as Jack would.

Her phone began to vibrate. "I've got a call coming in. Give me a minute?"

"No problem."

Alison's name flashed on the screen as she pulled out her cell. Not a call she had to answer, but it would give her a minute to think through her strategy for tomorrow.

She put the phone to her ear. "Hey. What's up?"

"Just checking in. You were pretty stressed at our lunch on Friday. I thought you might be glad to hear a friendly voice."

Bri peeked at her chauffeur. His friendly voice had already boosted her spirits, though there was no need to share that with Alison.

"I appreciate that after the day I've had."

"What happened?"

"Two flat tires."

"Seriously? That stinks."

"Tell me about it."

"So how can I help? Do you want a lift home tonight, or to a garage tomorrow after work to pick up your car? I'd offer to take you to work too, but I'm on early shift."

Her commuting options had expanded.

"Um . . . can I call you back in a few minutes? I'm tied up at the moment."

"Sure. Sorry you have to deal with such a mess."

"Could be worse. Talk to you soon. And thank you."

"Friends help each other out. Ciao."

As the line went dead, Bri slipped the phone back into the pocket of her jacket. Accepting a one-way lift from Marc shouldn't be too risky. They could discuss the case on the drive downtown in the morning. Keep everything business-like. Alison could pick her up.

"Turn left at the next light. We're getting close." She shifted her weight to relieve the ache that radiated from her hip to her knee. "I can get a lift home or to the garage tomorrow afternoon, but a ride to work would be appreciated if you're certain it's not too much bother."

"No bother at all."

"So what brought you back to St. Louis from Chicago?"

He shot her a quick look, as if the abrupt change of topic surprised him, but it was impossible to read his expression in the dim car. "Family."

"You're from here?"

"Yes. What about you?"

"Same."

"What did you do before you joined the Bomb and Arson Unit?"

Shoot. Getting into personal history hadn't been in her plans for today.

But if he dug into her past, there was plenty to find on the web. Why not give him a topline?

"I worked for a year as a fire investigator for an insurance company here, until a job opened up at County. I've also done firefighting."

"In St. Louis?"

"For a couple of years, early in my career. Then I moved west for eight years."

"Still firefighting?"

"Yes. Take a right at the corner. My apartment is three doors down. You can let me off in front. Is seven tomorrow too early for a pickup?"

"No. I'm used to rising at dawn."

"If anything comes up and you can't follow through, let me know and I'll make other arrangements."

"I'll be here."

"This is it." She motioned to her duplex.

He stopped the car at the curb. "I'll get your door."

"Not necessary. I appreciate your good manners, but you've done enough for me already today." She slid from the car and leaned back down. "Thank you again."

"It was my pleasure." The warmth in his tone seeped into her pores. "I'll see you tomorrow."

She closed the door and backed off, but he didn't pull away. Why was he—

Oh.

He must be hanging around until he was certain she was inside safely.

The man was a gentleman through and through.

Digging through her tote for her keys, she hustled to the door. Once it was open, she waved to him and pushed through, striding toward the kitchen to deactivate her security system. That task accomplished, she returned to the living room and peeked through the front window.

Marc was gone.

But in his wake he'd left a sweet stirring of tenderness, longing, and anticipation—along with a healthy dose of angst.

The timing for an appealing man to come into her life was all wrong, and sending even subliminal signals of interest to a coworker was a disaster waiting to happen.

Been there, done that, never going down that road again.

She flipped off the foyer light and wandered back to the kitchen. It was past dinnertime. She needed to eat.

At least Marc hadn't suggested they stop somewhere for food.

Because heaven help her, if he had, the self-discipline that had always been one of her core strengths could have failed her.

As it might still do if the first man in almost three years to

catch her fancy continued to infiltrate her heart and under-
mine her resolve.

THIS WAS NOT GOOD.

Not good at all.

I clenched my teeth as the headlights of the car disappeared
down Bri Tucker's street.

Luckily I'd found a spot on the outer road to continue my
surveillance after her mishap on the highway or I wouldn't
have seen Sir Galahad come to her rescue. The man had Fed
written all over him, so he must be the ATF agent who'd been
called in on the Kavanaugh case. And if I hadn't hung around,
I'd also have missed their visit to Pookie's childhood home.

I might not know what had led them there, but I did know
this.

My deterrence plan needed to shift into high gear.

Travis Holmes could take care of that for me—if he wasn't
already planning another strike of his own on Bri that could
do double duty.

Time to move on and see what he was up to tonight.

I put the car in gear and pointed it toward Marcia Blake's
house.

I'd learned quite a bit about Travis and Marcia since last
night. While Marcia had rented the car, Travis was listed as
a second driver. Like many rental customers, they'd left the
agreement in the glove compartment, and accessing the car
in the middle of the night had been a piece of cake. Though
I'd come armed with a lock-picking set, putty knife, strip of
plastic, and coat hanger, the tennis ball trick had worked like
a charm on my first try.

And once I had Holmes's name and home address, it had
been obvious he was the one with the connection to the
woman who was fast becoming a serious threat.

Why he had her in his sights wasn't yet clear, but that was unimportant. What mattered was that he'd appeared at exactly the right time.

For me. Not for him—or Bri Tucker.

And if he didn't have any other tricks up his sleeve to make her life miserable . . . if the flat tires had been a one-off . . . I'd have to convince him it was in his best interest to help me out. Unless he wanted the video I'd shot last night to wind up where it could cause him serious trouble.

NINE

BINGO. AGAIN.

Bri stopped scrolling through the Bomb and Arson Unit's report database as another match to the fires on Les's list popped up.

Renee Miller. Died of smoke inhalation in a blaze at her house ten months ago.

She jotted the woman's name down under Adam Long, who'd died in a similar fire fourteen months ago.

Michelle Thomas was already on the list.

That left one set of initials unaccounted for—the first date on the list. There'd been no match for that presumed fire from a year and a half ago.

Bri leaned back in her chair. The pattern was clear. Yet she'd come up blank with the first notation on Les's list.

Why?

Her cell began to vibrate, and she pulled it out.

The garage.

As soon as she answered, the guy on the other end gave her the bad news. "Sorry to tell you this, but the two flats aren't salvageable. You've got punctures in the shoulder of one tire and multiple punctures in both that are too close together to repair."

She squinted at the cursor on her laptop screen. "Multiple as in how many?"

"Three or four in each, and a third tire went flat after we

towed the car in. Same story. The fourth tire seems to be hold-ing air. Roofing nails were the culprit, by the way. Is someone putting on a new roof in your area?"

"No. There hasn't been any activity like that, or construc-tion of any kind, in my neighborhood."

"Huh. I've never seen anything like this before. It's pretty weird."

"So I need three new tires?"

"I'd suggest four. The tread is worn on all of them."

Sad but true. Replacing them was on her to-do list for down the road, after she beefed up her savings.

So much for that plan.

"Okay. Go ahead and put on four new ones. How much will that set me back?"

She cringed as he gave her the amount.

"That's assuming you want comparable tires. We could go with a cheaper model, but I'd recommend a higher quality tire if you're planning to keep your car for a while."

Yes, she was. A long while.

"The ones you suggested are fine. Can I pick up the car after work?"

"Sure. We're here till seven."

Seconds after she pressed end, her cell began to vibrate again.

This call she was happy to take.

"Morning again, Marc." She flicked a glance at her watch. Two-thirty already? Where had this Tuesday gone? "Or I should say afternoon."

"Your morning must have been as busy as mine."

"Nonstop. But I did manage to go through our database, and I've got matches for three of the four notations on Les's list."

"So your theory was correct. Have you had a chance to read the reports yet? Look for commonalities?"

"No. I was called out to a fire not long after you dropped

me off at work and only got back to the office an hour ago. Barring any other interruptions, I'm going to focus on culling through these this afternoon."

"If you want to send me copies, I can do the same. We could get together tomorrow or the next day to compare notes."

Another meeting with Marc?

That would definitely be the highlight of her week.

"I'm on board with that."

"What's the story on your car?"

A few beats of silence ticked by after she relayed the message from the service guy at the garage, and it wasn't hard to guess what he was thinking. Nor could she brush off his concerns as easily now.

"I have to admit I'm a bit spooked by the news, especially since I haven't been anywhere near an in-progress roofing job or construction zone." She doodled a bullseye on the pad on her desk. Scowled. Scratched over the scribble.

"You're certain there isn't someone who might have a grudge against you? Not just job-related but on a personal level?"

An image of Travis flashed across her mind, and Bri frowned.

That was crazy.

While their issue had been contentious, almost three years had passed. And he was far away. It was ridiculous to worry he'd—

"Your silence suggests you've thought of someone."

As Marc spoke, she pulled herself back to the conversation. "Like I said before, I assume there are people in my professional life who aren't happy with me for raining on their illegal parade. In terms of my personal life, I did have a bad experience with a guy out West. But I haven't had any contact with him since I came back to St. Louis."

"Was the experience bad enough to warrant concern about your safety if he was here?" Marc's tone was measured, but there was steel in his voice.

"No." Travis wouldn't risk his career by orchestrating petty pranks.

Would he?

Maybe she ought to contact Crystal. They hadn't touched base in a while, and while the other female smokejumper in their crew had also moved on career-wise, she'd stayed in Idaho. It was possible she had more recent intel on Travis.

"May I suggest being extra careful until we're certain this incident was a freak accident?"

"Goes without saying. I don't take chances."

"Good to know. I'll watch my email for those files."

"I'll send them over as soon as I hang up." Sarge appeared at her door, and she motioned him in. "My boss is here. Talk to you soon."

They said their goodbyes, and as she ended the call, Sarge strolled over to her desk. "Any news on Les's case?"

"Yes. I was just talking to my ATF contact about it." She relayed the latest. "But unless I can spot whatever caught Les's attention with these cases, this may go nowhere. And the missing match is bothersome."

"I wonder if it could be from another jurisdiction."

If so, finding it would be difficult. The FBI's Uniform Crime Reporting Program was woefully lacking in arson information, and the Arson and Explosives Incident System maintained by the ATF wasn't complete, either. Nor was it all that straight-forward to sort through. Searching those would be like looking for a needle in a haystack, and who had time for that?

Bri sighed. "If that's the case, it may forever remain a mystery. My plate is already full."

"I hear you—and I don't expect miracles. If Les couldn't crack whatever puzzle he stumbled across, it may not be solvable." He folded his arms and expelled a breath. "We're going to have to start ratcheting this back."

Disappointing, but not unexpected.

"Understood."

"Keep me in the loop, okay?"

"You got it."

As he disappeared out the door, Bri swung back to her laptop and emailed the origin and cause reports for the cases she'd identified, along with the autopsy results, to Marc.

Then she settled in to give them a thorough read.

By five o'clock, when Alison texted to let her know she'd arrived, Bri hadn't quite made it through both of them, thanks to several interruptions during the afternoon.

But she'd managed to pinpoint a few similarities.

All of the victims had been found in a room with an open window.

All of the fires appeared to have originated in a trash can.

All of the victims died of smoke inhalation near where the fire had started, and either drugs or alcohol were found in their system.

Plus, in addition to the missing clock reported by Les's daughter, the son of one of the other victims had asked about a monogrammed money clip, which he claimed his father always had on his person. However, it hadn't been found in the clothing he'd been wearing nor anywhere at the scene.

Were items from the other two victims on the list also AWOL?

That was a follow-up question for Michelle Thomas's father and the family of Renee Miller.

Bri packed up her laptop and notes and hurried toward the exit. This would be a working evening. Sarge was a patient man, but he was also practical. He'd cut her a reasonable amount of slack to continue delving into Les's puzzle, but current investigations would take priority. With their heavy caseload, it would be difficult to pursue this during normal business hours.

Not a problem. If she had to play with this riddle while off duty, so be it.

And that very diligence and determination could be why Les had considered enlisting her help, as Marc had suggested.

Alison pushed open the passenger door as she approached.

"Sorry to keep you waiting." Bri slid in, set her laptop, tote bag, and purse at her feet, and buckled up.

"No worries." Alison slipped her phone into a slot on the center console and put the car in gear. "I'm near the end of the romance novel I'm reading, and the swoon-worthy hero was about to come to the rescue." Lips bowing, she gave a sheepish shrug. "Despite my current situation, I'm a firm believer in happy endings. Even my own. I haven't given up on Nate yet."

"You really think the two of you might get back together?" Didn't seem likely after more than eighteen months, especially since Alison had hinted he was still battling the opioid issue at the root of their problems. But love could short-circuit common sense.

"We haven't shut down the lines of communication. But I sure wish that old back injury hadn't flared up and started him down a wrong path with painkillers." Alison wove through the rush hour traffic, toward the highway entrance ramp, and changed the subject. "What's all that?" She motioned to the material on the floor.

"Work."

Her volunteer chauffeur wrinkled her nose. "At least I can leave the job behind for the day after my shift ends. A hot new case?"

"No. Still dealing with the Les Kavanaugh investigation."

"You ever decipher that code you asked me about at the restaurant?"

"I've made a little headway, but it's led to more questions than answers. I feel like I'm trying to play a connect-the-dots game with half of the dots missing. And Sarge is starting to shut the investigation down. I'm going to have to relegate a lot of the work to after hours if I want to keep it alive."

Alison shook her head. "When I hear your stories and see the long hours you work, I'm glad I'm not a detective. Fire-fighting is hard, physical labor—and my alternate days playing paramedic have their own challenges—but on the plus side, my brain isn't fried at the end of my shift. And my free time is my own."

"I hear you. So how were your days off?"

"Quiet, other than my lunch with you on Friday. But I had my book to keep me company. This weekend's a different story. My sister's coming. Only for two nights, but I'll take it."

"That's great."

"I know." She accelerated onto the highway. "Even though Columbia isn't that far away, we don't get to see each other often. I've tried to convince Sophie to move to St. Louis, but she prefers life in a smaller town. Me, I couldn't wait to live in a big city. To each his own, I suppose. She loves the grade school where she teaches, even if her odds of meeting Mr. Right in that environment are small."

"Maybe she's happy being single."

"That's possible. After all, a woman doesn't need a man to lead a full, rich life—present company being an excellent example of that. To tell you the truth, I think my experience has made her gun-shy of marriage. Unless, of course, Nate and I end up back together." The corners of her mouth rose again in a wistful smile. "Hope springs eternal and all that."

"I'm all for whatever makes you happy, as long as he gets his act together. And I'd love to meet Sophie sometime."

"I have a full agenda planned for us already, but why don't we all get together during her next visit?"

"Let's plan on that."

The conversation moved on to other topics for the remainder of the drive. Not until Alison braked at the garage did the subject of work resurface.

"Good luck with that tonight." She waved a hand toward the laptop and tote bag.

"Thanks." Bri gathered up her belongings and opened the door. "I'll take all the luck I can get."

"You can always call on that ATF agent for help if you get stuck."

"He's already back in the loop."

Alison groaned and rolled her eyes. "I told you those Fed types like to be in charge."

"Not this one. He hasn't tried to take over."

"Glad to hear it. Is he nice?"

"Uh-huh." Very.

"Young?"

"Relatively speaking."

"Handsome?"

Oh yeah.

"That would be a fair description."

"Single?"

"As far as I know."

Alison grinned. "I wouldn't mind working with a Fed who had all those attributes, either." She glanced in the rearview mirror as another car pulled in behind her. "If you ever need another lift, give me a call."

"I will. Thanks again." Bri closed the door and hoofed it toward the garage while her chauffeur pulled out of the lot.

Some women would have let relationship problems sour them on marriage. But despite the bum hand she'd been dealt in the romance department, Alison still viewed the world through rose-colored glasses and saw Cupid's arrow everywhere.

Sweet, but dangerous. Because a starry-eyed outlook could also blind you. It was far safer to be pragmatic and learn from mistakes, as she had after her dreadful experience in Idaho.

Better to be slow and cautious than fast and sorry.

As Alison's taillights disappeared in the distance, Bri pushed through the door of the garage, rummaged through her purse for her wallet, and reviewed her priorities for the evening.

First, she'd grit her teeth and pay the hefty bill for four new tires. Then she'd go home, nuke a frozen dinner, pore over the mystery files again, and try not to dwell on Marc's worry that the flats were more than mere bad luck. That they were an attack . . . a payback . . . retaliation . . . revenge.

Ignoring that possibility would be foolish, however. And no one had ever called Bri Tucker foolish.

But if the flats did represent retribution, what was she supposed to do about it? She didn't even know where she'd picked up the nails. And how could she figure out who was behind it if she didn't have a clue what had motivated the attack?

She inched forward in the line, forcing herself to take a deep breath.

Worry and panic would get her nowhere. Those emotions had been dangerous and distracting during her smokejumper days, and they were dangerous and distracting now. She had to corral them, as she'd done on the disastrous day she'd almost lost her life.

And she would.

If someone was trying to make her life difficult, she wouldn't let them rattle her. She'd carry on and keep doing her best, as she always did.

There was one big difference this go-round, though.

Marc was in her corner.

Yes, they were new acquaintances. And yes, her instincts about men had failed her once. But her eyes were wide open now.

So unless fate was setting her up for a second spectacular fail with the opposite gender, Marc was the real deal.

Whether he'd end up helping her solve the puzzle Les had left remained to be seen, but one thing was for sure.

If she got stuck while trying to solve this case, or if someone really was trying to wreak havoc in her life, Marc was standing by as her backup.

That was comforting.

Nevertheless, as she paid her bill and the attendant handed over her key, Bri sent a silent plea heavenward that her future encounters with the charming ATF agent would be confined to the Les Kavanaugh puzzle rather than the consequences of someone bent on playing sick practical jokes—or worse.

TEN

MARC FINISHED RESPONDING to a text from his boss, hit send, and glanced toward the doors in the lobby of the medical office building.

No sign of Bri yet.

He pocketed his cell and leaned back in his chair.

Catching her on the fly to discuss the Kavanaugh puzzle wasn't ideal. A leisurely chat over another round of coffee and treats would have been far preferable.

But with the week he'd been having, this was as good as it was going to get—and it was better than a phone call.

The doors whooshed open, and Bri entered on a gust of late-afternoon autumn air.

He rose from the seat he'd claimed near the fountain in the center and waved to catch her attention.

Smoothing a hand over her wind-tossed hair, she hurried toward him. "It's blowing a gale out there. I think a front is moving in."

"That's what the meteorologists are predicting. Sorry to bring you out in all this."

"I've been in worse weather. You want to sit here, or talk somewhere else?"

"Here is fine." He motioned to the chair beside his.

"Everything okay with your grandmother?" She took the seat he'd indicated and set her tote bag and purse beside her.

"TBD. They x-rayed her wrist. Now she's waiting back at

her doctor's office for the verdict—and none too happy about it, either. She thinks I overreacted."

"I don't." Her response was instantaneous and adamant. "If someone I loved told me they'd lost their balance and fallen, I'd do the same thing. Especially if they were dealing with repercussions from surgery and radiation."

"Thanks for that." During their earlier phone call, Bri hadn't asked for more information beyond the quick briefing he'd given her on Nan's diagnosis and treatment regimen, but her support was comforting. "She's the only family I have, so I'm extra careful."

"I hear you. Family is everything. My brother and sister and I hovered over my mom too after her heart began to fail. Her deteriorating health was one of the reasons I moved home."

A woman with strong family connections.

Nice.

She pulled a notebook out of her tote and flipped it open. "I don't want to tie you up in case your grandmother needs you."

In other words, she was redirecting the conversation away from personal subjects.

Nothing new there.

"I know you want to keep the momentum going with the Kavanaugh case, and I have a packed day tomorrow. More packed than ever since I'll have to make up for this unexpected blip in my schedule. Otherwise I wouldn't have asked you to drive out here."

"I didn't mind. But we could have talked by phone."

True. Except in person was far better. With the cell pressed against his ear, he wouldn't have been able to see her expressive blue eyes or catch a whiff of the faint, spicy fragrance that wafted his direction with every shimmer of her blond locks.

Selfish, yes, but maybe she was enjoying this face-to-face visit as much as he was.

A man could hope, anyway.

"In-person meetings tend to be more productive."

She snorted at his lame excuse. "Not in my office."

"Let me rephrase. One-on-one meetings tend to be more productive—and satisfying."

Their gazes locked for a second before she pulled hers away. "Let's, uh, test that theory. I assume you reviewed the reports I sent?"

"Yes. I spotted a number of commonalities."

She nodded as he rattled them off. "I saw all that too. Les was the lead on one of the two fires I identified in our database. I talked to the investigator on the other one, who often worked with him. He remembered them chatting about the case. I assume that's how Les got clued in to the similarities. The fourth one remains a mystery. My boss suggested it could be from another jurisdiction."

"If that's the case, how would Kavanaugh have known about it?"

"After all his years in the business, he had a ton of contacts. Mostly in neighboring areas, meaning the case could be nearby. But it would take a fair amount of digging to unearth it, and there are only so many hours in the day."

While that was true, the woman sitting across from him was the type to find those hours, even if they had to be carved out of sleep.

"You're still going to try, aren't you?"

She brushed off a piece of dried grass the capricious wind had pasted on the bottom of her jacket. "I'll continue poking around whenever I have a spare minute. I noticed that in both Les's and Adam Long's cases, family asked about missing items from the fire scene."

"I saw that too. I presume you're going to talk to James Wallace and the other victim's family, see if that's a pattern."

"Already done. Neither noticed anything missing, although they couldn't say for certain there wasn't. Nothing much was left to find in any of these cases. Nor did either of them recognize the other names on the list."

"So what's next?"

She sighed and pushed her hair back. "I don't know. I'd like to find the name associated with the first date on the list. It's possible something in that case would spark an idea or two."

"But Kavanaugh had that information and it apparently didn't trigger anything for him."

"I know, but we also have the evidence in his case to work with as well. We know items were missing from two of the fires. Les may have suspected foul play, but the clock fragment gives that theory heft. An arsonist could have taken a souvenir."

"That's possible. I'll tell you what. Why don't we divide up the nearby jurisdictions, and as our schedules permit see if we can find a name to go with the first date on Kavanaugh's list?"

She tucked her hair behind her ear. "Seriously? Don't you have a full plate already?"

Yeah, he did.

But if he didn't offer to help, he wouldn't have an excuse to continue seeing her.

"No fuller than yours, I expect."

"I don't have an ailing grandmother to attend to."

"You have other family obligations."

A shadow passed over her features. "Not health related. Mom and Dad are both gone now."

So she was as parentless as he was—though he at least had Nan.

"I'm sorry."

"Me too." She watched a stooped, white-haired man trundle slowly by behind a walker, her expression melancholy. "They were older when they adopted us, but I hoped we'd have them longer than we did."

Bri and her siblings were adopted?

That was news.

Before he could try to ferret out a few details on that subject, she frowned, straightened up, and once again shifted back to business. "I'll go ahead and draw up a list of nearby jurisdictions, along with contact information for the fire investigation units, and send you a copy. You can pick as many or as few as you want to check out, and I'll tackle the rest."

"That works."

"Is there anything else we should talk about today?"

Yes. Her family background. The story behind her limp. Her career out West. Whether she'd be open to another Saturday morning get-together—one that wasn't work related.

But she was already stowing her notebook, preparing to end their impromptu meeting.

While patience wasn't his strongest virtue, perhaps he should leave his questions for another day. The lobby of a medical office building wasn't an ideal place to dive into personal subjects.

"Nothing that can't wait."

She threw him a cautious look as she stood. "I'll email you the list tomorrow, or later tonight."

Definitely not a nine-to-five woman.

He rose too. "I'll watch for it. Let me walk you to your car."

"Thanks, but I'm not far away and the wind is fierce." She retreated a step.

"Wind doesn't bother me—and you wouldn't want me to disappoint my grandmother with such a lapse in etiquette, would you?" He motioned for her to precede him.

After a brief hesitation, she started toward the door.

Outside, the shadows had lengthened and dusk was fast approaching as they trekked across the parking lot under the leaden sky. The gusty wind was also a force to be reckoned with. He'd have to pick Nan up at the door after she was done, even though she'd protest.

Like Bri had protested this escort.

What was it about him that activated her proceed-with-caution impulse? Was it him personally, or was she gun-shy about all men after the bad experience she'd referenced out West?

He mulled that over as the wind buffeted him, and more than once he had to fight the temptation to take her arm. Especially as her limp grew more pronounced the longer they walked.

And it was a long walk.

Bri wasn't parked as close to the building as she'd indicated. In fact, her car was at the far end of the thinning lot.

She spoke as if she'd read his mind. "Sorry for the hike. I'm a little farther away than I thought. The place was packed when I arrived."

"I don't mind the exercise. I was behind my desk most of the day—my least favorite place to be."

"I hear you. I loved the wide-open space out West, and despite all my fieldwork in this job, there are days the walls feel like they're closing in on me. But that's not a new—"

In the abrupt silence, he assessed her. Her lips were clamped together, and she'd picked up her pace.

What had she been about to say? Why was she plagued by a feeling of walls closing in on her?

It was clear from her furrowed brow, however, that she had no intention of answering those questions, either.

"I'm right here." She indicated her car with a flick of her wrist as she approached, then dug through her purse and extracted her keys without slowing her stride. As if she couldn't wait to relieve him of his escort duties.

Unfortunately, his phone cooperated with her. It began to vibrate as she rounded the trunk.

He skimmed the screen.

Nan.

She must be finished with her appointment.

Much as he'd like to eke out a few more minutes with Bri, he needed to get Nan home ASAP. After this latest setback, she'd be exhausted.

He put the cell to his ear. "All finished?"

"Yes. I'm in the lobby. Where are you?"

"Already in the parking lot." That should deflect any protests about curb service. "I'll pick you up in less than five minutes. What's the verdict on the wrist?"

"Slight sprain, like I told you. Nothing to be concerned about. I'll wait at the door."

He slid the phone back into his pocket and pulled out his keys.

"How's your grandmother?" Bri had already tossed her purse and tote bag onto the passenger seat.

"Fine. It's just a sprain."

"Glad to hear it." She angled away from the wind. "I'll get that list to you as soon as I can."

"I'll watch for it. Thanks again for meeting me here."

"No problem. It gave me an excuse to leave my desk behind earlier than usual. And for once, I'll beat my brother to the restaurant where we meet for dinner every couple of weeks. Talk to you soon."

She slid behind the wheel, closed the door, and started the engine.

Marc backed off as she pulled out, lifted a hand in farewell, and strode toward his car at the other end of the lot.

Nan was waiting when he pulled up at the entrance. As he set the brake, she opened the door and eased into the passenger seat.

"Why didn't you let me help you?"

"You can help me with the belt." She pulled it out with her uninjured right hand and extended it toward him. "Besides, I was afraid that wind would knock me over, and two falls in one day would be ridiculous. The sky is also threatening to open at any moment. And to tell you the truth, the faster I can get out of here, the better. I've had my fill of medical facilities."

"I don't blame you. What's the treatment for the sprain?"

She lifted it up with her other hand to display the elastic bandage. "The usual RICE advice—rest, ice, compress, elevate. After all your childhood bumps and bruises and sprains, I could have saved us both a trip here and treated this myself. I know the routine."

"I wanted to make sure it wasn't more than a sprain."

"You worry too much."

"Kind of like how you worried about me in my younger days?" He grinned at her as he exited the parking lot.

"Mothers—and grandmothers—are supposed to worry. It's in the job description. And for the record, I still worry about you. So why were you out in the parking lot?"

Of course she'd ask that. Radiation might tire her out, but it hadn't slowed down her mind.

It was unfortunate his meeting with Bri hadn't wrapped up five minutes sooner. If it had, he would have been back in the lobby before Nan was ready to leave.

"Since I had time to kill and work to do, I arranged for a colleague to swing by to discuss a case."

He caught the arch of her eyebrows in his peripheral vision. "In the parking lot? In all that wind?"

"No. We met in the lobby. I, uh, walked her to her car afterward. Like you taught me."

She shifted toward him, a glint of interest sparking in her eyes. "Was this a meeting with your intriguing woman, by chance?"

"Yes." Why lie?

"Does she have a name?"

"Brianne. She goes by Bri."

"Pretty. I bet she was impressed by your excellent manners."

"I think so—but I gave you all the credit." He accelerated toward the highway.

"I thought you said you probably wouldn't be seeing her again."

"The case heated up."

A beat passed, and he looked over again to find her watching him, her mouth set in a smug curve.

"That's not the only thing heating up, I'd wager." The glint turned to a twinkle.

He stifled a groan.

"She's a business associate, Nan—and she's given me no indication she'd like to be more."

"Rubbish."

"What does that mean?"

"A woman doesn't meet a man for coffee and scones on a Saturday morning, or trek to the lobby of a medical building for an exchange I imagine could have been done on the phone, unless there are sparks flying that have nothing to do with the fire you two are investigating. The evidence is all there."

"Sometimes evidence can be misleading." He pulled onto I-64 and picked up speed toward home. "I agree with you in principle, but whenever we're together she seems skittish. And she always shuts down if the conversation gets too personal."

"I wonder if there's some unpleasant history holding her back."

"She did say she had a bad experience with a guy in the past."

"There you go." Nan lifted her uninjured hand, palm up. "Don't give up on her too soon. I bet you'll win her over if you keep at it." She yawned and clapped a hand over her mouth. "Mercy. All at once I'm wilting like a thirsty daisy."

"Why don't you lean back and rest until we get home? I'll do a drive-through at Panera and pick up dinner."

"I believe I will." She settled into the corner and let her head tip back.

Within three minutes, her slight snoring confirmed she'd succumbed to sleep.

Fine by him. A few quiet minutes would be welcome after his adrenaline-pumping day racing to two high-profile fire scenes, plus his adrenaline-laced meeting with Bri.

What would it take for her to trust him enough to open up? To offer more than a tantalizing tidbit here and there about her background?

Would it help if he told her more about his own past?

He flipped on the wipers as rain began to sluice down the windshield, easing back on the gas pedal in response to the flash of brake lights on the car in front of him.

Maybe.

But he was no more inclined to talk about his history than she was to share hers. The passage of years could dull pain and guilt, but they never went away. And who wanted to dredge up unhappy memories?

Yet if doing so allowed him to breach the barriers she was erecting, might it be worth the risk?

Traffic picked up speed, and he exerted more pressure on the gas pedal.

A decision like that required serious thought, and it wasn't one he had to make today.

Yet he did need to make it soon.

Because if a door opened for that kind of conversation, it could shut again fast unless he was ready to step through.

THE WEATHER HAD COOPERATED, the dark clouds massed in the night sky had provided excellent cover, and the maple tree was in an ideal position, as he'd noted on previous stakeouts.

Anyone who left their car in the driveway overnight in a storm like this shouldn't be surprised if an accident happened.

Especially if one of the limbs whipping about overhead had been given an incentive to snap off.

Travis smiled and hunkered lower behind the wheel, keeping Bri's duplex in sight through the rain-spattered windshield.

No telling when she'd be home, but if she was having dinner with the guy she'd met up with outside the restaurant she went to after leaving that medical office building, it could be a while.

Marcia would wait dinner on him, though. She'd been most accommodating during his visit.

Most accommodating.

His smile broadened.

This trip was turning out fine on a number of fronts.

He rested his hand on the radio jamming device beside him that would disable Bri's remote opener once he flicked the switch. While that wouldn't necessarily keep her from pulling in, she'd have to trek to the front door in the rain, open the door from the inside, and brave the gale again to move her car inside.

Best case, she wouldn't bother. She'd leave the car outside until tomorrow, and the wind would do its job while she slept. The branch he'd doctored late last night, after he heard the forecast for tonight, would splinter and appear to be a natural break when it fell. Knowing how to cut trees was all part of his job.

If fate cooperated, it would fall on her car—and a branch that size could do a fair amount of damage.

But even if she came back out and moved her car inside, she'd have a mess to deal with in the morning. The driveway would be blocked, and she'd have to call for assistance.

Whichever scenario played out, the inconvenience would

seem like an accident. An act of God. No one would ever know he'd had a hand in it.

Because this wasn't the kind of neighborhood with security cameras everywhere. Or anywhere, near as he could tell. He hadn't spotted a single one on his stroll around the area during the reconnaissance phase of his mission.

The cell on the seat beside him began to vibrate, and he squinted at the screen.

Marcia was getting impatient.

He picked up the phone. Weighed it in his hand. Somehow he had to buy himself another hour. It was important to keep his hostess happy until he tired of his games with Bri and decided to head home.

And that would be soon. Another week, max. Six or seven more days would give him ample opportunity to create at least a couple more annoying, and hopefully expensive, disruptions to pay her back for all the trouble she'd caused him.

So after dinner tonight, followed by a bit of entertainment, he'd plot his next move. One that would also appear accidental.

Because no one must ever be able to prove that Bri's misfortunes were anything more than a run of very bad luck.

HARD TO TELL WHAT HOLMES WAS UP TO—but it wasn't good. Guaranteed.

From several houses down, I watched him watch Bri Tucker's duplex. He'd been there when I arrived an hour ago, but unlike his last visit, he'd never left his car.

Maybe he'd done his dirty work before I showed up.

Too bad I couldn't have come earlier.

But it was hard to do surveillance while holding down a demanding job.

Not that it mattered, though. Holmes wouldn't know when I'd been here, what incriminating evidence I had in hand. The nail-spreading photos would be enough to convince him I was on to him—and to cooperate. I could bluff the rest.

As another round of pelting rain kicked in and the wind picked up again, headlights swung around the corner.

My subject was home.

She pulled into her driveway. Stopped in front of the garage door. Sat there for a full minute.

Why didn't she open the door?

At last she emerged from the car and hurried toward the front door. Seconds later she disappeared inside.

Was Travis responsible for her dash through the rain? Had he somehow disabled the garage door?

But what was the point? No harm done, other than wet clothing and perhaps a minor repair.

Fifteen minutes passed.

Nothing happened.

All at once Holmes's car rolled down the street, lights off.

Should I follow him or hang around here?

A jagged slash of lightning illuminated the sky, followed by a crack of thunder that shook my car and sent a shiver rippling through me.

Decision made. I was out of here. Who wanted to risk getting fried in an electrical storm?

I twisted the key in the ignition, put the car in gear, and pulled away from the curb. I'd have to wait to find out what mischief Holmes had done tonight.

And I would.

My source was excellent.

But whatever petty plot he'd hatched, he was thinking way too small. For my brilliant plan to work, he had to up his game. Fast.

And I knew just how to convince him to do that.

ELEVEN

"YOU'VE GOT TO BE KIDDING ME."

As her garage door lumbered up, Bri gaped at her car—what she could see of it under the large maple tree limb that had fallen on the roof—while her shocked words echoed in the quiet, early morning air.

This was so not how she'd planned to start her Thursday.

The hint of a headache began to pulse in her temples, and she set the remote opener on the trash can. Leaving her laptop, purse, and tote bag in the garage, she slowly approached the Camry, circling around to the left for a better view.

At least the base—and heaviest part—of the limb was resting on the asphalt.

Summoning up her courage, she peered under the branches splayed across the roof and against the passenger side.

It was impossible to gauge the damage with a mass of fall-burnished foliage blocking her view, but if she tried to pull it off by herself, that could inflict more scratches and dents. It would be prudent to round up another set of hands rather than attempt to extricate the car alone.

A tall, dark, and handsome ATF agent came to mind, but she'd already accepted his offer of a lift downtown after the tire fiasco. Asking for a second favor could be pushing it.

Safest route was to call Jack. At this early hour, it was possible she could catch him before he left for work.

But when his cell rolled to voicemail and her text went unanswered after five minutes, she moved on to plan B.

Marc.

Unlike her brother, he answered on the first ring.

"Morning, Bri. Don't tell me you already have the list ready to divvy up."

It took a moment for his comment to register. Hard to think straight while you were gawking at what could be a very expensive repair.

"I did work on it last night, but no, I don't have all the contact information pulled together yet. That's not why I called. I have a favor to ask."

"Name it."

His quick response was heartening and a bright spot on this otherwise depressing day.

"I came out this morning to find a tree—or part of a tree—on my car. It must have fallen during the storm last night. I called my brother, but he's not answering. I could try to round up a neighbor to help me pull it off, but most of them are older, and my duplex mate is a night shift worker who isn't home yet. I hate to ask, and I know this is a huge imposition—"

"I'll be there in ten or fifteen minutes. And it's no imposition. You caught me as I was walking out the door, and you're not far away."

"Are you sure? I can always—"

"I'm sure. See you soon."

As the line went dead, her spirits lifted another few notches. Whatever hassles lay ahead with her car, Marc's willingness to assist helped mitigate them.

Slipping the phone into the pocket of her jacket, Bri reentered her unit through the garage to watch for him through the front window. Though the sun was out and no evidence of last night's storm remained—other than the tree on her car—there was a distinct fall nip in the morning air.

True to his word, Marc pulled up in front of her duplex twelve minutes later.

She exited the house and met him by her car. "Thank you for doing this. I was going to try to pull the branch off myself, but I was afraid I'd do more damage."

Fists propped on hips, he surveyed the Camry. "I'm glad you called. Four hands are probably better than two for a job like this." He looked up at the tree. Inspected the open garage door. "You left the car outside last night? In the storm?"

She made a face. "Not entirely by choice. The battery died in my garage door opener, so I was stuck outside after I got home from dinner with my brother. I thought about coming back out to get the car, but it was dark and cold and pouring rain, so I didn't. Now I'm paying the price for my laziness." She waved a hand toward the branch in disgust.

"I don't blame you for not wanting to brave the elements again. It was a bad storm. As for laziness—I may not know you well yet, but I'd bet a month's salary that isn't one of your faults."

Warmth bubbled up inside her, chasing away the chill in the fall air.

"I appreciate the vote of confidence. Shall we give this a try? I don't want to delay you any longer than necessary."

That was a lie.

If she had her druthers, she'd suggest another trip to her favorite coffee shop. Extend this visit as long as possible.

But they both had work to do, and she wasn't in the market for romance—especially with a professional colleague.

It would behoove her to remember that.

He motioned to the jagged end of the branch that had splintered off from the tree and was resting on the driveway. "If you'll hold that end steady, I'll lift the bulk of the branch off the car from higher up, then swing it away and drop it onto the driveway."

"That sounds reasonable." She moved into position.

Marc shrugged out of his jacket, revealing a crisp dress shirt that showcased his broad chest. After draping the jacket over the exposed part of the Camry's trunk on the other side of the car, he worked himself under the branch. "Ready?"

"Yes." She gripped the bottom of the branch, bracing her foot against it.

"On three. One . . . two . . . three."

The branch rose, and an instant later the base pivoted as Marc guided the limb to the left and let it fall to the asphalt.

It took a few moments for him to extricate himself, and when he finally emerged, a streak of dirt ran across the front of his pristine shirt. There was also a large smudge on one sleeve.

"Uh-oh." Bri pointed to the damage.

After a quick glance, he shrugged it off. "Dirt goes with the job of fire inspector. No one will pay any attention to this. Let's check out the car." He walked closer to the Camry and gave it a swift perusal.

Steeling herself for more bad news, she joined him.

"Could be worse. Mostly scrapes and scuffs." He homed in on a six-inch scratch on the front passenger door. "That's the worst one. And you've got a dent here." He ran his fingers over the edge of the roof. "I don't see any structural damage."

Neither did she.

But while the cosmetic blemishes weren't terrible, they wouldn't be cheap to fix. Nothing ever was on a car.

"As long as it's drivable, I can worry about repairs later."

"Your insurance should cover most of the cost, if you have comprehensive."

"I do, but the deductible's pretty high—and the four new tires already put a dent in my budget." Much as she'd loved fighting remote wildland fires out West, the job hadn't paid a whole lot even if the experience was priceless.

Twin furrows creased his forehead, and she braced for a

comment or question about her finances. Instead, he changed the subject.

"You said your remote was dead last night?"

"Yes."

"Did you try it again this morning?"

"Yes. After I changed the battery. It worked fine. Why?"

"Would you mind if I took a look at the old battery and the opener?"

She cocked her head and repeated her question. "Why?"

"Like I told you the day we met, I pay attention to my instincts. Same as you do. And I'm playing with a theory. Humor me?" He flashed her a cajoling grin. "It'll only delay you a few extra minutes."

The dirt on his shirt—damage incurred on her behalf—and his engaging smile made his request impossible to refuse.

"Okay. The remote's on the garbage can in the garage. I'll dig the battery out of the trash in the house. Give me one minute."

It took her a tad longer than that to rummage through the garbage and clean off the yogurt clinging to the battery from her on-the-run breakfast this morning.

By the time she returned, he'd donned his jacket again and was examining the branch he'd hefted off the car.

"Sorry. This was wearing part of my breakfast. But don't worry, I've removed all my germs." She held it out.

"I'm not worried about your germs." He took the battery.

The warmth of his fingers as they brushed against hers sent a delicious tingle down her spine, and she curbed an eye roll.

Oh, for pity's sake. She ought to be beyond such an adolescent reaction at this stage of her life.

He walked closer to the car, where he'd set her remote.

She followed but kept her distance. The man's appeal was way too potent.

Since he'd already removed the back of the opener, it took him only seconds to pop in the old battery and press the button.

The door rumbled down.

Bri stared at it. "That doesn't . . . I don't understand. It didn't work last night."

He waited until the door closed and pressed the button again.

The door rumbled up.

She clamped her hands on her waist. "What's going on? I thought the battery was dead. Could the storm have interfered with it?"

"Unlikely."

He set the opener on the hood and walked back to the branch. Dropped to his haunches and began examining the break.

Vague suspicions began to niggle at her, and as she joined him, they coalesced into a disturbing conclusion. "You think I was set up? That this was deliberate?"

He continued to examine the bottom of the limb. "That thought did cross my mind. This happening so close on the heels of the tire incident is suspect."

"Or a run of bad luck."

He pulled out his phone. "I'd like to think that's all it is, but my gut is telling me there's more to it."

Her own phone began to vibrate, and she pulled it out.

Jack.

"If that's a call, go ahead and answer. I want to take a few photos." He got up close and personal with the bottom of the branch and began snapping away.

Bri retreated a few paces and greeted her brother. "Sorry for the early call."

"No worries. I was in the shower and just noticed your text message and voicemail. What's up?"

She briefed him on her latest catastrophe. "I was hoping you could stop by and help me extricate my car, but I rounded up another pair of hands. On the bright side, the damage isn't too bad."

"Why did you leave your car out last night, anyway?"

She transferred her weight from one foot to the other.

This could get tricky.

If her brother ran true to form, he'd be as suspicious about the circumstances as Marc was. But she couldn't lie about what had happened.

After she answered his question and shared the news that the battery wasn't dead after all, she could almost hear the gears grinding in his brain in the silence that followed.

"I don't like this, Bri." A thread of worry wove through his terse comment. "First the tires, now this. Plus an unexplained battery malfunction. That's too much bad luck too close together to be coincidence."

Yep. He was running true to form.

But she couldn't argue with his conclusion.

"I admit it's suspicious. That's why Marc is—"

Whoops.

She clamped her lips shut, but the damage had been done.

"Marc who?"

She edged away from the man in question and lowered her volume. "When I couldn't reach you, I called the ATF agent I've been working with on the Kavanaugh case. I, uh, needed to talk to him anyway." Sort of true. "He wasn't far from here and came over. He helped me get the branch off the car."

"What's his last name again?"

"I never shared it—but nice try, Mr. Over-Protective Brother. Besides, like I told you on Sunday, he's a professional colleague. We're not in a dating relationship."

"Maybe not, but any guy who shows up at a woman's house at the crack of dawn to deal with a downed tree would like to be."

She peeked at Marc. He'd finished with his photos and was looking at his watch.

"No comment. Much as I'd love to continue this conversation, I have to get to work."

"Is the mystery man still there?"

"Yes, but I think he's getting ready to leave."

"This subject isn't closed."

Bri huffed out a breath. She should never, ever, ever have sought his advice about her problems with Travis.

"Yes, it is."

"TBD. I may swing by and take a look at the branch myself."

"I'm calling my landlord momentarily. If he's as responsive as usual, it won't be here long."

"I can be there in twenty minutes."

She swiveled away from the car, keeping her volume low. "I'll be gone."

"I don't need to see you. Just the branch."

"Marc already took photos. I can send you copies."

"I'll take my own. I want to nose around."

Of course he would.

"Fine. Anything else?"

"Yeah. Be careful."

"Always."

"Good. If anything happened to you, I'd miss our Tuesday night dinners—and Cara's too far away to fill in for you. Besides, she'd want to drag me to the Thai place she likes that sets my tongue on fire."

At his gruff comment, the corners of her mouth rose. Typical Jack. Under his wisecracking, tough-guy veneer, he was a total softie. "You should find yourself a wife. Dinner every other week with your sister isn't much of a social life."

"I'll get around to that one of these days."

"To borrow Danny Kaye's line from our favorite vintage family Christmas movie, my dear fellow, when what's left of you gets around to what's left to be gotten, what's left to be gotten won't be worth getting whatever it is you've got left."

"Very funny."

"Very true. You're not getting any younger."

"Neither are you. But with that ATF guy hanging around, you could be closer to the altar than I am."

She checked on Marc again. He'd pulled out his keys and was clearly ready to leave. "That may be a bit premature."

"I don't know. Mom always said she knew Dad was the one the first time they met."

"I have no intention of jumping to conclusions too early in the game. Not ever again." She suppressed a shudder as an image of Travis during their last encounter strobed across her mind. Getting friendly with a man who had obvious control and anger management issues—obvious in hindsight, that is—had been the biggest mistake of her life up to that point.

At least there'd been no lingering repercussions from that lapse, though. Unlike the second one a few months later.

"It's smart to be cautious. Keep that in mind with your ATF friend."

"I'm hanging up now."

A chuckle came over the line. "Message received." Then he grew more serious. "Listen, if you need a small loan to help with the car repairs, I have a few bucks stashed for emergencies. I know you didn't make a fortune in Idaho."

Pressure built behind her eyes, and she blinked to clear her vision. She and Jack and Cara might not be related by blood, but the bond of heartstrings could be just as strong.

"I'll be fine. But I appreciate the offer. Love you, Jack."

"Mutual, I'm sure." Naturally he'd counter with another line from *White Christmas*. "Hang in there, okay?"

"You got it."

As she ended the call, Bri rejoined Marc. "Sorry to delay you. I have an overprotective brother, and it doesn't help that he's a homicide detective."

Marc's eyebrows peaked. "With County?"

"Yes."

"Does law enforcement run in your family?"

"Hardly. My sister's a college professor specializing in historical anthropology, Mom was a homemaker who worked part-time at a floral shop, and Dad was an accountant. My brother and I were the outliers." Enough about that. "I don't want to keep you. I should be good to go now."

"Before you take off, why don't you start the car and drive up and down the street once to make certain there's no mechanical damage? I'll wait."

Not a bad idea.

"Let me get my stuff."

She detoured to the garage for her purse, tote bag, and laptop, stowed them in the car, and slid behind the wheel. As she backed down the driveway, Marc followed along and waited by his car.

A quick cruise up and down the street confirmed his assessment. No mechanical issues.

She pulled up beside him and lowered her window as he leaned down. "I owe you for this."

"Happy to help. Send me the list of jurisdictions once you have it together."

"Later today, I hope. Unless another case lands on my desk."

"I'll watch for it. Be careful."

Same instruction her brother had given her.

"I will. Did you notice anything suspicious while you were taking photos of the branch?"

"No, and it's usually not difficult to spot a man-made cut in a tree. Handsaws leave marks."

"Maybe you're looking for something that's not there." She hoped.

"Could be, but I don't like the timing."

Neither did she.

"If either of these incidents was deliberate, though, there doesn't seem to have been any intent to hurt me."

"Let's hope that doesn't change." He backed off after delivering that unsettling comment. "Talk to you soon."

She offered him a wave, rolled up her window, and drove away.

Yet when she checked her rearview mirror, Marc remained by his car, hands in pockets, watching her.

As if he was worried.

That made two of them.

She rounded the corner, and as she lost sight of him, a shiver rippled through her.

While it was possible her misfortunes this week were coincidence, more and more they were feeling intentional. As if someone was targeting her.

Was it the same person who'd targeted Les with deadly results? And if that was the case, could these incidents be the preamble to a more lethal attack?

Or was she being paranoid?

Except Jack and Marc were concerned too, and the sharp, perceptive ATF agent who'd come into her life a mere two weeks ago didn't seem like the type to worry without cause.

But if someone was lurking in the shadows, waiting for another opportunity to further upend her life, how could she ward off an unknown foe?

A yellow "Proceed with Caution" sign appeared on her right, and she slowed as she passed the work zone.

Not a bad warning to heed in the days ahead in her personal life, either.

Because much as she wanted to believe she was overreacting to the two car incidents this week, every instinct in her body said they were more than unlucky flukes. That nefarious intent was behind them.

And that there was more to come.

TWELVE

THIS WAS THE LIFE.

Travis stretched, yawned, and refilled his mug from the pot of extra-strong coffee his most hospitable hostess had brewed to his specifications before she left for work an hour ago.

Sleeping late, answering to no one, being waited on hand and foot—he could get used to this.

Too bad he had to work.

And too bad Bri had made that so difficult.

Scowling, he stalked over to the window and took a swig of the potent brew.

At least he was making her life difficult now. Or rather, continuing to make her life difficult. After all his surveillance, it was clear she was still dealing with repercussions from the Idaho incident.

That was satisfying.

Travis finished off his coffee in a few large gulps, shrugged into his jacket, and picked up the keys to his rental car. Maybe he'd tool over to Bri's, do a drive-by to see the damage from last night. That would be entertaining.

Afterward, he could drop by Marcia's gym, use her guest privileges to get in a workout. It was important to stay in peak physical condition. He had to be ready to hit the ground running when he returned to his job.

He left his dirty mug in the sink, let himself out the front door, and strolled toward his car.

Why not drop in at that diner he'd found too? The one with the attractive waitress. Eat lunch, flirt a bit, try to convince her to meet him for happy hour somewhere before Marcia got off work. That would be fun, and—

Travis halted as he reached the driver-side door. Frowned at the white square stuck under his windshield wiper.

What was that all about?

He leaned around and pulled it free. The small envelope bore his name.

Huh.

Sealed missive in hand, he opened the car door, slid behind the wheel, and used his key to slit the flap.

A single folded sheet of paper was inside.

He withdrew it, flipped it open, and read the short, typed note.

Seven words in, the acid from his coffee began to gurgle in his stomach.

I saw you at Bri's Sunday night . . . and since then. I have photos and video. Flat tires, trees falling . . . you've been busy. I need a favor. Call me.

A phone number was at the bottom.

Lungs locking, Travis crimped the sheet in his fist and banged his hand against the steering wheel.

No!

This couldn't be happening!

How could anyone know about those incidents at Bri's?

Was someone following him?

But that didn't fit. No one except Marcia knew he was in town.

Was it possible the note sender had just happened to notice him at the duplex and stumbled across an opportunity for blackmail?

The odds of that had to be minuscule. Yet what other explanation could there be? Most people who witnessed suspicious behavior like his would have called the police, reported him. They wouldn't have used the information to their advantage.

Unless they were up to no good too.

And if they were, he'd played right into their hands.

He spat out an expletive his father had often used during his frequent rants, averting his face as a UPS truck trundled past.

Unfortunately, sitting here bemoaning the situation wasn't going to fix the problem. Nor could he ignore it. If this person had evidence of his nocturnal activities, he could be dead meat if he didn't call.

First, though, he'd get a burner phone. This conversation had to be untraceable.

Once he had that in hand, he'd place his call. See if the note was a bluff—or a nightmare.

And if it was the latter, he had a sinking feeling that whatever favor the note writer wanted was only going to make the nightmare worse.

ZIP.

Marc reread the list of jurisdictions he'd agreed to research for Bri. It had taken a while to reach all the people on the contact list, but as Friday wound down, he was officially finished.

And there wasn't a match on his end.

Nor had there likely been one on hers. If she'd solved the puzzle of Kavanaugh's list, she'd have called or texted.

But he ought to let her know he was done rather than leave her with any false hope that he might still come up with a name.

Besides, aside from professional consideration, hearing her voice would be a pleasant end to a busy workweek.

Lips bowing, he pulled her number up on his screen and placed the call.

"Hi, Marc." She answered on the fourth ring, a bit out of breath. "Can you give me a minute?"

"Take your time. My day's over." He leaned back in his chair.

In the background, a siren blared—and from the other noises that came over the line it wasn't hard to figure out where she was.

A fire scene.

Two minutes later, the background noise began to recede as she spoke again. "Sorry. I'm at a fire."

"I can tell. You want me to call back later?"

"No. I'm getting into my car. It will be quieter there, and I could use a break." A few moments later, a door banged and all extraneous noise ceased. "That's better. What's up?"

"I wanted to let you know I'm done with my part of the list. I'm sorry to say there wasn't a match."

"Dang." Her frustration came through loud and clear.

"I assume you haven't had any luck, either?"

"Not yet. I have two more jurisdictions to contact. I was hoping to finish this week, but we've been slammed with fires. And since I doubt my counterparts would appreciate me interrupting their weekend, I won't be able to get back on it until Monday." She blew out a breath and switched subjects. "How's your grandmother doing?"

"Improving. Thanks for asking. She's also three-fourths finished with her course of radiation as of today. We're celebrating tonight—dinner at her favorite restaurant if she's not too tired."

An invitation to join them hovered on the tip of his tongue, but that was crazy. The odds Bri would accept were infinitesimal. And if by some chance she did, Nan's romantic fantasies would mushroom. Besides, hadn't he vowed to maintain a low social profile until Nan was out of the woods and he was settled into his new job?

Yes.

So asking Bri out was a bad idea all around, even if the temptation to throw caution to the wind was strong.

"A celebration dinner sounds lovely. I hope you both enjoy it."

"Thanks." He doodled on the notepad in front of him. "What's on your schedule tonight?"

She snorted. "The way this scene is going, I'll be shoveling soot and sifting ash until long after dark. Call me Cinderella, with no ball to go to afterward." Despite her attempt at humor, her words were etched with weariness.

Not surprising.

In addition to the demands of her busy job, she'd been dealing with all kinds of hassles on the personal front this week.

"Not a fun Friday night."

"Goes with the territory. I didn't sign on for this job expecting a barrel of laughs."

"Why did you sign on?" The question popped out too fast to restrain, and he grimaced.

Bad move. She'd shut down, like she always did if he—

"Sometimes I wonder about that myself."

At her pensive tone and candid admission, he stopped doodling.

Was that an invitation for further discussion on the topic? Might she be more comfortable talking about nonwork subjects on the phone rather than in person? Safety in distance and all that?

Only one way to find out—and it wasn't as if he had much to lose by trying. Worst case, she'd shut him down.

So what else would be new?

"Do I detect a hint of regret about your career choice?" He kept his manner conversational.

"No." Her firm response was immediate. "No regrets. The

work is satisfying. All my jobs have been satisfying. It's just kind of disheartening that I have so little to show for everything I've done. My brother even felt compelled to offer me a loan this morning. Sweet, but depressing." She sighed. "Sorry. You caught me at the end of a long and trying week. I shouldn't dump on you."

"Don't apologize. If you find someone with a willing ear, take advantage of it. Venting is healthy. And I hear you about income issues. Firefighting isn't the highest-paying profession, especially if you live in a smaller town or more rural part of the country. Is that where you worked out West?" He braced, waiting for her to change the subject.

She didn't.

"Yes. Towns don't get much smaller or more rural than McCall, Idaho."

McCall.

Home to a major smokejumper base.

Marc squinted at the squiggles on the pad. "Did you work for the city?"

A few seconds ticked by.

"No. US Forest Service."

The speculation he'd been playing with gained traction. "Were you a smokejumper?"

Another pause.

"Yes. After I logged five years of hotshot experience."

Wow.

Marc set his pen down, leaned back, and stared at the file folder he'd put on his laptop screen the day he'd taken his first job with the ATF but rarely opened anymore.

Bri had been part of the elite group of four hundred or so men and women who risked their lives parachuting into isolated, rugged terrain to fight wildfires up close and personal with only the equipment that dropped in with them and little hope of rescue if a situation went south.

In the firefighting world, they were the stuff of legends.

And he thought *he'd* led an exciting life.

"Can I say I'm impressed?"

"It's just firefighting on a different scale. There's no magic to the job. A willingness to work hard is the main prerequisite."

"Along with a boatload of courage."

"Lots of jobs require courage."

"Some more than others." He added modesty to her list of virtues and shifted the focus to practical matters, since she seemed uncomfortable with praise. "So why did you leave?"

"Parachute accident. My main chute didn't deploy properly, and the descent on the backup is faster. I had a bad landing. But I did live to tell the tale, albeit with a souvenir. I'm sure you've noticed my limp."

"Yes." Pretending otherwise would be disingenuous. "What happened with your main chute?"

"No idea. But I packed it, so the career-ending mistake was mine. A shattered femur held together with plates and pins isn't conducive to smokejumping or firefighting. When it comes to regrets, that slipup tops my list."

"I'm sorry." What else was there to say?

"Thanks. But I'd have aged out of the job eventually anyway. That's why I double majored in forestry and forensic science. Fire investigation was always where I wanted to end up—just not this soon. As Mom liked to say, though, we may not always understand God's timing as it unfolds, but in hindsight we can often see a purpose to it."

He moved his cursor to the file folder and circled around it.

What purpose could there be in a potentially fatal accident that had left her with a permanent limp?

"Have you?"

"Yes. Mom began to decline about the time of my accident, so after I recovered, I trained in fire investigation, got a job in a municipality within driving distance of St. Louis, and was ready to step into my present job when the opening came up. The accident allowed me to be closer to Mom in her final months."

Somehow Bri had found the bright side to an experience that would have made many people bitter and resentful.

Talk about making lemonade out of lemons.

"Nan has a similar philosophy." He moved the cursor away from the folder. As long as she was opening up, this could be his chance to find out if her career out West in the wide-open spaces had anything to do with her walls-closing-in comment. "I'm assuming the degree in forestry means you love the outdoors. Have you always—"

"Oops. I'm being summoned. I have to run." The sound of a door opening came over the line, and the background noise once again picked up. "I'll let you know as soon as I finish my list. Cross your fingers that I find a match. Otherwise, we may be at a dead end."

Their conversation was over.

Tempted as he was to try to detain her, duty was calling. The moment was lost.

"Enjoy whatever you can salvage of your weekend."

"Thanks." The background noise increased. "I'll give it my best shot. Talk to you soon."

The line went dead.

Marc pressed the end button, processing the history Bri had shared from the confines of her car—apparently a safer spot for her to have a personal discussion than while sitting within touching distance of him.

Useful information to tuck away for future reference.

He shut down his laptop and stood, unanswered questions scrolling through his mind.

Were her sister and brother blood relations, or had they all been adopted separately?

What had happened to her parents?

Had she been in the foster system?

If so, what kinds of experiences had she had there, and how had they shaped her?

What had gone wrong with the guy she'd known out West?

Had her bad experience left her gun-shy of romance, or was she simply not interested in *him*?

And if she decided she *was* interested, what was he going to do about it?

Excellent question.

For as he'd told Nan when he'd come home, romance was a low priority for the immediate future.

But all at once, her advice replayed in his mind.

"Don't close any door too fast. Some only open once."

So if Bri opened a door, he'd better decide soon whether he wanted to walk through—or perhaps spend the rest of his life regretting a lost opportunity with the most intriguing woman he'd ever met.

TRAVIS SWIPED OFF THE SWEAT beading above his upper lip, cracked his window to refresh the stale air in the car, and eyed the new burner phone clasped in his white-knuckled grip.

He had to call the note writer. He or she had left him no choice.

Yet once he did, his life would get way more complicated than it already was. He knew that as surely as he knew the summerlike warmth of these falls days wouldn't last.

But sitting in a parking lot stewing about the situation wasn't going to fix it. He ought to get the facts before he panicked.

He flexed his fingers to restore circulation and tapped in the number from the slip of paper.

After five rings, an androgynous voice greeted him. "Hold."

Silence followed.

He waited.

Three minutes later, the voice returned. "It took you a while to respond. Don't make that a habit."

"Who is this?"

"My identity doesn't matter. All that matters is how you can help me."

"Why should I do that?"

"I have information the authorities would find interesting."

"Like what?"

Seconds later, his phone pinged.

"I texted you a photo. Take a look. I'll wait."

Dread pooling in his gut, he clicked on the image.

He recognized himself instantly in the shadowy figure putting roofing nails on Bri's driveway.

But most people wouldn't be able to discern much. The image was on the dark side, and his features were murky. Maybe the cops could enhance it, identify him from this. Maybe not.

His predicament might not be as bad as he'd thought.

Pulse moderating, he put the phone back to his ear. "I'm not impressed."

"There's video to go with it that shows your face much more clearly, along with the license plate of your rental car—and your name on the rental agreement. I could post it on YouTube if you want to see it. Plus the one of you working on that tree at Bri's house."

His heart missed a beat. Raced on.

"No." The last thing he needed was an incriminating video splashed all over the internet for the world to see. That wouldn't help his situation back in Idaho. "What do you want?"

"A small favor. No more than a continuation of what you're already doing to your former colleague."

Someone else had it in for the woman who'd messed up his life?

He wrapped the fingers of his free hand around the steering wheel. "What's your beef with Bri?"

"Not important. All you have to do is follow my instructions. I have two potential assignments for you. The first one has to be completed by three o'clock Sunday afternoon. I don't care when or where you do it, as long as it's finished by the deadline. If you want an idea, though, she likes to walk in the park near her house early on Sunday morning. I assume you have a gun?"

Sweat broke out on his upper lip again, and he rolled his window up tight. Lowered his volume. "What if I don't?"

"Get one. But I'd be willing to bet a man with your background is never far from his gun."

What did this person know about his background?

This was getting worse and worse.

"I'm not shooting Bri." Mayhem was one thing. Murder was another.

"That's not part of this weekend's assignment. I just want you to take a shot at her. Come close, but miss."

A few yards away, a woman struggled to pull a shopping cart free from the nested line waiting to be trundled back inside, but it was stuck tight. "What are you trying to do, scare her or something?"

"Or something." A touch of amusement colored his blackmailer's inflection.

"It's too dangerous. I could get caught."

"Make certain you don't. And don't disappoint me, Travis. You won't like the repercussions. One more thing. Don't leave town until you hear from me."

The caller cut the connection.

Travis slowly lowered the phone and tried to control the shaking in his fingers.

How could this be happening, after everything had gone so well? From the day he'd left Idaho, he'd been in total control of the situation, had called all the shots.

Not anymore.

He set the phone on the seat beside him and wiped his palms down the denim covering his thighs.

Taking a shot at someone, even one not intended to kill, was dicey. If he got caught, no one would believe he hadn't had murder on his mind. They'd just assume his aim was bad.

But he had to do it. His blackmailer had left him no choice. The trick would be pulling it off in a manner that guaranteed he didn't get caught.

The question was how.

Minutes passed as he racked his brain for an answer.

None came.

He had two days to think about it, however. To plan. And with his smarts, he ought to be able to both satisfy the person on the other end of the burner phone and stay safe.

After all, it wasn't like the note writer had asked him to kill Bri. All they wanted him to do was scare her, which dovetailed with his own plans. While a gun hadn't been part of his aggravation arsenal, a shooting would shake her up. Much more than his pranks to date had.

That was a definite upside.

But there was also a definite downside.

Unlike flat tires and a fallen branch, a shooting would be deliberate. No one would classify that as an accident.

That jacked up the risk exponentially.

Still, he ought to be able to pull it off and escape unscathed.

Yet as he started the engine and put the car in gear, the knot in his stomach kinked tight.

Because even if he completed this task to his blackmailer's satisfaction, another potential assignment could be coming.

And if the first one involved a gun, odds were the second one would be at least as risky—and perhaps more dangerous.

He could only hope it never materialized. Or that if it did, it wasn't more lethal than the first.

THIRTEEN

NOT. ENOUGH. SLEEP.

Propping up her eyelids, Bri shoved her hair back from her face and padded barefoot into the kitchen. After her late night at the fire scene, another hour or two of slumber would have been bliss.

Alas, her internal alarm clock refused to be silenced.

And now that she was awake, why lie in bed staring at the ceiling instead of doing something productive? Like restocking her almost empty fridge or throwing in a load of laundry . . . or going over the case files from the Kavanaugh puzzle again in case she'd missed a nuance that would be helpful.

But first, coffee.

Yawning, she went through the motions with her one-cup brewer, then poured herself a glass of cranberry juice and sat at the table to wait for the caffeine infusion that would nudge her brain into gear.

As she sipped her juice, she squinted at her watch. Much too early to rouse Cara for their usual Saturday morning chat. Her night owl sister wouldn't appreciate a wake-up call at this hour.

But a quick pass through her email wouldn't bother anyone, nor would it tax her sluggish mind too much.

Chin propped in hand, she scrolled through the messages that had come in since she was summoned to the fire yesterday afternoon. Work . . . work . . . spam . . . a confirmation for a haircut . . . church newsletter . . . work . . . Crystal . . . reminder for—

Wait.

She backed up.

Crystal had finally responded to her email from Tuesday night.

She opened it and read the message.

Hey, girl! Sorry for my tardy response. I unplugged from all electronics and spent a few days camping in the backcountry.

Glad you got the job at County. I'm loving my ranger gig with the National Park Service. Wish I could have talked you into joining me instead of going home, but I know you wanted to be there for your mom.

Funny you should ask about Travis. I'm still connected to the McCall grapevine, and he is in one heap of trouble. After the furor died down between the two of you, he apparently reverted to his old ways—except his next victim did more than threaten to file harassment charges. She followed through.

Now he's on administrative leave until the matter is resolved, and the general consensus is that he's either taken off for parts unknown or is lying low and staying under the radar. That guy is a piece of work. (I'd use a stronger term, but you wouldn't approve! ☺)

As the last vestiges of sleep vanished, Bri skimmed the remainder of the chatty email about Crystal's current beau and the smokejumper crew, then reread the two pertinent paragraphs.

So Travis had pulled the same stunt again, after he'd promised under threat of a lawsuit and job loss to mend his ways?

Crystal was right.

Piece of work didn't come close to describing him.

And if he wasn't in Idaho . . . if he'd fallen off the radar there . . . where was he?

A quiver of unease slithered up her spine as suspicion began to swirl through her mind.

Surely he wouldn't travel cross-country just to play mean-spirited practical jokes on her, though.

Would he?

Frowning, she rose to claim the mug of caffeine she no longer needed, an image of his cold, angry eyes strobing across her mind. Eyes that had strafed her whenever they'd met after their squad leader took her concerns to his supervisor, who'd called her and Travis in for separate chats.

Of course Travis had said all the appropriate things. Agreed to respect her space and keep his distance. Put on a public show of conciliation and deference.

But while he'd honored his promise to leave her alone, rage had continued to burn in him. He'd masked it well around the other team members, hiding it behind the jovial demeanor that had fooled her at first too. On the few occasions they'd encountered each other at the base facility without witnesses around, however, the venom in his gaze had sent an arctic chill through her.

Instead of being grateful she'd refrained from pressing harassment charges, those glowering looks had made it clear the grudge he harbored wasn't going away anytime soon.

Bri took a sip of her brew, wincing as the hot liquid scalded her tongue.

Her own fault, though. If you got up close and personal with heat, you should expect to get burned.

Scrubbing a hand down her face, she moved to the fridge, pulled out a carton of half-and-half, and added a generous splash to her coffee.

Despite her suspicions, it was foolish to jump to the conclusion that Travis could be behind the tire and tree incidents.

Their clash was old news at this point. Besides, why come after her for problems he'd brought on himself because of his improper behavior with another woman?

That wouldn't be logical.

Yet anger could override logic, and he did have anger management issues.

Her doorbell rang, and her hand jerked, sending coffee spewing across the floor in a wide arc.

Oh, for heaven's sake.

She was getting all worked up over speculations that probably had no basis in reality.

After giving the java splatter a fast swipe, she hurried toward the front of her unit and peeked through the sidelight.

Did a double take.

Why on earth was Cara on her doorstep at this hour on a Saturday morning?

She flipped the lock and pulled the door open. "What are you doing here?"

Her sister's eyebrows arched. "Good morning to you too."

"Sorry. Good morning. Come in." She stepped back, ushered her inside, and closed the door. "But I repeat, what are you doing here?"

"Can't one sister drop in on another?"

"Yes—but trekking more than a hundred miles doesn't qualify as dropping in. And you never get up until after eight on weekends."

"Never is a slight exaggeration. I've been known to rise early on days off if the situation warrants it." She plopped into the overstuffed chair she always claimed on her visits. Skewered her with an accusing look. "And your eventful week warranted it. Were you ever going to tell me about the tires and the tree?"

Bri perched on the arm of the couch and folded her arms. "I see our dear brother has been telling tales out of school."

"No. He's been keeping me informed. Which is more than I can say for my dear sister."

"I would have told you about it on our call this morning." Probably.

"A toned-down version, no doubt. Like when you called after your parachute accident and told all of us you had a few minor injuries."

Bri shifted. "That was before I had the full diagnosis—and what happened this week wasn't anywhere close to the scale of the Idaho catastrophe."

"Then why is Jack worried?"

"Jack worries about everything."

"Not true. He worries about the people he cares about—like his sisters. He said you were fine, but I wanted to see for myself."

Bri held out her arms. "Satisfied?"

"On that score, yes." She continued to study her with an appraising expression. "He also said the ATF agent you've been working with on the case you mentioned last weekend came to your rescue with the tree."

Well, crud.

Knowing Jack, that's not all he'd said.

"For the record, I called Jack first." She tried for a nonchalant tone. "He didn't answer. My ATF colleague was my second-string choice. Luckily, he came through. I needed to consult with him on the case anyway."

Cara smirked. "That's what Jack said you'd say."

"It happens to be true."

"You don't have to get all flustered about it."

"I'm not flustered."

"The flush on your cheeks says otherwise, but hey. I think it's great if you've got a hot guy in the wings. It's about time one of the Tucker kids found someone interesting to date."

"I'm not dating him."

"Yet. Jack thinks it's only a matter of time."

"Since when has our brother's romantic radar ever been dependable? Remember that colleague of yours he predicted you'd fall for after you brought him to the wedding we all attended last summer? The business school professor who spent the entire evening talking about supply chain disruptions during the COVID crisis and how that would affect global macroeconomics?"

Cara winced. "Yeah. Mr. Snooze City. That was our first and last date. Fine. I'll concede Jack's call on that one was out in left field."

"I rest my case."

"However . . . I do trust my powers of discernment, and I saw how ruffled you got while we talked about your ATF guy at Jack's. So I'll reserve judgment."

"Don't get your hopes up."

"It's not my hopes that are at stake." She waggled her eyebrows.

Bri held on to her cool. Barely. "Can we move on to a different subject?"

"Sure. How about food? I've got a hankering for an almond croissant from Nathaniel Reid bakery." Cara stood. "Unless you already ate, which wouldn't surprise me, early riser that you are."

"Not yet. I had a late night at a fire scene and managed not to beat the sun up this morning." She rose too. "Give me ten minutes to change. Make yourself a cup of coffee while you wait."

"Don't mind if I do. After my almost predawn start, a caffeine infusion would be welcome—and the watered-down brew I got when I stopped for gas doesn't come close to the decadent Kona coffee you buy."

"One of my few indulgences."

"Trust me, I know." She started toward the kitchen.

"Cara." Bri touched her shoulder, waiting until her sister turned. "Did you really drive up here just to see me?"

"The truth? I have a list of errands I've been saving up for my next trip to the city, and Jack's news gave me an incentive to tackle them sooner than I'd planned. I do have to be back in Cape by one for a special session with one of my doctoral students, though." She played with the zipper pull on her jacket, faint creases marring her forehead. "Before we leave the subject of this week's incidents behind, is there anything to worry about?"

That was a tricky question—and too direct to dodge.

Until the email from Crystal had activated her yellow alert, it would have been easy to reassure Cara. Despite Jack's concerns and Marc's suspicions, the episodes had amounted to nothing more than aggravation. Expensive, yes, but not dangerous.

If Travis was involved, however—and if he had other tricks up his sleeve—one of them could have more serious consequences. Fury that hadn't dissipated in close to three years could be a potent and perilous force.

"Bri?" A hint of anxiety sharpened Cara's prompt.

"I don't think so." That was all she could offer without telling an outright lie. "But I can promise you this. I'll be watching my back, and I'll carry on and off the job if that will ease your mind."

"It would help."

"Done. Now let's think about more pleasant subjects. Like those sin-on-a-plate almond croissants."

The taut line of her sister's shoulders relaxed a hair, and her mouth flexed. "I'm ready whenever you are. Those alone are worth the drive up from Cape."

"Aha! The real reason for your trip comes out." Bri called up a grin.

"You know better. Go change. I'm starving."

"I'm on it."

While a mollified Cara continued toward the kitchen, her peace of mind somewhat restored, Bri headed to her bedroom.

Sad to say, her own peace of mind remained wobbly.

Why, oh why, couldn't Crystal have confirmed that Travis was in Idaho, where he belonged?

Still . . . pinning her woes on him seemed like a stretch, even if he was a vindictive jerk.

Bri pulled off her ratty sweatshirt and threw on a sweater. Proceeded to the bathroom to add a modicum of makeup.

If only she had someone to discuss this with. Someone impartial.

Certainly not Jack or Cara.

But what about Marc? His critical-thinking and deductive skills were sharp, and he'd be far more capable of putting aside his personal feelings than either of her siblings.

She pulled out her mascara. Rolled the tube between her fingers as she mulled that over.

No. If she wanted to keep him at arm's length, seeking his counsel on this wouldn't be smart. She'd already let too much slip about her past, thanks to the case of motormouth that plagued her in his presence. He was much too easy to talk to.

And for a woman who'd claimed she wasn't ready to dip her toes into romance again . . . who'd vowed not to get involved with a professional colleague . . . Marc was a clear danger zone.

She leaned forward and began stroking on mascara.

So who did that leave? Crystal, perhaps? They'd been simpatico back in Idaho, and she did know Travis.

But her fellow female smokejumper had a set-in-stone negative opinion about him, so she wasn't impartial, either.

Maybe she could—

Her phone began to vibrate, and she pulled it out of the pocket in her jeans.

Alison.

Bri finished her mascara and capped the tube. "Hey, girl. What's up? I thought your sister was in town."

"She is. We're going to brunch soon, but while she's in the shower I wanted to check in and see how you're doing after the taxing week you had."

"Hanging in—and playing with sort of a bizarre theory about the source of my problems."

A few moments of silence ticked by.

"Does that mean you don't think they were accidents?"

"I wouldn't go that far, but I did get a piece of unsettling information this morning."

"Now you have me intrigued. And more than a little worried."

A voice spoke in the background as Bri tucked her makeup bag back in the vanity. "Sounds like your sister's ready to roll. I don't want to keep you."

"Give me one sec." After a muffled conversation on the other end, Alison was back. "Listen, if you want to bounce ideas off someone, I'll be cooling my heels for forty-five minutes later this morning while Sophie gets the manicure I scheduled for her. I'd go too, but as you know, fancy fingernails and firefighting don't mix. If you want to get together for a quick chat, I could also introduce you to Sophie after she's done. I've been wanting the two of you to meet."

Alison's offer of an impartial, willing ear was too providential to pass up.

"Name the time and place." Bri crossed to the nightstand and pulled a pen and pad of paper from the drawer.

"Her appointment is at eleven, and there's an ice-cream shop next to the salon if I can tempt you to indulge."

"Count me in. If they have butter pecan, I'll be in heaven." Bri jotted down the name and address as Alison recited them. "Got it. I'll be there. Thanks a bunch, Alison. Your call couldn't have been better timed."

"Must be fate."

"Must be. See you soon."

Bri tucked the slip of paper with the meeting information into her pocket and pulled her belly band holster from the closet. After fastening it around her waist, she fitted it into her jeans, slid her compact Sig into the slot, and secured it with the snap.

Thanks to her promise to Cara, she'd be carrying for the foreseeable future.

But truth be told, it was a prudent tactical strategy. Whether Travis was behind the incidents this week or not, strange vibes were in the air.

Hopefully, Alison's read on the situation would be helpful. Her new friend appeared to have sound judgment—except with her own husband, perhaps—and it was possible she could offer a useful insight or two.

Yet as Bri flipped off the light and hurried toward the kitchen to join her sister, she couldn't help wishing she was meeting a handsome ATF agent instead.

Because much as she'd welcome Alison's input, Marc's steady presence and mellow baritone voice would be even more reassuring than the Sig she would continue tucking into her concealed carry holster until whatever latent threat she might be facing was neutralized.

FOURTEEN

THIS WAS NOT HOW HE'D PLANNED to spend his Saturday.

From fifty feet inside the police tape cordoning off the scene, Marc surveyed the popular mid-county restaurant crawling with law enforcement personnel from various jurisdictions. Typical when a fire resulted in multiple deaths, involved more than a million dollars in losses, and had potentially been caused by explosives.

While County was in charge, the request for ATF assistance wasn't surprising for a blaze of this magnitude.

"I'm gonna run out for a burger. You want to come?" The second ATF agent who'd been dispatched to the scene joined him, keeping his back to the crowd gathered on the other side of the tape.

"No thanks. I don't want to have a microphone shoved in my face." Marc hooked a thumb toward the large media contingent milling about, jostling for the primo filming position and waiting to pounce on anyone who ventured within badgering range.

His colleague grinned. "I hear you, but hunger is a powerful motivator. I'm going to try to sneak out the back. You want me to bring you anything?"

Marc surveyed the scene again. Could be a long day. "Yeah. Whatever you're having is fine with me. I'm not picky."

"You got it. I'll be back in thirty minutes." The other man began stripping off his gear as he walked away.

Marc turned back to the restaurant—or what was left of it. Now that the fire was out, the bodies of the two victims had been removed, and the injured were being transported to hospitals, the investigative work could begin.

It was a shame Bri hadn't been called in for this one. Not that she didn't deserve a day off after the week she'd had. But it would be far more pleasant to work with her on this case than the two older guys who'd shown up from the Regional Bomb and Arson Unit.

Oh well. It was what it was.

Hard hat under his arm, he struck off toward the remains of the building, where his County fire investigation counterparts were continuing to do a preliminary walk-through of the scene, trying to nail down the point of origin. Once they had that, it would be—

"Marc Davis?"

He stopped and swiveled back. A sandy-haired thirtysomething guy, almost as tall as he was, stood a few feet away.

"Yes."

"Our arson guys pointed you out." After motioning toward the two men Marc had been working with for the past hour, he moved closer and extended his hand. "Jack Tucker. Homicide."

It took a few seconds for the name to click into place.

Bri's overprotective brother.

Why had the man sought him out?

Marc returned his firm clasp. "Nice to meet you. I know we haven't met, but your sister told me you were with County."

"That's why I wanted to introduce myself. Bri's mentioned you to me too."

Mentioned?

Considering how her brother was sizing him up, she'd done more than that. Like, given him the impression she was interested in a certain ATF agent on more than a professional level, perhaps?

That was encouraging. Assuming he was interested too, of course.

Give it a break, Davis. You're interested.

Okay. Fine. He'd admit that—even if their meeting hadn't fallen within his timetable for reentering the dating world. And starting today, he was going to begin actively exploring that interest.

But what exactly had Bri said to her brother?

As Jack continued to study him, Marc put on his hard hat and searched for a diplomatic approach to uncover the answer to that question.

Jack saved him the effort.

"In case you're wondering how much Bri told me, she's been very closemouthed. The only personal detail I could pry out of her was your first name. After our arson people passed on your full moniker, I put two and two together."

Marc's spirits nose-dived. If Bri hadn't bothered to tell her brother his whole name, she must not be—

"Her reluctance to talk about you was telling." Jack angled away from the bright sun. "Whenever she clams up, it means one of two things. She's in trouble, or she's interested in someone. I'm assuming with you it's the latter. At least it better be."

Marc squinted at Bri's brother.

That sounded almost like a threat.

Apparently she hadn't been exaggerating about her brother's über protectiveness.

But what had prompted it? Normal sibling loyalty, or something more?

"I'm in Bri's corner—always." Marc dodged the sun's piercing rays too. "I'd prefer to save her from trouble rather than cause her trouble."

"Good to know."

"Also, just to set the record straight, we're not dating."

"So she said."

"Then why the subtle threats and third degree?" Two could play this in-your-face game.

Jack regarded him in silence for a few beats. "She tell you her history?"

"She shared some of her work background. Not much on the personal side. What should I know?"

"That's for her to decide. But she's had more than her share of tough breaks. All three of us have. So we watch out for each other, like the Three Musketeers. One for all, all for one."

And don't even think about doing anything to hurt either of my siblings or there will be consequences.

Jack didn't have to say that for the warning to come through loud and clear.

"Understood—and admirable." He folded his arms and adopted the wide-legged stance that was useful in situations where he needed to communicate strength and authority. "So do you want to tell Bri we had this conversation, or shall I?"

An important question, now that he'd decided to follow Nan's advice and walk through the door that appeared to be opening. Relationships should be based on trust and openness, and keeping this encounter with her brother secret wouldn't advance his cause.

Jack flicked a speck of ash off his jacket. Pulled out his sunglasses and slipped them on. Transferred his weight from one foot to the other. "There isn't much to say. It was just an introductory chat."

Marc waited him out.

When the silence lengthened, Jack cocked his head. "You think I came on a little too strong?"

"I'm more interested in what Bri would think."

Jack snorted. "Nothing complimentary, that's for sure. She thinks I overplay the protective brother role, and she isn't afraid to tell me to butt out if she thinks I've overstepped."

Yeah. That sounded like Bri.

But it was hard to fault a caring brother.

"I'll tell you what. Why don't I say we met at a crime scene and gloss over the protective part?"

"That works for me. I'd like to stay in her good graces. The three of us are pretty tight, and I wouldn't ever want anything—or anyone—to change that."

Marc flicked a glance at the empty ring finger on the man's left hand. "No spouses?"

"Not yet."

"Marriage will alter the family dynamics."

"We can always add a Musketeer or two, as long as they live by the code."

"Naturally."

Jack gave an approving dip of his chin and planted his fists on his hips. "So are you planning to ask my sister out?"

This was not a man who beat around the bush in the name of diplomacy. At least if people he loved were involved.

Also admirable.

But Marc wasn't going to be railroaded into answering. When he decided to ask Bri out, she should be the first to know.

"She hasn't given me much encouragement."

"There are reasons for that."

"I assumed as much." Maybe her brother would offer a few insights if he provided an opening. "She mentioned a bad experience with a guy out West."

Jack's forehead bunched. "That didn't help, but there's a lot more to her story. If you stick around long enough, she may decide you're worth trusting with it." He pulled out his cell. Shifted his attention to the screen. "I have to run. But I'll leave you with one thought. Nothing worth having comes easy."

As Bri's brother strode away, phone to his ear, Marc pulled on his gloves.

Was that parting remark a backhanded word of encouragement?

Possibly.

He crossed to the burned-out hulk of the restaurant, their conversation replaying in his mind. It was hard to dispute anything the man had said, especially the last comment.

But sometimes, no matter how hard you tried . . . no matter how much blood, sweat, and tears you invested in a quest . . . the goal was impossible to achieve.

Like his elusive search for resolution and peace of mind.

The folder on his computer desktop was a constant reminder of that.

He swallowed past the gritty taste of ash on his tongue and forced himself to shift gears. Lamenting the past was fruitless. He ought to focus on how to proceed with Bri rather than dredging up the unanswered questions from his childhood that continued to plague him.

Jack had implied that gaining Bri's trust would be difficult, but Marc was no stranger to hard work.

One thing for certain.

However much perseverance and patience it took to chip away at the wall she'd erected around her heart, it was becoming clearer by the day that the treasure waiting inside would be worth the effort.

"BRI! OVER HERE!"

At Alison's summons, Bri lifted a hand in acknowledgment, wove through the throng of patrons clustered near the ice-cream shop display cases, and slid onto a stool at the small, cocktail-height table her friend had claimed. "Have you been waiting long?"

"A few minutes. Mostly in line." Alison slid a cardboard cup across the table.

Bri began to salivate. "Is that butter pecan?"

"Yep."

"Oh, man. You know how to rack up brownie points with this girl. But I could have gotten my own."

"Waiting to place an order would have eaten into our limited time. Look at that crowd." Alison waved toward the throng planning to indulge in a high-calorie Saturday splurge. "Besides, what are friends for if not to lend an ear and provide ice cream?" She motioned toward the treat. "Dig in and give me the scoop on the new information you mentioned—no pun intended."

Bri picked up her plastic spoon. "It's relationship related."

"Ugh." Alison made a face. "Considering the state of my marriage, I hope you're not going to ask me for advice."

"No. This is about a relationship gone bad."

"Ah. That, I should be able to help you with. Unfortunately." She scooped up a spoonful of her mint chocolate chip. "What's the problem—and how does it relate to what happened last week?"

In between bites of ice cream, Bri briefed Alison on her experience with Travis in Idaho and the news she'd received this morning.

"I can't help but wonder if he's somehow connected to the so-called accidents that have been happening to me, but . . ." Bri sighed and shook her head. "Isn't that kind of far-fetched?"

Alison swirled her spoon in her softening ice cream, brow wrinkled. "Traveling cross-country seems excessive, unless this guy has gone off the deep end. I mean, why would he wait almost three years to exact revenge?"

"I don't know. I wonder if getting put on leave for a similar incident brought back all his anger at me for the first one."

"But this latest episode wasn't your fault. If anything, he ought to be grateful you cut him slack after the first harassment episode. Gave him a chance to clean up his act. His failure to toe the line, and the consequences for that, are his fault, not yours."

"I know. But he did have a victim mentality. Nothing that went wrong was ever his fault. That was true both on the job and off."

"Hmm." Alison pursed her lips. "You think, in some twisted way, he could be blaming you for the pickle he's in now?"

Bri drew a jagged line through her ice cream with the tip of her spoon. "I don't think it's out of the realm of possibility, but if he *is* behind the incidents this past week, he's covered his tracks. I can't prove he had a part in them."

"Do any of your neighbors have security cameras?"

"No. Most don't even have alarm systems. It's a quiet street in a stable neighborhood. And annoying as those incidents were, I can deal with them." She jiggled her foot, chased an elusive dollop of ice cream around the cup, and gave voice to her biggest fear. "To tell you the truth, I'm more worried about what he may be planning next—if anything. I'm wondering if this could ratchet up."

Alison stopped eating. "You think he might want to hurt you?"

Bri poked at her ice cream.

Did she?

Was he capable of actually inflicting harm?

"Bri . . ." Alison leaned closer, features etched with concern. "Your hesitation tells me the answer could be yes. If that's the case, it may be smart to take a few precautionary measures."

She glanced around the shop and lowered her voice. "I have. I started carrying off the job too."

"Wow. You must be really worried."

"This was more to appease my sister." She rested her hand on the slight bulge at her waist, beneath her sweatshirt.

"You want the truth? It makes me feel better too." Alison pushed aside her paper carton and linked her fingers on the table. "Is there any way you can find out where this Travis guy is?"

Bri scraped up the last of her ice cream. "Not easily. Besides, for all I know he's still in Idaho. But if he did leave town, he apparently didn't tell anyone there about it. And contacting airlines or rental car companies with nothing more than a name would be like searching for a needle in a haystack—if they even chose to cooperate. It's not like I can use probable cause to get a court order."

Alison rested her elbow on the table and propped her chin in her palm, her expression somber. "From what you've told me about this guy, I do think your concern is valid. People with anger issues can be loose cannons. It's possible the latest incident in Idaho lit his fuse. He can't get back at the woman who filed the charges because he'd be the obvious suspect if anything bad happened to her, but he could come after you without much risk given the time elapsed and the distance. Would he resort to actual violence? That's hard to predict."

Yeah, it was.

But his fury the day she'd told him once and for all to leave her alone, and his vise-like grip on her arm that had left long-lasting black-and-blue finger marks, suggested he could be capable of inflicting physical injury.

"I guess all I can do at this stage is keep looking over my shoulder. But that stinks."

"I hear you. At least with Nate I never worried about my physical safety. But he worried too much about me, thanks to my job. Another point of contention between us. For all I know, his concerns about my safety caused some of his issues." Alison exhaled and shook her head. "Relationships can be a can of worms."

"That's true." But not always. An image of Marc materialized in her mind. Nothing about him raised any red alerts, should she decide to venture down that relationship road.

As if Alison had read her thoughts, she spoke again. "Speaking of relationships . . . how goes it with that ATF agent of yours? You two still in touch?"

"Yes. I imagine we will be as long as Les's case is active."

"Is it?"

"As of today. But the leads are drying up."

"Did you ever crack that code his daughter passed on?"

She hesitated—but only for a second. Why not give Alison a topline? Unless one of the two jurisdictions left on her list panned out, she was at a dead end anyway.

"Yes. It was names and dates from cases. But I can't find the last name, and as far as I can see at this juncture, the list is random. If there's a connection among the people or the cases, I haven't found it. I was hoping the last name might help, but even if I do track it down, the link could still be elusive."

"It's possible the pieces will click into place eventually."

"Eventually could be too long. My boss has already told me to begin pulling back on the investigation."

"In that case, let's hope a clue turns up soon." Alison leaned sideways and raised a hand. "On a more upbeat note, Sophie's here. You two will finally get to meet."

As Bri twisted toward the door, a slender, dark-haired woman hurried toward them. Unlike her outgoing sister, Sophie didn't make eye contact with anyone as she traversed the shop. She kept her chin down and her purse clutched tight against the gray jacket she wore over her dark denim jeans, as if she didn't want anyone to notice her.

Once she joined them, Alison performed the introductions, then took Sophie's hand. "Let's see the manicure."

Bri examined the woman's fingers. The short nails weren't a surprise, but the hot pink polish was. The attention-grabbing color wasn't consistent with the shy, avoid-the-limelight vibes Sophie was transmitting.

"Beautiful." Alison beamed at her sister. "What do you think?"

The woman freed her hand and tucked her somewhat lank shoulder-length hair behind her ear. "Considering what she had to work with, the manicurist did a fine job. But I think the color may be too strong."

"No, it's not. It's vibrant. I knew the minute I picked it for you it would add a spark to your day."

Ah. Alison had chosen the color. That made more sense.

"It's kind of bright." Sophie didn't seem convinced.

"What do you think, Bri?" Alison deferred to her.

She smiled at Sophie. "I'm a fan of bright. And I bet your students will love it. Alison tells me you teach elementary school."

"Yes." Her demeanor lit up, and she slid her hands in her pockets, out of sight. "Second grade. I love how fast children absorb new material at that age, and their enthusiasm is infectious."

Bri chatted with her for a few more minutes about her job, and the longer they conversed, the more the other woman relaxed. It was clear she was in her element while talking about her students and teaching.

Finally, though, Bri picked up her purse and stood. "I have to run, and I know you two ladies have a packed agenda for the weekend. Alison, thanks for lending me your ear. It was a pleasure to meet you, Sophie."

"Likewise." The woman smiled back at her.

"We'll talk next week, okay?" Alison arched an eyebrow.

"I'll hold you to that."

"Good luck with the Kavanaugh riddle too. I'm glad my job doesn't require me to deal with cases like that."

"There are days I wish my job didn't, either."

After lifting her hand in farewell, Bri edged through the crowd and stepped outside. While the exchange with Alison hadn't solved her dilemma about Travis, it had at least reassured her that her suspicions weren't totally crazy. Her friend hadn't dismissed them, and in fact had offered a reasonable explanation for why Travis could have sought her out now.

But Alison's conviction that her apprehension wasn't misplaced only added to Bri's unease.

Because if Travis was out there somewhere, waiting and watching, how could she not worry that his next move would damage far more than her bank balance?

TRAVIS SLUNK LOWER IN HIS CAR, pulled down the brim of his baseball cap, and adjusted his shades as Bri left the ice-cream shop behind and struck out for her car.

Finding an ideal spot to take his shot was going to be a challenge, and his blackmailer's suggestion about the park tomorrow morning was fishy. What if it was a setup?

It would be safer if he picked his own location.

He gave the small shopping mall a slow scan. Somewhere busy like this would be less risky than a park with few people around. In an area with more activity, it would be harder to pinpoint the source of the shot, and in the mass confusion that followed, it would be far simpler to slip away unnoticed.

Bri stopped beside her car and pulled the door open. As she slid behind the wheel, he twisted the key in his ignition, his nerves kicking in.

He had to get this done fast.

Marcia hadn't been happy that his Saturday plans didn't include her. She'd expected him to devote his weekend to her. If he took off again tomorrow, she could get suspicious.

But it all depended on where Bri went from here. If she headed home and shut herself in her duplex, he was sunk. He might have to use the park as a fallback and come up with another excuse to ditch Marcia tomorrow morning.

Which would tick her off.

All he could do was hope Bri went somewhere today where a fair amount of people were gathered. A place that would offer him a clear line of sight and allow him to vanish as soon as the job was done.

Luck, however, hadn't been on his side in the past couple of days.

And if he blew this assignment, he'd be in a heap more trouble than the mess he'd left in Idaho.

Thanks to Bri. Again.

Rage began to simmer in his gut, but he reined it in. He had a lot more discipline than his old man. Except for the day Bri had warned him to back off and keep his distance.

His loss of control then had been a mistake.

One he wouldn't make again.

While he was livid that an anonymous person was pulling the strings at the moment and manipulating his behavior, giving in to anger could lead to slipups that would put him at even higher risk.

So he'd follow Bri, wait for an optimal setting in which to follow the instructions he'd been given—and hope the potential second assignment the blackmailer had mentioned never materialized.

FIFTEEN

WAS THAT BRI?

Nan's shopping list in hand, Marc paused midstride as he approached the grocery store and squinted at the woman who was trundling her cart under the shadowed overhang outside the entrance.

The instant she stepped into the light, his question was answered.

It was Bri.

His lips curved up.

After all the hours he'd spent at the fire scene today, she was a welcome sight. A reward for keeping his promise to Nan that he'd stop on his way home to get the items on her grocery list, despite his fatigue and desperate need for a shower.

Chatting with Bri for a few minutes would revive his waning energy.

He picked up his pace as she gave the parking lot a slow, deliberate one-eighty. The kind he often did in potentially dangerous situations, when he was on high alert for threats.

Odd.

She spotted him as he continued toward her, her eyes widening in surprise, the tiny lift at the corners of her mouth suggesting she was pleased to see him.

"Fancy meeting you here." He stopped a few feet away.

"I could say the same." She gave him a head-to-toe. "Let me guess. You worked today."

He grimaced and inspected his jeans. "Am I that grungy?"

"No, but I know from personal experience what your soot smudges mean. Like the one here." She tapped her left cheek.

He reached up and scrubbed the area she'd indicated. "Gone?"

"Yes." Her gaze dropped to the list in his hand, and a killer dimple appeared in her cheek. "Grocery shopping for your grandmother?"

"Yeah." He tried not to stare at the enchanting dent that juiced his libido. "She gave me her list before I got called to the scene this morning. To be honest, I wasn't in the mood to follow through on my promise. Now I'm glad I did."

A faint flush crept over her cheeks, and she leaned down to readjust a bag in her cart. "I, uh, don't want to hold you up. You must be tired."

"Not anymore." When her flush deepened, he tipped his head toward the lot and changed the subject. "Where are you parked?"

"Right there." She nodded to her Camry, three cars away, and started walking again.

He fell in beside her. "Why don't I help you load your groceries? I'm in no hurry to wander through the aisles inside. Seems like between every visit, they rearrange the store and it takes me—"

A loud, sharp pop cut him off midsentence, and he jolted to a stop.

Seconds later, another pop sounded, followed by a distinctive thump as a bullet pierced the back of her trunk less than ten feet away.

Heart lurching, he grabbed Bri and pushed her down beside the closest car. "Shots fired! Take cover!"

As he yelled out the warning, screams erupted around the parking lot.

He dropped down next to Bri, letting her cart wobble away as he used his body to shield her.

But it was hard to keep a person safe when the shooter's location was impossible to pin down—and when your duty weapon was locked in the glove compartment of your car.

Bri struggled to extricate herself from his protective tuck. "Marc, let me up!" She wiggled free, emerging a moment later clutching a weapon. "Where's the shooter?"

"Unknown."

"Call this in." She stayed low but jockeyed sideways to get a broader view of the lot, Sig gripped in both hands.

Since she had the gun, he pulled out his cell and did as she'd asked, relaying the pertinent information and location in a few clipped sentences after identifying himself as an ATF agent.

"Officers have been dispatched." The 911 operator's response was crisp and all business. "I'll stay on the line until they arrive."

"Copy that."

Marc surveyed the lot. Around them, people were cowering beside their cars. Next to him, Bri's posture was rigid.

"I don't see anything." A slight quiver snaked through her words. "Are you certain it was a shooter?"

He pressed the mute button on his cell. "Yes."

"I don't know." She caught her lower lip between her teeth as the faint wail of a siren heralded the approach of a patrol car. "A car could have backfired. Or it may have been—"

"Bri." He waited until she met his gaze. "The second bullet hit your trunk."

Her lips parted a fraction, and a wave of shock wiped all expression from her face. "How do you . . . do you know that?"

"I happened to be looking in the right place as it hit. And the sound of a bullet striking metal is distinctive." Marc continued to do a visual grid search of the parking lot as the siren increased in intensity. Another one joined in, creating a discordant melody.

"Do you think the shooter's still h-here?"

Though her tone was calm, the hiccup in her voice was telling.

Bri might be law enforcement, but fire investigators weren't often in the line of gunfire. Nor was that a high risk in *his* current job. But he'd been involved in dicey situations during his early days with the ATF. Dodged more than a few bullets. Dealt with a number of shooter situations.

This one, however, didn't fit the pattern for shootings in typically safe public locations.

"Doubtful."

"Why?"

"It's not an active shooter situation, which is more what you'd expect in this setting. Only two shots were fired. If the shooter had been trying to wreak havoc or kill multiple people, he'd have kept firing. Besides, most perpetrators of mass shootings pick a place where they can take out the most people as fast as possible. Think Columbine or the movie theater in Colorado or the Las Vegas tragedy."

"So what was the point of this?"

He stopped searching the parking lot long enough to spare her a measured glance. "Like I said, the second bullet hit your car."

Once more, shock blanked out her features as his message registered. "You think . . . you think this person was aiming for me?"

"I don't know, but it's disturbing in light of all that happened last week."

Three patrol cars with sirens blaring pulled into the parking lot.

"Agent Davis, are you there?"

At the 911 operator's question, he released the mute button. "Yes. Officers just arrived. Let them know no other shots have been fired."

"Copy. Please stay on the line."

Once more Marc muted the phone and spoke to Bri while keeping tabs on the activity in the lot. "Are you certain you can't think of anyone who would want to do you harm?"

When she didn't respond, he looked back at her.

Her forehead was puckered, and her complexion had paled.

Two other facts also clicked into place in rapid succession.

She was carrying off duty—and she'd paused to get a read on the lot as she'd left the store.

His pulse ratcheted up another notch.

"Bri?"

She massaged the bridge of her nose. Exhaled. "There was a new development this morning." In a handful of sentences, she told him about Travis Holmes. "But I have no proof he's involved in any of this. And I can't believe he'd travel almost two thousand miles to harass me."

"Don't you think it's worth finding out where he is?"

"I don't have any probable cause for a warrant to dig into his credit card records to check for charges that could track his whereabouts."

"Agent Davis, the responding officers have asked for your location."

He unmuted the phone again and provided the information.

"Stand by. One of the officers will come to you."

"Copy."

As he spoke, a uniformed man began working his way toward them, pistol drawn, staying low. The other officers fanned out in separate directions.

"We're about to have company." He indicated the man to Bri. "Was Holmes a decent shot?"

"He claimed he was. He liked to hunt, and I know he went to the range on a regular basis. Why?"

"If he was aiming for you, he missed by a mile."

"So maybe whoever was shooting wasn't aiming for me. Maybe it was a random incident."

While that was possible, it didn't feel right. The timing was too coincidental.

Yet it was hard to argue with Bri's reasoning about Holmes. Why would he travel cross-country just to make her life miserable?

If he had, though, why switch to shooting—clearly a deliberate attack—when the previous incidents, even if they'd been intentional, could have been dismissed as accidents?

There was no mistaking a shooting for an accident.

Meaning if Holmes was behind this, he'd decided that camouflaging his pranks as an unfortunate but innocent run of bad luck was no longer important and was willing to put himself at risk.

Why?

What had changed?

No answers came to him as the officer rounded the car and joined them.

At the man's request, Marc repeated the information he'd provided to the 911 operator. "Also, since the bullet entered the back of the trunk, I'm assuming the shot came from that direction." He pointed east.

"Okay. Stay put. If there hasn't been any activity in the past ten minutes, I'm thinking the shooter is gone. We'll verify that before we give the all-clear."

The man moved off as several more patrol cars piled into the lot.

Wincing, Bri shifted her position and settled onto the asphalt, knees bent, legs drawn up, back against the car, Sig still in hand.

Marc remained crouched beside her, one knee resting on the pavement. "Is there anyone else you could contact who might know where Holmes is?"

The grooves remained embedded in her brow. "No. He didn't hang around with the other smokejumpers during off-duty hours. I know he had a network of acquaintances around the country, but he never mentioned their names."

"Are you planning to identify him in your statement?"

She sighed. "It doesn't seem fair to sic law enforcement on him when I'm not certain he's involved. Much as I dislike him, linking him to today's shooting—or my other issues—would be pure conjecture."

You had to admire a woman who didn't want to complicate someone's life, even if that someone had apparently complicated hers.

"Let's see what the police find."

But forty-five minutes later, after it was determined the shooter had fled and no one interviewed in the parking lot had seen the person, the responding officers didn't have a single clue that would help them identify the perpetrator. While they'd do a cursory search for the first bullet, finding it would be difficult even if it had survived intact.

They were, however, very interested in extracting the bullet that had pierced Bri's trunk.

In the end, Bri kept Holmes's name to herself. Marc didn't push her. It was a leap to think someone would pursue a woman after a gap of almost three years or escalate from puncturing tires to shooting.

Nevertheless, as he collected her wayward cart while she talked with the officers about timing on the release of her car, he couldn't shake the feeling that something wasn't right about Holmes.

So why not see if she'd tell him more about what had happened with Holmes? It was possible that after dodging bullets together, she'd feel more comfortable confiding in him.

Even if she shut down, though, letting this die would be a mistake. Every instinct in his body told him that finding the whereabouts of the man who'd caused Bri grief during her life as a smokejumper should be a top priority.

As the officer moved on in response to a summons from one of his colleagues, Marc trundled the shopping cart her direction. "What's the word?"

Bri wrinkled her nose. "It could be an hour or two before they're ready to release it."

Fine by him.

"In that case, let me give you a lift home."

She hesitated, a flicker of indecision darkening her irises. "I've already imposed too much for one week."

Unless he was reading her wrong, she was tempted to accept.

"To tell you the truth, I'd love to have an excuse to defer shopping, and there's nothing on Nan's list that can't wait until tomorrow. Besides, you have groceries that will spoil if you don't get them home soon."

"I don't know . . ."

"A piece of advice? Don't overthink this. You'll actually be doing me a favor." He offered her his most engaging grin. "And Nan will be fine with this, trust me." More than fine, in light of all her questions about Bri. Assuming he decided to tell his grandmother why her shopping had been deferred.

Bri rested her hand against the car, and all at once her scraped-raw knuckles registered. Two of them had bled.

"Hey." He positioned the cart to keep it from rolling and circled around it to join her. "What happened here?" He took her hand.

Her brief, sharp intake of breath suggested his simple touch had the same electrical effect on her that it generated in him.

"I, uh, must have grazed them when you pushed me down."

So the damage was his fault.

His stomach kinked. "Sorry about that."

"Better than getting shot. They'll be fine." She tugged her hand free.

"Why don't you let me take you home? It's been a tough afternoon on the heels of a tough week. I'm parked over there." He waved toward his car, several spots away in the adjacent aisle. "Or you could call your brother to pick you up. Unless he's still at the scene where I spent most of my day."

She blinked. "You met Jack?"

His ploy to pique her interest had worked.

"Yes. He tracked me down."

Her eyes narrowed. "Why?"

"I'll tell you all about our chat if you let me drive you home." He snagged her cart as it began to roll, hoping she'd take the bait he'd dangled.

But if she didn't, he'd try again. Push harder. The time had come to get answers to at least a few of the questions that had been plaguing him since the day they met. And perhaps one of those answers would offer a clue about the odd happenings of the past week.

Because if someone was targeting Bri, they needed to figure out fast who it was before one of these incidents turned deadly.

SIXTEEN

AS THE WARMTH OF MARC'S TOUCH lingered on her skin and seeped deep into her pores, Bri's resolve to keep her distance from the man standing inches away wavered.

Not good.

She brushed a smear of parking-lot dust off the sleeve of her jacket as he waited for her answer.

If she didn't want to get involved with him, she should refuse his offer of a lift. Call Jack to pick her up.

Yet much as she loved her brother, it would be oh-so-nice to spend a few more minutes with Marc. Strength and competence radiated from him, and she could use a bit more of those until she regained her equilibrium.

Besides, if she called Jack, she wouldn't get the straight story about the exchange between the two men.

Decision made.

She lifted her head to accept, but at the tender expression in Marc's soft, unguarded brown eyes—and the hope in their depths—the words got stuck in her throat.

Maybe this was a mistake.

As if he'd sensed her sudden hesitation, his demeanor morphed from serious to playful. "Not that I'm trying to rush your decision, but your frozen flounder is beginning to thaw." He indicated one of the bags in her cart. "If you don't get it home fast, you'll have squishy fish."

That was true. And this was only a ride home, after all, not a lifetime commitment.

Taking a deep breath, she took the plunge. "If you're certain you don't mind, I accept—as long as you keep your promise to fill me in on your conversation with Jack."

"I never break a promise." After holding her gaze for a charged second, he swept a hand out for her to precede him. "Shall we?"

She struck out for his car, and once they loaded her groceries in the trunk, he circled to the passenger door and pulled it open for her.

"I can't say I'm sorry to leave this parking lot behind." She held onto the frame as she eased into the seat, trying not to be too obvious about favoring her bad leg. The tumble to the pavement had taken a toll on more than her knuckles.

"Old injury bothering you?" Marc leaned down, concern etched on his features.

The man didn't miss anything.

"It'll be fine. I'll sit on a soft cushy chair after I get home and prop my feet up."

"Then let's get you there ASAP." He closed the door and walked around the hood to the driver's side, giving the area a sweep as he took his place behind the wheel. "Everything here seems back to normal."

While he put the car in gear and backed out, she surveyed the lot. Two police cars remained stationed at the perimeter, but the lack of witnesses hadn't left law enforcement much to work with. The first bullet hadn't been found, and the one in her car might or might not be helpful. The stores in the strip mall were back in business, and customers were once more bustling about as they completed their Saturday errands.

"It's hard to believe that forty-five minutes ago we were all taking cover from a shooter. At least there were no injuries."

"Except your knuckles."

"They'll heal." She shifted the conversation to a more important subject. "Tell me about you and Jack."

Marc hitched up one side of his mouth. "Bottom line, he wanted to check me out."

"Why?" was the obvious next question—but she already knew the answer.

More to the point, what had her brother told Marc to explain why he felt it was *necessary* to check him out?

As the silence lengthened, Marc glanced over at her. "Your brother's a straight shooter."

She stifled a groan.

Considering how he and Cara had ribbed her at their family dinner last weekend, who knew what he'd said?

Bracing, she gripped the seat belt strapped across her rib cage. "Did he go into protective mode?"

"That would be a fair assessment. And his comments were underscored with a very clear warning, which I took in the spirit it was intended." Marc flipped on his blinker.

She narrowed her eyes. "What kind of warning?"

"That if I messed with his sister, he'd break my legs—or worse."

Oh, for crying out loud.

"Please tell me you're kidding."

He threw her a grin. "I'm kidding."

Thank goodness.

Otherwise she would have had to do serious bodily harm to her dear but overbearing brother.

"I'm glad to hear that. Jack isn't always the most tactful person."

"I found that out. But it's hard to fault a brother who loves his sister and wants to keep her from getting hurt."

"Unless he takes that brotherly love too far."

"No worries. We came to an understanding."

What did that mean? Had Jack shared his assumptions about her romantic fancies?

She squirmed in her seat. "I'm thinking I should apologize for whatever he said. For some reason, at our family dinner last week, he got the impression I was, uh . . . that our relationship was, um . . ." As she stumbled around, trying to come up with an explanation that didn't give her feelings away, Marc stepped in.

"More than professional?"

That was a genteel way to put it.

"Yes. He has a habit of jumping to conclusions, and he may have read more into my comments than I intended."

"Did he?" Marc's tone was casual, but the look he gave her was anything but.

The man beside her was as direct as her brother.

"I'm not certain what you're asking." Not true, but the stall tactic bought her a few seconds to come up with a plan on how to play this.

Marc passed a slow-moving car. "May I be direct?"

She huffed out a small laugh. "You're asking me that now?"

"Touché." His lips twitched. "Let me rephrase. May I be more direct?"

Bri fiddled with the zipper pull on her jacket, tamping down the sudden uptick in her pulse.

She could say no, and Marc would respect her wishes. Of that she had no doubt.

But why put off this discussion? The voltage in the car was already in electrical-storm range. Pretending otherwise would be immature and disingenuous. They should discuss the attraction between them like two reasonable adults and decide how to proceed.

Assuming she could get the left side of her brain in gear.

"Bri?"

She exhaled. "Yes. You may be more direct."

After all, what danger could there be in listening to what he had to say? Especially since he had both hands on the wheel and no further touching was possible? This was about as safe as she could get for an in-person discussion.

He maneuvered into the turn lane and hung a left. "Unless I'm misreading your cues, you're interested in me. If I'm off base, tell me—but be aware the feeling is mutual."

O-kay. That was direct. No pussyfooting around with this guy.

What a different approach than Travis had taken when he'd decided to respond to whatever subliminal signals she was sending in the days before she'd realized his jovial demeanor hid a much darker side. Waiting to catch her alone, then backing her up against a locker and invading her personal space, had been a major turnoff.

Marc's approach, on the other hand?

Opposite effect. It only increased his appeal.

And his honesty deserved honesty in return.

"You're not off base. But in the spirit of candor, you're not in my game plan."

"You weren't in mine, either." His tone remained conversational. As if they were discussing the weather.

The knot in her shoulders began to loosen. Talking about their mutual attraction rather than stewing over the sparks zinging between them had been a wise choice.

"I wanted to get my career established here before I ventured into the dating scene."

"Same here. Plus, I wanted to be available for Nan. I was also coming off a long-term relationship that was going nowhere. I didn't intend to plunge back into the social realm until I had a few months to regroup. But it seems God may have other plans for me."

Long-term relationship.

That comment deserved further exploration.

"You were involved with someone in Chicago?"

"Depends on how you define *involved*. If you're asking me whether we lived together—or slept together—the answer is no."

Another forthright response. And a direct answer to the nosey question that had immediately popped into her mind. One she would never have voiced.

"I'm not trying to pry into your personal business, Marc."

He made another turn and sent her a smile. "It's not prying when the information is freely offered. Serena's a smart, ambitious, career-focused prosecuting attorney, and we had a number of things in common. We clicked, we dated, we fell into a pattern that suited us both. It was pleasant and uncomplicated, but while we enjoyed the hours we spent together, it was understood from the get-go that our jobs came first. We were, to use a cliché, married to our careers."

"That happens to a lot of people, yours truly included. But dramatic wake-up calls can force you to realign your priorities." Like a career-ending accident.

"I hear you. Nan getting sick was mine. I realized what Serena and I had was a relationship of convenience. What I wanted was what my parents and Nan and Pops had. The decision to relocate to St. Louis also gave me the impetus to reevaluate and, in the end, walk away."

"Was she upset?"

"About the shakeup in her routine, yes. Losing me? Not so much. Understandable, given the superficial nature of our relationship." He swung onto her street. "Home safe and sound."

As he drove toward the house, Bri rummaged for her house key, mind whirling.

While Marc had told her a great deal of personal history on the short drive from the mall, if he was in a talking mood, it was possible he'd tell her even more if she invited him in.

Like, why he'd been raised by his grandparents. What had compelled him to become an ATF agent. How he felt about changing his plans and dating someone sooner rather than later in St. Louis.

Learning more about him over a shared pizza would be a pleasant end to this stressful day.

The only downside to that?

He'd expect to learn more about her too.

She pulled out her keys. Weighed them in her hand.

Telling him about her experience with Travis would be manageable. While it would be embarrassing to admit she'd been taken in by his rugged good looks and jovial, down-to-earth facade, she'd extricated herself from the situation once he showed his true colors.

But if she asked Marc about his younger years, it was logical to expect him to reciprocate—and talking about those days would be difficult.

He pulled into her driveway, set the brake, and unlatched his trunk. "I'll get your door, then help you carry the bags in."

As he slid out of the car, she took a long, slow breath.

She could tell him to leave the bags on the porch, thank him for his assistance, and wait until he left to take them inside. That would be the smart course if she wanted to avoid sharing any more confidences and keep the childhood details few people knew about locked inside.

Mom and Dad had been privy to many of them, of course, thanks to the social worker who'd placed her with them during her foster days. And Jack and Cara knew quite a few. But not all. Talking about them had always been too painful.

Yet for some strange reason, the notion of sharing them with Marc didn't twist her stomach into a pretzel.

It would help to have a few more minutes to think through the ramifications of that unexpected reaction before making her decision, but that wasn't going to happen.

He pulled her door open. "If you can take two bags, I think we should be able to do this in one trip."

"That works." She swung her legs out, trying not to flinch at the twinge in her hip and knee. A long, hot bath later would be bliss.

Marc handed over the two plastic sacks dangling from the fingers of one hand. "I'll get the rest." He swiveled away and returned to the trunk.

She started for the door, but he caught up with her as she set one of the bags down on her small porch and fitted her key in the lock. "Give me a minute to shut off the security system."

"Okay. I'll wait here."

She let herself in and hurried to the door in the small laundry room that led to her garage, the command in her mind keeping beat with the rhythmic *beep, beep, beep* of the security system.

Decide, decide, decide.

From a pure politeness perspective, she should ask him to stay. Despite spending a long day at a dirty fire scene and dodging bullets, the man had volunteered to give her a lift home. He'd also gone above and beyond this week as she'd tried to cope with the other disasters that had beset her.

The least she could do was feed him dinner as a thank-you—and perhaps share a few bits and pieces about her past.

She punched in the code, and the house went silent save for the sudden, erratic thump in her chest that pulsed in her ears with an almost audible throb.

"All clear?" Marc's voice echoed from the front door.

"Yes." She wiped her palms down her jeans. "Come on in."

When he didn't join her after half a minute, she retraced her steps and found him waiting inside the front door.

"Would you like me to take these into the kitchen for you?" He hefted the plastic sacks.

He was asking permission to venture past her threshold.

And no wonder. From the day they met, she'd been prickly and stand-offish, setting clear boundaries and sending loud keep-your-distance signals.

If she wanted to open the door to more than her house, she'd have to spell it out.

"Yes, thanks. It's in the back." She moved aside, following him after she shut and bolted the door.

"Where would you like them?"

"The counter is fine." She nodded toward the expanse beside the stove as they entered the kitchen.

He deposited the sacks and gave the room a once-over.

She did the same, trying to see the space through his eyes.

Verdict? Bland and boring.

"Kind of bare bones, I know." She forced up the corners of her mouth. "I have to admit I've never devoted much effort to embellishing my digs. With the long hours I've always spent at work, decorating has never been a priority."

"Same here. I lived in my condo in Chicago for ten years, and it was as impersonal the day I moved out as it was the day I moved in. My living space was never top of mind. Another priority I want to shift once Nan is on her feet and I find a place of my own." He pulled out his keys. "Well . . ."

Bri's pulse picked up.

It was now or never.

She straightened a chair at the small café table that held her laptop. "I expect you have to get back to your grandmother"—at the breathless chop in her words, she forced herself to inhale—"but if you're hungry, there's a neighborhood spot a couple blocks away that has terrific pizza. They deliver."

Dead silence.

She risked a peek at him and caught the surprise on his face giving way to a slow grin.

"Sold—if you don't mind sharing a table with someone who has soot in his hair."

Her spirits took a decided uptick. "As long as you don't get any on my pepperoni, I can live with it."

"If you'll point me to the bathroom, I'll remove as much of the grunge as I can."

"Straight down the hall, first door on the right. I'll order the pizza. Do you have any favorite toppings or crust styles?"

"Any crust is fine. I've never met a carb I didn't like. And I'm not too picky about toppings—unless your idea of a three-cheese pizza is brie, gorgonzola, and Havarti. Or you like to top it with pears, arugula, and prosciutto."

She gave him a get-real look. "Who'd eat a pizza with those combinations?"

He arched his eyebrows.

Ah.

Bri tried to tame her smile. "Serena was into gourmet pizza?"

"Gourmet is a generous term. Our taste in pizza was one of the things we didn't have in common."

"I think the pizza makers at Sal's would have a stroke if I requested any of those ingredients."

"My kind of place. Whatever you order will be fine. Give me five minutes. Ten if the soot is worse than I think it is."

"Don't hurry. Sal's is fast, but it'll take a minimum of twenty minutes."

"In that case, I'll also call Nan while I'm in there and let her know I'll be later than expected."

With that he disappeared down the hall.

Bri remained where she was until the water was turned on half a minute later as her unexpected guest cleaned up for their shared dinner.

Shared dinner.

A delicious tingle rippled through her, but she squelched it at once. She shouldn't let herself get carried away. This was a simple thank-you for all he'd done for her this week. Nothing more.

Oh, come on, Bri! Who are you trying to kid?

Expelling a breath, she pinched the bridge of her nose and faced the truth.

She'd had the hots for the handsome ATF agent since the day he'd shown up at Les's fire. No, he didn't fit her dating timetable, but why not give the man a chance? It wasn't as if she had to rush into anything serious. She could open up a little, test the waters. What did she have to lose—except her heart?

Bri pulled out her phone and crossed to the table. Lowered herself into one of the chairs. Settled her aching leg on the other one.

The relief was immediate.

But a broken heart wouldn't be soothed as easily.

And while it was too early in the game to be certain she and Marc would click once they got to know each other better, if she were a betting woman she'd wager they would—and that this man could end up claiming her heart.

A situation rife with danger if the sparks fizzled on his end.

Yet wasn't life all about risk? Hadn't she spent months jumping into raging wildland fires, braving voracious flames and capricious winds that could turn on her in an instant, trapping her in their angry path? Risking her life with every callout?

Yes.

But somehow, the possibility of getting burned by Marc was even scarier.

She scrolled through to Sal's number, tapped on the screen, and put the cell to her ear as she homed in on the magnet Mom and Dad had given her the day she'd left for college, which had been front and center on her fridge ever since.

You cannot always wait for the perfect time. Sometimes you must dare to jump.

Her lips curved up.

How well they'd known her. Always the planner. Always the girl who tried to achieve the best outcome by seeking the optimal moment for every move and preparing for every contingency.

Yet during her smokejumping career, she'd followed the advice on that magnet literally. Learned to conquer her fear, trust her abilities and instincts, and leap into the unknown.

Maybe it was time to do the same in her personal life.

SEVENTEEN

SHE'D INVITED HIM IN.

How about that?

Lips bowing, Marc finished scrubbing the soot from under his fingernails and lathered his hands.

Of course, an invitation to share pizza didn't mean she was ready to share anything more. But it was a start.

He dried his hands, finger combed his hair, and rejoined her in the kitchen. "I'm afraid this is as good as it's going to get. Not much I can do about the soot that seeped through my coveralls." He tugged on the sleeve of his T-shirt, marred with a dark smear.

Plates in hand, she stopped setting the table and swiveled toward him. Gave his shirt a quick inspection, lingered for a millisecond on his bicep, then quickly transferred her attention to his face. "Soot is insidious."

"That's an understatement. May I?" He crossed to one of the chairs and held his jacket over the back.

"I can hang that up for you."

"This is safer." He draped it over the chair. "If it's harboring any soot, I'd rather the ash fall on a tile floor than rub against anything in your coat closet. How can I help?"

"Not much to do with takeout pizza." She set the second plate on the table.

He zoomed in on her knuckles. Cleaned up, but raw. They

had to hurt with every finger flex. "I could pour drinks or set out silverware."

"No utensils necessary with pizza, but you can get the drinks. There's Diet Coke and water in the fridge. If you prefer coffee, I'd be happy to brew a cup."

"I'll go with the Coke. What would you like?"

"Coke is fine."

Marc crossed to the fridge, taking a quick inventory as he extracted the two cans. Yogurt, milk, cranberry juice, deli turkey, eggs, and an array of vegetables and fruit. Mostly healthy, nothing fancy. Two takeout containers suggested she ventured farther afield if she wanted to eat more than the basics.

He set one of the sodas beside her as she placed paper napkins on the table, popped the tab on his, and took a long pull. "This hits the spot. I didn't have enough to drink today."

"Help yourself if you want a refill." She opened her own soda. Rested her hand on the back of the chair as she took a sip, favoring her right leg.

That parachute injury had had long-lasting repercussions.

"Why don't you claim the soft cushy chair you mentioned in the parking lot and put your legs up while we wait for the pizza?"

"I like that idea."

Her immediate capitulation confirmed his suspicions. Her leg had taken a hit during her tumble in the parking lot.

He followed her into the living room, sitting on the couch after she claimed a padded recliner.

"I know this isn't a typical younger person's chair, but it was a godsend during my recuperation." She pushed on the back to elevate her legs. "Hopefully one day I won't need it."

"How long ago did the accident happen?"

"Two and a half years. I was mobile after twelve weeks, more or less, but not fully functional for six months. I still do PT every day. At this stage, I'm thinking it will be part of my routine for the rest of my life. But those are the breaks—or the aftereffects of literal breaks." She flashed him a smile. "Did you talk to your grandmother?"

The discussion about her accident was over, and her message was clear.

Don't coddle me, and don't feel sorry for me. Because I don't feel sorry for myself. I've accepted what happened and moved on.

She rose another few notches on his admiration meter.

"Yes. She was watching an old movie and told me not to hurry. She said there were plenty of leftovers from our dinners over the past couple of days and that she was going to make it an early night anyway."

No need to tell Bri that Nan had probed for details about his unexpected plans for the evening or that she'd managed to nail them with her first guess. While the cancer treatments had slowed her down physically, they hadn't put a dent in her intuitive powers.

"Did you tell her about the shooting?"

"No. She worries about me too much already. I keep assuring her my job isn't as dangerous as she seems to think, but it's a hard sell."

"Understandable. Everyone knows any job in law enforcement is risky. More so these days."

"Going grocery shopping at a mall can be too."

"Sad but true. Few places are safe anymore." The doorbell rang, and Bri set her Coke on the table beside her. "That's the pizza. They were fast today."

Before she could stand, he rose. "I'll get it." He deposited his soda on a side table and hustled toward the door, digging out his wallet as he entered the small foyer.

Tip money in hand, he unlatched the lock, twisted the knob—and found himself face-to-face with Bri's brother.

Hard to tell who was more surprised, but Jack's monumental jaw-drop gave him a slight edge.

After several charged seconds, the other man narrowed his eyes. "I didn't expect to find you here. Especially after our conversation today. I thought you said the two of you weren't dating."

"We're not."

"Then what are you doing here on a Saturday night?"

"Getting ready to share a pizza with Bri." He tried hard to restrain his amusement at Jack's befuddlement.

"And that's not a date?"

"Not a planned one. You want to come in? I'll let Bri explain why—"

"Jack?" At Bri's query, Marc turned to find her hovering on the threshold of the living room. "What are you doing here?"

Her brother lifted the bag in his hand. "Delivering your favorite frozen custard. After the week you had, I thought you could use a pick-me-up. But I see someone beat me to it."

"This wasn't planned." Bri folded her arms.

"So I heard. I'm more interested in why you didn't—"

"Stop." She held up her hand. "Don't give me a hard time for not calling you, okay? I'm fine."

Jack squinted at her. "What are you talking about? I was referring to all my unanswered texts from this afternoon. Why wouldn't you be fine?" He looked back and forth between the two of them. "What don't I know?"

Whoops was written all over Bri's face as she came to the same conclusion Marc reached.

Despite his inside track to law enforcement news, her detective brother didn't know about today's shooting incident.

Should he step in or let her handle this?

Bri didn't give him a chance to debate the pros and cons of those options. In a few pithy, rapid-fire sentences she told Jack the story.

As she finished, her brother's jaw dropped again. "You were shot at?"

"I said shots were fired. No one was hit. The shooter disappeared. Marc drove me home because the police have my car, and I invited him to stay for pizza that's being delivered as we speak." She inclined her head toward a car pulling up at the curb. "End of story."

Jack frowned at her. "I don't like this, Bri."

"I'm not thrilled about another ding in my bank balance, either. I can ignore a few scrapes on the car, but a bullet hole is a different story."

"I'm not talking about the cost or inconvenience. I don't like the timing." Jack finally turned to him. "I bet you don't, either."

Marc leaned a shoulder against the wall and fitted his fingers into the pockets of his jeans. "Bri and I have already discussed that."

"Yeah?" Jack folded his arms. "And?"

"Jack." His hostess inserted herself back into the conversation. "We can talk about this later. Unless you want to join us for pizza."

Her brother glanced at him again.

Marc remained silent, but his expression should be sending a clear "say no" message if Jack was astute enough to pick it up.

He was.

"I'll pass—as long as you promise to call me later."

"I can do that."

"Why don't you keep these for dessert? My waistline won't appreciate two custards, and I'll eat them both if they're in my house." He held out the bag.

Bri's features softened as she crossed to her brother and took it. "Thanks. We'll go there together soon. My treat." She leaned over and gave him a hug.

He held her tight for a long moment, until the pizza guy cleared his throat at the bottom of the porch steps. "Enjoy your dinner." His comment encompassed both of them.

"We will—and our dessert." Bri lifted the bag.

"Nice to see you again." Marc pushed off from the wall.

"Yeah." Jack's response may have been affirmative, but his inflection suggested he wasn't entirely certain he was happy about this turn of events. "I'll leave you two to your dinner." Bri's brother sidled around the pizza guy and strode down the walk.

"I'll take care of this, Bri." Marc moved back to the door. "Why don't you grab our sodas and I'll meet you in the kitchen?"

"Sorry about the unexpected visitor." She motioned toward her departing brother.

"No worries. And if that bag holds Ted Drewes, it was worth the interruption."

She hefted the sack again and swung it back and forth. "Guaranteed."

"Next time, I supply the dessert *and* the pizza."

After a brief hesitation, she pivoted and headed toward the back of the duplex without disputing that there'd be a next time.

A win, as far as he was concerned.

By the time Marc rejoined her, pizza in hand, she'd set their sodas on the table and claimed a chair.

He took the seat across from her and flipped open the top of the box. "Does your brother know about Holmes?"

"He knows about my history with him. That's one of the reasons he's overprotective." She helped herself to a slice. "He doesn't know Travis has fallen off the radar in Idaho. I didn't know that either, until this morning."

"You plan to tell him?"

"Yes. And he won't be happy. Like I said, he knows the background."

"You want to fill me in on that? It's hard to evaluate the risk without complete information." He took a piece of pizza too, keeping his manner relaxed and conversational, hoping she was receptive to his question. Because if the cozy setting on her home turf didn't create a comfort zone conducive to sharing confidences, there wasn't much chance she'd open up anywhere else in person. He might have to resort to more phone conversations.

She wound a strand of hanging cheese back onto her pizza and replied at once, putting that fear to rest. "When I joined the unit, all I saw was Travis's charm and good looks. I expect I sent subliminal signals indicating I was attracted, and he responded. We started chatting on breaks, over meals. I was friendly. Interested, even. Until the day he cornered me in the locker room and showed his true colors."

Marc stopped eating. "Are you saying he assaulted you?"

She picked a piece of burnt crust off her pizza. "No, but he did come on strong. Very strong. I resisted. But I don't know what would have happened if someone hadn't interrupted us. The incident shook me up pretty bad. I'd never had a guy grope me like that before."

"Did you report it?"

"No. I was embarrassed. Also worried I'd sent the wrong signals. That what happened was at least partially my fault." She waved a hand over the box. "Keep eating or the pizza will get cold."

Marc took another piece, but his mind wasn't on food anymore. "For the record, if a woman says no and a guy ignores that message, he owns his bad behavior."

"I won't dispute that, but when you're in a situation like that, it's hard to be objective. In any case, I spoke with him after that and told him in no uncertain terms to leave me alone."

"Did he?"

"There were no more physical incidents, but he began hanging around outside my apartment, showing up at the coffee place I liked, sending harassing notes. Once, I was in a supply closet at the base and the door swung shut and locked on me. I could never prove he did it, but I'd bet a week's salary it was him. And I don't like confined spaces." Her voice hitched, and she took a drink of soda. Helped herself to another piece of pizza.

Coming on the heels of her admission a few days ago that she often felt as if the walls were closing in on her, that comment was worth following up on. But first, he needed to hear the rest of the story about Travis.

"How did you deal with all that?"

"I threatened to get a restraining order. When that didn't stop the harassment, I spoke to my boss, who had a long talk with Travis. I think once he knew his job was on the line, he realized he'd better clean up his act. He stayed away from me after that, but he never got over being angry—and a few weeks ago he pulled the same maneuver with another woman. Except she didn't just threaten him. She took legal action. It sounds like he's in a boatload of trouble."

"He also appears to be MIA." Marc continued to eat, though his appetite had diminished. "I agree with your brother. I don't like this. But why would he come all the way to St. Louis to heckle you? He's already up to his neck in problems. Why complicate his mess?"

"What other explanation could there be for everything that's been going on?"

He finished chewing his bite of pizza, wiped his mouth with a paper napkin, and laid out the theory that had been gaining traction in his mind. "I don't think we should discount the fact that all of these incidents occurred in rapid succession after Kavanaugh's death—and after you began digging into his fire and delving into the puzzle he left behind. Someone who doesn't want any of that investigated may be trying to discourage you from uncovering incriminating evidence."

Her expression didn't change, suggesting she was already thinking along the same lines.

What she said next confirmed that. "I can't refute your theory. If Les was getting close to figuring out how the cases on his list were linked, and if foul play was involved in those, that could provide the perpetrator with a strong motive for murder."

"As you've suspected from the beginning. It took me a while to get there, but you have impressive instincts. You had a feeling something was wrong with the Kavanaugh case, you pursued it, and you've uncovered evidence that suggests your intuition was spot-on. That could be making someone very nervous."

"Or Travis could be behind everything that's happened. Or it could be someone else. Or I might be the victim of a series of unlucky coincidences."

Marc picked up another piece of pizza. "I'm not buying the coincidence explanation. And while there could be a wild card at play here, if you have two legitimate possibilities, those seem like the obvious place to start." An image of the file folder on his desktop materialized in his mind, and he picked up a wayward mushroom that had dropped onto his plate. Repositioned it on his pizza. "Although pursuing the obvious doesn't always lead to answers."

A few beats ticked by.

"Why do I get the feeling you're suddenly speaking from personal experience?"

At the question, he looked over to find Bri watching him, those insightful eyes of hers trained on him, their probing intensity at odds with her casual tone. Proving once again she had sound instincts and that not much got past her.

She'd also given him an opening to share a few details about his past.

And the temptation to confide in this woman who hadn't even been in his life a month ago was strong.

Strange, when he'd never shared his darkest secret with anyone.

Also scary.

Because there was no going back once he made that leap.

But if he didn't answer her question, how could he ever expect her to trust him with the secrets of her heart?

It was a dilemma of the first order. And he had only a handful of moments to choose which fork in the road he was going to take.

EIGHTEEN

SHE'D OVERSTEPPED.

Stomach clenching, Bri pushed her plate aside and knitted her fingers together on the table. "Sorry. Ignore that last question. I don't expect you to—"

"Wait." He held up a hand. Took a deep breath. "This isn't a subject I talk about—ever—but you should hear the story."

"Why?" The response spilled out before she could stop it.

He locked on to her gaze. "If people are interested in deepening a relationship, I don't think there should be any secrets between them. Do you?"

Silence fell between them as Bri digested his comment . . . and his question.

He was putting his game plan for them out there and asking if she was willing to share her secrets too.

It wasn't an unreasonable question. Why should one person in a relationship expose his warts and foibles and vulnerabilities unless the other person was prepared to reciprocate?

But was she ready to make that sort of commitment?

Bri gathered up a few crumbs of crust and put them on her plate. "No. But don't you think it's kind of soon to be having such a serious discussion? We've only known each other three weeks."

"It seems longer to me. Maybe because I felt a strong connection to you from the beginning. Like Nan always said she felt with Pops. Unless my instincts are off, you felt it too."

If he was willing to lay it all out there, she may as well do the same.

"Your instincts aren't off. But what if it's nothing more than physical attraction? Hormones can't sustain a relationship long term."

"They're a start, though." He grinned and lifted his can in salute, then grew more serious. "But I think the potential is deeper than that, which is why I'm willing to tell you a secret about my early life that no one else knows. Not even my grandmother. Definitely not Serena."

Her pulse skittered.

Wow.

Their share-a-pizza-and-a-little-background dinner was rapidly morphing into a no-holds-barred soul-baring session.

She examined her raw knuckles. "I appreciate your honesty, but I have to admit I'm a tad nervous about the pace you're setting."

"You know what they say about he who hesitates." He flashed her a smile, breaking the serious mood as he took a sip of soda. "But I'm willing to table this discussion for now if you want to think about whether you're ready to take the leap with me."

He was giving her an out.

Should she take it? Play this safe? Let fear rule her life?

She flicked a glance toward the magnet on her fridge.

Sometimes you must dare to jump.

Could this be one of those times?

She inhaled long and slow. Listened to her heart. Made her decision.

"Let's go ahead and talk."

He gave a slow blink, as if he'd already psyched himself up to shut the discussion down and shift gears. Then he lifted his empty soda can. "Mind if I get a refill first?"

"Help yourself."

He pushed his chair back and stood, taking longer than necessary to rinse his empty can and claim another Coke.

Hmm.

Was he reconsidering the wisdom of this step?

"In case you're wondering, I'm not second-guessing this move. I'm organizing my thoughts." He rejoined her and took his seat.

She stared at him. "Is mind reading one of your super-powers?"

He hitched up one side of his mouth. "That could come in handy, but no. I attribute my insight more to us being on the same wavelength. Another positive sign." He opened his soda, the carbonation releasing with a quiet hiss. "I should warn you, though. My story isn't pretty—and it's not necessarily suitable for mealtime telling."

"I've seen plenty of ugly, and I have a strong stomach. If you're worried about shocking me, don't be. Besides, I think we're about finished with dinner." She nodded toward the single piece of pizza left in the box.

"Okay. Then let's give this a try." He took another long swallow of his soda. "You've probably wondered how I ended up being raised by my grandparents."

"Yes."

"My parents were killed in a house fire in Chicago when I was ten."

Bri's throat contracted. "Oh, Marc! I'm so sorry. What a terrible tragedy for all of you."

"Yes. It was. And it didn't have to happen."

At that unexpected comment, she frowned. "What do you mean?"

"This is the part I've never told anyone." A muscle in his cheek spasmed, and the can crinkled beneath his fingers. "I may have been able to prevent their deaths."

Her heart stammered.

What?

Linking her fingers, she studied the man across from her—the grim set of his mouth, the soul-deep torment in his eyes, the sudden collapse of his broad shoulders—as she scrambled to formulate a careful response that didn't add to the burden of guilt weighing him down.

"Why don't you tell me why you feel that way? Let me see if I come to the same conclusion."

He lifted his hand again to take another sip of soda.

It was trembling.

Sweet mercy.

Seeing this rock-solid man get the shakes was Richter-scale jolting.

Just how bad was the story he was about to relate?

Bri braced as he continued.

"I'll give you the condensed version of what happened." While his voice was controlled, calm, and matter-of-fact, tremors continued to vibrate in his fingers. "My mom broke her leg a few days before the fire. I was supposed to go camping that weekend with a friend and his family, but Dad wanted me to stay home in case she needed help. He was an investigative reporter, and he was working on a hot story that was taking him away from the house on nights and weekends. But after I begged and pleaded ad nauseam, Dad gave in. Unfortunately."

He scraped a dried speck of cheese off the table with his fingernail and deposited it in the pizza box. "I didn't find out about the fire until I got home Sunday afternoon. It had started in the middle of Saturday night. Dad called 911 after the smoke alarms went off, then tried to help Mom out, but it was slow going with her cast. They both succumbed to smoke inhalation in the hallway and were gone before the firefighters got to them."

Despite her strong stomach, Bri had to fight back a wave

of queasiness as she forced her brain into gear—and came up with the obvious disconnect.

She leaned forward, keeping her manner gentle and empathetic. "As tragic as that story is, Marc, I don't see how you could have stopped what happened."

He gave her a bleak look. "I was strong for a ten-year-old. If I'd been there to help my dad, I think we could have gotten my mom out. And they both would have survived."

Not necessarily. Or even likely, if the blaze was bad enough.

But if Marc believed otherwise, a trite, placating comment would do nothing to assuage his guilt.

Bri laced her fingers together on the table. "Did your grandparents think that too?"

"No. They didn't know I'd pressured my dad to let me go camping. In fact, they were grateful I wasn't home. Nan always said that losing all three of us would have destroyed her and Pops. She considered it a blessing I was gone that weekend."

It was clear from his tone he didn't share that opinion.

"Did the fire investigators figure out what happened?"

"Yes. There was abundant evidence of arson. Several points of origin outside the house, and indications an accelerant had been used. The house was wood and very old. It didn't take much to set it ablaze. It was also on a large lot and backed to a park, so an arsonist could do his work in relative isolation and escape without detection."

"But why would someone set your house on fire?"

"That was never determined. If you want my opinion, though, I think it was connected to the story my dad was working on that involved a local crime boss who was shaking down restaurant owners in certain areas of the city for 'street taxes.'"

"Were the police able to find any evidence linking it to him?"

"No. Nor to anyone else. The case was never solved. That's why from day one on my job there's been a folder on my computer desktop with everything I've been able to piece together about the fire."

"Did you join the ATF because of your parents?"

Marc finished his soda and crimped the empty can with his fingers. "I was interested in law enforcement anyway, but the fire pushed me toward the ATF and fire investigation. Justice wasn't done in my parents' case, and I didn't want to see that happen to anyone else."

"Are you still searching for answers?"

"No. I haven't opened the file since the crime boss died five years ago. Not that I think he set the fire. That job would have been assigned to an underling. But every lead I found led to a dead end or dried up. I finally had to make peace with the reality that the arsonist would never be found."

He may have tried to do that, but he hadn't succeeded. Not if the folder remained on his desktop, continuing to stoke his guilt.

"I don't know what more you could have done, Marc."

"Except been there the night of the fire."

"You might not have survived, either."

His eyes grew bleak. "You want the truth? There have been days I think that would have been a better outcome."

A pang of tenderness echoed in her heart for the grieving, guilt-ridden little boy who lived inside the strong, capable, determined man across from her.

"Did your grandparents know how you felt?"

"No. In the beginning, I was afraid they'd blame me if I told them. That they wouldn't want me around. And I had nowhere else to go."

"Based on everything you've said about them, I don't think that was a realistic worry."

"It wasn't. But by the time I realized that, I'd also realized that if I shared my fears and doubts, they'd hurt for me worse than they already did—and they'd endured more than their share of suffering. So I kept everything inside." He set his mangled can aside and twined his strong fingers with hers. "Until now."

At his touch, her respiration went haywire—but she made a yeoman's effort to remain focused on their conversation. "How did your grandparents feel about the case remaining unsolved?"

"They handled it with more grace than I did. They believed the police did everything possible to track down the perpetrator, and they found solace in their faith. They prayed for comfort, and that whoever had set the fire would repent and seek forgiveness. But that prayer was never answered."

"Maybe it was. Maybe he did repent."

Marc's jaw hardened. "If he did, it was between him and God. He never came forward to pay the legal price for his crime. That's not justice."

No, it wasn't. And she wouldn't try to convince him otherwise. In his place, she'd feel the same.

"The one bright side I can see to your story is that you had wonderful grandparents who were willing to take you in."

"I know. That's a blessing I give thanks for every day." He examined their entwined fingers, then looked back at her. "I'm sure adoption was no picnic, but it sounds like you ended up with wonderful parents too."

At the sudden pivot in the conversation, Bri's pulse lost its rhythm again. "I did. The best."

"How old were you when you were adopted?"

"Six."

"May I ask what happened to your parents?"

She gripped her soda can with her free hand. Of course he'd be curious about that. Anyone would be.

But the thought of answering that question set off a blender in her stomach.

"Hey." He stroked his thumb over the back of her hand.

"We can save this for another day if you prefer. I already dumped a boatload of heavy stuff on you. It may not be a bad idea to let all that settle out before we—" He stopped. Pulled out his phone. Frowned at the screen. "Normally I wouldn't check this in the middle of a conversation like we're having, but I'm trying to be available for Nan. This is her."

"Answer it, by all means." She started to rise, but he tightened his grip.

"Don't leave." He put the cell to his ear. "Hi, Nan. What's up? . . . Never too busy to talk to you . . . Uh, no." He glanced down at their entwined hands. "Nothing that can't wait a minute . . . Sure, I can pick that up . . . Got it. I'll get two for you . . . You're not. See you soon."

As he ended the call and slid the cell back into his pocket, the gist of the one-sided conversation wasn't hard to grasp. Marc's grandmother needed something, and their impromptu pizza dinner was coming to an end.

In other words, she'd been granted a reprieve.

So why wasn't she as thrilled about the delay as she should be?

"Do you mind if we continue this conversation another day? The backup tube of skin cream Nan thought she had is nowhere to be found, and the radiation burns are bothering her. She's ready to go to bed, but she won't be able to sleep until she gets some relief." He rose.

"No problem." Bri freed her hand and stood too, still sorting through her odd reaction to the delay. Heck, a few minutes ago she hadn't even been certain she was willing to tell Marc her story. What was with this vague sense of letdown?

"You want to pick this up tomorrow?" Marc pulled his jacket from the back of the chair. "I'll be free once Nan goes down for a nap after church."

"Um . . . I'm booked in the afternoon."

"Meeting your siblings for a family meal again?" He shrugged into the jacket and settled it on his shoulders, brushing off a wayward speck of soot.

"No. That's a once-a-month date. I volunteer through church with a group that does chores for people who could use a helping hand. Most are older. My assignment tomorrow is fall yard cleanup for an elderly man who isn't quite up to that job anymore."

Creases appeared on his brow. "Are *you* up to it, after everything that happened today?"

From anyone else, that question would activate her bristly defense mechanisms.

Strange that it didn't with Marc.

"I can manage yard work." Though it would leave her aching by evening.

"Would another pair of hands speed up the job?"

She did a double take. "You're volunteering to give up your Sunday afternoon to do yard work?"

"I wish I could claim my offer was motivated by altruism, but in the interest of candor, my reasons are more selfish. I'd like to spend a few hours with you tomorrow and continue our interrupted conversation."

That wasn't a bad trade-off. If Marc helped, she'd be less sore tomorrow night. Besides, putting off her story wasn't going to make the telling any easier.

"Sold."

"I could swing by and pick you up around one."

"That works."

"Let's go get your car. They ought to be ready to release it by now."

She waved off his suggestion. "Don't worry about that. I'll call Jack later. He'll be glad to swing by and give me a lift. I'm sure he's chomping at the bit for the scoop on our evening." She crossed toward the door. "Take care of your grandmother."

"Are you going to tell him we've decided to date?"

She paused at the door. "Have we?"

"I'm game if you are."

"I'm not certain it's wise to mix business and pleasure."

"Our business should be winding down soon."

Sad but true. Unless she made serious headway on Les's case or his list in the next few days, Sarge was going to tell her to let it go.

"Why don't we give it two more weeks?"

Marc let out a theatrical sigh. "I guess I can hang on for fourteen days." He pulled out his keys, but as he faced her, all humor faded from his expression. "You want to schedule an official date for two weeks from today?"

His question wasn't just about a date.

He was asking her if she was willing to explore the attraction between them with serious intent.

And while dating hadn't been on her agenda for the next few months, it would be nuts to pass up the opportunity that had dropped into her lap to get better acquainted with the most amazing man she'd ever met.

"That sounds great."

A slow smile warmed his eyes, and he leaned toward her, his intent clear.

She let her eyelids drift closed and tipped her chin up, but all he did was brush his lips across her forehead.

Well, shoot.

"A preview, to whet your appetite for what's to come." His promise was a whisper of warmth against her skin before he backed off.

"That was"—her voice rasped, and she tried again—"that was, uh, tantalizing."

"Hold that thought. See you tomorrow."

"Okay." With her heart banging against her rib cage, a one-word response was all she could manage.

She waited until he reached his car and lifted a hand in

farewell. Responded in kind. Closed the door and wandered back to the kitchen after he drove away.

They never had gotten around to dessert.

But much as she loved Ted Drewes, the creamy, rich sweetness of frozen custard came in a distant second to the sweetness of the kiss Marc had trailed across her forehead.

And best of all?

There would be more to come as soon as she put the Kavanaugh case to bed.

THE END WAS IN SIGHT.

Finally.

An owl hooted in the blackness—a forlorn, eerie sound in the silent forest—and I shuddered as I adjusted my night-vision goggles. Peered at the tent.

All was quiet, as it had been for the past half hour. As it should be, after the ground-up Ambien I'd slipped into his coffee while he'd been off in the woods, doing his business.

That had been the trickiest part of tonight's operation. The one with the highest risk of detection.

Yet I'd pulled it off. He hadn't spotted me.

I flexed my fingers inside my latex gloves and gave the dark, wooded area another scan.

Weird how anyone could find such solitude and isolation relaxing. And who could possibly enjoy the constant fight with mosquitoes, the primitive facilities, the hard dirt for a bed beneath a sleeping bag that provided minimal cushioning?

But his preference for dispersed camping in national forests provided a tailor-made location for my task, even if getting here had been a bear and would require me to forfeit a chunk of this night's sleep.

Worth it, though, to ensure the last person on my original list got the justice he deserved.

Thank goodness he kept the same evening schedule on his camping trips as he did in the city. It would have been difficult to get here in time to doctor his coffee if he went to bed earlier than ten.

I opened the backpack at my feet and extracted the syringe of fentanyl. Not an over-the-top amount, but combined with the Ambien, it would suggest to whoever investigated this tragedy that drugs had played a role in the death.

Just as they'd played a role in the other deaths.

Leaving the backpack at the edge of the clearing, I crept toward the tiny one-person tent, the fabric too flimsy to offer protection from a storm or an animal . . . or a sharp needle.

Since he always slept pushed up against the side, I circled around to the back, where the thin polyester outlined his body.

Exactly as expected.

I knew my targets well. And what I didn't know, I researched.

Keeping watch for any nocturnal creatures that might be prowling about, I moved in close, positioned the syringe beside the appropriate bulge, and slid the needle in nice and smooth.

He didn't stir.

Step number two finished.

The rest would be easy.

I crossed to his stash of dried, seasoned wood, gathered up several kindling-sized pieces, and placed them in his campfire, which had gone dark for the night. But the ash was warm, and it took mere seconds for my butane candle lighter to ignite the wood.

While the kindling burned, I moved the small pile of firewood next to the tent.

Of course, no one should stack logs close to a tent or go to bed until a fire was out for the night, but if you were drugged up, you could forget those rules. And in a breeze like the one blowing tonight, glowing embers were apt to drift.

Perhaps toward that stack of firewood.

I pulled the fine-nosed pliers from my pocket, knelt in front of the zipper on the tent, and worked a few teeth loose near the bottom, above the pull. To ensure the zipper would stick, in case he roused enough to try to escape.

Not much likelihood of that, but it was important to plan for all contingencies.

I stood, returned to my backpack, and pulled out the two fire-starter logs I'd cut in half. Back at the wood pile beside the tent, I tucked them in among the logs.

Done.

No need to collect a souvenir here. I already had one more significant than anything in this bare-bones campsite.

It was time to ignite the pyre.

After crossing to the edge of the clearing, I hefted my small backpack into position and settled it on my shoulders. The walk back to my car in this oppressive darkness held zero appeal, but I'd do it fast. And before anyone spotted the blaze at this off-the-beaten-path campsite, I'd be long gone. Heading home to try to catch a few hours of shut-eye.

Candle lighter in hand, I crossed back to the stack of logs beside the tent. Held the flame against all of the fire-starter sections. Backed away, into the shadows of the surrounding forest, waiting until the pile was ablaze.

It didn't take long.

How sweet it would be to stay. To experience this final cleansing moment.

But I didn't have to watch the last act. I knew how it was going to end.

As I turned and jogged through the darkness toward my car, tucked out of view on the national forest road, a sense of elation . . . of euphoria . . . swept over me.

I was free at last.

Unless Bri Tucker continued to dig for details she should leave undisturbed.

A branch slapped me in the face, and I shoved it aside.

Like I wished I could shove *her* away from the whole Kavanaugh mess. Killing an innocent person had never been in my plans.

Yet as another owl hooted, and a rustle of fallen leaves hinted at the presence of other woodland creatures who deemed darkness a friend, I accepted the truth.

If all the misfortune that had befallen her over the past week wasn't sufficient to distract her and eat up any after-hours time she was devoting to the Kavanaugh fire and the man's dangerous list, she'd leave me no choice.

Because after all my efforts to secure my freedom, anyone who threatened it had to be purged.

NINETEEN

BRI WAS STANDING IN FRONT of her duplex when Marc swung into her driveway Sunday afternoon, all set to go.

Not surprising.

She wasn't the type of woman who would keep people waiting.

As she came down the walk from the front door, he got out of the car and gave her a swift, appreciative perusal. Her limp was almost imperceptible today, and she was dressed for yard work in worn jeans and an oversized sweater, her pair pulled back and secured at her nape.

Despite her understated attire and minimal makeup, she was still the most attractive and captivating woman he'd ever met.

"You're prompt." She smiled as she closed the distance between them.

"Always. Another lesson Nan taught me. She said punctuality was a sign of respect, and that it was rude to devalue other people's time by being late."

"I like this grandmother of yours."

"You'll have to meet her one of these days." It couldn't be soon enough for Nan after the grilling she'd given him over breakfast about his unplanned date last night. But Bri would have to be comfortable with that step first. "Any hitches getting your car?" He walked around to the passenger side and opened her door.

226

"No, but I had to endure an inquisition from my brother while he scarfed down the custard I shoved in his face when he came to pick me up. Unfortunately, it didn't keep his mouth too busy to ask questions." She slid in.

"About us?"

"Bingo. Also about the shooting—and Travis."

"We'll continue this once I get behind the wheel." He closed her door, circled the car, and took his place. "So in the interest of keeping our stories straight, what did you tell your brother about us?"

"That the status had changed."

He put the car in gear and backed out of the driveway. "And . . . ?"

"And then I filled him in on the news about Travis, which distracted him. I think he's planning to connect with a few of his airline and rental car company contacts, see if they'll unofficially run Travis's name through their reservation databases. He's got decent connections."

"That can't hurt." He stopped at the end of the driveway. "You'll have to direct me."

"Go left and hang a left at the next corner." She buckled her seat belt. "May I ask a favor? Let's take a break from heavy subjects for a little while. Talk about our favorite book as a kid, or the funniest thing that ever happened to us, or the place we'd most like to visit someday."

Not a bad idea. Some lighthearted conversation—the kind most people engaged in during the early stages of a relationship— would add a touch of normalcy after the tension and stress that had characterized their interactions up to this point.

"I'm on board with that."

They stuck to that plan during the remainder of the drive and for the next two hours as they raked and bagged leaves, snipped dead flowers, and pulled weeds in a yard long overdue for attention.

"This place really got away from the owner, didn't it?" Bri examined the back of the house as they prepared to fill yet another bag with yard debris.

Marc inspected the peeling paint on the foundation and the back-porch railing that was missing a few slats. "Yeah. I wonder if he has any family nearby."

"He doesn't. I got a quick history along with the assignment. His wife died four years ago, they didn't have children, and his few distant relatives don't live in town. Meaning he's on his own. The house is too much for him, but he doesn't want to leave."

"Understandable. Nan's like that too. She was able to keep up with everything until she got sick, but I didn't want her to end up like this." He inclined his head toward the deteriorating house. "Another factor in my decision to come home."

"You're a good grandson." Bri smiled at him, and the warmth radiating from her chased away the slight chill in the October air.

"She and Pops took care of me when I most needed taking care of. The least I can do is return the favor."

"I felt the same about Mom and Dad." She surveyed the man's unkempt garden, filled with a tangle of weeds and frost-nipped flowers that had shriveled and died. "You want to tackle that next?"

"Sure. I think the rest of the yard is done."

She crossed to the flower bed and lowered herself to her hands and knees while he dropped down beside her.

"This is a mess. It won't be easy to clean it up." She surveyed the overgrown plot.

"Second thoughts?"

After a brief hesitation, she turned to him, her demeanor serious. "Sort of."

Uh-oh.

She wasn't referring to the flower bed.

Bracing, he shifted toward her. "About us?"

"No." The swiftness of her reply kick-started his heart. "About dredging up the ugliness from my past." She prodded a clump of dirt with her index finger until it disintegrated. "But I also have to confess that jumping out of planes into wildland fires was less scary than jumping into serious dating—and that has nothing to do with you personally."

"Why does it scare you?"

"Because relationships can go wrong or falter or fizzle out for a bunch of reasons." She expelled a breath and faced him. "I don't often admit to fears, but the truth is, I'm afraid of getting hurt."

"You don't have to worry about that with me. I won't hurt you, Bri."

As his assurance hung in the air between them, her complexion lost several shades of color. Fast.

Frowning, he touched her arm. "What's wrong?"

Her throat contracted, and he had to lean close to hear her whispered reply. "That's what . . . that's what my birth father always used to say."

Marc's stomach clenched.

It didn't take a genius to figure out why she had trust issues.

A man who should have loved her, who'd assured her he wouldn't do her harm, had reneged on that promise. And a betrayal like that from a father would leave lasting scars.

No wonder she was wary of opening up in general—and perhaps with men in particular.

"Do you want to tell me what happened?" He gentled his voice.

"No." She swallowed and turned her attention to the garden. Grabbed a dead stalk and yanked it out of the ground with more force than necessary. "I don't like thinking about him."

"But you do, don't you?"

"Not by choice." She hurled the shriveled, deformed plant into the waste pile a few feet away. "I'd like to forget him. Erase every single memory of him from my mind."

"Maybe talking about them instead of holding them inside would help you let them go."

Her lips twisted. "That's what the social worker told my mom and dad." She waved a hand over the garden. "If you don't jump in, we'll be scrambling to finish before the sun sets."

Message received.

He grasped a warped stem devoid of life and gave her space to decide what, and how much, she wanted to share.

After two or three minutes of silence, she resumed speaking.

"Mom and Dad took me to counseling, but it didn't solve my problem. The counselor was nice, but my trust level was zero. The only therapy that helped was being outside, in the sunshine, with my parents close by." Her hands froze, and she peeked over at him. "I still sleep with a light on in my room."

A suspicion began to form in his mind. One that twisted his gut.

"Why?" It took every ounce of his self-control to keep the rage building inside him in check. "What did your birth father do to you in the dark?"

She focused on yanking the roots of a distorted plant free from the hard, unyielding ground. "Not what you're thinking."

Thank God for that.

"So what happened?"

"He never wanted me. He always called me a mistake. My biological mom ran interference for me while she was alive, but she died of a drug overdose when I was four."

All at once, the plant she'd been pulling released its hold. As she teetered backward, he grasped her arm in a steadying grip until she regained her balance.

"Thanks." She tugged free of his hold and went back to work on the parched earth in front of her. "My father's favorite punishment for any transgression or any deviation from the long list of rules he had was to lock me in the basement. There weren't any windows down there, and the only light was controlled from the kitchen. He never t-turned it on."

As she paused, he digested what she'd shared.

A four-year-old, locked in a dark basement alone, for who knew how long.

That was the stuff of enduring nightmares.

The temptation to pull her close . . . hold her . . . comfort her . . . was strong, but her rigid posture sent a clear keep-your-distance message.

"Before he went to work every day, he locked me in the basement too, but he left a light on then." Her voice became flat, devoid of all emotion. "Sometimes he forgot I was down there after he got home. If I banged on the door or called for him to let me out, he wouldn't feed me until the next day."

The anger churning in Marc's stomach became harder to contain. "And no one knew about this? Or suspected?"

"Not for a long while. I was too young for school, and my father told neighbors he took me to daycare. When I was five, though, a new couple moved in next door. I don't know what made the wife suspicious, but she started watching him leave in the morning for work. After days went by and she never saw me, she called social services. They investigated, and the rest is history." She brushed a few flecks of dirt off her hand, but the residue stained her skin.

"What happened to your father?"

"His parental rights were revoked and he went to prison for nine years."

"Where is he now?"

"Somewhere hot, I hope." A touch of bitterness crept into her tone. "He died five years ago."

"You kept in touch with him?"

"No!" She jerked her head toward him, eyes blazing. "I never wanted to see him again after they took me away."

"Then how do you know what happened to him?"

Her mouth twisted. "Get this. He bought a life insurance policy and named me as his beneficiary. A reparation of sorts, I suppose. Like that was supposed to fix everything."

"He never attempted to contact you in all those years?"

"No." She picked up a fallen maple leaf that hadn't yet withered, its brilliant colors vibrant and unfaded. "I donated the insurance money to an organization that sponsors house parents for kids from troubled homes."

That sounded like the Bri he was coming to know.

"And you were placed with your foster parents after you were taken away from him?"

"Yes—and they became my real parents in every way that mattered. They lavished me with love, gave me siblings I cherish, and created a home where I felt safe. They also raised me in a faith-filled environment. But even though I attend church every Sunday, I can't reach deep enough to find forgiveness for my birth father. Which doesn't make me a very good Christian, I suppose."

"Then I'm not a good Christian, either, because despite my weekly church attendance, I can't imagine ever forgiving the person who set the fire that killed my parents."

She sat back on her heels and looked at him, moisture clinging to the tips of her eyelashes, the late afternoon sun burnishing her skin. "Maybe we can work on learning to forgive together."

"I like that idea."

The corners of her mouth rose a hair. "You know, that social worker may have been spot-on when she told Mom and Dad it would be healthy for me to talk about my bad memories. But I think you have to do it with the right person." Her gaze locked on his as a sudden breeze feathered the wisps of hair framing her face. "You feel like the right person, Marc Davis."

Warmth spread through him, as comforting and invigorating as the balmy caress of sun after a long, cold winter. "That's one of the nicest compliments anyone's ever paid me." His reply came out husky. "We're about finished here, so why don't—"

The back door banged, and they swiveled toward it in unison as the owner appeared on his small porch, juggling a tray in both hands, a cane hooked over his arm—and looking none too steady.

In a dozen long strides Marc covered the distance to the porch and relieved him of the tray. "Let me help you with that, sir."

"Thank you, young man. And the name's George. 'Sir' is much too formal." He motioned toward Bri as she joined them. "I thought you and the missus might be thirsty. I'm not too handy in the kitchen, but my wife did teach me how to make proper lemonade."

Marc sent Bri a sidelong glance.

Soft color flooded her cheeks as she responded. "We're not married. Marc just came along to help me. But that lemonade will hit the spot."

"It's delicious, if I do say so myself." George rested both hands on top of his cane. "So you two aren't a couple. I must be losing my touch. My wife always told me I had a sixth sense about people who were paired up—or should be. Well, you two enjoy the lemonade."

As the homeowner disappeared back inside, Marc nodded toward a bench at the edge of the patio. "Shall we?"

Bri crossed to it, taking the glass Marc handed her and claiming a spot as he deposited the tray on an adjacent table. "The sun's beginning to sink."

"We're lucky we finished before we lost the light." He sat beside her. "What are your plans for the rest of the—"

She held up a finger and pulled out her phone. Knitted her brow. "This number isn't familiar, but I don't like to let calls roll. You never know when a tip might be coming in. Do you mind if I answer? I'll make it quick."

"No. Go ahead." He could finish his question after the call.

Bri put the cell to her ear. "Hello . . . Sophie? . . . Yes, of course I remember you." Bri went silent for quite a while, her expression morphing from curiosity to shock. "I'm so sorry. How is she doing? . . . I'm sure she is. Will you tell her to call me if I can do anything? . . . Yes, I'd appreciate that. And thank you for letting me know."

As Bri lowered the phone and ended the call, Marc leaned toward her. "Bad news?"

"Yes." She scrubbed at her forehead with a hand that wasn't quite steady. "I have a firefighter friend in one of the local municipalities. She's separated from her husband but had great hopes for a reconciliation. That was her sister. My friend found out this morning her husband was killed in a camping accident last night."

No wonder Bri had paled during the conversation.

"That had to be shattering news. I'm sorry for her. For both of them."

"Me too. She has to be devastated." Bri stared into the depths of her lemonade. Took a sip. "Sometimes, when tragedies like this happen, don't you wonder what God is thinking?"

"Always." That question had plagued him for years after the death of his parents. "Life often doesn't seem fair, and the suffering of innocents is hard to fathom given how much of the evil in this world goes unpunished."

"I struggle with that too. In the end, I always fall back on a verse from Isaiah."

"Let me guess. 'For my thoughts are not your thoughts, nor are your ways my ways. For as the heavens are higher than the earth, so are my ways higher than your ways, my thoughts higher than your thoughts.'"

Her eyebrows peaked. "You know your Bible."

"Not well enough, but I do know that passage. It's my go-to verse whenever life throws me a curve."

"One more thing we have in common." She took a long drink. "I think I'll take food over to Alison's house tonight. That's what my mom always did after a family suffered a death. I used to think the gesture was odd. I mean, who has much appetite if they've lost someone they love? But Mom said it was less about the food and more about the kindness and caring it represented."

"Wise woman." Marc finished off his lemonade in a few swallows. The quick dinner he'd been about to suggest wasn't going to happen, but at least he had a real date to look forward to in two weeks. "You ready to call it a day?"

"Yes." She stood and held out her hand for his glass. "Give me a minute to return these to George and I'll help you haul the yard waste bags out to the curb."

By the time she took care of the first chore and chatted with the owner for several minutes, Marc had finished carting out the debris. He met her at the car.

"You didn't let me help." She surveyed the lined-up bags.

"Giving a lonely man company for a few minutes was more important."

She conceded the point with a dip of her head. "George asked that I pass on his thanks."

"Happy to help." He opened her door, and she eased in, clearly stiffer than she'd been upon arrival.

Once behind the wheel, he put the car in gear and aimed it toward her house. "Do you want to stop and pick up food for your friend?"

"No, thanks. There's a grocery store between my house and hers."

"Have you two known each other long?"

"Only about three months. After I took the job with County, we ran into each other at a fire, started chatting, and set up a lunch date. It grew from there."

"Did you ever meet her husband?"

"No, but she almost always mentions him during our conversations. It was obvious she never stopped loving him." Bri stretched out her leg, as if seeking a more comfortable position. "I have no idea what I'll say to her."

"Based on your conversation yesterday with a guilt-ridden guy I know, I have a feeling you'll find the right words." He reached over and gave her hand a squeeze.

"Thanks for the encouragement." She exhaled. "You know, we never did get around to talking about bucket list vacations. Tell me where you'd go if money was no object."

She needed a respite from heavy subjects for the remainder of the drive home.

Following her lead, he launched into a travel discussion, and that topic carried them through until he walked her to her front door.

"Thank you again for helping me today at George's house." She pulled out her key and fitted it into the lock.

"Thank you for taking the leap and trusting me with your secrets." He leaned close and made do with another lip brush across her forehead, but he had to call up every ounce of his willpower to stop there—especially when he backed off and the longing in her eyes sent a signal that was hard to ignore.

"I'll be counting the days until our official date." Her comment came out a tad breathless.

"Me too." He stroked a finger along the line of her jaw, then stuck his hand in his pocket in case it decided to misbehave. "Let me know if you have any luck tracking down the last case on Kavanaugh's list."

It took her a moment to switch gears. "Yes. I will."

"If I don't hear from you, I'll touch base with you in a couple of days."

"I'll count on that."

Before he succumbed to the impulse to give her a proper goodbye kiss, he swung around and strode toward his car.

He didn't dare look back until he was on the street and preparing to drive away.

She remained where he'd left her. Watching him.

Waving a hand through the window, he pressed the gas pedal and guided the car down her street.

Two weeks until their date.

An eternity.

But without a break on the Kavanaugh case, there would be no official excuse for them to see each other in the interim. And since the odds of any new clues emerging grew longer by the day, phone calls would have to suffice.

Unless Bri's unknown tormentor returned to continue their make-her-life-miserable campaign.

Eyebrows dipping, he flicked on his blinker.

That remained a real and worrying possibility. And she didn't need any more hassles. Especially if the attacks ratcheted up and became even more dangerous.

Also a very real and very worrying possibility.

TWENTY

"BRI! WAIT UP!"

Retracting her finger from the elevator button at headquarters, Bri glanced back toward the hall.

Sarge was bearing down on her.

Well, crud. This could be the official end of the Kavanaugh case and the retired fire investigator's puzzle.

Her boss motioned her off to the side as one of the city detectives approached the elevator, waiting until she joined him before he spoke again. "I've been trying to catch you all week for an update on Les's case."

Suspicion confirmed. This was about the Kavanaugh investigation.

Not a discussion she wanted to have.

Except she did have to talk with Sarge about another matter, and with Friday only two days away, she'd have had to touch base soon anyway.

"I don't have anything new to report. I was never able to link a case to the last unidentified set of initials and date on Les's list." Sadly, neither of the two adjacent jurisdictions she'd pinned her hopes on had yielded a match. "And I don't have any new leads on a potential arson suspect in Les's fire, either."

Her boss raked his fingers through his hair, the permanent creases on his forehead deepening. "I think we're at a dead end."

Much as she wished she could dispute that, the evidence supported his conclusion.

"I hear you, but I hate to give up."

"I know you do. You're like Les in that regard. The man was a bulldog—and that's a compliment, in case you're wondering." He flashed her a grin, then grew more serious. "He and I had this same conversation on more than one occasion, by the way. It never went over well, but he always officially closed the file on whatever case we were discussing."

In other words, while Sarge wasn't authorizing further investigation on the Kavanaugh case during working hours, if she wanted to continue to pursue it during her off hours, he wouldn't object.

"Understood. I'll follow his example."

A fan of lines appeared at the corners of Sarge's eyes. "That's what I figured. Keep me in the loop if anything develops."

"I will. I also wanted to let you know I have to attend a memorial service on Friday afternoon. The husband of a firefighter friend. You may have heard about the death on the news. It was a camping accident."

Sarge squinted at her. "Is this the guy who died in a tent fire?"

"Yes."

"Yeah, I heard about it. Sad case."

Very. More so because drugs had been involved. According to what Alison said yesterday during her thank-you call for the food Sophie had accepted at the door Sunday night, her husband's expedited tox report had indicated elevated levels of controlled substances.

Evidently the drug issue she'd hoped he'd kick had instead been a contributing factor in his death.

"I know. It has to be devastating for my friend."

"From the scuttlebutt I heard, the guy was divorced."

"No. Separated."

"Goes to show you can't trust the grapevine. No problem on the service. Take as long as you need."

"Thanks."

"You heading out to the fire on Sycamore?"

"That's where I was going when you flagged me down."

"I'll let you get to it, then." Lifting a hand in farewell, he took off down the hall.

Once again, Bri crossed to the elevator, reached toward the down button—and froze as the door slid open.

Jack was on the other side.

She did a double take. "What are you doing here?"

"Taking care of County business that spilled over into the city. I was going to swing by your office and see if you were in, but this works." He took her arm and tugged her off to the side again, away from the elevator traffic.

Apparently this was the day for hallway conferences.

"What's up?" She shifted toward him as he stopped by the wall.

"I've been working my airline and rental car company contacts. They all ran Holmes's name through their databases. Nothing came up."

"So he's still in Idaho."

"I didn't say that. All I said is he's not showing up as a customer with any of the major carriers that service St. Louis. Have there been any more incidents?"

"No. I'm beginning to think my run of bad luck last week was nothing more than a bump on the road of life."

His dubious expression said he wasn't buying that. "In case there's more to it, watch your back."

"I always do."

"You want me to connect with the McCall cops, have them do a drive-by and see if his car's at his apartment? That could be helpful—unless he's got a garage."

"He doesn't. Or he didn't while I was there. He used to complain about snow blowing into his covered spot. It may be worth a try. But an empty space doesn't prove he's out of town. Not many people want to tackle a twenty-six-hour drive."

"I know a few guys who like cross-country trips. If the cops do spot his car there, though, we should be able to assume he likely didn't drive here."

"It can't hurt to have someone take a look."

"Done. I'll let you know what I find out." He folded his arms and propped a shoulder against the wall. "So how goes it with your ATF agent?"

"Nothing new to report. Now I have a question for you." Putting her brother on the defensive should distract him. She hoped. "Why did you tell Cara about the shooting? She called yesterday and was all over me about it."

"It came up in conversation during a phone call."

"Right."

"You know she doesn't like to be left out of the loop."

"And you know I don't like to make her fret unnecessarily. Having two siblings in law enforcement is enough of a stressor."

"I played it down."

"Didn't sound like it."

He narrowed his eyes. "You're trying to avoid talking about Davis."

Drat. He'd seen through her ploy.

"There's nothing to talk about. By the way, did you know Cara's thinking about trying to barbecue again for our next Sunday get-together at her place?" If the prospect of another tooth-breaking meal didn't distract her food-loving brother, nothing would.

He straightened up. "Did she tell you that?"

Mission accomplished.

"Yes."

"We have to convince her to stick with omelets."

The elevator swooshed open, and Bri backed away. "I tried. Your turn. Gotta run."

She escaped inside, pressed the first-floor button, and fluttered her fingers at Jack as the doors slid closed.

Brothers.

One of these days, she was going to have to have a long talk with him about his overzealous interest in her love life. Remind him that the situation with Travis notwithstanding, she was a grown woman and didn't need his help screening her potential dates. Nor did she appreciate his intrusion into her personal affairs.

What she did appreciate were his efforts to check with his airline and rental car contacts about Travis, and his offer to have the local cops see if they could spot the man's car. If it was there, and his name hadn't shown up on any carrier databases including rental car companies, odds were he was in Idaho.

The elevator stopped on the first floor, and she exited as soon as the doors opened, psyching herself up for the fire scene investigation awaiting her on this Wednesday afternoon. A chore that could stretch into the night.

But it wasn't as if she had anything else to do with her evening. She'd been the one who asked for the two-week delay on dating, after all, so unless there was a new development in the Kavanaugh case, it would be ten days until she saw Marc.

Unfortunately, new developments at this point seemed doubtful.

Sarge had her pegged, however. While she'd back-burner the case going forward during her official working hours, she wasn't going to let it go.

In the end, maybe it would remain unsolved, like the one that had claimed the lives of Marc's parents and refused to yield its secrets despite his diligent efforts to uncover them. Perhaps the links in Les's list would never be found, either.

Yet as she stepped into the gusty wind whipping about under menacing skies, she couldn't shake the feeling that the connection she needed was tantalizingly close. That she was one elusive break away from cracking the code and nailing the culprit not only in Les's death but also in the other cases on his list.

An image of James Wallace's haggard, grief-stricken face strobed through her mind, the conviction in his voice as he tried to convince them his daughter's death hadn't been an accident echoing in her ears.

Justice hadn't been served in that case. She knew that in her bones. Nor had it been served in Les's case, or likely in all the others.

And as she hurried toward her car, dodging the raindrops beginning to fall, she vowed that somehow, some way, she would find out who the final set of initials and date belonged to. And once she did, she'd do her best to discover the link that had eluded Les and track down the person who had destroyed countless lives.

No matter how much personal time she had to invest.

"YOU'RE VERY PREOCCUPIED TONIGHT, SWEETIE. What did you do all day while I was at work?"

Marcia's petulant question registered as background noise, but Travis kept playing with his phone. Maybe if he ignored her, she'd go back to stacking the dishwasher.

While his lodging arrangement had been a godsend at the beginning, allowing him an off-the-radar place to stay, it was getting old.

Marcia was getting old too.

Causing Bri grief had been fun in the beginning, but now that a blackmailer was involved, it had lost its appeal.

Especially after the shooting on Saturday.

Yeah, he'd picked an excellent spot and escaped unscathed, but it had been risky. The repercussions of a shooting were a whole lot more serious than wrecking tires or damaging a car.

He had to get out of here.

But he couldn't. The blackmailer had said to sit tight until further notice.

He bit back a curse.

"Travis? Are you listening to me?" Marcia's tone sharpened.

"Yeah. I'm listening." He snapped out the response.

"Hey." She stuck her hands on her hips. "I asked a simple question. What's with you tonight?"

He reined in his temper. Ready as he was to leave St. Louis, as long as he was here, he ought to be smart and keep the owner of his safe house happy.

Reaching deep for a smile, he tried for a placating cadence. "Sorry, babe. With my vacation winding down, I'm a little bummed."

Her face fell. "You're leaving?"

"In a few days. I do have to work, you know." Surely the other person who had a grudge against Bri didn't expect him to hang around forever.

"Maybe you could get a job here." She wiped her hands on a dish towel and joined him at the table.

"I don't think there's much call for smokejumpers in St. Louis."

"No, but we do have fire departments. Fighting fires is fighting fires, right?"

Not even close. There was nothing like the adrenaline rush of diving into a raging inferno and taming it.

"Smokejumping is different." He left it at that. Why bother trying to explain the thrill to Marcia? She'd never understand.

"But you can't do that kind of work forever. And there would be other compensations if you moved to St. Louis." She rested her hand on his. "Why don't you—"

"Hold on a sec. Call coming in." He picked up his vibrating phone and checked the screen.

Unknown.

This could be his mystery nemesis.

His breathing hitched.

"I have to take this. Give me a few minutes." He shoved his

chair back, strode to the door that led outside, and pushed through onto the deck before he answered.

"Nice job on Saturday, Travis. I'm glad I can count on you." The same genderless voice from the first call responded to his greeting.

"I did what you asked, and I waited until you called, like you told me to. But I have to go home."

"Not yet."

He gripped the banister on the deck and stared into the dark hedge at the rear of Marcia's property that blocked her house from the view of nosey neighbors. "I can't stay here forever."

"You don't have to rush home. You're on leave. And I'm sure Marcia has made you feel welcome."

Travis turned his back on the darkness. Inside the kitchen, Marcia had gone back to loading the dishwasher. "How long do you expect me to hang around?"

"Until the threat is gone."

"What threat?"

"You ask too many questions, Travis. Just sit tight until further notice."

"If I have to wait much longer, I'll run out of cash."

"Ah. No credit card use, no way to track your location. You're smarter than I thought."

"Look . . ." Sweat popped out on his forehead despite the chilly evening breeze. "At least give me a timeframe."

"Let's say two weeks, at the most. You could, of course, leave sooner—but you wouldn't want to have to make the long drive back if I end up having another job for you, would you?"

"You'd seriously ask me to do that?"

"We all do what we have to do, and we use the tools at our disposal. You're a very valuable tool, Travis, and I may require your assistance with another assignment."

Marcia glanced his direction, and Travis moved toward the

door. If he didn't go in soon, she'd come out to investigate—and he didn't want her hearing any of this conversation.

"I'll stay for a while."

"I thought you would. I'll be in touch. Enjoy your evening with Marcia."

The caller severed the connection.

Travis kept the phone to his ear and held up a finger as Marcia walked toward the door, buying himself a few moments to think as he pretended to converse over the dead connection.

After a pause, she went back to the counter.

Backhanding the sweat off his forehead, he forced his brain to shift into analytical mode.

His blackmailer had again broached the idea of another assignment. One that appeared to be contingent on factors he wasn't privy to.

And he wanted no part of it. The first one had been bad enough. Who knew what he'd be asked to do in a second go-round? He'd been lucky to pull off the shooting without any repercussions, but pushing your luck was never smart.

Because luck always ran out.

In his peripheral vision, a movement caught his eye. He twisted toward it.

Backlit by the illumination from the kitchen, a spider was spinning his web, the delicate strands forming an intricate and deadly trap for any prey that ventured too close.

His stomach kinked at the all-too-apt analogy.

While it was possible this would all end well, that he'd get permission to leave without being asked to do any more dirty work, he had a sinking feeling the worst was yet to come—and that when it did, all the trouble he'd left behind in Idaho would seem like a minor annoyance compared to what lay ahead.

TWENTY-ONE

EIGHT MORE DAYS UNTIL HIS DATE WITH BRI.

Picking up his pace as he walked the short route from the ATF office to the US Attorney's digs, Marc smiled.

It was time to call and establish concrete plans they could both look forward to. End his week on a high note, even if he wouldn't clock out for another seven hours.

Besides, talking with Bri would help energize him for the boring press conference he'd been tapped to attend on this Friday morning as the ATF representative. While he'd boned up on the four-month, multi-agency initiative to stem violent crime, the odds he'd be singled out to answer any questions were minuscule given all the higher-ranking law enforcement officials on the attendance roster.

Marc pulled out his phone as it began to vibrate.

He and Bri on the same wavelength again?

No.

The number that flashed on his screen was the main office line.

He put the phone to his ear and greeted the operator.

"Agent Davis, a call came in on the general number a few minutes ago from a woman who wanted to speak with you ASAP. She wouldn't say why. I do have her name and contact information."

"Hang on a sec." Keeping tabs on his surroundings, he moved out of the middle of the sidewalk, extracted a notebook and pen, and flipped to a blank page. "Go ahead and give me the information." He jotted it down as she spoke. "Thanks. I'll follow up."

Once he ended the call, he read the name he'd written.

Laura Butler.

It didn't ring any bells.

He googled the area code.

Kansas City.

Nothing clicked there, either. Near as he could recall, he didn't know a soul in that area.

He checked his watch. Fifteen minutes until the meeting started. That ought to give him sufficient time to cross this item off his to-do list.

After calling the woman's number, he picked up his pace. Lingering too long in this part of the city wouldn't be smart, even for a federal agent who was carrying.

The woman answered on the second ring, and after Marc identified himself, he got straight to business. "I understand you wanted to speak with me. How can I assist you?"

"Thank you for your quick response. I'm actually calling on behalf of my father, Joseph Butler."

Marc ran the name through his mental database as he pocketed his notebook. Came up blank. "I'm sorry. That name isn't familiar to me."

"He told me you wouldn't know him, but he says he needs to talk with you. And there isn't much time." Her voice cracked, and she cleared her throat. "He's in hospice with pancreatic cancer. The doctor thinks he only has a few days l-left. I don't have any idea what this is about, and he won't answer my questions."

Marc skirted an empty vodka bottle. "I'll be happy to talk with him if you want to put him on the line."

"This is where it gets tricky. He says he has to talk with you in person, and that it's very important."

Marc tamped down a surge of annoyance. If the man had an urgent message, why couldn't he relay it by phone?

"Did he say if this is related to a case I'm working on?"

"No. He wouldn't give me any information. I'm sorry."

"You're in the Kansas City area, correct?"

"Yes, and I know this is a huge imposition. I tried to reason with Dad about it, but he got very agitated. It's hard to say no when someone you love is d-dying."

Marc turned the corner, his destination in sight. "Would a Zoom call work?" He'd try to accommodate the man, but eight hours behind the wheel was far more than his boss would expect or sanction without clear justification.

"I suggested that. He said no. He insists it has to be in person. And he's not hallucinating or anything, in case you're wondering about that. Mentally he's as sound as ever. He won't even take many pain meds."

This was getting weirder by the minute—and beginning to set off alarm bells. While Bri claimed she didn't have any known enemies, after a dozen years with the ATF, he had his share. And a few of them wouldn't hesitate to exact revenge if they got half a chance.

Legit as this woman sounded, it could be a setup.

"I'm sorry, Ms. Butler. With so little information to go on, I can't devote a full day to a trip to Kansas City." He paused at the entrance to the US Attorney's office and dug out his creds.

"He told me if you wouldn't come, I should pass on a piece of information." A crinkling noise, like a sheet of paper being unfolded, came over the line. "He said to mention the date July 22."

Marc froze.

The day his parents died.

Then she recited their address.

His lungs locked.

What did this man know about the tragic events of that day?

Did Joseph Butler hold the key to solving the mystery contained in the file that had been on his computer desktop all these years?

If so, had the approach of death convinced him to share whatever he knew about the crime that had been committed that night?

"Agent Davis?"

At the woman's prompt, he fumbled for his notebook again. "Yes, I'm here."

"Does that information mean anything to you?"

"Yes." He pulled out his pen, a trip to Kansas City suddenly becoming a distinct possibility. But not until he ran background. Fast. Before the man who could perhaps bring closure to the unsolved case took his last breath. "I need more background."

She provided everything he asked for over the next few minutes as he fired questions and jotted furiously. Family history, names, addresses, social security numbers, birth dates. Anything that would help him try to nail down what this man might know and whether his information merited a very long drive.

As the clock inched toward the beginning of the press conference and he finished scribbling his notes, Laura spoke again. "Are there any other questions I can answer to help convince you to come?"

"No. Give me a few hours. I'm going into a meeting as we speak, and I'll have to do a bit of research."

"To make sure I'm not a nutcase."

He hesitated. "I wouldn't put it quite that way."

"You wouldn't hurt my feelings if you did. If I got a call

like this, I'd be as skeptical as you are. But I assure you this is on the level. When you run us through your background check, you'll find everyone in the family is legit. I don't know what has Dad agitated, but I do know he's a fine man and a responsible citizen. If he says he has important information to share with you, he does."

"I don't doubt your sincerity. Expect a call from me later today."

"I'll be here with Dad. None of us are venturing too far away at this stage. Thank you for your willingness to consider my request."

As soon as the call ended, Marc stowed his phone, notebook, and pen and pushed through the door into the office building.

He'd go to the press conference. Represent the ATF, as he'd been assigned to do. Formulate responses to questions, should any arise about his agency's role in the violent crime initiative.

But his mind wouldn't be on the meeting that had no doubt already begun.

It would be on the computer desktop folder that had stared at him every day for twelve long years—and on the possibility that maybe, at long last, the mystery that had eaten at his soul since his parents died was about to be solved.

IT WAS OVER.

The long, terrible ordeal had ended.

Alison stepped out of her heels, unbuttoned the jacket of her sedate dark suit, and locked the door of her bedroom.

In a few minutes, after they exchanged their funeral attire for more casual clothes, she and Sophie could decide how they wanted to spend the remainder of this day.

But first, one important matter to attend to.

She crossed to the closet. Pulled out the Nike shoebox. Flipped up the lid and surveyed the contents.

The nautical emblem from Larry's cap. Adam's monogrammed money clip. The necklace she'd spent a week's salary on for Renee. Les's Waterford clock. The class ring that should have been hers, until her so-called best friend Michelle had stolen Daniel from her and he'd given it to his Pookie instead.

Just one item to add.

Alison carried the box to the dresser and set it on the corner. Opened her jewelry box and reached into the back. Pulled out Nate's wedding ring.

The one he'd flung at her the night he said he was leaving.

The one she'd spat on the day he filed divorce papers.

The one that had convinced her to exact revenge for all the wrongs done to her by the people in her life who'd professed to care for her and then proved otherwise.

Mashing her lips together, she threw the ring into the box and closed the lid.

Every person who'd betrayed her had gotten exactly what they deserved. She was the wronged one here, not them.

What she'd done was called justice.

And it had nothing to do with the borderline personality disorder label that quack shrink had slapped on her after she'd acquiesced to Nate's ultimatum that she either get help or their marriage was over.

What a farce—and a waste—those garbage sessions had been. All those hours she'd endured listening to his drivel hadn't saved her marriage anyway.

Gritting her teeth, she pulled off her jacket and hurled it onto the bed.

The truth was, she didn't have a disorder of any kind. The people with the problem were the ones who'd hurt her. Betrayed her. Deserted her.

But now they were gone, and she was free of the past.

Forever.

As long as Bri shelved the Kavanaugh case and the man's stupid list.

Alison picked up the crystal clock. Ran her finger over the broken, jagged corner.

Tenacious as Bri was, it was possible she'd continue to poke into the mystery. Like Les had. But she was at a dead end. If neither she nor that ATF hotshot had been able to put the pieces together despite all the hours they'd devoted to the case, there wasn't much chance they ever would.

Which was good.

Because hurting Bri would be hard.

She set the clock back in the box and brushed her fingers over the other items.

Getting rid of people who were disloyal was easy.

Getting rid of a friend like Bri, who'd shown up at a memorial service for a stranger to demonstrate her support, was a whole different matter.

But if it became necessary . . . if left with no choice . . . she'd have to—

"Alison?"

As Sophie called through the door, she swept the box off the dresser, carried it back to the closet, and shoved it into the dark corner where it belonged.

"Hang on a sec, hon." After smoothing her hands down her skirt, she strode over to the door and flipped the lock. Pulled it open.

Her sister had already changed into jeans and a fleecy, oversized sweatshirt, her pale face and big eyes evidence of the body slam Nate's death had dealt her.

Poor Sophie. Always so sensitive. Always so in need of protecting.

But that's what big sisters were for, especially when it was the two of you against the world.

"Come on in." Alison smiled and swept a hand toward the room. "You changed fast."

"Comfortable clothes help me relax."

"I hear you. I ditched my heels the second I walked in the room." She motioned to the discarded pumps. "After I change, you want to go out for lunch?"

Sophie wrapped her arms around her middle. "Are you up for that?"

As a matter of fact, she was starving.

But it wouldn't do to admit that to Sophie, who thought her sister was grieving the loss of her estranged husband.

"I've been hungrier, but we have to eat, and I'd rather not cook. Why don't you sit on the bed while I change?"

After a tiny hesitation, Sophie walked over to it and perched on the edge, back stiff.

"So what kind of food are you in the mood for?" Alison moved to the closet and began riffling through her clothes.

"I don't care. Whatever you want is fine." Tension vibrated through her words.

Alison glanced over at her. "You okay?"

"Yeah. I guess."

At the unsettling vibes quivering in the air, Alison pulled a blouse off a hanger and pivoted toward her. "What does that mean?"

For a long moment, Sophie studied the toe of her sport shoe. "How come you never told me you and Nate were divorced?"

Alison crimped the blouse in her fingers and bit back a word that would make her sister cringe.

She should never have left Sophie alone while she made a quick trip to the ladies' room after the service in the funeral home chapel. Someone had either told her sister the truth, or Sophie had overheard it. What other explanation could there be?

That had been the one danger of attending Nate's service with Sophie in tow. But after her still-in-love-with-my-husband act all these months, not attending would have raised too many questions.

Alison crossed to the bed and sat beside her sister. "Did someone tell you that?"

"Not directly. I overheard two of his friends talking while I waited for you to come back from the bathroom."

Conclusion confirmed.

Brain clicking at warp speed, Alison set the blouse beside her. "I'm sorry to say he did go through with the divorce, but we also continued to talk. Both of us wanted to work through our issues. I had great hopes we'd end up back together. And we might have, if the camping accident hadn't happened."

Sophie searched her face. "Why didn't you tell me this before? Why pretend you were just separated?"

Calling up every ounce of acting skill she could muster, Alison coaxed her eyes to tear. "I suppose I didn't want to admit we had problems, or disillusion you about love." She slipped her arm around Sophie's shoulders. "I've always tried to protect you from the harsher realities of life."

Her sister once again focused on the toe of her shoe. "I know. Going all the way back to Larry."

At Sophie's soft reply, Alison sucked in a breath and straightened her spine. "What do you know about Larry?"

"More than you think I do."

Anger began to build in her. "Did he ever—"

"No!" Distress darkened Sophie's pupils as their gazes met. "He never touched me. You watched me too close. But later, when I was older, I figured out what happened during those trips to his boat." She swallowed, and her complexion lost a few more shades of color. "You were only what . . . ten, eleven . . . when it started? What he did was terrible, Alison." Her voice choked, and she swiped at her lashes. "Why didn't you ever tell anyone?"

Alison retracted her arm and stood. Paced over to the window and glared out as the ugly memories came roaring back. Of those nightmarish weekend trips with her step-uncle, taken with the full knowledge and blessing of her stepfather—may he rot in hell as the cancer had rotted his liver. Of all the things Larry had done to her below deck while her sister played above, oblivious but safe as long as Alison cooperated and kept her mouth shut.

That had been the terrible bargain.

But it had worked. It had protected Sophie.

And that was all that mattered.

"Alison?"

She straightened her shoulders. She would never regret what she'd done to safeguard her sister. "Because with Mom gone, our stepfather wasn't going to side with us over his big-shot lobbyist brother. You know how close they were. And he . . . he promised to leave you alone if I went along."

"Oh, Alison." The bed squeaked as Sophie rose. "I'm sorry you—"

She spun around, anger quivering through her. "Don't feel sorry for me, okay? I survived, and I'm still here. He's not."

Sophie stared at her. "What . . . what do you mean?"

Blast.

She'd said too much.

Fighting back a wave of panic, she forced herself to calm down. To put a lid on her emotions and engage the left side of her brain.

She had to act as if it was no big deal. If she treated the remark like an offhand comment, Sophie would too.

Calling up an indifferent expression, she shrugged and strolled back to the bed, keeping her tone casual as she picked up her blouse. "Out of curiosity, I googled him a few months back. I found his death notice. No great loss, if you ask me." She put an arm around her sister's delicate shoulders again. "Let's not talk about any more unhappy subjects today. Give me ten minutes to finish changing, then go out to eat with me. Somewhere bright and cheerful. Deal?"

"Sure. I guess." Sophie eased out of the hug. "I'll wait for you in the living room."

"Think of where you want to go. My treat."

With a dip of her head, her sister slipped through the door and closed it with a soft click.

For several moments Alison remained motionless, processing the conversation.

So much for keeping the trauma of those boat visits a secret and saving Sophie an undeserved guilt trip. But it wasn't surprising her sister had figured it out eventually. She might be the quiet type, but as they said, still waters ran deep—and her insights had always been keen.

As were Bri's.

Another reason skipping the service that had tipped off her sister about the divorce hadn't been an option.

If she'd bailed after Bri, loyal friend that she was, had insisted on attending, that would have raised all kinds of questions too.

Alison headed for the bathroom to remove some of the makeup she'd applied with a heavy hand this morning, as any distraught widow would, to camouflage signs of grief.

At least Bri hadn't overheard anything. She'd come in less than a minute before the service began, woven through the crowd the instant it was over to offer her condolences, then disappeared out the door.

Only Sophie had learned that her separation story was a fabrication.

Yet much as she wished her sister hadn't heard that snippet of conversation, no harm had been done.

Nor would Sophie worry too much about Larry's demise, even if she'd been shocked to learn of his death.

Because Sophie was in her corner, just as she'd always been in Sophie's.

And sisters stuck together.

No matter what.

TWENTY-TWO

LAURA BUTLER WAS LEGIT.

Arms folded on his desk, Marc reviewed the basics again.

Age twenty-two, born in KC, honor student, recent college grad, five-month tenure with the respected marketing firm in Kansas City where she'd interned, no criminal history. Not even a traffic ticket.

Everything she'd told him was consistent with what he'd found after running a background check, googling, and reviewing her social media sites.

Likewise for her younger brother and mother.

Her fifty-one-year-old father was the question mark.

Marc rose, shoved his hands in his pockets, and wandered over to the window.

Other than a birth certificate from St. Louis and a social security number, there was almost no data on Joseph Butler prior to the house fire.

Very suspicious.

His daughter had mentioned in passing that he'd had a tough childhood he never talked about, but why were there so few records of his life once he'd reached adulthood—until after the fire?

What was his link to the tragic event that killed two people and changed a young boy's life forever?

Marc forked his fingers through his hair. Expelled a breath.

To get that answer, he was going to have to drive to Kansas City.

Like, tomorrow.

If the man died before they talked, what could be the last chance to close the file on his desktop would perish too.

But what would he tell Nan about the trip?

Or *should* he tell Nan about the trip?

He inspected the darkening sky. Twisted his wrist to see his watch.

It was getting late. He should go home.

After he called Bri.

Pulling out his cell, he crossed back to his desk, propped his hip on the corner, and dialed her number.

She answered at once. "A friendly voice at the end of a long day. You have excellent timing."

The smile in her inflection loosened the knot of tension in his shoulders. "I meant to call sooner, see how the funeral went, but it got crazy."

"I hear you. Same here. The service was sad, but I'm glad I went to lend moral support. What made your day crazy?"

He gave her a fast briefing.

"Wow." A squeak came over the line, as if she'd dropped back in her office chair. "Are you going to KC?"

"I think so. If I don't, I'll always wonder if he knew a detail or two about the fire that could lead me to the truth."

"What will you tell your grandmother?"

"The very question I was wrestling with before I called you. Any thoughts?"

A few seconds of silence passed. "From what you've shared, it sounds as if she made her peace with the status quo long ago. In your place, I don't think I'd stir up old memories unless the trip actually produces answers or a resolution."

Another indication they were on the same wavelength, and a validation of his own reasoning.

"That's how I was leaning." He shifted toward his laptop and powered it down.

"When will you go?"

"I'd like to leave now, but an overnight trip would be out-of-pattern and raise more questions with Nan. I'll probably head out early tomorrow."

"How will you explain the trip?"

"If I take off early enough, I can leave a note and just say there was a break in one of my investigations. That won't be a lie, and Nan will assume I'm somewhere in town. I don't like being four hours away in case a medical emergency arises, but there's not much I can do about that."

Several beats ticked by. "If it would ease your mind, you could call me if you hear from her. I'd be happy to step in and help. Unless you don't want her to start asking questions about us."

He swallowed past the lump that rose in his throat at her kindness. "She's already asking questions. I can handle a few more. Thank you for that offer."

"After all you've done for me in recent days, this is the least I can do." Her tone softened. "I hope the trip gives you the answers you've been searching for, Marc."

"I do too. I'll call you tomorrow after my visit."

"I'll be waiting. Drive safe."

They said their goodbyes, and Marc stood, snagged his coat off the stand in the corner, picked up his laptop—and quashed the nudge from his conscience about keeping the trip a secret from Nan.

Yes, it was a deviation from his usual honest and straight-forward approach with her, but why open old wounds when this could end up producing nothing?

If the man did have pertinent information to offer, however, the situation would become more complicated. He'd have to weigh the pros and cons of how much of it to share, perhaps tap into Bri's sound thinking again.

But for tonight, he'd eat dinner with Nan, celebrate the end of her radiation, and hope whatever he found tomorrow would lead to closure on the most difficult chapter in his life.

TRAVIS'S CAR WAS IN IDAHO.

And since he hadn't shown up in any of the airline or rental car company databases, odds were he wasn't behind her run of bad luck.

Bri exhaled.

"Thanks for connecting with the McCall police, Jack." She shoved aside the remains of her nuked dinner and booted up her laptop. "That's one less worry on my plate."

"What else is eating at you—pardon the food pun."

"The Kavanaugh puzzle, for one thing. I'm about to have another go at the autopsy reports."

"You have any new leads?"

"I wish."

"If nothing's happening, why are you working the case on a Friday night?"

"Because the time I put into it now is on my own dime."

"Your boss wants you to shut the investigation down?"

"Officially."

"If neither you or your ATF buddy have been able to find anything to back up your suspicions, maybe there's nothing to be found."

"That was Sarge's conclusion too." She opened the medical examiner's report on Michelle Thomas. "He could be right."

"But you're not giving up."

Jack knew her well.

"Not yet."

"You know, there's more to life than work."

"Says the man who views cold case files as recreational reading."

"Ha-ha. Why aren't you out with Davis? It's date night."

"We're waiting another week, just in case a new lead does surface and we have to work together. We want to keep our personal and professional lives separate." And now that she was done discussing that topic, an offensive play was in order. "Why aren't *you* out on a date?"

"Haven't met anyone who's piqued my interest."

"If you socialized more you might."

"I'm not into the Friday night bar scene, and there aren't any eligible women at church who appeal to me."

Bri arched her eyebrows.

Instead of blowing her off with a flippant remark, as usual, he'd given a serious answer. And was there a hint of wistfulness in his voice?

Was Jack the loner finally beginning to show some interest in dating?

She closed her laptop screen halfway and gave the conversation her full attention. "If you want to spice up your social life, there are reputable dating apps out there."

"That feels too artificial. If it's meant to be, someone will come along. Look how you met Davis. You want to ride together to church on Sunday?"

In other words, subject closed. And if she pushed, Jack would clam up like he always did when anyone poked too hard into his private affairs. Sisters included.

"Sure."

Once they decided on a service and his ETA at her place, Jack signed off without returning to the subject of his lackluster social life.

Nevertheless, it was still on her mind.

What was up with her brother?

Did Cara know?

She put in a call to her sister.

Cara answered on the first ring, alarm raising her pitch. "Bri? What's wrong?"

Well, crud. She'd upset Cara. A pox on Jack for telling her about the shooting.

"Nothing. Calm down. Can't a girl call her sister?"

"Yeah. Sure. But you never call on Friday night."

"I do have an ulterior motive." She relayed her conversation with Jack. "Do you have any idea what's going on with him? He seemed . . . I don't know. Lost, I guess. And lonely."

"He gets like that in October."

"Since when?"

"For the past three or four years, I guess."

"Why?"

"No idea."

"Why haven't I ever noticed this?"

"Idaho's not close, and after the accident you had other priorities. Like recovery. I tried to ask a few discreet questions in the beginning, but he always dodged them."

Bri rested her elbow on the table and propped her chin in her palm. "I think he needs a wife."

"I don't disagree, but he's a big boy. If he wants to get married, he can figure out how to go about finding the right woman. Speaking of dating . . . how's Marc?"

Bri lifted her gaze to the heavens and shook her head. "Let me guess. Jack filled you in on my love life."

"I wouldn't go that far, but he did mention the two of you were planning to see each other. Why do I always hear everything secondhand?"

"I was going to tell you during our usual weekly call tomorrow." She picked up her soda can. Shook it. Empty—and she was nearing her daily limit. "However, this could go nowhere. Don't get carried away."

"I was about to offer you the same advice."

She stood and wandered over to the fridge. One more jolt of caffeine would keep her sharp as she reread the tedious autopsy reports. "Trust me, I'm going into this with my eyes wide open and keeping my expectations in check."

"You know, it's kind of sad we're all in our thirties and none of us have ever had a serious romantic relationship."

"Understandable though, in light of our backgrounds. Trust doesn't come easy."

"True. But you and Jack should have found someone by now who could get past the walls you've built. I mean, I understand why it's more difficult for me. I'm not exactly a perfect specimen."

Throat constricting, Bri grabbed her soda and shut the fridge. "You're perfect in all the ways that matter."

"Spoken like the loyal sister you are—but I do have issues."

"Any guy who can't look past those isn't worth having."

"I'll hold that thought. You still going to call me tomorrow morning?"

"Wouldn't miss it." And she'd return to this topic then, since Cara didn't seem inclined to discuss it now. If her sister's old self-esteem issues were rearing their ugly head, she and Jack would have to tag-team a boost-her-spirits campaign. "By the way, I know you were thinking about barbecuing for our next family get-together, but Jack mentioned to me this week how much he likes your omelets. I do too."

"Good. I was having a few doubts about tackling the grill again anyway. I wouldn't mind reverting to my old standby."

Thank you, God!

"That gets my vote. Maybe you could make your cheesy potato casserole too. That would be a treat."

"Consider it done. I'll add it to the menu." A yawn came

over the line. "Sorry. Early class today, and I have a stack of papers to grade. That's what I'm doing on my Friday date night, such as it is."

"I'll let you get back to your red pen. We'll have a longer chat tomorrow."

As Bri closed out the conversation and severed the connection, she leaned back in her chair, weighing the cell in her hand.

Brunch menu problem solved.

Jack owed her.

Now she could concentrate on more important matters.

Like solving the Kavanaugh puzzle. Praying Marc's trip tomorrow would yield answers that helped heal his hurting heart. Psyching herself up for the Tuesday lunch date Alison had suggested during their brief chat after the memorial service.

And on a happier note, breaking the long dry spell in the romance department that had, until a certain ATF agent came into her life, appeared to be the destiny of the Tucker siblings.

In eight days, a new chapter in her life would begin. And with the Travis threat apparently discredited, nothing was going to stop her from turning the page and writing the first scene in her story with Marc.

Nothing.

SOMETHING WASN'T RIGHT.

Wrapped in her softest fleecy sweatshirt, Sophie cowered against the headboard and stared at the screen of her laptop as it booted up—the only source of light in the midnight darkness of her sister's guest room.

This clandestine digging didn't feel right, either—but with questions swirling around in her brain, how was she supposed to sleep unless she found some answers?

Like . . . why had Alison spent more time consoling her about Nate's death than vice versa at their lunch earlier today? And why had her sister's mood seemed almost . . . upbeat . . . if she'd just lost the man she'd claimed to love?

Suppressing a shiver, Sophie typed in their step-uncle's name and called up a story about his death.

As she scanned it, her stomach bottomed out.

Larry—the predator of little girls—had died in a boat fire while in a drug-induced stupor.

And Nate—the faithless, rejecting husband—had died in a tent fire while in a drug-induced stupor.

Was it merely a fluke that two men who'd hurt her sister had perished in a similar, tragic fashion?

Maybe.

Unless . . . could there be others? People who'd also done Alison wrong and met a similar fate?

As that insidious thought snaked through her mind, a name bubbled up from the recesses of her memory.

Michelle Thomas.

Alison's boyfriend-stealing best friend.

Her sister had been devastated by that betrayal.

Still, that had happened long ago. Surely Alison hadn't held a grudge against her for all these years.

But what if she had?

Slowly, fingers trembling, she typed in the name.

Gasped at the first hit that came up.

Stopped breathing as she read the article.

Michelle had died too. In a house fire, while in a drug-induced state.

No.

No!

There couldn't be a connection between these three deaths.

Alison would never do such horrible things.

Yet the coincidences seemed too . . . coincidental. And too

close together, all bunched over the past eighteen months, after the divorce.

And what if there were more?

Stomach twisting, Sophie moved her laptop aside and buried her face in her hands as shivers coursed through her.

She had to be crazy to harbor such vile thoughts—didn't she?

The sister who'd nurtured her . . . protected her . . . stood by her through all of life's storms . . . couldn't be capable of such loathsome acts.

It was impossible.

And she was despicable for letting such doubts poison her mind.

After all, the night Nate died, she and Alison had both been asleep in this house.

Except . . .

Sophie gulped in a lungful of air and pulled the covers up to her chin as the faint wail of a distant train whistle keened through the night.

Except she'd been super tired that night. Barely able to keep her eyelids propped open after she and Alison had indulged in her sister's homemade carrot cake. When Alison had waved her off to bed far earlier than usual, she hadn't protested.

And while it had been a bit strange to suddenly run out of energy, she'd had a busy week at school. Plus, Alison had packed their Saturday with activities from sunup to late afternoon. A hectic schedule like that would tire anyone out.

But that didn't explain the drugged-like sleep she'd fallen into the instant her head hit the pillow or her groggy sluggishness the next day.

Drugged-like.

Groggy.

Sophie's breath hitched, and she pulled the pillow in front of her. Hugged it tight against her chest.

Had Alison put some sort of sedative into her dessert?

Knocked her out, then slipped away unnoticed and driven to the national forest where Nate had been—

No!

It couldn't be true!

But . . . but what if it was?

A wave of nausea swept over her, and Sophie flung the pillow aside. Stumbled toward the bathroom. Heaved what little was left of her late lunch into the toilet.

For several minutes, she remained there, clutching the edge of the vanity for support until her retching was reduced to dry heaves.

Finally, legs wobbling, she lurched back to bed, cocooned herself under the covers, and focused on the dark ceiling. Why bother closing her eyes? There would be no sleep this night. Not with a decision to make that could change her life, and Alison's, forever.

Yet how could she betray the sister who'd sacrificed too much to protect her? Who'd put the welfare of an innocent little girl she loved above her own?

And what if she brought her suspicions forward and ended up being wrong?

Alison would never forgive her, and their two-person family—the sole blood link either of them had—would be destroyed forever.

But if she remained quiet, and Alison was responsible for those deaths, that was like condoning murder. Wasn't it?

Sophie's temples began to throb, and she reached up with quivering fingers to massage her forehead. If the headache got worse, she could always take aspirin. That would relieve the pain.

Unfortunately, there was no such simple remedy for the situation with Alison. It had no painless answers.

Because no matter what she decided to do, the outcome would be rife with hurt.

So she'd spend the long, shadowy hours until morning thinking about the problem, and pray that by the time dawn announced the start of a new day, she'd be granted guidance—as well as the courage to do what had to be done.

Even if that ended up destroying her bond with the only person who'd loved her since the day their mother died.

TWENTY-THREE

THIS WAS IT.

Marc set the brake in front of Joseph Butler's small but well-kept ranch house. It was the sort of home a man would own if he'd spent his working life as a church custodian—or the last couple decades of his working life, anyway.

Mentally prepping himself for whatever lay inside, Marc exited the car and strode up the walkway.

A young woman with faint purple shadows in the hollows beneath her eyes opened the door as he approached the porch. "Agent Davis?"

"Yes." He closed the distance between them and extended his hand. "Ms. Butler, I assume."

"Yes. Please come in."

He followed her into a tiny foyer, and an older teen rose from a chair in the living room on the right to join them.

Marc shook his hand as Laura introduced her brother.

"Mom's in the bedroom with Dad. The hospice nurse will be here soon, and our pastor is coming by too." Laura pulled out a tissue and swiped it under her nose. "Sorry. It's been a stressful night. Can I get you something to drink after your long drive?"

"No thanks. I stopped for breakfast and coffee on the road."

"Then let me take you back. Dad declined overnight, and

he's sleeping more and more, but he's still lucid when he's awake."

She led him down a short hall to the last room on the left.

As she pushed the half-closed door open, a pale woman with grief-filled eyes and dark hair in need of brushing rose from her vigil beside the hospital-style bed, blocking Marc's view of the face that went with the sheet-covered form next to her.

"Mom, this is Agent Davis." Laura kept her volume low as she motioned her mother into the hall.

After a brief hesitation, the woman swiveled back to the bed and leaned down. "I'll be back in a few minutes, Joe."

If Butler responded, it was audible only to his wife.

As she crossed to the door, Laura backed up to allow her to join them.

"Thank you for coming. I think Joe's been hanging on just to talk to you." The man's wife extended her hand, and Marc took it.

Tremors coursed through her icy fingers.

"It was an easy decision, in light of the information your daughter shared with me."

"Do you know what it's all about?" The older woman's puzzled expression suggested she was clueless about the reason for his summons.

"The information has meaning for me, but I have no idea what your husband knows about it—or how he knows about it."

"If it convinced you to make this long drive on short notice, it must be important."

"It could be. I'm hoping it is."

"Mom." Laura touched her arm. "I should take Agent Davis in."

"Yes, of course. I didn't mean to delay you. I'm not thinking very straight. Thank God Laura has handled most of the details. She's been a rock." The woman touched her daughter's cheek, gratitude and love displacing the grief in her eyes for a brief instant. "I'll wait in the kitchen until you're finished." She edged around Laura and continued down the hall.

Laura turned toward him. "Dad asked that we give the two of you space to have a private conversation. After I introduce you, I'll join Mom in the kitchen until you're finished." Her brow crinkled. "We're all baffled by this whole thing. I hope whatever Dad has to say makes your trip worthwhile."

So did he.

"Only one way to find out."

She took his cue and entered the room.

He followed and got his first clear view of Joseph Butler—or the wasted body that was left after his battle with the cancer that was about to take his life.

His frame was skeletal beneath the sheet. His sunken eyes were closed, his cheeks hollow, his skull bald save for a few patchy spots of hair that must have survived chemo, his skin an unnatural yellowish hue. His bony hands lay unmoving beside him.

He looked already dead.

Only the slight rise and fall of the sheet indicated his heart continued to beat.

Despite the ravages of disease that had no doubt altered his appearance, one thing was clear.

This was not a man he'd ever met.

"He's asleep again." Laura whispered the words over her shoulder before leaning closer to her father. "Dad. Agent Davis is here."

When he didn't respond, Marc's pulse stuttered.

Was he too late?

"Dad." Laura placed her hand on her father's arm. Gave him a tiny nudge. "Dad, wake up."

After a few seconds, Butler's eyelids fluttered open. "Laura."

The corners of his mouth lifted a hair. "My sweet angel daughter." He tried to lift his hand, but the effort appeared to be too much for him, and he let it drop back to the bed.

Laura took it and folded it in hers. "Dad, the ATF agent you wanted to talk to is here." She angled sideways so her father could see him.

The older man shifted his focus, and a slight spark appeared in his dull irises. "You came."

"Yes." Marc moved closer to the bed. "The date and address you passed on were too compelling to ignore."

"I hoped they would be." The man's voice was faint. As if speaking required him to dip deep into his waning reserves of energy. "Laura, would you raise the head of the bed?"

She did as he asked. "We'll wait in the kitchen, Dad—but if you need anything, tell Agent Davis and he'll come get us."

"I'll be fine for a few minutes."

As she disappeared out the door, closing it with a quiet click behind her, the man motioned him over. "Sit. I know you had a long drive."

Marc took the chair Butler's wife had vacated and opened the leather notebook with the ATF logo on the front. The one he used for important meetings that required detailed note-taking.

Rather than waste the man's precious time and energy on social niceties, he dived in. "You know about the fire that killed my parents."

"Yes."

"I've been trying to find answers about it for years."

"I had a feeling that might be the case, given your profession. And I'm the only one left who knows what happened that night. That's why I couldn't leave this world without talking to you."

Marc tried to tamp down his frustration—and anger. "If you had information that could bring the person who set the fire to justice, why did you keep it secret all these years?"

The man locked on to his gaze. Moistened his parched lips. "Because I was a coward." His emaciated fingers crumpled the sheet, but he never broke eye contact. "I started that fire, Agent Davis."

As the man's confession hung in the silent air between them, a roaring vortex swirled around Marc, sucking the oxygen from the room.

The most he'd hoped for from this trip was a new clue. A piece of information that would give him a lead to follow as he tried to identify the perpetrator.

Instead, he was face-to-face with the man who'd killed his parents and forever changed the landscape of his world.

Struggling to fill his depleted lungs, he shot to his feet. Dropped his notebook on the chair. Paced to the end of the bed. Turned his back on the man.

And found a crucifix in the center of his vision on the wall in front of him.

A symbol of sacrifice. Hope. Redemption. Love. Forgiveness.

A reminder of all the principles his faith taught.

None of which he was inclined to follow at this moment as he tried to untangle his jumbled thoughts.

"I thought you'd want to hear the story." Joseph spoke behind him, his rasp of a voice barely there. "That's why I asked you to come. I want to answer your questions and tell you how sorry I am for the terrible deed I did that night—which wasn't supposed to end with anyone dying. I went to the house ahead of time and looked through the windows. I could see smoke detectors on the ceilings."

Marc lifted his hand to slide his pen back into his shirt pocket. Stared at his fingers.

They were trembling.

Badly.

And speech had deserted him.

"Please, Agent Davis. Let me tell you what happened—and what led up to it."

No.

He wasn't ready for this conversation.

Not until he could reconcile himself to being in the same room with the man who'd murdered his parents.

But much as he wanted to bolt . . . to put as much distance between himself and this man as possible . . . to go somewhere quiet to try to process what had just transpired . . . he didn't have that luxury. If he left, Butler could be gone before he felt ready to hear the story.

It was now or perhaps never.

Forcing air into his lungs, Marc slowly pivoted and lurched back to the chair on wobbly legs. "I'm listening." His own voice sounded like gravel.

"Thank you." Joseph drew an unsteady breath and bunched the edge of the nubby blanket that rested near his fingers. "I was twenty-six that summer. Working as a day laborer. There weren't many other jobs open to a high school dropout. It was a dead-end life and I knew it, but if you come from a bad home environment and find yourself on the street at fifteen, that's where you can end up. So when the opportunity to make a few easy if not quite legal bucks came along, I grabbed it. I didn't realize I was getting involved with a crime syndicate, or how much power they'd have over me once I got trapped in their web."

The man grimaced as if in pain and shifted in the bed. "I was assigned to set the fire at your parents' house. They didn't explain why. I didn't ask. I found out from the news stories afterward that your dad was an investigative reporter and put two and two together. But I never intended to kill anyone. There should have been plenty of time to get out."

A muscle in Marc's jaw spasmed. "Not if someone in the house has a broken leg."

Sadness filled the man's eyes, so profound it infiltrated Marc's defenses and stirred a faint ember of compassion to life deep in his heart.

He snuffed it out at once.

"I didn't know about that until I read the news story. The guilt was overwhelming. I decided I was no good to anyone, that my life was worthless and the world would be better off without me. So I decided to commit suicide."

Marc hardened himself to the man's pain. Joseph Butler didn't deserve one iota of pity.

"I assume you changed your mind."

"No. I went through with it. Late one night about a week after the fire, I drank myself into a stupor and jumped off one of the Chicago River's highest bridges. I didn't have strong swimming skills, and I assumed the booze would weaken them. All I wanted to do was sink to the bottom of the river and die."

"Obviously that didn't happen."

"No—and the sequence of miracles that followed convinced me I wasn't yet meant to leave this earth."

He wasn't going to let the man's sad personal history soften his heart, but the reference to miracles was intriguing.

"What kind of miracles?"

"Despite the late hour, someone saw me jump off the bridge and dived in after me. A bona fide hero. That was miracle number one. He also managed to find me in the dark. Miracle number two. I don't remember anything from the moment I hit the water until I woke up hours later in the hospital. No one—"

Butler's breathing suddenly faltered, and as he began gasping, Marc vaulted to his feet. "I'll get your daughter."

"No." The command came out in a wheeze. "Wait."

Marc hesitated.

"Sit."

At the sudden strength in that command, Marc complied. Half a minute later, the man's respiration evened out.

"Happens . . . more and more. But God won't take me until I finish this." He drew a few more shallow breaths. "I'd left all my IDs in my apartment, and after I regained consciousness the doctors and nurses asked for my name. That's when I realized I'd been given a chance to start over. All I had to do was get out of town, pick a new name, and the syndicate would never be able to track me down. Miracle number three."

"Is that what you did?"

"Yes. I pretended I couldn't remember who I was, and as soon as I felt strong enough, I slipped out of the ER. I went back to my apartment, grabbed a few things, and hitched rides west, sleeping in alleys or vacant buildings, going through garbage cans for food. One night here in KC, I took shelter in an unlocked storage shed at a church during a storm. Father Bob found me the next morning—miracle number four. After we talked, he gave me breakfast, rounded up a set of clean clothes, let me use the shower in the church basement, and offered me a job. I've worked there ever since."

"And somewhere along the way you got married."

"Yes." He flexed his fingers, releasing the edge of the blanket as the tension in his features eased. "Miracle number five. I met my wife at a church function. She saw past all my rough edges. Tapped into goodness I didn't even know was there. Made me believe I was worth loving. Father Bob helped on that score too."

"Did he also help you secure a new ID?"

"No. Tyler Joseph Butler was my roommate for a few months before I got involved with the crime syndicate. He was killed in a street fight, and while I was going through his stuff, I found a few personal documents—social security card, birth certificate, an old driver's license. I kept them. It was as if I had a premonition they'd be useful someday."

"And your family knows nothing about any of this?"

"No." His breathing hitched again, and his withered fingers fisted. "And I never want them to. I haven't spoken about it in years."

"Why now?"

"Because I didn't want to die without telling you the truth and letting you know I asked for God's mercy and forgiveness long ago. I also want to ask for yours. Not today, but after you think all this through. I hoped that by meeting me in person, you'd see how sincerely sorry I am."

"Remorse and regrets don't bring the dead back to life, Mr. Butler. You killed my parents. Two wonderful, caring people who had much to offer this world and who never got to see their son grow up." His reply came out harsher than he intended, but so be it.

"I know that." With his tale told, Butler's voice faded, as if his strength was ebbing. "And I've lived with that guilt for twenty-five years. I'll take it with me to the grave. But at least now you know what happened. Maybe it will bring you a sense of closure and give you a few insights into why I did what I did."

If the man was hoping for sympathy, he was out of luck.

"Many people from tough backgrounds manage to overcome them."

Like Bri.

"The strong ones do. That didn't describe me back in those days. But I never intended to harm anyone that night. I was certain everyone in the house would get out."

"It's hard to move fast with a newly broken leg."

"I know. And I'm so sorry. More sorry than I can say." His eyelids fluttered closed, but he managed to lever them up once again. "Do you have any questions?"

"No." In the space of a few minutes, Butler had given him all the information he'd sought for a quarter of a century. There was nothing left to ask.

"Thank you for coming." Again, his eyelids flickered shut. This time they remained closed.

Marc stood. "I'll tell your family we're finished."

The man gave an almost imperceptible nod.

Tucking the leather cover with the blank notebook under his arm, Marc let himself out.

Once he closed the door behind him, he paused in the hall and took a long, slow breath. Surveyed the walls lined with photos of backyard barbecues, Christmas mornings, fishing outings, graduations, recitals, soccer games.

The kinds of family activities he and his own parents had enjoyed together for only a short while, thanks to the man in the room he'd just left.

Anger churned in his gut.

It wasn't fair.

Maybe Joseph Butler had repented. But that didn't change the fact that he'd killed the two people Marc had loved most in the world and deprived another family of the life he himself had gone on to enjoy.

A door opened down the hall, and a gray-haired man in a clerical collar emerged. He hesitated for a second, glanced at the closed door of Butler's room, and extended his hand as he approached. "Father Bob Allen. I'm the pastor at Joe's church."

Marc exhaled and returned his firm grip. "Mr. Butler mentioned you."

"I assume the two of you are finished?"

"Yes."

"I know he appreciated your willingness to make the long drive to meet with him in person. I hope the conversation gave you some answers."

Marc studied him.

The man who'd killed his parents may never have told his family any of his background or shared the sins that darkened

his soul, but based on the cleric's comments, Butler had un-
burdened himself on the priest who'd extended kindness to
the lost soul in his storage shed on that long-ago morning.

Marc offered him a clipped nod. "It did."

"If it's any consolation, Joe's led an exemplary life since the
day I met him. He volunteers at the food bank. He does his
job, humble though it may be, with diligence and dedication.
He raised two wonderful children, and he treats his wife with
love and respect. He's always the first to pull out his wallet
or roll up his sleeves to help anyone in need."

"None of that erases the past." He didn't attempt to mask
his bitterness.

"No. Our past is always part of us. Some people are victims
of it and remain so until the day they die. Others overcome old
traumas and mistakes and go on to create a new and better life."

"That doesn't condone wrongs. Or give me and my parents
back the years we should have had together. The years Butler
had with his own family."

"No, it doesn't." The priest's tone was empathetic and
nonjudgmental. "That's why mercy and forgiveness are so
difficult."

Marc wasn't about to argue with that. He was nowhere
near either.

"I'll say goodbye to his family before I leave." He motioned
down the hall.

"They're very grateful for your efforts to fulfill Joe's last
wish." The priest stepped aside to allow him to pass.

"My motive was purely selfish."

"Nevertheless, it was a gift to everyone in this family. Your
kindness will be long remembered. God be with you on your
drive home."

As the cleric moved toward the bedroom door, Marc continued down the hall. He'd say goodbye, offer a few perfunc-
tory words of condolence, and take his leave.

Then he'd have four hours during his trip back to St. Louis to think through everything that had occurred in the past half hour—and try to figure out how much of this visit he should share with Nan, who'd long ago made her peace with the events of that terrible night.

TWENTY-FOUR

Rather talk in person than by phone.
May I stop by around 2:30?

I'll be waiting. See you soon.

Bri reread her text exchange with Marc, then peered through the front window again—her third detour to the living room in the past twenty minutes.

If he'd come here straight from KC, he should be arriving any second.

And if he wanted to talk out the encounter, that must mean he'd learned important information. Perhaps he was hoping to bounce ideas off her about how much to share with his grandmother.

As she let the curtain drop back into place, a car turned onto her street.

She snatched up the fabric again.

It was Marc.

After a quick dash to the bathroom to run a brush through her hair, she zoomed back to the door and was waiting as he came up her walkway.

He called up a weary smile as he approached the door. "You were watching for me?"

"Yes." She stepped back and waved him in. "Would you like a cup of coffee?"

"I would. Thanks. I had an early start, and it's been a long day already."

The brackets beside his mouth and the fan of lines at the corners of his eyes were evidence of that.

"Why don't you make yourself comfortable and I'll bring the coffee into the living room?"

"Okay."

But he trailed along behind her as she headed for the kitchen.

The man was seriously distracted.

She brewed two mugs of coffee, handed one to him, and led the way to the living room, where she sat on the couch and patted the cushion beside her.

He didn't need a second invitation.

Once he settled in, she shifted toward him. "Was the trip worth taking?"

"Yeah." He took a slow sip of the coffee. "Get ready for a bombshell. Joseph Butler set the fire that killed my parents."

Her breathing hitched.

Sweet heaven.

Marc had come face-to-face with the man who'd taken the lives of his mother and father and forever changed his future.

Heart pounding, Bri set her mug on the coffee table and twined her fingers with his. "Tell me what happened."

He recounted his visit, ending with the man's request for forgiveness and his brief encounter with the priest.

As he finished, Bri exhaled. "Wow."

"That about sums up my feelings. The term emotional roller coaster doesn't come close to describing the past five hours."

There were probably a dozen things she could say—should say—but instead she followed her heart. "Could you use a hug?"

In reply, he pulled her close, wrapped his strong arms around her, and held on tight.

For a long time.

When he at last drew back, he let his hands slide to her waist, keeping her close. "Thanks for that."

"Hugs can be the best medicine." Even if they elevated your pulse and jacked up your adrenaline.

But this was about dispensing comfort, not creating a prelude to romance.

She needed to focus.

"Agreed. And I could also use some advice. I've been trying to figure out what to tell Nan, but my brain's fried. I thought I'd tap into your sound thinking."

"What are your instincts telling you?"

He released his hold on her, leaned back, and picked up his coffee. "I've always tried to be honest with her, but I don't tell her everything—especially about my job. Why make her worry more than she already does? In terms of the fire, she accepted long ago it would never be solved. Made her peace with that. Stirring it all up again could reopen old wounds."

"Or provide closure." Bri leaned toward him. "You told me your grandparents prayed that whoever had set the fire would repent and seek forgiveness. It may comfort her to know that prayer was answered."

He took a long draw on his coffee. Stared into the half-empty mug. "I did think about that on the drive home, but you want the truth? Butler may have squared himself with God, but he didn't have as much success with me. If Nan asks, I'll have to admit I couldn't summon up the compassion to forgive him—as she no doubt will, once she hears his story."

"Would she hold that against you?"

"No. That's not her style. But she'd be disappointed."

A man who worried about disappointing his grandmother. Touching.

Bri picked up her own coffee and carefully composed her

reply. "I think your concern about not living up to your grandmother's high standards is a testament to your character and your compassion."

One side of his mouth quirked up. "I appreciate the flattering take, but there's also a bit of ego involved."

"You're honest too. Another fine quality."

"But what does it say about me that after all these years I can't dredge up one ounce of mercy for a man who never intended for his actions to have fatal consequences and who spent the rest of his life following the straight and narrow?"

"It says you're human. Forgiveness is hard. I've never gotten there with my father, either."

"You have scant evidence he ever reformed."

"That's not supposed to be a requirement for forgiveness." She sipped her coffee. Refocused on the matter at hand. "Here's my two cents. Give yourself time to digest this new information. See how you feel about it in a week . . . or a month . . . or a year. Our faith may tell us to forgive seventy times seven, but as far as I know, there's no timetable attached to that."

The corners of his mouth rose again. "I knew you'd offer wise advice."

Warmth filled her. "Suggestion, not advice. What are you going to do about your grandmother?"

He drained his mug, stood, and tugged her to her feet. "I'm going to tell her the truth. You're right on that score too. I think it will comfort her to know her prayers were answered, even if my ego takes a hit. Walk me to the door?"

He was leaving already?

Well, of course he was. He'd gotten up before dawn, spent eight hours behind the wheel of his car, listened to a man confess to murder, and now he had to share that news with his grandmother. He couldn't sit around here all day with her, much as she might want him to.

"Sure." She followed him to the foyer. "Let me know how it goes with your grandmother."

"I will." He paused on the threshold and turned toward her. "Are we still on for a date next Saturday?"

"Absolutely."

"I was on the verge of calling you yesterday to set up concrete plans when Joseph Butler's daughter contacted me."

"I can see why that would have been distracting."

"So is a certain fire investigator." He reached up and fingered a few strands of her hair. "What do you say to a picnic in the wine country?"

"I'm in."

"Let's make a day of it."

"Sounds great."

"Unless, of course, there's a break on the Kavanaugh case."

She made a face. "I'm not holding my breath. There aren't any new leads on the fire at his house, and the connections on his list are eluding me as adeptly as they eluded him. The only consolation is that we won't have to postpone our date."

"There is that." He leaned down and brushed his lips across hers. "A sample of what's on the menu for our picnic."

Her heart stopped. Raced on.

Oh man.

"I, uh, may want a full serving of that."

"I'll be happy to oblige." He waggled his eyebrows and winked. "I'll call you later."

"Good luck with your grandmother."

He gave her a thumbs-up and strode down the path to his car.

Bri watched until he drove away. Once she lost sight of him, she closed the door and ambled back to the living room. Picked up their empty mugs. Continued to the kitchen and eyed her laptop on the table.

She could review the origin and cause reports again for the fires on Les's list. Give the autopsy reports one more skim.

But she'd done that last night, and her efforts had yielded zilch.

Maybe it was time to admit the truth.

Unless a new clue dropped into her lap, the puzzle Les had left her—along with the identity of the arsonist who'd set the fire at his house—would forever remain a mystery.

"WHAT DO YOU MEAN YOU'RE LEAVING?" Alison frowned at Sophie as her sister hovered in the living room doorway, suitcase in hand, laptop case slung over her shoulder. "I thought you were staying until tomorrow?"

"I was, but our organist texted me to ask if I'd play at the nine o'clock service tomorrow. A family emergency came up."

"You have a family emergency here."

Sophie shifted her weight from one foot to the other. Readjusted the strap on the laptop case. "You'll be fine. You've always been strong. And I really need all day tomorrow after church to prep for school this week. I'm behind."

Setting aside the magazine she'd been reading, Alison studied her sister.

Ever since her slip yesterday about Larry, Sophie had seemed subdued. Preoccupied. Troubled. She'd gone to bed early last night and hadn't appeared in the kitchen until midmorning, yet the shadows beneath her eyes suggested she hadn't slept well.

Why?

Could she possibly suspect her big sister had played a role in the demise of Larry and Nate?

No.

Sophie loved her, and if you loved someone, you believed in them until they gave you cause to do otherwise.

She'd never done that. And a mere mention of Larry wouldn't be sufficient to set off any alarm bells.

"Are you certain you feel okay?" Alison rose and crossed to Sophie. "You don't have one of your headaches, do you?"

"I did last night. It's not as bad today."

Ah. That could explain why she looked tired. The stress-induced headaches that had always been the bane of her existence could knock her flat, and this had been a stressful week.

"Another reason you should have said no to the organist."

Sophie rummaged through her purse for her keys. "I'll be fine by tomorrow, and playing the organ relaxes me. I'll call you later tonight."

"Are you certain I can't convince you to stay?"

She eased back. "No. I want to sleep in my own bed tonight. Get back to my normal life."

"I hear you about getting back to normal. Let me take your suitcase for you."

They walked out to her car in silence, and once everything was stowed in the trunk, Alison pulled her into a tight hug. "Thanks for being here for me this week."

"That's what sisters do." Sophie endured the hug, but her stiff posture didn't encourage prolonging the embrace.

Alison released her. "Drive safe."

"I will." Her sister hurried around the car, slid behind the wheel, and took off with a quick wave through the window.

Like she couldn't get away fast enough.

Also strange.

Shoving her fingers into the pockets of her jeans, Alison wandered back to the house and quashed the sudden case of nerves roiling the chicken Caesar salad she'd eaten for lunch.

What was the point of worrying, after all? On the off chance Sophie suspected her big sister knew more about certain deaths than she'd admitted, she wouldn't do anything that would put the only family she had in jeopardy. Sophie was too loyal.

She was also too meek. Her timid, docile sibling didn't have one proactive, assertive bone in her body.

So no matter what doubts she might harbor about Larry and Nate, she'd keep them to herself.

Alison entered the house and closed the door behind her. Locked it.

Put her fears to rest.

Because unlike all the other traitors in her life, Sophie would stay true to her to the end.

WHERE WAS NAN?

Marc tossed his keys on the kitchen counter and cocked his ear.

All was quiet.

Was she taking a nap?

He tiptoed down the hall and peeked through her half-open bedroom door.

Empty.

A quick circuit of the house was also a bust.

So where was she?

As if in answer to his question, the back doorknob rattled and she pushed through.

"Marc! Finally! I was beginning to think you'd deserted me." She removed her gardening gloves and brushed a wisp of hair back from her flushed cheeks.

"What are you doing?"

"I've been pruning my roses. They've been sadly neglected these past few weeks. Isn't this one a beauty?" She held up a pink rosebud that was beginning to open.

"Very pretty. But are you up to that sort of work?"

"Gardening refreshes the soul—and the body."

"That's not what I asked. And what about your wrist?" Despite the spark in her eyes, fatigue was evident in her features.

"Put away your interrogation skills with me, young man. I kept the elastic bandage on my left wrist and only used my right hand for pruning. Being out in the fresh air and working with my flowers is wonderful medicine."

"Unless you overdo it."

"I didn't. I've only been out there for half an hour. I won't push it until I get my stamina back, and I'll take a nap when I need one. Like now." She tipped her head. "You look as if you could do with a nap too. Whatever case took you out at the crack of dawn must have kept you hopping."

"It was an eventful day." He gripped the back of the chair beside him. "I'd like to tell you about it, unless you'd rather take that nap first."

Her gaze flicked down to the fingers he'd wrapped around the chair. Returned to his face. "The nap can wait." She set her gardening gloves on the table, claimed a chair, and waited expectantly.

Marc's pulse picked up as he pried his fingers off the chair, pulled it out, and sat. "I drove to Kansas City this morning."

Her eyes widened. "Good heavens. I thought most of your cases were in the city, or at least nearby."

"The ones I handle for work are. This one was personal. I've had the file on my desktop since the day I joined the ATF."

The flush faded from her cheeks, and a slash of pain ricocheted through her eyes. "Oh, Marc. The house fire." She laid her hand over his.

"Yes."

"You never let that go."

"No. But I never found any answers, either. Until today."

"Tell me what happened."

He relayed the whole story, beginning with the phone call yesterday up to the moment he'd walked out the door of Joseph Butler's house.

When he finished, Nan didn't say a word. After a few seconds, she picked up the long-stemmed rose, walked to the sink, and rummaged around in the cabinet underneath until she found a bud base. Filled it with water and slid the stem in, keeping her back to him.

"Nan?"

Slowly she turned, vase in hand.

Tears were streaming down her cheeks.

His gut clenched, and he vaulted to his feet. "Nan, I'm sorry. I shouldn't have—"

"Sit." She waved him back down, carried the vase to the table, and joined him again. "I needed a few moments to take in everything you said." She fished a tissue out of her pocket and dabbed at her lashes. "It's quite a shock after all these years to finally learn what happened that night. I assumed we'd never find out the truth."

"I did too, until that call came in from out of the blue."

She fingered one of the rose petals poised to unfurl. "So your grandfather's prayers and mine were answered." Her voice was soft. "The person did repent. I'm glad."

As Bri had suspected, that piece of news had given her comfort.

But didn't the rest bother her?

While Nan examined the delicate petal, Marc frowned at the thorns along the stem, mind whirling.

Why wasn't she angry, as he was, that the man had hidden his deed for a quarter of a century, lived a life of deception?

"You think I should be upset, don't you?"

At Nan's quiet question, he refocused on her. "I guess I'm a little surprised you're not. He never paid for his crime. He went on to live a normal and happy life despite all the pain and death he caused. That wasn't right."

She inhaled the sweet scent of the rose. Stroked the velvety petal. "He may have paid a higher price for his crime than you think. Living with the knowledge that you've done wrong, keeping secrets from your family, struggling to salvage what remains of your life—none of that would be easy."

"It's not like serving prison time."

"There are many kinds of prisons." She let out a gentle breath. "And he did come forward at the end with the answers you've always wanted."

How could she be so calm and cavalier about this?

"Nan." He leaned forward. "He killed your son and daughter-in-law."

She laid her hand on his again, sadness dimming her eyes. "And I'll never get over that loss as long as I live. But hating a man who never intended to kill, and who worked hard to lead a virtuous life for the past twenty-five years, won't bring them back. If God has mercy on a repentant heart, shouldn't we follow his example?"

"In theory, yes."

"Practice is much harder. I know." She fingered the rose petal again. "How providential that this was the last one blooming. In the language of flowers, do you know what pink roses represent? Gratitude."

His shoulders stiffened. "I'm grateful for the answers, but nowhere near mercy."

"It will take me a while to get there as well, despite everything I've just said. I have a lot of emotions to sort through. You should give yourself time too."

The same advice Bri had offered.

"Have you talked to your friend Bri?"

Marc did a double take.

Had she read his mind?

"I swung by her place on the way home."

A slow smile curved Nan's lips. "I must meet this intriguing young woman soon." She pushed herself to her feet and motioned toward the counter. "I baked a batch of your favorite brownies. They should hold you until dinner. We're having pot roast. It's been in the oven for hours."

All at once the savory aroma permeating the kitchen

registered—a measure of the depth of his distraction if he'd missed that enticing scent.

"You were busy while I was gone. I would have picked up takeout for us."

"We're done with takeout. I want to get back into my routine. And I want you to start giving your own life top priority." She leaned down and inhaled the sweet fragrance of the rose. "The end of radiation, a decades-old mystery solved, answers to prayers—I'd say we're on the cusp of a new beginning. I'm going to take that nap now. Wake me at five for dinner." She bent down, pressed a kiss to his forehead, and continued down the hall.

Marc remained at the table long after she left, mulling over all she'd said and staring at the symbolic rose.

Maybe one day he'd make his peace with the fire, as she had. Even dredge up the forgiveness Joseph Butler had asked for.

Maybe.

But he was in full agreement with Nan's comment about new beginnings.

And unless an unexpected break emerged on the Kavanaugh case in the next seven days, come next Saturday he was going to launch a new chapter in his life that had nothing to do with mayhem and murder.

TWENTY-FIVE

NO, NO, NO, NO!

Sophie adjusted her laptop screen to cut the glare from the afternoon sun and stared at the news story from fourteen months ago, heart thumping against her rib cage.

Adam Long was dead too.

The guy Alison had fallen for in college.

The guy she'd expected to marry.

The guy who'd dumped her.

And he'd also perished in a fire.

Sophie shoved the computer aside and tried to shut off the blender in her stomach that was cranked up to puree.

All of these fiery deaths couldn't be a coincidence.

She rose and began to pace, trying to call up an image of Adam.

Failed.

Who knew why his name had even popped into her mind? She'd met him . . . what? Twice? Hard to remember a guy who hadn't made much of an impression. Nor had he appeared to be that interested in Alison, even though her sister had hung all over him like he was the center of her world and been devastated when he moved on to someone else.

Why, oh why, had she googled him?

That was a huge mistake.

Because now she had a . . . what did lawyers call it? . . .

a preponderance of evidence to suggest there was a link between all these deaths and her sister.

But why would Alison target these people? Yes, she was all
about loyalty. Yes, they'd all done her wrong. But while Larry's
behavior was criminal, the other breakups were just how life
worked. Sometimes friendships—or marriages—fell apart.

You didn't kill people for that.

Sophie stopped at the window in the living room, wrapping her arms tight around herself as a hawk circled in the
sky above, searching for prey.

At least normal people didn't.

And Alison was normal.

Wasn't she?

Yes, of course she was—other than being a tad paranoid,
perhaps. But who wouldn't be, after what she'd gone through
with Larry? Was it so wrong to want people she cared about
to reciprocate and treat her with kindness?

No.

Not unless you decided to punish those who didn't.

Had Alison done that?

Sophie resumed her pacing.

Maybe she ought to call her. Somehow introduce one of
these people's names into the conversation. Michelle, perhaps.
Why not find a way to work her into the conversation, see
how Alison reacted? If her sister had anything to hide, she'd
pick it up. The two of them had been super close back in their
younger days.

Yes. Calling was a smart idea.

Besides, she'd promised to touch base before the weekend
ended.

Wiping her palms down the oversized sweatshirt that hit
her leggings mid-thigh, she altered her course and hurried to
the kitchen. Pulled the charging cord from her phone. Placed
the call.

After three rings, as Sophie prepared to leave a voicemail, her sister answered.

"Sophie! I've been thinking about you. How did the organ gig go this morning?"

She crossed back to her computer, where the story about Adam Long dominated the screen. "I was a little rusty, but I got through the service and no one complained."

"I'm sure it was fine. You've always been too critical of yourself. Did you get caught up on your lesson plans?"

Sophie surveyed the material spread over the kitchen table.

Not even close.

It was hard to concentrate with worry and indecision clouding your brain.

"I have a bit more to do." She wandered back toward the living room. "But there are a few hours left in the day."

"You work too hard."

"I like what I do." She nestled into the super-comfortable, overstuffed, estate-sale-find wing chair—her go-to retreat on hard days. Pulled her legs up. "You work hard too."

"I also make time to play. Get together with friends. Like Bri. You met her last weekend."

This could provide the segue she needed.

"Yes. The fire investigator." Sophie squeezed her knees closer to her body with her free hand. "You know, she reminded me of Michelle, that girl you were friends with in high school. Remember?"

Silence greeted that comment.

When it lengthened, Sophie spoke again. "Alison? Are you there?"

"Yes. I just . . . I haven't thought about her in years. How does Bri remind you of her?"

"The blond hair, I suppose. I remember Michelle had beautiful hair. I always thought she was glamorous. I wonder whatever happened to her."

"I have no idea. We didn't stay in touch after she stole my boyfriend."

"It's a shame a fleeting high school romance ruined your friendship. You two were tight."

"It wasn't fleeting for them." A hint of bitterness etched her words. "They ended up getting married."

Sophie rested her cheek against the soft velveteen fabric and focused on the scene through her window, where the deepening shadows portended the arrival of dusk. "How do you know? I thought you didn't stay in touch?"

Another beat ticked by. "We didn't, but we had a few mutual friends."

"You ever think about trying to reconnect?"

"No. What's with all the questions about ancient history?"

"I don't know. I guess death puts me in a pensive mood."

"Well, I had no interest in reconnecting with her. She wasn't the kind of person you could trust."

Had.

Wasn't.

Both past tense.

The bottom dropped out of Sophie's stomach.

Her sister knew Michelle was dead.

Suspicion about Alison's involvement morphed to probable, and bile rose in her throat.

Choking back the acrid taste, she shot to her feet and dashed toward the bathroom. "Sorry. I have to go. Call coming in."

Without waiting for a reply, she severed the connection, opened the toilet lid, and once again lost the contents of her stomach.

When she stopped heaving, she closed the lid, sat, and buried her face in her hands.

All of the fires she'd read about had been deemed accidental.

But they weren't.

Someone had set them.

Probably someone who knew about fires.

Someone like Alison, who had grudges against the victims.

All innocent people except for Larry.

And innocent people deserved justice.

Yet how could she betray her sister? The one who'd always watched out for her? Who'd protected her from Larry at great personal expense? Whose concern for her welfare had never wavered?

How could she do that?

Shoulders slumping, Sophie pushed herself to her feet and stumbled back to her chair, legs shaky. Sank into its welcoming depths and cuddled up in the sheltering wings.

Could she provide law enforcement with the facts she knew, leave her sister's name out of it, and let them try to make the connection? See if they could find proof of her suspicions? After all, that was their job.

Yes. That approach would be fair to everyone involved.

But how could she anonymously pass on what she knew?

Sophie played with her phone.

She couldn't call or email. Both were traceable.

A note would have to do. Mailed from a post office close to St. Louis, so the postmark couldn't identify her location, and printed in the block letters she taught her students.

As for where to send it—why not that fire investigator Alison knew? Bri Tucker. The woman had come across as smart and buttoned-up. If she didn't want to deal with the information, she could pass it on.

And it was possible nothing would come of it. If the information languished, or law enforcement failed to connect the dots, so be it. Her conscience would be eased, and Alison would never know.

Yet as Sophie rose from her chair and headed to the kitchen

to find a piece of notepaper and an envelope along with a pair of latex gloves from her COVID stash, she couldn't shake the feeling that she was about to set off a chain of events that would have dramatic and long-lasting repercussions.

"THERE'S AN UNUSUAL ONE FOR YOU, DETECTIVE. Looks like a prop in a B movie." As the guy from the mail room deposited the day's delivery in Bri's inbox, he grinned and motioned toward the envelope on top with her name and address printed in block letters.

She plucked it off the stack. "Yeah. It does." She turned it over. No return address. "Or someone with a complaint who wants to remain anonymous."

"Could be that too." He gave her a mock salute as he exited. "Have a nice day."

Not likely. After spending too many hours yesterday on her feet at a fire scene, her knee and hip were aching.

Too bad she'd agreed to meet Alison for lunch today.

But bailing on a grieving widow who could probably use an empathetic ear would be heartless.

She'd have to suck it up and go—as soon as she opened this curious piece of mail.

After slitting the flap, she pulled it out and read the single folded sheet.

Under the heading "These fires may be connected," the writer had listed four names and dates.

Bri stopped breathing.

Michelle Thomas was on the list.

So was Adam Long.

But Nate Stephens? That was a shocker.

And who was the fourth guy? The name wasn't familiar, nor did it—

Wait.

Pulse hammering, she fumbled for Les's list in her drawer. Pulled it out. Zeroed in on the one entry she'd been unable to identify.

Yes!

The initials and date matched.

This was the missing piece.

But who was he? Where had he died?

And why was Alison's husband on this list?

Mind racing at warp speed, Bri resorted to Google.

A number of hits came up for Larry Walters.

Age sixty-two, he'd died in a boat fire seventeen months ago. A longtime lobbyist, he'd lived in Springfield, Illinois, for most of his life. Cause of the fire had been listed as accidental, and drugs and alcohol had been found in his system during the autopsy.

Same as the verdict for all the other fires on the list, which encompassed three different jurisdictions.

But what was the common denominator that would lead to the killer?

Bri pulled a pair of latex gloves from her desk and flipped the envelope over.

The postmark was from Monday morning in . . . she squinted at the smudged ink . . . Wentzville. Thirty-five or forty miles west of St. Louis.

Who was this person, and what else did they know?

Bri snapped photos of the envelope and note, then deposited both items in an evidence envelope. Given the generic block lettering designed to disguise handwriting, there wasn't much chance the cautious writer had left prints anywhere, but it couldn't hurt to have the lab check.

ASAP.

She picked up her phone. A call to Marc was in order, since it seemed their case could be heating up again.

After returning his greeting, she filled him in.

"That's an interesting development. You not only found the missing name, you have a new name."

"But still no clue how or why they're connected."

"Your friend may be able to offer an insight or two, since her husband's name is on the list."

Bri jiggled her foot and studied a scuff mark on the wall across from her. "I thought of that, but bringing this up in the midst of her grief would be awkward. I'm having lunch with her, though."

"It may be worth trying. If that doesn't produce anything, we could always run the list by James Wallace again, now that we have a few more names. Someone out there must know what the connection is. I don't like the fact that the list keeps getting longer. That may mean the person behind all these deaths isn't finished yet."

That was true.

Marc was also right about bringing up the subject with Alison. In light of their imminent lunch, her friend was the logical place to start. If the conversation didn't produce a lead, they could see if the names meant anything to James Wallace.

"I'm with you on all counts. I'll try Alison first. If she's clueless, I'll move on to Wallace. Want to join me if that happens?"

"Count me in. You know, there is one downside to this new lead."

"What?"

"We may have to delay our date—unless you've changed your mind about mixing business and pleasure."

Well, crud. Why had she raised that as an issue?

"Not in theory. In practice, however, I'm wavering. Why don't we wait and see what turns up this week and hope for a quick resolution?"

"Fingers crossed on my end. Let me know what comes out of your lunch."

"Will do."

As they said their goodbyes and Bri ended the call, she stood, plucked her jacket off the chair across from her desk, and strode toward the elevators.

Not that she was in a hurry to see Alison. Their lunch would have been subdued in any case under the circumstances, but her new agenda would likely put a damper on both their appetites.

But maybe . . . just maybe . . . once Alison got past the shock of seeing her husband's name on the list, she'd be able to help put this case to rest once and for all—and prevent any more deaths.

TWENTY-SIX

WHAT WAS UP WITH BRI?

As Alison sipped her margarita, she eyed her friend over the salt-encrusted rim of the glass.

Those twin creases on her forehead often showed up while she was talking about a thorny case, but since her initial "tell me how you're doing" query, all they'd discussed while perusing the menu and placing their lunch order had been the weather.

An innocuous topic if ever there was one. Nothing that should produce worry lines.

Was it possible Bri was fretting about the grieving widow and wondering what she could say or do to cheer her up?

She should put her mind at ease on that score, lighten up the atmosphere, or the pall hanging over the table would ruin both their appetites.

Alison swirled the contents of her glass. "This hits the spot."

"I'm glad." Bri offered her a smile that seemed strained around the edges.

"Thanks again for squeezing this lunch into your busy schedule. It helps restore a semblance of normalcy to my life." She set the glass down and leaned forward. "Tell me what's going on at work. Hearing about routine stuff will also get my mind off gloomy subjects."

Instead of dissipating, the furrows on Bri's forehead grew more pronounced. "It's been hectic."

"Par for the course, right?"

"Yes. But I thought . . ." Bri straightened her fork. Swallowed. "I thought the particular case that's on my mind was winding down."

A muted alarm bell began to ring in Alison's mind. "Which case?"

"Les Kavanaugh."

The word that flashed through Alison's mind wasn't appropriate for polite company.

Keeping her expression and tone as neutral as she could, she picked up her drink again. "I thought you were out of leads."

"I was. Until this morning." Bri folded her hands on the table, her taut features evidence of her distress. "Alison, I hate to add more stress to your life, but I need to tell you about a new development and get your input."

She took a sip of the margarita. "This sounds serious."

"It is." Bri's knuckles whitened. "The tip that came in was a list of victims who died in fires. Whoever wrote it said they could all be related. Three of them were on Les's list." She took a breath. Let it out. "The fourth was Nate."

Somehow Alison managed to call up a shocked, what-in-the-world-is-this-about look, but it took every ounce of her acting skill.

Because she knew exactly what this was about—and who was behind it. Only one person could have sent that list.

Sophie.

That's why her sister had been acting rattled on Saturday. Why she'd left sooner than planned. Why she'd brought up Michelle and Larry. She'd realized their deaths, and Nate's, weren't accidental, as the official reports had concluded, and had alerted law enforcement.

Searing hurt scorched Alison's heart.

How could the sister she'd loved and protected and stood up for all these years sic law enforcement on her, when all the people who died had deserved their fate?

Unless . . .

Alison's brain kicked back in.

Maybe Sophie hadn't done that.

Bri had mentioned receiving a list and a suggestion the fires could be connected. Nothing more. Given Sophie's honesty and integrity, not to mention the deep faith she'd developed a few years back, her conscience would have compelled her to take some sort of action if her suspicions were strong.

But no culprit must have been mentioned, or she wouldn't be sitting here with Bri, drinking a margarita. She'd be in an interview room at headquarters.

The most prudent plan was to buy herself a few minutes and find out everything she could before panicking.

"I'm sorry." Alison set her glass down and rubbed her temple. "I'm trying to take in what you said, but it's not computing. Why is Nate's name on that list?"

"I was hoping you could tell me." Bri pulled out her phone, scrolled to a photo, and held it out. "Here's the list of every name I have that's connected with Les's case. Since Nate's name is among them, I thought you might see a connection we've missed."

In other words, despite the tip Sophie had passed on, Bri was no closer to figuring out the link than she had been a week ago.

Excellent news.

Alison leaned forward and pretended to study the list. Slowly shook her head. "The only ones I recognize are Nate's and Les's." She leaned back and feigned a shudder. "Is whoever sent that suggesting those fires weren't accidents?"

"That's my assumption." Bri slipped her phone back into

her purse. "Alison, did Nate have any enemies that you know of?"

"No. Everyone liked him." She fished out a tissue and dabbed at the corner of her eyes. Sniffed. "This is bizarre."

"I know, and I'm so sorry to upset you. But with Nate's name on the list, I had to ask."

"I understand—and I wish I could have helped." She swiped at her nose. "What will you do next?"

Bri leaned back as the waiter set her soup and sandwich combo in front of her. "Talk to any relatives of the other victims we can find, ask the same question. If that doesn't produce anything, we're back to square one."

"Any chance of tracing the sender of the note?" Alison surveyed the chicken club sandwich the waiter set in front of her, but her appetite had evaporated.

"Not unless the lab finds fingerprints, which I'm not expecting."

"Where did it come from?"

"Wentzville."

So Sophie had driven seventy-five or eighty miles to mail the letter.

Smart.

"I guess that doesn't help much."

"No." Bri picked up her spoon. "What do you say we switch to more pleasant topics for the rest of the meal?"

"I'm all for that." Alison hoisted her glass again and took another sip of her drink.

But alcohol couldn't dull her nagging worry as she picked at her lunch.

Bri wasn't much interested in food, either. They both ended up taking a substantial portion of their meals home.

As they parted in the parking lot forty minutes later, Bri gave her a hug. "Take care of yourself."

"I will."

"Sorry I cast a damper over our lunch."

"Hey, you were just doing your job. Let me know if anything comes of the tip."

"I will."

With a wave, Bri struck off for her Camry.

Alison continued to her car, slid behind the wheel, and watched her friend back out of her parking spot.

It was possible she was safe. Sophie had done what she had to do to salve her conscience, but she hadn't provided specifics, and no one related to the people on that list would have a clue what linked all the names. None of the victims had known each other.

No one other than she and Sophie were privy to the connection, and her sister's suspicions weren't provable. If there'd been any evidence left at the fires to point a finger toward the culprit, it would have been found.

She should be safe.

Except Bri was tenacious. Would she really let this go now that she was more convinced than ever those deaths were the result of foul play? And what if she figured out the link?

That would be very bad news.

An icy shiver rippled through Alison, and she took a long, slow breath. Faced the truth.

Bri was a threat.

Bri would always be a threat.

Her new friend was as persistent as Les had been.

That was the harsh reality—and it left her only one choice.

Alison twisted the key in the ignition as Bri's car exited the lot and disappeared from view, the little lunch she'd eaten churning in her stomach.

Eliminating all the others had been easy.

But putting a friend in the crosshairs?

Much, much harder.

Yet Bri had told her to take care of herself, and she'd be foolish to ignore that wise counsel.

Even if that meant she'd also have to take care of Bri.

Once and for all.

MARC SET HIS BRAKE in front of James Wallace's house and surveyed the few cars parked on the street.

No Toyota.

Bri wasn't here yet.

He was a few minutes early, though. Of course, that had nothing to do with being anxious to see her.

Right.

Mouth curving up, he pulled out his phone and began scrolling through texts and email. Saturday couldn't get here too fast for him—assuming Bri didn't bail on their date, thanks to the new development in the case.

But unless Wallace or someone else related to one of the people on the expanded list offered more than her friend had at lunch today, they were back in a holding pattern.

Not great news for the case, but a green light for romance.

A reasonable trade-off, as far as he was concerned.

His smile broadened as Bri's Toyota turned the corner and pulled up behind him. This might not be a date, but it was better than nothing.

He met her in front of her car.

"Thanks for coming, even though you may have wasted your time." She angled away from the wind that had picked up over the afternoon. "I tried to call him again half an hour ago. Another roll to voicemail."

"Spending a few minutes with you is never a waste of my time."

A hint of pink bloomed on her cheeks. "You have a silver tongue."

"You inspire eloquence."

"See what I mean?" She shot him a teasing look. "Getting back to business . . . in light of how hard Wallace pressed us to keep his daughter's case on our radar, I doubt he'd ignore a call from me. So I assume he hasn't received my messages."

"Possible. He could be out of town and out of cell range. Or he could be having phone issues."

"If it's the latter, he may be here. Let's give it a shot."

He fell in beside her as they walked up the stone pavers toward the front door, but halfway there, a fiftyish woman exited the adjacent house, lifted a hand in greeting, and crossed the lawn to join them.

"May I help you? James isn't home."

"We were hoping to talk with him." Bri pulled out her creds and displayed them for the woman. "Do you know when he'll be back?"

After giving Bri's ID a quick read, the woman furrowed her brow. "Is this about his daughter?"

"It's a related matter."

"That was such a terrible tragedy. She was all he had left in the world. A lovely young woman."

"She seems to have been." Bri returned her creds to her purse and steered the conversation back on track. "Do you know when Mr. Wallace will be home, or how we could reach him?"

"He's at his little cabin near Steeleville. The cell service there is spotty. I do have the sheriff's number down there in case of an emergency. I could give you that if it's urgent. James won't be home until Thursday afternoon."

"Our business can wait until then." Bri pulled out her keys. "Thanks for the information."

"No problem. Sorry for butting in, but I always get his mail and keep an eye on the place while he's gone. You people appeared to be reputable, but it never hurts to be careful."

"That's true. Thanks again." Bri pivoted and started back toward their cars.

Once out of earshot of the woman, Marc spoke. "Do you want to contact family members of the other people on the list or wait until we talk to Wallace?"

"Let's wait. I spoke early on with the ones who were related to the victims on Les's original list, and they'd all accepted the accidental ruling. Wallace was the one most interested in further investigation."

"Okay. Once you hear from him and set up a meeting, let me know and I'll be here."

"I hate to take you away from your other work again for what could be a conversation that leads nowhere—like the one I had with Alison at lunch."

"But two heads are better than one. And I have a vested interest in seeing this wrap up fast. Like before Saturday."

She flashed him her dimple. "I hear you. I'll text you the minute I hear from Wallace."

"Sounds good." He paused beside her car and opened the door for her. "What was your friend's reaction to finding her husband's name on the list you got?"

"Shock, as you'd expect. I'm still shocked too. I did get a copy of his police report and autopsy findings. I can't fault the accidental ruling—and it's not my case to investigate—but that conclusion doesn't feel right. Alison told me once he loved to camp and was very experienced. Why would someone like that stack logs next to his tent?"

"People can do foolish things if they're under the influence of drugs."

"I know. I factored that in. But I can't shake the feeling that it's all too neat and tidy. Like the other cases were—not to mention the similarities among them. Instincts don't take the place of concrete proof, though." Bri sighed and slid behind the wheel. "On a more positive note, at least my personal run of bad luck seems to be over. No tire or car issues this week."

"Let's hope that continues. Drive safe." He closed the door, lifted his hand in farewell, and returned to his car.

But as Bri drove past James Wallace's house, *safe* suddenly felt far away.

Because his instincts were weighing in, as Bri's had about her friend's husband. And as he'd told her the day they met at the Kavanaugh scene, he listened to his gut too.

So why was it suddenly sending a red alert?

HIS PHONE WAS VIBRATING.

Again.

Travis stifled a curse and tossed back the last of his scotch.

Marcia was driving him crazy.

Being at her beck and call every minute she was off work was too high a price to pay for the hospitality and accommodations she'd provided.

He had to get out of St. Louis.

The vibration stopped, and he signaled to the bartender for a refill. Gave the crowded, noisy bar a sweep. Homed in on a couple of chicks who were eyeing him from a table not far from the seat he'd claimed at the bar.

He gave them a leisurely perusal. Not bad. They could be amusing for an hour or two. As soon as he had his drink, why not—

The vibration started up again.

This time he spat out the curse.

Enough.

He yanked the phone from his pocket to let Marcia have it—but froze as he skimmed the screen.

An anonymous caller.

Aka the person responsible for keeping him in town far longer than he'd expected to stay.

Was this a reprieve or a new assignment?

Pulse accelerating, he picked up the drink the bartender set in front of him, took a fortifying sip, and pressed talk.

"It's about time." Though the voice remained genderless, the caller's annoyance was clear.

"I wasn't in a position to take calls." He slipped off his stool and went in search of a quiet corner.

"It doesn't sound like you are now, either. Are you at a bar?"

Since there was no escaping the loud music and raucous conversation inside, he pushed through the door that led to the patio.

It wasn't much quieter there. The revelry had spilled outside too. But the noise had more area to dissipate.

"Travis?"

"Yeah. I'm trying to find a private place to talk. Hold on a minute." He wove through the partiers and tucked himself into a corner of the terrace, his back to the crowd. "I'm set."

"I have another job for you."

Not the news he wanted to hear.

"It better not be risky, like the last one."

"It doesn't have to be. I'll leave the execution up to you. And I'll have no further need of you after Thursday."

Best news he'd had in weeks.

"What's the job?"

"Thursday afternoon, Bri will get a message directing her to be in the pumpkin patch at the Kirkwood farmers' market at four o'clock. I want you to intercept her there and escort her to a different location."

Travis frowned. "You mean show my face?"

"Unless you can think of another approach."

He stared into the darkness beyond the string of white

lights that delineated the outdoor party zone. "Are you crazy? If she sees me, I'm toast. Besides, she won't go anywhere with me."

"There are ways to persuade people to do your bidding. I'm sure you have such a tool on your person as we speak."

The pressure of the concealed carry holster in the small of his back registered, even as his heart stuttered. "That's kidnapping. I'll end up behind bars for the rest of my life."

"No, you won't. If you plan this well, no one will be able to identify you. That's what disguises were made for."

The person on the other end of the line was certifiable.

"Bri will know it's me, no matter how much I try to disguise myself."

"That doesn't matter. Bri won't be around to identify you."

Travis's hand began to shake, and the scotch sloshed onto his fingers. He set the drink on the railing that enclosed the patio, glanced around, and lowered his voice. "I'm not going to kill anyone."

"I'm not asking you to. All you have to do is deliver her to the location I specify. I'll take care of the rest."

"You're going to kill her?" That was almost as bad. It would make him an accessory.

"You'll be gone before that happens. I'll handle the actual deed. And I don't plan to get caught."

"I don't like this." Pranks were one thing. Killing—directly or indirectly—was another.

"Tough. The alternative is that I go to the police with evidence of your other lapses in judgment."

That would be a disaster, coming on top of the problem waiting for him in Idaho.

He was stuck.

Swallowing past the sour taste on his tongue, he gripped the edge of the railing and did what he had to do. "Fine. I'll deliver her. But that's it."

"Get ready to take down directions."

"Hang on." He fumbled in his jacket for a pen and a slip of paper. Extracted the receipt where he'd jotted the phone number for the waitress who'd shared a few happy hours with him. Flipped it over. "Ready."

He scribbled the directions as his blackmailer reeled them off, digging out another scrap of paper when he ran out of room.

"Do you have that?"

"Yes. What do I do once we're there?"

"Wait."

"For what?"

"You'll know when you see it."

"What does that mean?"

"You ask too many questions, Travis. Trust me. You'll know. Two pieces of advice. Be careful approaching Bri. She'll probably be armed. And knock off the booze until your job is done."

The line went dead.

Slowly Travis slid the pen and pieces of paper back into his pocket. Weighed the phone in his hand.

He could call back. Demand more specifics.

But in all likelihood, the call would roll to voicemail. Whoever was behind this plan was done communicating.

He picked up his drink and downed the remains in several long gulps. Quashed the temptation to order another.

His tormentor was right.

To pull off this next assignment, he'd need a clear head.

But after it was done . . . after he walked away and left Bri to the mercy of the person who had a deadly vendetta against her . . . he'd stop at the first bar he found and drink until he obliterated the memory of his part in murder.

TWENTY-SEVEN

THIS COULD BE IT.

Bri stopped in front of James Wallace's house, set the brake, and inspected her face in the rearview mirror.

Her makeup was impeccable, but it couldn't hide the faint lines of fatigue at the corners of her eyes.

Having to wait two days to meet with him hadn't been conducive to nighttime slumber.

But her Thursday afternoon would perk up considerably if he was able to provide a piece of useful information.

She pulled her key from the ignition and checked out the street. No sign of Marc yet, but she was a few minutes early. It was also possible the meeting he told her about two hours ago when she called to let him know she'd connected with Wallace could be running long.

If he wasn't here by three, she'd shoot him a text and let him know she'd get started without—

Ping.

Message coming in, likely from Marc.

She pulled out her cell.

Yep.

Bri—Sorry to bail on you. Nan has a hundred and one temperature, and she told me one of the blisters on her irradiated skin seems to be infected. I'm with her at urgent care now.

> Probably overkill again, but after all she's
> been through I didn't want to take a chance.
> Let me know how it goes.

Quashing her disappointment, she set her thumbs in motion.

> No worries. Hope all is well.

After putting her phone back in her purse, she picked up the file folder from the seat beside her, got out, locked her car, and strode toward the front door.

James Wallace pulled it open before she could ring the bell. "I've been watching for you. Come in, please."

"Agent Davis had hoped to join us, but a family emergency came up."

The older man closed the door behind her. "I know all about those. Let's sit in the living room again. May I offer you coffee or a soda?"

"No, thanks." Bri took a seat on the couch.

Michelle's father sat in the upholstered chair across from her and leaned forward, hands clasped. "I assume you have new information about the fire at my daughter's house."

"I do, but it hasn't yet led me anywhere concrete." Bri explained about the expanded list of names and the tip she'd received that they were all connected. "I know I already ran the initial list by you, but I wanted you to review it again now that I have more names. I'm hoping if you see them all together, it will trigger some connection between them." She withdrew a copy of the list from the folder, handed it over—and held her breath.

Wallace gave the names his full attention as almost half a minute ticked by.

But in the end, he shook his head. "I'm sorry. None of these names mean anything to me." He held out the sheet.

Bri swallowed past her disappointment. Her best hope of

finding a link had just gone down the toilet. "Why don't you keep that, in case anything comes to mind later?"

He set the list on the coffee table. "Do you think talking to another relative of someone on the list may help?"

"That's my next move." She picked up the folder and her purse. No reason to linger—or tell him she wasn't holding out much hope for a breakthrough there.

"You'll let me know if you find out anything?"

"Of course." She stood.

He accompanied her to the door, and once they said their goodbyes she returned to her car, trying to quell her frustration.

They were so close. She could feel it.

But close didn't count in a crime investigation. A miss was a miss, even if the answer was a mere whisper away.

As she started the car, her cell began to vibrate.

Marc with an update?

No. It was the main office number.

The operator got straight to the point. "Detective Tucker, a call came in for you five minutes ago. The person asked that I pass along a message. They said they had more information about the list you received in the mail and asked that you meet them at the pumpkin patch in the Kirkwood farmers' market at four o'clock. I don't know if it was a man or woman. The connection was bad. They wouldn't leave a name or contact number, either, and caller ID was blocked."

Bri's pulse picked up.

This could be the break she'd been hoping for.

"Thanks. I'll follow up." She severed the call, checked her watch, and texted Marc with an update.

He pinged her back immediately.

Suspicious. Why would whoever this person
is show their face? Take backup.

No surprise he was concerned. She was too.

But there was no time to get anyone from County to the market. The most she could do was ask Kirkwood to have an officer or detective show up and keep a discreet distance during the encounter.

Besides, it wasn't as if she was meeting someone in a dark alley. You couldn't get much more public than the Kirkwood farmers' market.

> Will contact Kirkwood PD re: backup. Stand
> by for update.

Bri tossed the phone onto the seat beside her, buckled up, and sped toward the close-in suburb known for its small-town feel.

As she arrived at the bustling downtown area and began the often-difficult search for a parking place, her cell began to vibrate again.

She snatched it up as she did another circuit of the loop between a row of businesses and the farmers' market.

James Wallace.

Pressing talk, she jammed on her brakes as a patron of the quaint garden supply store began to back out of an angled parking spot. "Mr. Wallace, can you hold a moment?"

Without waiting for a response, she set the cell on the passenger seat, staccato-tapped the steering wheel as the shopper executed a slow-motion exit from the spot, then pulled in, set the brake, and picked up the phone. "Sorry. I was in the midst of parking. What can I do for you?"

"Well, after you left, I read through your list again—and that prompted me to go through the photo album I put together of Michelle. The one I showed you on your first visit. I thought one of those shots might jog my memory. I found one that did."

Bri twisted her wrist. She had fifteen minutes to connect with the Kirkwood PD and cross the street to the farmers' market. Could this wait?

No.

If Wallace had information to share, she needed to hear it.

"I'm listening, Mr. Wallace."

"The Larry name on the list may be a loose connection. I remembered it when I got to Michelle's sweet sixteen birthday photo—the shot of her with a group of friends. I never heard the man's last name, but there was a guy named Larry who was somehow related to Michelle's best friend in high school. I know her friend didn't like the man."

Bri's blossoming hope wilted.

Wallace was grasping at straws.

Hard to blame him, in light of all the trauma and tragedy he'd endured. In his position, she'd be turning over every rock too, no matter how obscure.

She had to let him down easy.

"I suppose there could be a connection, Mr. Wallace. I'll keep it in mind as I contact other family members of the victims."

"Michelle's best friend could tell you if the man's last name matched the one on your list."

Humor him, Bri. He's only trying to help.

"I could certainly consider calling her. Why don't you give me her name and any other information you have about her?" Bri fished out her pen again and pulled the sheet of names from the folder.

"I don't have any recent information. She and Michelle had a falling-out in high school, so all I have is her maiden name. Alison Lawrence."

Bri frowned.

Alison?

Strange coincidence that Michelle's best friend shared a name with Alison Stephens.

Or was it?

A tingle of suspicion began to niggle at her.

"Where did your daughter go to high school, Mr. Wallace?"

"Nowhere you'd recognize. We lived in Springfield back then."

Where Alison had grown up, based on a passing reference she'd once made about her childhood.

The tingle spread, setting off a vibration in her nerve endings as she tried to visualize the photo. The vague composition materialized, but none of the faces came into focus. She'd been too busy inhaling Marc's aftershave as they paged through the album to pay attention to the details of the pictures.

"Mr. Wallace, could you snap a photo of that picture and text it to me?"

"I'd be happy to as soon as we hang up."

"Where in the photo is Alison?"

"To Michelle's left. Has this been helpful?"

"It may be. I'll let you know if it leads to anything."

Less than a minute after they ended the call, her phone pinged with the photo.

Bri opened it at once. Homed in on the girl to Michelle's left and enlarged the image.

The hairstyle and color were different, and twenty years had passed, but the mouth and nose were the same.

It was Alison Stephens.

But Alison said she hadn't recognized any of the names on the list.

If Alison and Michelle had had a falling-out, however, it was possible she hadn't known Michelle's married name. And the Larry on the victim list might not be the same Larry that Wallace had mentioned. The one Michelle's friend hadn't liked.

Yet the man had died in a boat on Lake Springfield. Near Alison's hometown.

He'd also died in a fire, like all the others, with drugs in his system.

And Alison knew fires. Plus, as a firefighter/paramedic, she would have access to drugs.

Heart hammering, Bri tried to organize her scrambled thoughts.

Was it possible her margarita-loving friend could have played a role in multiple deaths?

It seemed absurd.

But if the Larry that Wallace had mentioned was the same one Michelle's friend had talked about, Alison had a connection to at least three of the people on the list. Perhaps more.

That was a fact.

A very disturbing fact.

She needed to talk to Alison. ASAP.

First, however, she had a date at a pumpkin patch. One that could potentially lead to more answers.

Bri skimmed her watch again. No time to go through clearances at the Kirkwood PD to get police backup. She'd have to call Sarge, give him a fast download about her rendezvous, and ask him to place that call. He could cut through red tape faster than she could. And surely Kirkwood would be able to get someone here in the next few minutes. It wasn't that large of a town.

Ten seconds later, Bri connected with her boss, gave him a rapid-fire briefing along with a description of her attire, left her car behind—and tried to tamp down an unwarranted surge of unease. Getting spooked was silly. She had her Sig, and there was plenty of activity in the area.

As she hurried toward the pumpkin patch peopled by mothers and toddlers, dog walkers, and a few older folks sitting on benches, she examined the area. Customers were coming and going at the surrounding businesses, and street traffic, as usual, was brisk.

If someone wanted to stay under the radar or was up to no good, this wasn't an optimal location for a meeting.

Taking a calming breath, Bri continued toward the display of pumpkins, gaze sweeping left and right. Nothing appeared to be amiss. A mother took a selfie with her little boy in front of a stack of pumpkins. A middle-aged woman kept a tight grip on the leash of her German shepherd as she inspected the merchandise. A gray-haired man with a cane and glasses paused to adjust his tweedy Irish cap and peer at a sign about the upcoming Christmas market.

Everything was quiet and—

Boom!

As an explosion in the vicinity of the historic train station across the street reverberated through the air, a collective gasp went up. Cars screeched to a stop. A woman screamed. People began running.

What in the—

Someone took her arm in a firm grip and pressed up close behind her. "Don't turn around, Bri. Walk toward the black Chevy Cruze parked eight cars west of yours." A blunt object nudged her in the side.

A gun?

Yet it was the voice that made her heart stumble.

"Travis?"

"So you do remember me. I'm flattered. Move." The gun pressed harder. "And don't even think about reaching for your weapon."

She lurched forward, trying to wrap her mind around what was happening.

Travis was here, after all? He was the one who'd called and asked her to meet him today?

But what could he know about the fires . . . or Les's list . . . or any of the victims, all of whom lived a long way from Idaho? And how was Alison involved? Or was she?

None of this was making sense.

As they crossed the street on the north side of the farmers' market, she glanced toward the west. A crowd had already formed a wide perimeter around the explosion site, and a police officer was sprinting toward the smoke.

Probably the officer Sarge had rounded up to keep an eye on her.

Wonderful.

"Did you do that?" She tried to swallow past her fear.

"Cell-phone-activated fireworks. A simple but effective diversion. No one got hurt. When we get to the car, enter through the front passenger door and hand me your weapon. No tricks, or one of the nice people close by will pay the price. Understood?"

"Yes." Smart of him to threaten an innocent bystander. He knew she'd never intentionally put anyone in danger.

"After you give me the gun, slide behind the wheel."

Bri followed his instructions, though parting with her Sig hollowed out her stomach.

As she scooted behind the wheel and got her first glimpse of the man she'd hoped never to see again, she did a double take.

The old gent with the cane and glasses and gray hair?

"I see you're impressed by my disguise."

She ignored that. "What's going on? Why did you want to meet me here? What do you know about the list?"

"You always did ask too many questions." He held out the key. "Start the car."

"Where are we going?"

"You'll find out when we get there."

She hesitated. Maybe if she—

Travis dropped the key onto the console and rolled down his window but kept his gun aimed at her. "See that older woman by the birdfeeders in front of the garden store? She's history if you don't follow my instructions."

Bri hesitated.

Would he really shoot her? He might be a lowlife with women, but picking off a stranger would be—

"I missed in the parking lot, Bri. On purpose." A hint of steel in his voice replaced the cockiness from moments ago. "I won't miss again." He lifted the gun.

324

"Fine." She snatched up the key and shoved it in the ignition. She'd wait for an escape window that didn't put anyone else in danger. But until she found it, why not ferret out as much as she could about what he'd been up to?

He spoke as if he'd read her mind. "No more talking. Just follow my directions. Take out your phone and turn it off. Then set it on the floor at my feet."

Panic spiked her adrenaline.

The phone was her lifeline. The only way anyone would be able to track her. Without that, she was—

"Now, Bri." He tipped his head toward the oblivious older woman again.

Putting a life at risk to protect herself wasn't acceptable.

She did as he instructed.

"Circle the block and make a left at the intersection."

After maneuvering the car out of the parking spot, she left Kirkwood behind by the back route he dictated—and peppered him with questions.

He ignored them all as they traveled north and merged onto I-64 west.

And as the miles whizzed by and the metropolitan area faded into the distance, Bri prayed.

Hard.

Because with a gun aimed at her heart and a man who, at this juncture, had nothing to lose, it was going to take a miracle for her to get out of this alive.

TWENTY-EIGHT

WHY HADN'T BRI CALLED OR TEXTED HIM?

Marc checked his cell again as he filled a glass with water and shook out one of the antibiotic pills the doctor at urgent care had prescribed for Nan.

"I can get that myself, Marc." Nan appeared in the kitchen doorway, weariness etched on her features. She'd already changed into her comfortable sweats and seemed ready to fold.

"Too late." He held out the glass and pill. "Why don't you rest for a couple of hours after you take this?"

"That's my plan." She popped the pill in her mouth, washed it down with the water, and sighed. "I didn't need an infection on top of a sprained wrist and the cancer treatments. Neither did you."

"We'll survive."

"Yes, we will. And then you can get on with your life."

"I *am* getting on with my life—and you're a big part of it."

She waved that comment aside. "All you do is wait on me hand and foot and hover like I'm a snowflake about to melt. I'm stronger than I look. And much as I appreciate everything you've done, I don't want to put a crimp in your personal life. Have you heard back from Bri yet?"

"No." If he hadn't been checking his phone constantly for the past half hour, Nan would never have asked him what was up, nor would he have had to explain. Not that he'd told her much, other than the fact he was trying to connect with Bri.

"Keep trying. She sounds like a woman worth pursuing. Once I get over this latest episode, I'd like to meet her."

"I think that could be arranged."

"Wake me in two hours."

"I will. Drink all of that water."

She rolled her eyes but took the glass with her as she retreated down the hall.

Once she was out of sight, Marc tried Bri again—with the same result. No reply to his text, and the call immediately rolled to voicemail.

Her lack of response suggested her phone was off or disabled. Neither scenario was comforting.

Now what?

She'd promised to contact the Kirkwood PD, so that was worth following up on. But the query would get faster attention if it came from her own people at County.

Unfortunately, she'd never mentioned her boss's name.

But he did know one County detective who could track her sergeant down and who would give this assignment top priority.

Calling up his most commanding ATF special agent persona, he put in a call to County, told the operator he had urgent official business to discuss, and asked for Jack Tucker.

"TURN RIGHT UP AHEAD."

As Travis issued his second instruction since directing her to exit I-64 west of the Missouri River, Bri frowned at the sign.

A conservation area?

"Why did you bring me here?"

He remained silent, as he had during the long drive from Kirkwood except to provide directions.

Once she swung into the entrance, however, he spoke more often, reading off a series of turns from a crumpled sheet of paper filled with scribbles.

As Bri navigated the narrow gravel lanes that took them farther and farther away from the main road, her stomach knotted. With the day waning and shadows lengthening, there was almost no activity in the conservation area—especially on a weekday. Nor were there any cars in the small, remote lot where Travis told her to park.

Her fingertips began to tingle.

This was looking worse and worse.

Not a soul knew where she was, and no one would ever think to search for her in such an off-the-beaten-path location.

Meaning she was on her own to find a way out of this.

And since it was obvious Travis's earlier pranks had escalated to one with lethal intent, there was no downside to an escape attempt. Better to die trying than go meekly to her demise.

She just had to wait for the right moment.

"Leave the key on the console." Travis kept the gun aimed at her. "Get out of the car, walk ten feet away, and face me."

Respiration quickening, she set the brake and did as he instructed.

He slid out of the passenger side and retrieved a combination flashlight/lantern from the back seat, gun never wavering from her. "Now we're going to take a hike. Follow the path behind you."

She pivoted. A narrow trail led into the woods.

Snuffing out the fear short-circuiting her brain, she forced herself to take a calming breath and put her gray matter to work.

Based on the strength Travis had exhibited the day he'd cornered her in the locker room, she'd never be able to overpower him in a hand-to-hand fight. But if she could lure him close, maybe she could snatch up a downed limb, take a swing, and perhaps stun him long enough to get one of the guns.

Maybe.

Perhaps.

An iffy plan, but it was all she had.

"Move!"

At Travis's command, she jolted forward.

A few yards down the path that could once have been a one-lane dirt road, she glanced back.

He was following but keeping a significant distance between them.

That wasn't conducive to an assault. He'd have to be no more than an arm's length or two away for her plan to work. At most she'd have a couple of seconds to dive for a tree limb and swing it.

She had to come up with a strategy to draw him closer—and do it in an optimal location.

Ten minutes later, as if in answer to a prayer, she rounded a bend to find a downed tree blocking the trail. A casualty from a not-too-recent storm, in light of the moss growing on the side of the trunk.

If she could spot a club-like limb that would serve her purposes, this could offer an opportunity to coax Travis nearer.

She did a visual search for potential weapons in the area.

There. Near the trunk. A thick branch, which would do considerable damage if wielded with sufficient strength and aimed with precision, had broken off.

She paused, as if contemplating the barricade.

"Go around it."

Pulse tripping into double time, she veered off to the side, the dead, fallen leaves crunching under her feet.

As she approached the spot that would provide the optimal access to her makeshift weapon, she gave a small yelp and went down on one knee, her hand resting on the branch destined to become a club.

"What's wrong?"

"The ground's uneven. My leg gave out. I had a parachute accident, remember?"

"Oh yeah. I remember."

Was that odd nuance in his tone satisfaction?

She crimped her brow as she angled toward him. "You seem happy about that."

He shrugged. "I'm not sorry."

"That's sick." Disgust turned her stomach.

The smirk he gave her was downright evil. "No. It was justice."

It took a few moments for his implication to sink in, and when it did, a shockwave rippled through her. "Are you saying . . . did you sabotage my parachute?"

"You deserved it after all the grief you gave me."

Sweet mercy.

All this time, she'd assumed the accident was due to an error on her part. Instead, it had been deliberate, cold-blooded revenge.

She stared at him. "You tried to kill me in Idaho too?"

"No." His smirk faded. "I just wanted you to pay for causing trouble. I knew you'd survive. You had a backup chute."

"I don't today."

He shifted his weight, and a muscle ticced in his jaw. "For the record, killing wasn't part of my plan. The tires and the tree were more my style."

So he *had* been the one behind her recent run of so-called bad luck.

"But now you've upped your game." Fury began to swirl through her as the havoc this man had wreaked on her life began to fully register.

"I'm done talking." His lips settled into a grim line. "Get moving."

She tightened her grip on the limb. "My leg hurts too much."

"We don't have far to go."

"I'm telling you, my leg hurts too much. Thanks to you."

He edged in a couple of feet. "And I'm telling you, we can't stay here."

She made a halfhearted attempt to push herself to her feet. Sank back to the ground. "I need a hand."

"Use the tree trunk and push yourself up."

Keeping a firm grip on the limb, she pretended to try, then let loose with a whimper and collapsed against the trunk.

He edged nearer, and she peeked at him.

Not as close as she'd like, but within striking distance if she took him by surprise.

"Try again." The gun wavered. "We have to keep moving."

Now!

Gripping the branch with both hands, she sprang upright, pivoted, and lunged for him. Raising her improvised club, she swung for his temple as she came within target range.

It should have worked.

Would have worked if she hadn't stepped into a hole left by a foraging raccoon or a squirrel burying his winter stash.

Instead of a bullseye on the temple, all she managed was a glancing blow to his chin.

Not near hard enough to stun him.

But it made him mad.

Very mad.

Growling deep in his throat, he came at her swinging.

She tried to duck, but the metal flashlight connected with the side of her face. Hard. Fireworks went off in her field of vision, and she staggered.

A follow-up punch to her nose sent her sprawling to the ground.

Flat on her back, chest heaving, she tried to clear her vision through a haze of pain.

The darkening sky gradually came into focus through the shriveled leaves clinging to the trees above her, but the horrendous ache radiating through her head rippled the image, like a rock dropped into water.

All at once, Travis blocked her view of the heavens and glowered down at her. "Get up."

Impossible.

He nudged her none too gently with his toe, the barrel of the gun aimed at her. "I said get up."

Would he shoot her here if she didn't?

And what difference would it make if he did? There was no question that was his intent, either now or later. And barring divine intervention, there was no chance she'd be able to stop him. He had a gun and strength on his side, and she—

Stop that, Bri Tucker! Pull yourself together and stand up! You're not a quitter. Give your brain a few minutes to recalibrate. This isn't over till it's over.

Hard as she tried to smother that insistent voice, it continued to loop through her mind.

Fine. She'd soldier on as long as she could.

Wincing, she rolled to her side, heaved herself onto her knees, and stood. Swayed as she swiped at the blood flowing from her nose.

A blurry Travis glared at her. "I'm not falling for any more tricks. Walk."

Not easy to do when your leg throbbed, pain reverberated through your face with every step, and blood dripped down your chin.

But she put one foot in front of the other and continued down the path.

Thinking.

Trying to come up with a way out of this mess.

Praying.

Because she wasn't ready to die. Not even close. Not after surviving a failed parachute. Not after the surgeries she'd endured and the countless hours of excruciating PT she'd suffered through to regain the use of her leg. Not after meeting a man who'd made her believe in the possibility of happily-ever—

"Stop. We're here."

Bri jerked to a halt.

A dozen yards to the left, a weathered concrete structure loomed behind a denuded tangle of branches. About fifteen feet high in the middle, flat above the rusted steel door but with sides that sloped down to the ground, it was covered with earth and vegetation. A large number was painted on the door.

It was like a set from a horror movie.

"Wh-what is this place?"

"World War II munitions bunker. Go up on the concrete platform and stand on the far right side."

She squinted at the structure. Between the deepening dusk and the swelling in her eye, it was getting more and more difficult to see, but the large stoop-like platform in front of the building was easy to make out.

Pushing aside brambles, Bri limped toward it. Hoisted herself up and moved to the side.

Once she was at a safe distance, Travis joined her on the platform and crossed to the door.

Near as she could tell, it was bolted shut and padlocked.

How in the world would he know about this place, let alone have a key for it?

Except he didn't. After fiddling with the lock, he detached it and swung the heavy door open. Swept his light around inside. Backed up and motioned her forward. "After you."

He wanted her to go inside this tomb-like structure?

Her stomach revolted.

Is that where he planned to finish her off? Pull the trigger within the confines of the thick concrete that would muffle the shot, then leave her there until someday someone came across her bones?

No.

If he was going to kill her, he could do it out here.

She folded her arms. "I'm not going in there. If you're planning to shoot me, do it here."

"Don't make this hard, Bri."

She was done obeying orders.

It was time to create some noise. Perhaps an armed ranger or hunter in the area would hear her and come to investigate. Even if it was too late to save her, they might catch Travis. The crime wouldn't go unpunished.

Bracing for a bullet, she let loose with a piercing scream.

Instead of firing, Travis cursed and hurled himself toward her.

Without letting up on the scream, she swiveled around at the edge of the concrete platform. But Travis was on her before she could jump off.

He grabbed her, slammed his hand over her mouth, and twisted her arm behind her back.

The more she tried to resist, the more he bent her arm.

She was sunk.

But at least she'd sent a distress signal, if anyone other than a few deer was within earshot.

Propelling her toward the bunker, Travis didn't loosen his hold. Only after they were inside did he release her, shoving her away from him with such force she face-planted while he secured the door.

He clicked the flashlight lantern on as she struggled to her feet and fought back a wave of nausea while the suffocating blackness outside the small perimeter of light clawed at her windpipe.

"Don't get any ideas about venturing into the dark where I can't see you, Bri, or I'll have to use these." Travis waved several zip ties at her.

No worries on that score. She was drawn to the lantern like a moth to light.

"Move farther back in the building."

Creeping forward, she skirted a few boards, a coil of fencing, several cardboard boxes, and the edge of what appeared to be a sink—all of which suggested that the bunker had become a junk repository.

"Stop there. Sit on the right side, by the wall." He motioned with the lantern.

Bri found a cleared area and eased herself onto the concrete floor.

Once she was seated, Travis set the lantern on a box near the opposite wall, about twenty feet away. Her breath hitched as shadows engulfed her, and dampness from the concrete seeped into her slacks.

Her silence seemed to spook Travis—and loosen his tongue.

"Why'd you get so quiet all of a sudden? You were always the mouthy type."

Was that a tremor of trepidation in his voice? Like his nerves were kicking in? If so, could she use that to her advantage? Get a few answers to her questions, even if she couldn't escape?

"Tell me what you know about the list."

"What list?"

Unless he was a better actor than she remembered, he was genuinely confused.

"The list that got me to the farmers' market."

"I don't know anything about a list."

She shoved her tangled hair back and swiped at her bloody nose, trying to make sense of his comment.

"Aren't you working with Alison?"

"Who's Alison?"

Again, his puzzlement seemed sincere.

She touched her throbbing cheek.

Why weren't the pieces of this puzzle fitting?

Or maybe they were, and her brain was too rattled from the blow to her head to connect the dots.

"If that's true, why did you bring me here?"

"You'll find out."

"When?"

"When it's time."

"What does that mean?"

"Just shut up, okay?" The man appeared to be seriously nervous now. "No more talking while we wait."

"Wait for what?"

Silence.

And as the tomb-like quiet expanded to fill the underground bunker . . . as tension vibrated off the walls . . . as her fate grew more and more precarious with every second that ticked by . . . one fact was crystal clear.

While the munitions this place had once stored were long gone, one part of the bunker's history was alive and well.

Its legacy of death.

TWENTY-NINE

JACK TUCKER HAD ARRIVED.

As Bri's brother swung into an empty parking spot near the iconic garden store in Kirkwood and vaulted from his car, Marc waved at him from beside Bri's Camry.

The other man joined him, forehead wrinkling as he examined the car. "This isn't good."

No kidding.

"It was the first thing I spotted. I already did a walk-through of the farmers' market." He waved a hand across the street. "No one working there remembered seeing Bri. They were all focused on a blast near the train station that turned out to be fireworks in a trash can, hooked up to a timer, according to the cop who had Bri in his sights until he took off to investigate. An obvious distraction ploy."

Jack squinted at him in the fading daylight. "You've been busy since I passed on the cop's name."

"With nothing to show for it. What did Bri's boss say?"

"Only what you'd already told me about the call that came in holding out the promise of a tip on the Kavanaugh case." Jack forked his fingers through his hair and surveyed the scene. "We have to track her down."

"Tell me something I don't know."

"Let's canvass the businesses on this side of the street. It's possible one of the shopkeepers noticed her."

"I already hit a few. We can divide up the rest and—"

"Excuse me. Are you the law enforcement guy?"

Marc turned.

The lanky teenager who'd addressed him stood about six feet away.

"Yes. So is Detective Tucker." He motioned toward Jack. "How can we help you?"

The teen tipped his head toward the garden shop. "My boss said you were asking questions about the woman who owns that car." He motioned toward the Camry.

"Yes. We're trying to locate her. What can you tell us?"

"I saw her when she got out of her car. I was loading a sack of birdseed into a customer's trunk, and I, uh, noticed her blond hair, so I, uh, kind of watched her." The teen shoved his hands in his pockets. "I wasn't going to bother her or anything, though."

"No worries. Watching someone in a public place isn't against the law." Marc forced up the corners of his lips. The more he could defuse the teen's nervousness, the more likely he'd offer a useful tidbit. "And she does have amazing hair." The scowl Jack sent him registered in his peripheral vision. He ignored it. "What else did you see?"

"I snuck a few peeks at her while she was at the market, in between working. After the explosion went off, I saw an old guy come up behind her. Real close. Then they both walked to a black Cruze parked a few cars down from here. She looked worried. And it was weird how they both got in on the passenger side and she scooted over behind the wheel. I mean, why wouldn't she get in on the driver's side?"

Marc glanced at Jack. From the grim set of her brother's mouth, they were tracking the same direction.

She'd been forced to walk to the car under duress, and whoever the old guy was, he'd wanted to keep her within arm's reach once they got there.

"You have excellent observation skills." Marc pulled out a

notebook. "Can you describe this man in more detail and tell me which direction they went when they left?"

He jotted as the teen spoke.

"I also checked the license plate as they drove away. Would you like that too?"

Jack jumped into the conversation. "You wrote it down?"

"No. I memorize fast, especially if it seems important—or sort of weird, like this."

"We'll take the number." Marc wrote that down too.

So did Jack. "I'm going to run this while you wrap up here." Without waiting for a response, he jogged back to his car.

Marc got the teen's name and contact information, but despite a few additional questions, he had nothing more to offer.

Not a problem.

The license plate was huge.

After finishing with the teen, Marc strode toward Jack's vehicle as the other man slid out of his car.

"It's a rental. I played the exigent circumstances card and got the info on who rented it. Credit card belongs to a Marcia Blake. I'm waiting on a call back for more details on the contract and any additional drivers." Jack read off the notes he'd written. "Marcia's record is clean. She lives about fifteen minutes from here. I already put out a BOLO alert on the vehicle."

"We need to pay Ms. Blake a visit."

"Agreed. Let's take my car."

Marc suppressed a surge of frustration. With his tricked-out duty vehicle back at the office, thanks to a short day due to Nan's emergency, he had no grounds to object. Otherwise, he'd have lobbied for the driver's role, which would have given him control of the accelerator.

If Jack didn't have a lead foot, he was going to hear about it.

Thankfully, Bri's brother shared his sense of urgency, and Marc remained silent during the white-knuckle drive.

Distracting a man on a high-speed mission would be fool-hardy. Besides, he was busy tracking down Marcia Blake's cell number, in case she wasn't home.

The instant Jack stopped in front of her house, Marc un-hooked his seat belt. "How do you want to play this?"

"According to her driver's license, she's thirty-seven. So it's doubtful the old guy is a spouse or brother. Could be a father. She may have no idea the car was used for nefarious purposes. I say we tell her we're investigating a disappearance, give her the guy's description, and see what she says."

"That works. Let's go."

Marc was halfway up the walk before Jack caught up with him, and he took the porch steps two at a time. Leaned forward and pressed the bell.

Thirty seconds passed.

He tried again.

If she wasn't home, they'd have to resort to a phone call. But that was never as effective as a face-to-face chat. Body language was—

The lock clicked, and a woman who fit the age profile opened the door.

"Ms. Blake?"

"Yes."

Marc pulled out his creds and displayed them. "County Detective Tucker and I would like to speak with you for a few minutes."

She frowned. "Is something wrong?"

"Did you rent a black Chevy Cruze?"

"Yes. What's going on?"

"Is the vehicle on the premises?"

"No."

"Where is it?"

"A friend is using it. I rented it for him. Why? Is he in trouble?"

Jack joined the conversation. "Ms. Blake, we need your

Union West Regional Library
704-283-8184 opt. 3

Customer ID: **********2094

Items that you checked out

Title: Into the fire /
ID: 871091008613964
Due: Monday, July 15, 2024

Total items: 1
Account balance: $0.00
Checked out: 4
Overdue: 0
Hold requests: 3
Ready for pickup: 0
7/1/2024 11:40 AM

assistance with an urgent investigation. May we come in for a few minutes?"

Impatient as he was for answers, Marc couldn't fault the other man's technique. Marcia was clearly rattled, and hammering her with questions on her front porch wasn't ideal interview protocol.

But every minute they spent trying to put her at ease was a minute less to work with if the clock was ticking for Bri.

"I guess so." She backed up, opened the door, and motioned to her left. "We can sit in the living room."

At least Jack didn't waste time once they claimed seats.

"If you could tell us the name of the friend who's using the car, that would be helpful." He pulled out his notebook.

"Is he in trouble?"

"Are you aware of any reason he should be?"

"No."

Jack waited.

Smart man.

After a few moments, she tucked her hair behind her ear. "I mean, I don't know him all that well, so I can't say for certain. And I don't know what he does while I'm at work. He's in town on vacation, and I offered him a place to stay. We met years ago, and we've kept in touch on and off, but it's not like he's told me much about his life."

Translation? She wasn't 100 percent certain about the character of her houseguest and wanted to cover her butt.

"Why did you rent a car for him?"

"He had engine trouble during the trip here and didn't want to risk driving his car around town until he has a mechanic look it over."

"Why did you rent the car instead of him?"

"He said he was transitioning out of his old credit card and his new one hadn't arrived yet. But it's not like I'm paying for it or anything. He gave me cash for it."

This guy had covered all his bases.

"Where is your friend tonight?"

"I don't know. He said he had to take care of some personal business. He didn't offer any details." A disgruntled note crept into her tone.

"What's his name and cell number?"

"Travis Holmes."

She rattled off a number, but the rushing sound that filled Marc's ears drowned it out.

A quick glance at Jack confirmed he was having the same reaction.

"I thought you said he was in Idaho." Marc narrowed his eyes at Bri's brother.

"I said his car is in Idaho. At least there's one there with a license registered to him."

"You know who he is?"

At Marcia's question, Marc shifted his attention back to her. "We've run across his name." But the description the teen at the garden center provided wasn't meshing. "Is it possible he loaned the car to someone else?"

"I don't think he knows anyone else in town."

"Give me his cell number again." Jack jotted it down as she recited it.

"It's not a smartphone, though. It's one of those throw-aways. He said his regular phone broke and he hasn't replaced it yet."

Another red flag.

Jack's somber expression indicated they were again on the same wavelength. "The description we got of the person who was driving the car was an older man. Gray-haired, glasses, used a cane."

Marcia seemed bewildered. "I have no idea who that could be."

"Jack." Marc waited until the other man looked at him.

"Sometimes appearances can be deceiving. Why don't you get a track on that number in the works, and maybe Ms. Blake will let me see her guest's quarters."

If Jack was smart, he'd pick up on the subtle message that a search could produce evidence of a disguise. That would prove useful if Holmes later claimed the old gent hadn't been him. And no warrant was necessary. Exigent circumstances gave them sufficient cause to act.

Bri's brother shared his sibling's astuteness. "That works. Ms. Blake, you wouldn't have any objection to Agent Davis taking a quick look around, would you? He won't disturb anything, and law enforcement always appreciates cooperative citizens." He offered her the kind of smile a lot of women fell for.

Marcia Blake was one of them.

"No, of course not. I'm happy to help in any way I can. I've always been a great supporter of law enforcement. It's a hard job in this day and age. You guys rock." She batted her lashes at him.

Marc curbed an eye roll.

"Thank you." Jack rose. "Marc, I'll step outside to place my call and join you in a few minutes." With that, he hustled toward the front door and let himself out.

"What would you like to see?" Marcia rose.

"Your guest's sleeping quarters, the bathroom he uses, and his luggage."

She moistened her lips. "Um . . . okay. It's down the hall."

Pulling out a pair of latex gloves, Marc followed her until she paused at a door. "This is the, uh, guest bedroom. Travis uses the hall bath." She motioned behind her. "Most of his stuff is in these rooms."

"Where's the rest of it?" Marc snapped on the gloves.

"Um . . . there are a few things in my room."

In other words, she was providing more than a place to

sleep for her visitor. The one she claimed not to know all that well.

But he wasn't here to make judgments.

He was here to get answers about Bri.

"I'll only be a few minutes."

"No rush. I'll, uh, wait in the kitchen."

He called up a smile similar to the one Jack had given her. "Actually, ma'am, I'd appreciate it if you'd stick close. It's always better if a homeowner witnesses a search." That was stretching it. But it would be smart to keep her in sight until Jack finished, in case she decided to straighten up her room—and maybe give Holmes a heads-up.

She appeared to be susceptible to *his* smile too. "I don't mind hanging around. I'll stay back here, out of your way." She withdrew into the hall as he entered.

His search was fast but thorough, and it didn't take long to unearth a can of gray hairspray from a bag buried in a suitcase in the closet or find traces of gray on the vanity in the bathroom.

It was clear Travis was their guy. But how was he involved in the Kavanaugh case?

Marc was still puzzling over that when Jack returned with a few evidence envelopes and the good news that his boss was working on the phone track.

After discreetly sharing his hairspray find out of view of Marcia and depositing it in one of the evidence envelopes, Marc continued the search with Jack's assistance.

No more clues emerged.

But what they had was more than sufficient to tie Travis to today's abduction.

His connection to the Kavanaugh case, however, remained a mystery.

As they wrapped up, Marc pulled off his gloves, rejoined Marcia in the hall, and handed her a card. "We're finished here. If you hear from Mr. Holmes, or he returns, please give me a call—day or night. And please don't try to contact him."

"He's in big trouble, isn't he?"

"Let's just say he's a person of interest. If he does come back, be careful. He may be armed and dangerous."

Her complexion lost a few shades of color, and she wrapped herself in a hug. "Goes to show you can't trust anyone anymore."

"It never hurts to be cautious." Jack nudged him toward the door. "Thank you for your assistance, Ms. Blake."

Once they were outside and striding toward Jack's car, Marc spoke. "How long until we get a location on the phone?"

"My boss said he'd call as soon as he had it."

"What are we supposed to do in the meantime? Twiddle our thumbs?"

"You have any other ideas?"

He blew out a breath. "No."

Jack rounded the car and slid behind the wheel. "What's your take on how Holmes is connected to the Kavanaugh investigation?"

"I don't have one. He's not from this area. I don't see how he could have been involved in any of the fires on Bri's list."

"Yet there has to be a connection. It would help if we could figure it out."

"If you have any brainstorms, let me know. I'm going to call the victim's father Bri met with. See if he can shed any light on the subject."

Jack started the engine and put the car in gear. "I'll pull down to the end of the block and park. We can watch the house in case Holmes shows up while we're waiting for a location from the cell provider."

"Can't hurt."

But it might not help, either. Whatever nefarious plan Holmes was involved in, he was in it up to his neck. And he wasn't going to show until the job was finished.

In fact, considering all the people on Bri's list who'd died—including Kavanaugh, who'd no doubt been targeted after he got too close to discovering the perpetrator's identity—Holmes's absence was a positive omen. It likely meant the plan was still in progress.

Yet in his gut, Marc knew that with every passing second, the danger to Bri was escalating.

THIRTY

A MUTTERED OATH ECHOED in the tomb-like bunker as Travis paced in front of the flashlight lantern, and Bri peeked at her watch.

Six forty-five.

They'd been here almost two hours.

And Travis was getting more and more agitated.

His edginess, along with the fact he hadn't yet killed her, suggested he was either waiting for further instructions or someone was supposed to meet him here to do the final dirty work.

Perhaps the killer connected to Les Kavanaugh's expanded list.

In light of her discovery today after James Wallace's call, one name came to mind—but wrapping her head around the notion that Alison was behind all the murders was difficult, even if the pieces did fit.

Travis whipped out his cell phone. Scanned the screen. Cursed again.

There wouldn't be any service inside this vault. A realization he'd apparently just come to.

After snatching up the flashlight, he strode toward the door. "Don't try anything stupid, Bri. I'm not taking my eyes or my gun off you."

She didn't respond.

It wasn't as if there was anything she could try, after all.

347

He had the sole source of light—which could have been a weapon used to blind him had he ever moved more than six feet away from it—and if she attempted to fumble around in the dark, she'd end up flat on her face. Again.

The door opened.

Although the sun had set, a full moon gave the woods outside a ghostly glow.

Travis set the lantern in the doorway and stepped out onto the concrete platform, facing her direction as he punched at his phone and put it to his ear.

After fifteen seconds, he spewed out more obscenities, shoved his fingers through his hair, and picked up the lantern before reentering and closing the door behind him.

As he set the light back on the box and resumed his pacing, she spoke. "Look, it's obvious you're waiting for something. Can you give me a clue what's going on? It's not like you have anything to lose at this point. I assume the plan isn't to let me out of here alive. Who will I tell?" Despite the quivers rippling through her body, she managed to keep her voice steady.

Several beats ticked by.

She tried again. "Will you at least tell me who's calling the shots?" Because it wasn't him. That was becoming clearer by the minute.

More silence.

But just when she thought he was going to remain mute, he spoke.

"I don't know."

The headache pounding in her temple and the throb in her nose must be messing with her brain, because that answer didn't compute.

"I don't understand. Why would you get involved in a crime like this with someone you don't even know?"

He stopped. Kicked at a box. "They saw me plant the nails and cut the tree."

Ah.

Now this was beginning to make sense.

"You're being blackmailed."

"Yeah. I had no choice about this. I already have a boatload of trouble waiting for me in Idaho, thanks to you."

No. Thanks to himself.

But antagonizing him would get her nowhere.

"You don't have to do this, Travis. A couple of vandalism incidents is a whole different ball game than accessory to murder."

He began prowling back and forth again, like a caged animal in a zoo. "My career is toast if the police find out about those. I can't take the chance."

How to play this?

Could she appeal to his logic? Convince him he was making a huge mistake? Promise to let him off?

Anything that had the potential to save her life was worth trying.

"There's no risk if I don't press charges. If I forget any of this ever happened."

He swung toward her, his backlit features difficult to read. "Why would you do that?"

Unless she was mistaken, there was a tiny hint of hope in his inflection. Like he was grasping for a way out of this.

She could work with that.

"I don't believe in holding grudges. It's not who I am."

"Even about the parachute?"

"That's history. If I brought it up now, it would be my word against yours—and I can't prove you did it. Plus, I've recovered. I'd rather have my life than exact revenge."

He shifted his weight. "You're lying. The minute I let you out of here, you'll call the cops."

"I *am* the cops, Travis. And I don't lie. If you help me get out of this, I promise you I won't press charges. It sounds like you already have plenty of problems waiting for you in Idaho, and I'm not a vindictive person."

"I don't know . . ."

He was wavering.

Yes!

"Have you ever seen me break a promise?"

"No. You were always a straight shooter. I guess—"

The door creaked open, and Bri jerked toward it.

So did Travis.

An instant later, a bright light was aimed at her abductor. He angled his head away and shielded his eyes while a figure slipped inside and shut the door.

"Hello, Travis. We meet at last."

A mere six words, but Bri knew that voice.

It was Alison.

Her heart stumbled. Raced on as the suspicion that had taken root in her mind this afternoon solidified.

The woman who'd befriended her at a fire scene months ago and with whom she'd shared companionable lunches was the killer in Les's puzzle.

As Bri tried to absorb that bizarre reality and shift her strategy, Travis peered toward the new arrival. "I did what you asked."

"Yes, you did. Your job is almost done." She moved farther into the bunker but stopped about fifteen feet back from the lantern. "Put your gun and Bri's beside the light, on the box."

"Why do you want my gun?"

"Let's just say my trust level is on the low side. You understand how that is. Once you do that, back away. After I have them in hand, your work here will be finished."

"I don't like giving up my gun."

Alison lifted her latex-encased hand to reveal a pistol. She aimed it at Travis, within the circle of her light so he could see it. "I understand that, but I must insist. There's too much deception in the world. Set them on the box and back off."

After another pause, Travis did as she instructed.

"Very good. You take instructions well." Alison continued forward.

As the other woman approached the box, Bri gave her a swift perusal.

She was dressed for stealth, in all-black attire, her hair tucked under a black knit ski cap. Like someone in special ops on a life-and-death night mission.

Emphasis on death.

Alison picked up Bri's gun first. Examined it for a moment.

Then she strolled toward Travis, aimed the Sig at his chest, and popped off two shots in rapid succession.

As Travis crumpled to the floor, Alison shot him again.

Bri vaulted to her feet and gaped first at him, then at Alison.

Dear God.

She was doomed.

While there was a slim possibility she could have talked Travis into letting her go free, a woman who killed in cold blood, with no hesitation, no display of emotion, wasn't going to be swayed.

Alison set her gun and Bri's on the box beside her, picked up Travis's, and swung the harsh light her direction.

Fear clogged Bri's throat, and her heart lurched into a gallop.

"Oh, Bri." Concern etched Alison's features. "Did he do that to your face?"

What?

The woman who was preparing to kill her was upset about her injuries?

Bri recalibrated.

If Alison did harbor any affection for her, that could be a tool.

Maybe all wasn't yet lost.

"Yes."

"What a scumbag." Her disdain echoed off the walls. "I didn't tell him to hurt you."

No. Only deliver her to this execution site.

The disconnects were causing a short circuit in her brain.

And that was bad.

She had to strategize.

Could she perhaps try to build on their bond, remind her they were friends, play on her empathy?

It wasn't much, but it was all she had.

"Travis is no great loss." Bri forced out the words, striving to match Alison's contempt.

It wasn't hard.

"Isn't that the truth." Alison sent him a withering look, then turned her back on the dead man. "You solved Les's puzzle, didn't you?"

"Some of it."

"Sophie's tip had to help. She connected a few dots after Nate died, while she was here for the funeral."

Another shockwave rippled through Bri.

Alison's sister was the one who'd sent the list? Revealed that the names were related?

But that made sense. No one else would have been privy to the links.

"It gave me more to go on, but everything began to fall into place when I recognized you in a photo today from Michelle Thomas's sweet sixteen birthday party."

"I remember that day. She was my friend once, until she stole my boyfriend." Alison lifted the gun, and Bri stopped breathing. "I really hate to do this, you know." Regret edged out the bitterness in her tone. "You've been a good friend. The best one I ever had."

"You don't have to kill me."

She sighed. "Unfortunately, I do."

"Will you let me ask a few questions first?" She had to buy herself time. "You know how hard I've tried to solve this case. It would mean a lot to me to have some answers."

A beat ticked by.

"Yes. I can understand that. I know how determined you are with your cases." Alison lifted her wrist, glanced at her watch, and perched on the edge of a packing crate. "I suppose I can spare a few minutes, but I don't want to linger long. This place gives me the creeps. What do you want to know?"

Bri scrambled to formulate a coherent question as she eased onto the edge of a large box.

"Tell me how you knew about this bunker."

"Nate brought me here once. I always tried to be enthusiastic about his passions—including history and the outdoors—even though I hated tents and ticks and tramping through the woods, and I found history boring. But he was excited to show me this. He'd discovered it before we met, realized the lock wasn't solid, and thought I'd get a kick out of seeing the inside. As if. Still, it ended up being useful."

"So what happened between the two of you? You did love him, didn't you?"

"Yes. Until he turned on me." Her voice hardened. "He said I was too controlling. Too possessive. Too demanding. He forced me to go to a shrink and listen to that parasite rattle on about borderline personality disorder. If you ask me, Nate was the one who needed help. He didn't appreciate true love. When the counseling didn't take, he dumped me. Like all the other people who've used me during my life did. That's not right, Bri."

"No, it isn't." Not by Alison's convoluted logic, anyway.

"So after Nate filed for divorce, I decided they all had to be punished. Larry, the child molester. Adam, the unfaithful boyfriend. Renee, the friend who took my gifts but decided she didn't want to be my friend anymore. Michelle, who not only stole my boyfriend but married him."

A suspicion niggled in Bri's mind.

"Daniel died too. Michelle's husband. Were you responsible for his accident?"

"No. He was on my list, but a drunk driver took care of him for me."

Her dismissive tone turned Bri's stomach, as did her obvious satisfaction at someone else's tragedy. If nothing else, Alison and Travis had that in common, given the man's sick attitude toward the parachute incident.

"What about Les? He wasn't an old enemy."

"No. That was unfortunate. But he wouldn't let go of cases that bothered him, even after he retired. When you told me he'd set up a meeting with you, I had a feeling there was going to be trouble."

"Your staging of his fire was impressive." Somehow Bri instilled a hint of admiration into the compliment. "How did you manage to make his death look like an accident? Make all of them look like accidents?"

"Careful planning. I excel at that." A smug note crept into Alison's inflection. "The short timeframe with Les was a challenge, though. I'd studied the others for weeks, but with him, I had to think fast. In the end, I decided to stop by his house with Ambien-laced brownies to congratulate him on his retirement. Once he was out, I vaporized bourbon in a nebulizer and had him inhale it. Voila—a drunk, drugged former fire investigator. Ingenious, wasn't it?"

Bri swallowed past the bile rising in her throat at the woman's gloating manner. "Very."

"Ambien was useful with Sophie the night I took care of Nate too. It kept her sound asleep while I was gone."

And gave Alison an alibi.

The woman had dotted all the i's and crossed all the t's.

"You took Les's Waterford clock, right?"

"Yes. A small souvenir. Dropping it was my one mistake. I

think you'd have shelved the investigation if you hadn't found the broken corner. Of course, it didn't help that his daughter gave you the list she found, either. I knew you'd dig in after that."

"Is that when you decided I was a threat?" Bri gave the area around her a discreet inspection, searching for something . . . anything . . . that could help her escape this crazy woman.

"I did start to worry. So I began following you, watching your patterns, in case I had to take drastic action. That's how I was able to enlist the help of our friend there." She waved the pistol toward Travis.

"It's amazing how you've pulled all this off." Bri continued to surreptitiously scrutinize everything within arm's reach.

"Like I said, I have excellent planning skills." She stood, and Bri's pulse surged as she snapped her attention back to the woman. "Tonight included."

"Tell me about that." She had to come up with a plan. Fast. "Why do you think you won't get caught?"

"Because Travis is clearly the culprit. Once authorities find the rental car in the parking lot and discover the history between the two of you, the obvious assumption will be that he came to town to seek revenge. Which he did. Maybe not to this extent, but law enforcement won't know that. They'll come to the logical conclusion."

"But he's dead."

"Yes. Poor guy. It happened while you two tussled—and you have the injuries to prove that. He does too. I noticed the abrasion on his chin. In the struggle, you shot him with your gun. But he also got off a couple of shots. Neither of you survived."

The plan was audacious, clever, and pure evil.

Somehow, Bri managed to hide her revulsion.

How could she ever have been fooled by this woman?

355

Yet based on all the victims who'd preceded her, she wasn't alone.

Except she didn't intend to follow in their footsteps. She was going to win this battle of wits by using the idea that suddenly popped into her mind.

Her weapon of choice would be Alison's Achilles' heel—furry little creatures that prowled around in the dark.

Yes, the odds were against her—but in a hand-to-hand skirmish with another woman in similar physical condition, she'd be better able to hold her own than she had in the scuffle with Travis.

If she got that far.

"You've really thought this through." Bri bent down on the pretext of massaging her leg, searching the debris around her.

A few loose pebbles at her feet would do the trick.

"Yes, but I didn't expect it to end like this. I'm sorry, Bri. Don't hold it against me, okay?"

Did she seriously want absolution?

Didn't matter. It was important to tell her what she wanted to hear.

"I understand the predicament you're in."

"I hoped you would." She examined Travis's pistol. "This is going to be hard."

That was her cue to act.

Praying for strength and fortitude, Bri filled her lungs with the stale air in the bunker, bent forward to scoop up a few pebbles while rubbing her leg, then leaped to her feet and gave a shriek.

Alison jerked back a few steps. "What's wrong?"

"I think a rat brushed up against me." She hopped from one foot to the other, waving her arms.

"Oh, geez. I hate those things." Alison's gaze darted away. Long enough for Bri to hurl the pebbles behind the other woman.

As they skittered on the floor, Alison let out a yelp and whirled around, giving Bri the window she'd hoped for.

Without hesitation, she sprinted for the firefighter-turned-murderer, dived for her legs, and prepared to wage the battle of her life.

THIRTY-ONE

"WHAT IF WE'RE WRONG?" Marc gripped the edge of his seat as Jack executed a hard left on Highway 94 off I-64.

Posture taut, Bri's brother accelerated. "We can't be. This is where triangulation led us—smack dab in the middle of a state conservation area. A perfect place to take a victim if you're up to no good. And the gaps in service before and after the carrier picked up the last transmission are fishy. Why would someone turn on their phone only long enough to make a call?"

"To conserve the battery?"

"Not buying that in this scenario." He zoomed past a slow-moving vehicle, lights flashing. "I think he's—call coming in." Jack took one hand off the wheel and yanked out his phone. "Tucker . . . Where? . . . Got it. We're five minutes out. I'm putting my colleague on the line." He held it out. "The conservation agent I talked to did a drive-through of the area. He spotted the rental car at a trailhead parking lot. See what else you can find out."

Marc took the phone and identified himself. "Tell me what you have."

"Like I told Detective Tucker, the car you're looking for is here. There's only one other vehicle in the whole place, in the next lot over, so the one you were after was easy to spot."

Two cars in relatively close proximity, in an isolated area, after dark?

Suspicious.

"Is it unusual to have people there at this hour?"

"This time of year, yes. We have very few visitors after dark. That's why I took down the other license, in case you wanted it."

"Go ahead and give it to me." He pulled out his notebook, squinting in the dark as he jotted down the information. "Tell me about the trail off the parking lot. Where does it go?"

"Into the woods. There's nothing much to see on that hike except an old WWII munitions bunker."

Marc's antennas went up.

If Holmes was using that bunker, it could explain the gaps in his cell signal.

"Is it accessible?"

"No. We have a hundred of them, and they're all padlocked."

Unless someone picked one of the locks.

"How far down the trailhead is it?"

"At a fast clip, about eight to ten minutes. Slower in the dark. You want me to go in and check it out?"

Jack swung into the entrance of the conservation area and killed his flashing lights.

"No. It would help us more if you ran the plates on the other car."

"Roger."

Marc ended the call and gave Jack a rapid briefing. "We need to get the St. Charles PD in here with backup."

"Agreed. Go ahead and punch in County. They can take care of the coordination." He recited the number, then reached for the phone as he did a one-handed turn.

By the time he swung into the parking lot three minutes later, he'd barked out a string of orders, including an instruction that all law enforcement vehicles congregate here with no lights and no sirens to wait for further orders—and that a paramedic crew also be dispatched.

The conservation agent got out of his car and strode over as Jack set the brake. "I ran the other plate. It's registered to an Alison Stephens from St. Louis."

Why was that name familiar? Where had he—

"Alison Stephens?" Jack did a double take. Directed his next comment to him. "She's Bri's friend. The one whose husband was killed a couple weeks ago in a camping accident."

That was why he'd recognized the name. She was the firefighter Bri had mentioned.

Firefighter.

Marc sucked in a breath.

"I wonder if she was lured here too for some reason." Jack fisted his hands on his hips. "We could be dealing with—"

"Jack." Marc touched his arm, pulse skittering as his nebulous suspicion began to coalesce. "She may not be a victim."

Bri's brother cocked his head, forehead bunched. "What are you talking about?"

"Think about it. All of the victims on Les Kavanaugh's list died by fire, including Alison's husband. She's a firefighter. Bri was getting close to solving the puzzle, and the perpetrator couldn't let that happen. Bri could have shared pieces of the investigation with her friend."

Jack's sudden pallor had nothing to do with the blanching effect of the moonlight. "But how does Holmes fit in?"

"Unknown."

"Wait here for backup." After aiming the directive at the conservation agent, Jack took off running toward the trailhead. "Let's go."

Marc was close on his heels as they sprinted down the path through the darkness, the mournful *whoooo* of an owl as it prepared to soar on silent wings in search of prey accompanying them.

But the pounding of his heart reverberated in his ears like the bass beat of a rock band.

If his hunch proved accurate, they weren't just dealing with a man bent on revenge, whose original goal had been confined to troublesome pranks.

They were also dealing with a cold-blooded killer who'd already murdered multiple people.

And unless they got to Bri in time, that killer's new best friend would be the next victim—and the future he'd begun to dream about would be nothing but ashes.

THE ELEMENT OF SURPRISE HAD WORKED.

So far.

But Alison's strength was formidable as they began to grapple.

At least Bri's initial tackle had knocked Travis's gun from the woman's hand, sending it flying into the dark. Alison had also dropped her high-powered light. It lay on the floor, propped against a pile of trash and aimed toward a far wall.

The other two guns were on the nearby box, barely visible in the faint light.

She had to get to them first.

As Bri scrambled toward the box, Alison latched on to her ankle.

Gritting her teeth, she tried to yank it free, ignoring the pain that radiated up her bad leg.

Alison's grip didn't waver.

Changing strategy, Bri scooted closer to the woman and kicked with her free leg. It connected with flesh, and Alison gave an *oomph* as her hold slackened.

Bri yanked again. Extricated her ankle. Combat crawled to the box and grabbed both guns.

A second later, Alison was on Bri's back, clawing toward the weapons. Bri lost her grip on one of the guns, and it clattered to the floor. Out of sight.

Blast, blast, blast, blast, blast!

Rolling to her side, she took Alison with her—away from that gun.

The other woman groped for her hand. The one that held the pistol she controlled.

"I . . . I don't want . . . to shoot you, Alison. But . . . I will." She tightened her grip on the gun as they writhed on the hard concrete.

"You won't." Alison mashed a palm against her face, crushing her tender nose and bruised eye while she flailed for the gun with her other hand.

Pain exploded in Bri's head as she threw her leg over the other woman, forced her onto her back, and pressed down hard on her windpipe with her free hand.

Alison clutched at her hand as she struggled for air, thrashing beneath her.

After maintaining pressure for another few seconds, Bri rolled off and hauled herself to her feet. Limped several feet away as fast as her shaky legs would carry her.

A few moments later, Alison sprang up too, half crouched as if intending to continue the fight.

But Bri had the gun, and she pointed it at the other woman. "Stay where you are."

"What if I don't?" Alison's irises glittered in the pale, eerie light.

"I'll shoot you."

"I don't believe that. You're not a killer."

"I can kill in self-defense."

"Are you certain of that?" She edged closer, as if to test Bri's conviction.

"Yes." Bri spoke with far more confidence than she felt. Of course she'd always known that in a life-threatening situation, any law enforcement officer could be called upon to kill. You accepted that or you found a different career.

But it was a lot harder to pull the trigger in practice than in theory, even if the woman in your sights would do the same to you in a nanosecond without giving it a second thought.

"Then I guess you'll have to." Alison took another step.

Bri retreated a few more paces. "Don't make me do this, Alison." She kept the gun aimed at the woman's center mass, as she'd been trained to do.

But fire investigators rarely had to put that training to use.

"Look, what do you say we call a truce? We're friends, right? We can sort this out." Alison's gaze flicked for the barest second to the ground to her left.

Bri gave the spot a quick glance.

Travis's gun lay within Alison's grasp.

A beat ticked by, and the other woman dived for it.

Oh, God, no!

That plea, however, didn't change the harsh reality.

She was seconds away from death.

There was no time to think. To plan. To consider other options.

So Bri did what she'd been trained to do.

She pulled the trigger.

Alison jerked back and went down on one knee.

Operating on instinct and adrenaline, Bri snatched up Travis's gun and backed toward the door. There was another gun in here somewhere, and it was possible she could muster the strength to search for it while Alison was doubled over.

But hanging around, poking through the rubble in the hopes she'd find it before the other woman did, would be foolish.

She was out of here.

Bri continued backing toward the door. Once there, she pulled it open, slipped outside, shoved it closed, and took off down the path she'd trod earlier with Travis.

Praying Alison wouldn't find the gun and come after her before she could get to Travis's car, turn her phone back on, and send an SOS.

"HOLD ON." Marc grasped Jack's arm, jerking him to a stop. The rustle of leaves in the distance indicated someone—or something—was on the move.

"I hear it." Jack motioned him to the side. "Find cover there. I'll take the other side."

Marc tucked himself beside a cedar tree that allowed him to see the path—or as much as was visible in the darkness. The light from the full moon wasn't sufficient to be more than marginally helpful.

A pair of night vision goggles would come in handy about now.

The rustling grew louder.

Possibly a deer . . . but deer tended to mosey along unless spooked. This sounded like a flat-out run, and it appeared to be coming from around the curve in the path up ahead.

Five seconds later, a dark figure barreled into view.

From the distance, it was impossible to discern features. But several things registered in the dim light.

The form appeared to be female.

She had long hair.

And despite her fast clip, she was limping.

It was Bri.

A shuddering wave of relief passed through Marc.

Whatever had happened, she was alive.

That was all that mattered.

Fighting an almost overpowering impulse to run to her and fold her in his arms, he remained where he was. If someone was following her, alerting that person to the presence of other potential foes could be dangerous.

Hopefully, Jack had also recognized her and would hold his ground until she got close.

As she drew near, Marc searched the path behind her.

Clear.

The instant she passed him, he took cover behind the tree and spoke softly. "Bri—it's Marc."

She gasped. Faltered. Swung around, arms stretched out in front of her, a pistol clasped in both hands and pointed in his general vicinity.

"I'm here too, Bri. Jack."

She swiveled his direction, her gun unwavering.

Then she hiccupped a sob and lowered the gun.

Marc was beside her in a heartbeat.

Jack wasn't far behind.

"We c-can't stay here. She m-may be following."

Bri swayed, and Marc grasped her upper arms, absorbing the tremors that coursed through her body. Despite the darkness, her puffy face and swollen-shut eye registered.

His gut clenched.

"We have to get her out of here. She needs medical attention." He directed the comment to Jack, even as he took Bri's arm and urged her forward.

Jack fell in behind them, keeping tabs on the path that led into the woods. "Are you talking about Alison, Bri?"

"Yes. I sh-shot her and left her in the b-bunker, but I don't know how badly she's hurt. She could have come after m-me."

"Where's Holmes?"

"In the bunker too. He's d-dead."

"Let's hold off on the questions until we get out of here." Marc picked up the pace, keeping his arm around Bri, propelling her forward, while Jack took up the rear.

The walk out seemed far longer than the race in, but finally the parking area came into view.

Thank you, God!

Once they emerged onto the lot, Marc left Jack to brief the conservation agent and the officers who'd arrived at the scene while he escorted Bri to the waiting paramedics.

Not until she was secured behind the shelter of several

vehicles and the paramedics put a light on her did the extent of the damage register.

He almost lost the late lunch he'd eaten.

In addition to the injured eye, the entire side of her face was bruised, her nose was puffy, and her jacket was covered with blood.

But her grip on his hand was strong, and she didn't seem inclined to relinquish her hold.

Fine by him.

Marc stayed with her as the paramedics treated her injuries, leaving Jack to deal with law enforcement coordination. This wasn't ATF jurisdiction, anyway, and Bri's brother was more than capable.

When Bri declined hospital transport, Marc squeezed her hand. If she had any idea how she looked, she'd rethink that. "You may want to reconsider. The visible injuries aren't pretty, and there could be others we can't see."

"Listen to him, Bri." Jack joined them, dropping down on his haunches beside her. "Get yourself checked out."

She offered them a shaky smile. "Don't gang up on me, okay? After all the surgeries and rehab I've been through, I know my body. The damage is confined to my face, and nothing's broken."

"You can't be certain of that." Jack used the stern tone that probably served him well in interrogations.

It had no effect on his sister.

"Yes, I can." She held up a hand. "But if it will ease your mind, I promise I'll go to urgent care if anything gets worse or new symptoms appear overnight."

"Not acceptable." Jack turned to him. "Talk to her."

"I already tried. And I'm fine with Bri's plan." Not really, but he'd learned to read that mutinous tilt of her chin. Once she dug in her heels, arguing with her was a lost cause. "But I'll keep an eye on her."

"*I'll* keep an eye on her tonight."

"What?" Bri's attempt at a glower morphed into a wince.

"I'm staying at your place tonight."

"That's not necessary, Jack."

"Here's my offer—ER or overnight houseguest. Take it or leave it."

Marc's mouth twitched.

There was a definite stubborn streak in this family.

At last she huffed out a breath. "Fine."

Her quicker-than-expected capitulation suggested she hurt more than she was letting on. Or perhaps her last reserves of energy had evaporated. More likely, a combination of the two.

Much as Marc wanted to get her home ASAP, County and St. Charles didn't finish taking her statements until after eight.

The moment they wrapped up, he hustled her to Jack's car and joined her in the back seat, his fingers linked with hers, while her brother drove. Using Jack's vehicle tonight had ended up working to his advantage after all.

Bri snuggled against him, a cold pack propped against her bruises, her voice soft in his ear as the miles sped by. "I still can't believe you showed up tonight. I want to hear the story behind that." Her words slurred.

"I'll tell you all about it tomorrow. Go ahead and sleep now. I've got you covered."

She didn't respond.

But he'd spoken the truth.

And once she recuperated and the mystery of Les Kavanaugh's list was finally resolved, he intended to honor that promise for as long as she'd let him.

THIRTY-TWO

SOMEONE SHOULD ARREST THE DRIVER of the truck that had run over her.

Groaning, Bri gingerly turned on her side and squinted at the sunlight peeking through the shades on the window across from her bed. Checked her watch.

Nine thirty?

She'd slept twelve hours?

That was a first.

Then again, the physical and emotional turmoil of an abduction was a first too.

And hopefully a last.

The door to her room edged open, and she tensed—until Jack stuck his head in.

"Are you awake?"

"Getting there."

He pushed the door open all the way. "I was beginning to think those paramedics had drugged you."

"Sorry." She eased her legs over the side of the bed and pushed herself upright. "Why aren't you at work?"

"I was on the job until late last night, as you may recall. I'm due a few comp hours. Cara's here too."

"What?" Bri stared at him. "She has classes today."

"She said her schedule was light and her teaching assistant could take over until this afternoon."

"She didn't have to drive all the way up here. What did you tell her?"

Cara nudged Jack aside and took his place in the doorway. "Yes, she did—and all Jack told me were the facts without embellishment. They didn't *need* any embellishment to launch me into my car and convince me to drive like a bat out of you-know-where to get here. I had to see you for myself."

Pressure built in Bri's throat.

This was what family was about. The drop-everything-because-you're-important-to-me kind of love that made miles traveled and hours of sleep lost irrelevant.

The kind the three of them had always shared.

"Thank you for that. And thank you both for being here."

"Of course we're here." Cara propped her hands on her hips. "We're the Three Musketeers, remember? Tell us how you're feeling."

Jack snorted. "How do you think she's feeling? Look at her."

"Gee. Thanks for the ego boost." Bri tried to make a face at him, but it hurt too much. "To answer your question, Cara, I'm on the mend. You can stop worrying."

"You should tell that to your other visitor too." One side of Jack's mouth quirked up. "He's been waiting with us for Sleeping Beauty to awaken. And if you think we're worried, you should see him."

Bri's pulse stumbled. "Marc's here?"

"Since seven this morning. He beat Cara to your doorstep. He also brought bakery stuff, which we've put a dent in while we cooled our heels and you snoozed."

Cara elbowed their brother. "Speak for yourself. Marc and I waited for Bri."

"Hey. I was hungry, okay? I missed dinner last night, and there wasn't much to forage through in Bri's refrigerator. You need to up your game in the provisions department, Sis."

"I'll take that under advisement. Give me a few minutes to shower and dress." No way was she letting Marc see her in her sleep shirt with bed hair.

"Take your time. No one's going anywhere."

Well, shoot.

Not that she didn't appreciate her siblings' concern and attentiveness, but a few minutes alone with Marc would have been wonderful.

Cara winked at her. "Speak for yourself, Jack. I have to hit the road once I see Bri up and about. And don't you have follow-up to do from last night?"

Her sister's intuitive powers were formidable, and Bri telegraphed her a silent thank-you.

"It can wait."

Jack wasn't getting the message.

Oh well. Marc would hang around until they both took off. She hoped.

"Before you two leave me to my shower, give me a quick update. What happened with Alison?" Bri pushed herself to her feet, suppressing a grimace.

"Gunshot wound to the shoulder. She was armed when they intercepted her on the path."

"So she did come after me." A shiver rippled through her.

"Yes, but she's behind bars now." Jack's expression was grim. "And I doubt she'll ever get out."

"Come on, Jack." Cara nudged him. "Let's give Bri space to clean up and get dressed."

They left, closing the door behind them, and Bri didn't dawdle. Not with Marc waiting for her two rooms away.

Unfortunately, the shower took longer than she expected. Who knew water spray glancing off a cheek could be so painful? Nor did her face like the hot air from the blow dryer. As for the bruises, swollen eye, and puffy nose—makeup couldn't cover everything, and most of the area was too tender to allow for a heavy application anyway. What she managed to put on wasn't nearly enough, but it would have to do.

Smoothing a hand down her leggings, Bri took a deep breath and limped down the hall.

She found her three guests waiting in the kitchen.

Jack was chowing down on a piece of coffeecake and Cara was helping herself to a coffee refill, but the man she zeroed in on vaulted to his feet and gave her his full and undivided attention. As if nothing else in the world mattered.

Whew.

A look like that could turn a girl's head and steal her heart.

"Good morning." She squeaked out the greeting.

"How are you feeling?" His question came out husky.

At least she wasn't the only one affected by the electricity arcing between them.

Nor had Jack been exaggerating about Marc's worry. If the shadows beneath his lower lashes and the parallel creases embedded on his forehead were any indication, he hadn't clocked more than an hour or two of shut-eye last night.

"I'm holding my own. Give me a day or two, and I'll be back in fighting form."

"Let's hope there are no more fights in your future."

And there wouldn't be, if he had anything to say about it. He may not have verbalized that, but the message was written in his eyes. If there was any way he could protect her from future trauma, he would.

The warmth in Bri's heart spilled over.

Cara took a sip of her coffee, watching the two of them over the rim of her mug. "What do you say we all have one of these sweet treats Marc brought? I do have a class to teach this afternoon, and I know Jack has places to be—or a few z's to catch up on after racking out on your sofa last night."

"I'm not in any hurry." Their brother reached for a Danish.

"Yes, you are." Cara elbowed him.

He shot her a scowl but remained silent.

"Why don't you sit here, Bri?" Marc picked up a mug of coffee from the counter, set it on the table for her, and pulled out a chair.

She moved to it and lowered herself onto the seat. He took the adjacent chair and twined his fingers with hers.

It seemed he wanted to send a clear message about his intentions to her siblings.

No problem.

Cara claimed a chair too. "I'm sure Bri has a million questions."

Actually, she didn't. And the ones she did have had nothing to do with the case that had monopolized her for weeks and almost cost her her life. They were much more personal than that.

But she could deal with those after her siblings left.

"I think I got most of my answers directly from the source, but I do have a piece of news I didn't share last night. With Travis dead, it wasn't relevant. My parachute accident wasn't an accident. He sabotaged my chute."

Marc's grip on her hand tightened, and Jack almost choked on his coffee.

After hacking for a few moments, her brother swiped at his mouth with a napkin, face red. "He tried to kill you in Idaho?"

"Not according to him. He knew I had a backup chute. He claims he just wanted to scare me. Part of his retribution plan."

"What a scumbag."

"That's what Alison said."

"Now there's a woman who's a piece of work." Marc stroked his thumb over the back of her hand. "I wonder how she pulled off the camping 'accident' with her ex?"

"We'll find out." Jack's resolute tone left no doubt of that. "I do have one other development to report. A stash of souvenirs was found in Alison's house during the search. We assume they're from her victims. Les Kavanaugh's retirement gift was among them."

"I'm glad his daughter will get that back. It will mean a lot to her." Bri sighed, then forced up the corners of her lips. "Why don't we chat about more pleasant topics while we eat these pastries? I, for one, would rather forget about yesterday for a little while."

"I second that." Cara lifted her coffee mug in agreement, selected a pastry, and kept the conversation humming for the next fifteen minutes, at which point she stood. "Jack and I should be going. I'll call you later, Bri."

Bri pushed herself to her feet, and Marc rose at once, giving her an assist. "Thank you both for coming. You for the long drive"—she touched Cara's arm—"and you for suffering through a night on my couch." Jack remained sitting, so she laid her arm on his shoulder.

"See us out?" Cara tugged Jack to his feet.

"Sure."

"I'll get a refill and wait for you here." Marc picked up his mug.

After a flurry of goodbyes between him and her siblings, Bri followed her brother and sister to the door.

"I really do appreciate you guys being here when I woke up." Bri leaned back against the wall as Jack opened her front door. Any support at this stage was welcome for her aching hip and knee.

"One for all, all for one." Cara leaned close and gave her a gentle hug. "I like your guy." She whispered the comment in Bri's ear.

Bri returned the squeeze. "Me too."

As Cara backed off, Jack moved in, kissed her uninjured cheek, and echoed Cara's sentiment. "For the record, Davis seems like an okay guy."

"I'm glad you approve."

"But don't rush into anything."

She gave a mock salute. "I'll keep that in mind."

"And go sit down before you fall down."

Based on Cara's nod of agreement, they'd both deduced the reason she was holding up the wall. Or vice versa.

"Next on my agenda."

After they filed through the door, Bri waved them off and returned to the kitchen.

Marc stood again and tapped her chair. "Sit. You look ready to fold."

Did everyone in this house realize how shaky she was?

She slipped back into her seat without argument. "I have news. You've received the family stamp of approval."

"Good to hear." He rested his elbow on the table, propped his chin on his fist, and played with the ends of her hair. "But I'm more interested in getting the stamp of approval from a blond I know."

Her respiration lost its rhythm. "Consider it done."

He scooted his chair closer. "Prove it."

"I thought we had a dinner planned tomorrow to launch our transition to dating?"

"The dinner's still on the books, but I'm accelerating the dating timetable—with all its perks. Any objections?"

A delicious flutter rippled through her as she draped her arms around his neck. "Not a one. But we'll have to work around parts of my face."

"No worries. I would never, ever do anything to hurt you, Bri." His voice hoarsened.

"I know that." Her own throat clogged. "I would trust you with my life, Marc Davis—and coming from a woman who's stingy with her trust, that's about the highest compliment I could pay you."

He stroked her uninjured cheek with a feather-light touch, the tenderness in his eyes filling her with warmth and joy and hope. "Thank you for that. And now I have an admission to make."

"Lay it on me."

"I had a feeling the day we met at the fire scene that the sparks between us were going to lead to something big."

She gave him a slow smile. "Is that a prediction or a promise?"

"It's a promise. Starting now."

With that, he oh-so-carefully claimed her lips.

Bri leaned into the kiss, giving back 100 percent as gratitude flowed through her.

For who could have guessed, back on the September day they'd met amid ashes and cinders, that the man who'd invaded her professional turf would end up staking a personal claim on her heart? Or that she would cede that private, guarded territory so fast and take a gamble on a happily-ever-after with him?

But in truth, it wasn't much of a gamble. Marc was the real deal. Men didn't come any finer than the ATF agent who'd partnered with her on the Kavanaugh case.

And unless her instincts were failing her big-time, another sort of partnership was waiting for them in the not-too-distant future. One that would be filled with the kind of love dreams were made of.

In fact . . . if she were a wagering woman, she'd bet the house—and her heart—on that very outcome.

EPILOGUE

HE WAS A MARRIED MAN.

Grinning, Marc tugged open his black bow tie, unfastened the top button of his shirt, and took a long, slow, satisfied breath.

Until Bri had walked down the aisle in her knockout bridal gown, it had all seemed too good to be true. Like a fantasy that comes in a dream and then slips away, no matter how hard you try to hold on to it.

But this was real. She'd said I do, he had the ring on his finger to prove his new husband status, and the two of them had checked into the bridal suite of one of St. Louis's high-end hotels as man and wife. Tomorrow they'd wing east for their Paris honeymoon, with a side trip to the Pyrenees.

What could be more perfect?

As Bri flipped on the faucet behind the closed door of the bathroom, Marc shrugged out of his tux jacket, pausing at a crinkle sound in his pocket.

Oh, right. The envelope Nan had slipped him as he and Bri prepared to leave the reception, with an instruction to open it tonight.

Must be one of the sweet notes she often penned him on

special occasions—and perhaps another reminder from her that he should count himself blessed to have found such a wonderful woman for a partner.

He'd also been blessed that his grandmother and Bri had clicked from the moment they met.

Lips still curved up, he pulled out the envelope, crossed to the sitting area, and sank into an upholstered chair. He ought to have a few minutes to skim this before Bri emerged.

He slit the flap to find a short note written in Nan's hand inside, along with another envelope that said "To Marc—On Your Wedding Day," also scrawled in a familiar penmanship.

A letter from his father?

His smile faded as he read Nan's note.

Marc: After the fire, I found this among your father's important papers. I've kept it for you all these years. Have a wonderful honeymoon!

Swallowing past the lump in his throat, Marc opened the other envelope, ran his fingers over the chicken-scratch his father had called writing, and began to read the note that had been penned on his first birthday.

My dearest son,

I am writing this as you sleep beside me in your crib, my heart full of joy for the gift you have been to your mother and me. Praying life will be good to you, and that I am with you on this happy day many years in the future. But life holds no guarantees. Plus, my work can be dangerous, as you'll have learned by now. Yet the fight for truth and justice is worth the risk, as is any worthwhile endeavor.

Including love.

In this early stage of marriage, I'm no more than a novice. But I've already learned three things I want to pass on to you.

First, don't let the trials to come—and they will come—divide you. Stick together during the tough times. Be allies and friends as well as lovers.

Second, remember to appreciate all the fine qualities that drew you to your wife in the beginning, and let her know you value them. Gratitude for each other is the foundation for a happy marriage. Put that into words and live it. Every day.

Third, don't be afraid to say I'm sorry—and always be willing to forgive. Mistakes happen. Sometimes bad ones. If they're yours, apologize. If they're hers, be gracious and generous. If God can forgive, we can too.

My wish for you this day, my son, is a marriage as joyous and fulfilling and blessed as the one I share with your mother. I hope I can hand you this letter in person. But if that isn't to be, know that I am with you in spirit always.

As Marc got to the scrawled *Dad* at the end, his vision blurred.

The heartfelt message sounded like the father he remembered. A man who treated his wife like a partner, who loved her in words and deeds, who never held grudges and was always willing to forgive both her and his sometimes disobedient son. Who followed God's example and offered mercy and pardon without reservation.

Slowly Marc stood and walked over to the window that offered a panoramic view of the city on this August night.

If Dad were here, there was no question what he'd advise about Joseph Butler.

But while he'd inherited his father's fight-for-justice gene, his dad's generous spirit had passed him by.

At least in terms of Butler.

A door behind him clicked, and he straightened. Turned.

Bri emerged, still clad in the filmy pink sheath she'd changed into before they left the reception, but minus the shoes. And she hadn't touched her elaborate updo.

At his request.

He wanted to remove, one by one, the dozens of pins she'd said the hairstylist had used to create the flattering, elegant style.

She walked toward him barefoot, her steps silent on the carpet, and slipped her arms around his middle. "You look serious."

"Nan gave me this as we were leaving." He held up the notepaper. "It's a wedding message from my father, written on my first birthday. Nan found it among his papers."

Her mouth formed an *O*. "What an amazing gift."

"Would you like to read it?"

"I'd be honored."

He twined his fingers with hers and led her to the turned-down bed that had been strewn with rose petals in anticipation of their arrival. Drew her onto the edge beside him and held out the sheet of paper.

Angling it toward the soft light that suffused the room, she read it through in silence.

"Wow." She handed it back, her voice hushed. "What a beautiful letter."

"And great advice."

"For both spouses."

"I wish I could have lived up to the forgiveness part with Joseph Butler." He exhaled and refolded the letter. "I doubt I'll ever be as fine a man as my father."

She smoothed out the wrinkles in his brow with a gentle touch. "You're plenty fine in your own right, Marc Davis. Close to perfect, if you want my opinion."

"Nowhere near perfect."

"You're perfect for me."

The tenderness in her expression fed the flame in his heart. "You're biased."

"Maybe a little. But I'm also a realist, and I know a treasure when I see it. As for forgiveness . . . you may get to that someday."

"I'm a realist too, and I don't think so. I've made progress since my trip to Kansas City, but I have a feeling I've come as close to forgiving as I'll ever get. So you know what? I'm going to follow the example you've set over the past few months with your birth father. I'm going to give it to God. Let the pain and anger and bitterness go. Wash my hands of the past and look to the future—with you." He set the letter on the bedside table and methodically began to remove the pins from her hair.

Bri's eyelids drifted closed, and she gave a deep, satisfied sigh. "You know what's perfect? This moment."

"If you think this is perfect, wait until Paris."

Her lashes fluttered open, and not even the famed glittering light show on the Eiffel Tower that they'd soon witness would be able to rival the megawatt glow of love in the depths of her sapphire eyes. "Perfect is anywhere with you, Marc Davis."

She reached up, and as she traced a finger along the line of his jaw, he captured her hand. Pressed his lips to her palm. Eased her back onto the sheets, among the rose petals.

And as their sweet perfume swirled around them . . . as he captured her mouth in a kiss that hinted at the passion to come . . . as he pulled her close against him until their heartbeats mingled . . . Marc gave thanks.

For imperfect as he was, God had blessed him with a gift beyond value. One more precious than gold.

A woman whose goodness and convictions and kindness and empathy had filled his world with joy and grace and contentment through the fall and winter and spring and summer when their love had grown and blossomed.

As they would during all the seasons of his life to come— and for all the magical and memorable years ahead that they would spend together as man and wife.

Can't get enough of Irene Hannon?

Turn the page and journey with her to Hope Harbor!

COMING SOON

GOOD GRIEF.

What on earth had Kay gotten herself into?

Matt Quinn braked, gravel crunching beneath the tires as his Mazda came to a stop in front of his sister's new business.

No. Scratch new.

Beachview B&B might be new to Kay, but that adjective didn't come anywhere close to describing this cedar-shake-covered structure with the whimsical turret on one end.

Exhaling long and slow, he wiped a hand down his face as his hopes for the much-needed R&R that had fueled his long drive from San Francisco evaporated.

His sister may not have summoned him for help with her business, but how could he ignore the elephant in the room?

An elephant that likely wouldn't be here if he'd done what he should have done and asked way more questions when she'd told him about the plan she'd hatched nine months ago to buy a B&B on the Oregon coast. Or even come up here to look the place over. He could have accomplished that in a weekend trip if necessary.

One more regret to feed the gnawing guilt that had been his constant companion for two long years.

Knuckling the road grit from his eyes, he tried to coax the ever-present knot in his stomach to untwist. After all, it was possible the few rotted pieces of shake siding above the foundation, the missing roof shingles, the potholes on the inn's access drive, and the listing shutter on the second floor weren't an omen of what was to come inside.

Nevertheless, the empty parking lot suggested he wasn't the only one who'd been put off by negative first impressions.

Did his sister have *any* customers?

The knot cinched tight again, like a hangman's noose.

But this whole scenario did have one bright side.

385

There would be plenty to distract him from his own problems while he was here.

The front door opened, and Kay stepped out, shadowed under the large A-frame roof above the entryway at this twilight hour.

Since it was too late to drive away even if that had been an option, he pulled into a parking space, set the brake, and pushed the engine stop button.

She jogged over, waiting to speak until he opened the door and slid from behind the wheel. "I've been watching for you." Her lips tipped up, fine lines feathering at the corners of her eyes as she held out her arms. "Welcome to Oregon on this beautiful June day."

"Thank you." He gave her a hug.

After returning the squeeze, she eased back to scrutinize him. "You look tired. Tell me you took a couple of breaks during the drive."

"I did." But only long enough to fill up with gas.

"This wasn't an emergency, you know. You didn't have to make it a marathon."

"A nine-hour drive isn't exactly a marathon."

She rolled her eyes, just as she'd been doing for the past twenty-six years whenever he exasperated her—which had been often in the early days. Few eighteen-year-olds thrust into a dual parenting role were equipped to deal with a grieving nine-year-old who tended to get into a lot of messes.

If Kay had ever resented being saddled with such a heavy responsibility at that young age, though, she'd never let on.

One of the many reasons he loved her.

"Hey." He put one hand on her shoulder and used the pad of his other thumb to smooth out the furrows on her brow. "No frowns allowed. I'm here, safe and sound."

Her features relaxed a hair. "That's one worry off my plate, anyway."

Meaning there were others. Plural.

And one of them had to include the condition of the inn.

But that discussion could wait until he'd clocked some z's and his brain was fully functional again. Better to focus on the situation that had summoned him here.

"Is Cora still trying to convince you not to go back to Boise for her surgery?"

"Yes. But it's a major operation, and she doesn't have any family. I'd hate for her to go through that alone."

"I would too. She may not be related to us by blood, but I'll always think of her as a grandmother."

"Me too. I don't know what I would have done if she hadn't unofficially adopted us after we moved into the other half of her duplex. She was always there to lend a hand or offer advice when I was at my wit's end."

He propped a hip against the car and folded his arms, mouth bowing. "Not to mention the chocolate chip cookies she plied us with."

"That too." The twin creases reappeared on Kay's forehead. "I know bypass surgery is a common procedure these days, and her heart is healthy other than the blockage, but she's getting up in years."

"She'll be fine, Kay. She's a strong woman, physically and mentally."

"Do you talk to her often?"

"Yes." Though that was more Cora's doing than his over the past two, dark years. How often, when he'd most needed to hear an encouraging voice, had he answered the phone and found her on the other end? Too often to count. It was as if she'd sensed his plunges into despair across the miles. "She told me the doctors gave her a very optimistic prognosis."

"I heard the same story." Kay sighed and brushed back a few strands of wind-ruffled hair. "I've missed her these past five months. I mean, I love the ocean, and this inn is a wonderful opportunity to start a new chapter in my life, but . . ." Taking a deep breath, she put on a bright face. "Let me help you with your bags." She circled around to the trunk and waited.

Rather than probe for more information about her regret-infused *but*, he took her lead and followed her to the trunk. There should be ample opportunity to get the lay of the land with the inn and with her before she left for Boise in three days.

After giving her the smaller of his two bags to tote, he picked up the heavier one, closed the trunk, and followed her inside to the spacious foyer.

A quick perusal revealed a small room to the left that appeared to be an office. A wide doorway on the wall that faced the front door offered a glimpse of the sea through windows at the rear of the structure. A staircase led to a balcony above the foyer, and two doorways on the second level were visible before a hallway disappeared to the right.

At first glance, there were less obvious signs of wear and tear inside than out.

That was encouraging.

"Do you want to drop your bags here and have something to eat, or would you like to freshen up first?" Kay stopped in the center of the foyer. "I made the spaghetti sauce you always liked."

His stomach rumbled, and he gave her a sheepish grin. "Sorry. My last meal was hours ago." And the drive-through burger he'd wolfed down hadn't put much of a dent in his hunger. "Give me five minutes to dump my bags in my room and wash my hands."

"That'll work. I'll get the noodles going. Your room is up the stairs and down the hall, last door on the left."

"Got it." He took the smaller bag from her. "See you in five."

He had no trouble finding the spacious if cluttered room—

nor spotting a few signs of wear as soon as he entered. While the space appeared to be spotlessly clean, scrubbing couldn't erase the faint vestiges of two sizeable stains on the carpet. Nicks in the doorframe and baseboards were past due to be touched up. A few mars above the luggage rack suggested the entire room could use a fresh coat of paint.

But the view from the sliding door that led to the balcony? World class.

Matt left his bags at the foot of the bed and crossed to the far side of the room.

Through the expanse of glass, the azure ocean stretched to the horizon past several dramatic sea stacks. Billowing clouds tinged with gold and pink massed where sky met sea as the sun began its grand exit for the day. To the left, on a tree-covered headland, the top of a lighthouse soared over the distant point. And straight in front, visible through the branches of the spruce and pine trees that nestled the inn? A gorgeous, secluded beach that extended as far as he could see to the right behind a long stretch of low dunes.

Wow.

The location alone would sell this place to potential customers—if they could look past the obvious deficiencies in the inn itself.

So why hadn't Kay corrected them? Had she spent every dime of her husband's insurance money on the purchase price alone? Was she living on fumes and regretting her hasty purchase?

Those were among the questions he'd ask before she left for Boise.

But that discussion would have to be handled with kid gloves, and after almost a full day on the road, it would be wiser to keep their conversation on the lighter side tonight.

Except Kay had other ideas.

After giving him five minutes to wolf down a significant

portion of the large serving of pasta she set in front of him, she wrapped her fingers around her glass of iced tea and angled toward him on the stool at the counter where he'd elected to eat. "So tell me how you're doing—and how you managed to take a month off from your vet practice. You didn't give me a straight answer on the phone."

The last bite he'd taken stuck in his windpipe, and he fumbled for his glass of Sprite. Took several gulps while he tried to formulate a response that was short on details but sufficient to satisfy his sister.

"I'm fine. I got a glowing report at my physical six weeks ago. And my backlog of unused vacation days was getting unwieldy."

She narrowed her eyes. "You know I'm not talking about your physical health, and unused vacation days never compelled you to take time off in the past. Especially four weeks in a row. It's not like you to leave your partner in the lurch for that long."

If he told her Steve was the one who'd suggested he not only take a break, but one even longer than he'd finally agreed to, he'd have to tell her why.

Another discussion he didn't want to have tonight. Or ever.

ACKNOWLEDGMENTS

Launching a new series is always fun, and this one is off to an exciting start! The Tucker siblings are a force to be reckoned with, and I hope you enjoy meeting them as much as I'm enjoying writing about them.

As always, there are many people behind the scenes who help make my books the best they can be.

On the professional front, I'd like to offer special thanks to retired Chief/Fire Marshal Marc Ulses, who answered my questions about all things fire-related for this book. His expertise was invaluable. I also want to single out the amazing team at my publisher, Revell—Jennifer Leep, Kristin Kornoelje, Michele Misiak, Karen Steele, and Laura Klynstra. You are the best!

On a personal level, my husband Tom is my staunchest supporter. There are days I'm sure he wonders why he married a novelist who has a penchant to angst over story ideas and disappear into her head to weave plot twists, but I'm glad he did! And though my mom and dad are gone now, their legacy of unconditional love and support live on in my heart and continue to bless my life—and my writing—every single day.

Looking ahead, please watch for book 10 in my Hope Harbor series—*Sandcastle Inn*—coming in April. I think you'll enjoy this story of new beginnings in the little town where hearts heal . . . and love blooms. And next October, I'll bring you Jack Tucker's story in book 2 of the Undaunted Courage series. It's quite a tale!

Until then, stay well—and happy reading!

IRENE HANNON is the bestselling, award-winning author of more than sixty contemporary romance and romantic suspense novels. She is also a three-time winner of the RITA award—the "Oscar" of romance fiction—from Romance Writers of America and is a member of that organization's elite Hall of Fame.

Her many other awards include National Readers' Choice, Daphne du Maurier, Retailers' Choice, Booksellers' Best, Carol, and Reviewers' Choice from RT *Book Reviews* magazine, which also honored her with a Career Achievement award for her entire body of work. In addition, she is a two-time Christy award finalist.

Millions of her books have been sold worldwide, and her novels have been translated into multiple languages.

Irene, who holds a BA in psychology and an MA in journalism, juggled two careers for many years until she gave up her executive corporate communications position with a Fortune 500 company to write full-time. She is happy to say she has no regrets.

A trained vocalist, Irene has sung the leading role in numerous community musical theater productions and is also a soloist at her church. She and her husband enjoy traveling, long hikes, gardening, impromptu dates, and spending time with family. They make their home in Missouri.

To learn more about Irene and her books, visit www.irene hannon.com. She posts on Twitter and Instagram but is most active on Facebook, where she loves to chat with readers.

Love Irene's Romantic Suspense Books? Don't Miss the Triple Threat Series!

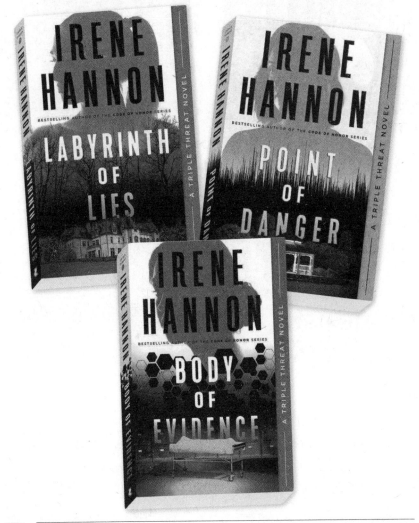

Don't miss Irene Hannon's bestselling
HEROES OF QUANTICO series

"I found someone who writes romantic suspense better than I do."—**Dee Henderson**

MORE FROM THE

"Queen of Inspirational Romantic Suspense"

(Library Journal)

DANGER LURKS AROUND
EVERY CORNER

Meet
IRENE HANNON
at www.IreneHannon.com

Learn news, sign up for her mailing list,
and more!

Find her on